STARS FALLEN SERIES

AKE'S ASCENT

BOOK TWO

NADINE ABRAHAMS

The Written Word Publishing
Australia
Contact: keltoidrui@hotmail.com
https://nadineabrahams.wixsite.com/author

ISBN: 978-0-6457722-8-9 (paperback)
        978-0-6457722-9-6 (ebook)

Cover design by Mibliart: https://miblart.com
Family tree created by Nadine Abrahams and Jenn Zabinskas

This book is dedicated to all those who have been through painful experiences. Your wounds may be internal, but they are your battle scars. Remember, you are warriors.

The Primal Heartbeat, book one, was first published in 2004. Originally meant to be a trilogy for my *Stars Fallen* series, it took me many years to be inspired to write the sequel.

The books are centred around the characters' enduring love, despite going through terrible ordeals. These novels helped me through my own experiences. They are dedicated to all those who can still love and find beauty in the world despite the sad things other humans cause them to endure. It is also a story of redemption, and never losing hope that your dreams will be fulfilled in the end.

Chapter One

'The sun's weak rays streaked across an overcast winter sky. Snow had fallen, heavily covering roofs and doorways precariously. A clump of snow slid from the roof of the cabin and down the window, knocking the shutters.' The old man sipped his tea, and he smiled as his grandson gulped, his face a mixture of suspense and excitement.

'Well, Grandfather.' The boy frowned. 'Please continue.'

The old man smiled and began to tell the rest of the story.

Lan's eyes fluttered open and he rolled over to glance at his wife, she was turned away from him. A year later and they were still working through her ordeal in Regis.

For five years Ake had been forced to be the bride of Emperor Cephas. Cephas had battled the pair with the aid of his militia and left Lan for dead. Ake had borne six children in that time and Lan knew most had died except for two sons, Mandami and Sia, who resided with Ake's former captor.

Ake wanted another baby and tried to initiate intimacy, and this had led to an argument. They were not in a situation to worry about another child, when a dark goddess wanted to kill their six-year-old son, Amities. The child was supposed to bring about the downfall of the dark goddess, Drianna.

Ake would not even look at him when she tried to initiate love-making. He wanted her to be fully on his level if he was to make love to her again. Lan couldn't stand the thought of her being frightened of him while engaged in such an intimate situation. So, he had turned her down.

Ake had begged and cried which broke his heart, but Lan was determined to have her heal before he would sleep with her. He reached out and caressed her cheek. She smiled in her sleep. *I wish I could bear this burden for her.* Tears started in his eyes, and he swallowed hard, trying to stop them from falling.

Lan got up and forced open the shutters of a window. They were fully snowed in. *I will have to keep the children busy; we can't go out again.* He crawled back into bed. They were warm in their little sanctuary. Lan was very intelligent and after drawing up some plans he had created their own space. He had divided, their little room from the main area of the cottage with a wall and doorway. Lan had done so well it looked like it belonged to the original plan.

Someone knocked and opened the door. Amities walked in.

'Father, I'm hungry,' said the little boy.

Amities had the elven look of his father: dark hair, obsidian eyes, pointed ears and pale skin. Lan had built a bond with his son this past year. When Amities and his twin brother, Mandami, the acknowledged son and heir of Cephas, had been born, Amities had been sent to live among slaves, separated from his mother and his father, Lan, who Ake had thought dead.

A year ago, the elven kingdom of Relequis fell when the elves tried to rescue Ake from Cephas. Ake's relatives died when their ship *Syl* sank. Ake and Amities had slipped aboard the ship before it sunk and were reunited with Lan and his great nephew Hau. They had managed to escape on a lifeboat and ended up on the island.

Lan left the room and proceeded to make breakfast for the cottages' inhabitants. This included Carolina, the four-year-old daughter of the previous farmers, Hau, Amities, Ake and himself.

—⁓—

Ake's eyes fluttered open. She rolled over to try and convince her husband to love her, but he was already gone. She heard the comforting noise of her family's morning routine. The clatter of forks on plates, general conversations and the playful laughter of the children. She wanted a large family. Ake had been an only child abandoned by her tribe because her mother had defied her parents and loved a child of the gods. The wounded child in Ake felt the need to have a large family surrounded by love and happiness.

Ake's daughter had been a breath of fresh air at a terrible time, looking nothing like her Regian father. She had looked like her mother. Ake had imagined the baby as Lan's. The child had given her peace, but she only lived three weeks.

She wanted another daughter, but Lan was unwilling to consider it. She understood. They were on an island far away from others. They had to sustain themselves on this little farm and starvation was always a possibility if the crops failed when the weather was unpredictable. Still, it didn't change her mind.

Lan had said he would not make love to her until she wasn't frightened of him. He had said he didn't want to cause her any more trauma and she loved him even more for that. Ake could never be frightened of him.

Ake couldn't look him in the eyes because she was ashamed of her past and how she had been forced to be another man's bride under pain and fear of the death of her son Amities. Ashamed she had shared that part of her life that she wanted to reserve only for Lan. Ake knew she had nothing to feel guilty for, but trauma had a way of making one feel guilty for something they are not in control of. The once-proud woman now struggled to look at a man intimately again.

Ake knew Lan understood the trauma as Drianna had cast a spell over him forcing him to perform terrible deeds with his enslaved sister. Lan still dealt with the guilt and bitter memory. She just didn't get why he was adamant she look him in the eyes. Ake sighed and got up for breakfast.

CHAPTER TWO

Ake jumped at the cries of combat in the main room of the snowed-in cottage. Hau sparred with Lan. The teenage half-elf blocked a punch aimed at his face with an upper block using his forearm to prevent it crashing into his fine boned face.

'Good. Now your turn to counter.' Lan took a step back.

Hau nodded; his sea green eyes filled with determination. He rushed Lan but didn't take into account his footwork. Lan swept his feet out from under him, and he landed on the ground. The boy spluttered and spat the tendrils of his chestnut hair out of his mouth.

'You should tie your long hair back. It can be an easy target in battle.' Lan offered Hau a hand. The lad accepted and rose to his feet.

Amities rushed his father from behind, Lan turned and grabbed the boy and swung him up onto his shoulders. The boy squealed with delight. Hau attempted to use a snap kick to Lan's chest. Lan's head was turned, but he grabbed Hau's foot with an open palm. With a hand movement too quick for human eyes, Hau was flung away from him. Hau stumbled and found his feet. Lan set Amities down.

Lan was a master in unarmed combat and had been instructing the boys for the past year. He had once had powerful magic at his fingertips and had been the headmaster of the ancient mystic school, Caelestis.

Lan had conjured fire with a simple thought, controlled the weather and struck his enemies with bolts of lightning. Lan had been so skilled in unarmed combat he had once moved like a dancer on the battlefield, dodging enemies with little effort. Horrific injury after injury had left him damaged and devoid of magic. Ake's blood ritual had healed most of his physical deformities, but magic seemed lost to him.

He made the boys do some strengthening workouts before getting them to spar with each other. Winter was no reason to slack off when they could be attacked by supernatural forces at any time.

Carolina sat at Ake's feet shelling walnuts into a wooden bowl. Ake sat reading an ancient tome Dane had given her when he last visited a month ago. She glanced up and saw Lan interacting with their son and her cousin and smiled. Dane's apprentice Orilan had not come with him. Lan had threatened to kill him last time he had seen him. She shivered and rubbed her shoulders; grateful he hadn't attended.

Orilan had been raised by the dark goddess Drianna. Ake's son was meant to bring about Drianna's downfall, so Drianna concocted a plot to have Orilan sire a child on her.

Lan wanted to punish his son Orilan with his own hands for her honour. He hated the fact his father, Dane, had trained the demon as his replacement after the passing of his previous apprentice, Het. Dane appeared to favour his grandson over his son. Dane and Lan were still at odds and the visit was brief and awful.

Ake slammed the tome shut. She despised the contents of the book and grumbled as she haphazardly chucked it on a table nearby. Carolina looked up at her foster mother, worry etched on her little face. Ake smiled at her.

'I'm okay, sweetheart. Thank you for shelling the walnuts. Would you like to help me prepare dinner?'

'Yes, please.' Carolina scrambled up and followed Ake.

Chapter Three

Ake's hands trembled as the butterflies in her stomach threatened to swarm. *I hope I am not doing the wrong thing. I don't want him to hate me for this ritual that I am about to perform.* Dane had warned her it had to be done without forewarning the recipient. Ake still hated that fact. Apparently, coming to terms with fear and the unknown were the healing agents for unlocking the power within a victim of great trauma, according to the spell.

Ake had told Dane on his last visit that the spell was very cruel and asked if there was another way. He had shaken his head sadly and told her if Amities was to survive, Lan had to deal with his past.

Lan's eyes fluttered open. An awful, indiscernible chanting filled the dark room, the air was hazy as the acrid smoke of incense burned nearby, powerful enough to dull his strong elven senses. Lan's eyes scanned the room searching for Ake, her side of the bed was void of her presence.

Lan tried to move his arms and couldn't. He tried to call out, but the incense made his voice falter. Lan began to drift as the rhythmic chanting and incense lulled his brain into a false sense of rest.

Lan remembered the countless times magic had been used to harm him, control him or destroy those he loved. He revolted against the painful memories. He hated the fact those with high magic—druids and dark goddesses alike—used it to manipulate the destinies of others. *How can I fight that?*

'I hate magic, I hate it,' he yelled out. 'When has it ever done me any good?' His eyes flashed with anger.

Memories washed over him. He had used magic to defend Ake and those he loved. Lan had used magic to create the music box that played a song he had written for Ake when he had fallen in love with her. Magic had been used in great acts of healing during the Astazian plague that took the lives of thousands. *I guess I don't hate magic but rather those that use it for evil.*

Lan felt a burning pain start at the bottom of his feet. He winced as it spread throughout his body. Lan resisted it until he felt the silky touch of magic winding its way through his veins and he relented a little. *No. No, I don't want this.* He fought against the intrusion, struggling against his ethereal bonds. His body betrayed him and welcomed the rush of magic as it swept through him.

Lan broke the spell cast on him with a simple thought. He sat up and reached for the incense and blew it out. He felt his body shake with anger and he scowled. The magic surged in him threatening to overwhelm his newly awakened body. He looked around expecting to see druids invading his home.

Ake stopped chanting. 'Sorry,' she whispered, her eyes full of concern. There was a small candle burning nearby and she closed the tome quickly.

Lan scowled. 'Ake, I was happy being just a man. No longer a weapon for druids and goddesses. Why?'

'I thought you missed it. You are always trying to convince me things would be easier if I used my magic,' she said.

'You naïve woman. Dane gave you that book. The druids needed their tool back,' said Lan.

'He said Amities needed you whole to survive. But you not being whole makes me sad.' She gave him a gentle smile.

'Emotionally whole or magically whole are two different things, Ake. You are either aware Dane means the latter, or you have been tricked.' Lan stood up.

'Why are you pushing me to use magic if you're against it yourself?' she asked.

'You're the woman in the prophecy, Ake. We can't have you losing any magical aptitude if Drianna comes for you.' He grimaced.

'So, I have to still be a part of it, but you don't?' asked Ake.

'I guess that is a fair question.'

'I can't do this on my own, Lan. You were chosen and must own your actions.'

'My actions?' Lan blinked in surprise.

'How did we come to this point, Lan? You have been a pivotal player on the stage of my destiny. You don't get to back out whenever it suits you,' said Ake.

Lan thought about the meaning behind her words. The storm he had created as a teenager had led to the events of Ake's birth. If he hadn't cast the spell, Ake would never have been born. His eyes widened in sudden realisation. *All I wanted to do was help a friend.*

He had been forced to seek out Ake and bring her to Caelestis. Lan had never wanted to be beholden to Ake. Being an elf, he matured much slower than a human and had no idea what he was to do with her. He became wrapped up in his school and often overlooked her. Lan had left for years to try and find his kidnapped son.

Ake matured rapidly while he was away. Lan realised she had become his equal. He unwillingly fell in love with the loving, beautiful and courageous woman she had become.

His biggest sin was he was well versed in the prophecy. Lan knew full well her son would become a tool for good. Yet he had pursued her, he loved her and no one else was good enough for her.

Lan had been very proud and believed he could protect her with his magic and fighting skills and no one else could. He had vowed to do so. Lan couldn't keep his word without his magic. Lan was annoyed that the druid knew this before he did and had tricked Ake into making sure Lan kept his word.

Ake's childhood friend Het had a similar history to the partner of the woman in her prophecy. Interpretations were a shady process. Het had grown up with Ake and was with her all those long years he was away, her confidant and mentor. *Did I rewrite Ake's destiny?*

Lan frowned 'Ake, did you love Het at all?'

'Het was like a brother to me, Lan. I would never have married him. I had already decided by the time you returned that I was in love with you and only you would be my husband,' she said.

Lan's eyes widened and he closed his mouth when he realised it was open in shock. 'You decided? How could you have known that at such a young age when I was unaware still?'

Ake laughed. 'I was an eighteen-year-old human woman, Lan; you were an elven youth. By then I was more mature than you.'

'You are here because I cast that storm to help a friend.' He stared at her forlorn.

'You couldn't have known, Lan. If it wasn't you, don't you think someone else would have done it? With all these people involved in making sure the prophecy is fulfilled, I'm sure someone else would have intervened if you hadn't. They do it because they must. You do these things out of love and compassion.' She smiled at him.

That shocked Lan. He had always harboured guilt that he had involved himself in her prophecy.

'But I made this prophecy a reality. Look at Amities,' he said.

'I wanted you, Lan. I could have chosen Het. We even kissed. There was no romantic spark for me. He was destined for someone else,' she said.

Lan felt the tendrils of jealousy squeeze his heart. *I am being ridiculous.* Lan laughed.

'What is so funny about it?' asked Ake.

'I was a little jealous of Het just now. I was laughing at how immature that was,' said Lan.

Ake laughed. 'What is there to be jealous about, you silly elf? You really are sometimes very immature.'

Lan grinned sheepishly at Ake.

'I will rectify that.' Ake winked at Lan and walked over and kissed him.

'Still not resolved.' Lan drew her against him and indulged in a passionate kiss. 'Much better.'

'I can't sleep now.' Ake sighed.

'I am restless as well, being cooped up in this cabin.' Lan went over to a drawer and pulled out a deck of wooden cards. Ake lit the lantern.

The cards were inscribed with various elven words.

'What game is that?'

Lan gave her a cheeky smile. 'It's an elvish game called *Din and Dage* or safety and danger. I used to play it with my friends when I was young. I got bored so I made these cards.'

Ake smiled. 'It was popular when I was at school too. I was invited to play with some girls and Thane Norris's son, Campbell. Het wouldn't let me attend. I never even got to see the cards.'

'I am glad he didn't. With the wrong people it can be a dangerous game. Want to play with me?' Lan smiled mischievously.

'Sure. Explain the rules.'

'We shuffle the deck and each take turns drawing a card. You see these four different symbols on the various cards?'

Ake nodded.

'When at least two symbols match on various cards a player calls out *dage*. The other players stop and the player who called out Dage must form an action from the words on all the cards on the table with a max of five words. The other players then perform it. Those that don't want to perform the task call out *din* or safety and are out and must do a favour for the player. Elvish pride often leads to interesting results as very rarely will an elf decline to do the task. The used cards are shuffled and returned to the deck. Cards can be removed from the deck to make it more family friendly.'

Ake watched as Lan began to remove the cards for passion and love.

'Why are you removing *sion* and *ley*?'

'I don't think you're ready for those kinds of games. Do you?' Lan gave her a gentle smile.

Ake sighed. 'I guess not.'

They sat on the bed and Lan shuffled the cards. They each drew four hands before Ake called out.

'*Dage*.' She smiled and looked over the eight cards. 'Let's see we have: *sastn* to eat, *musen* music, *ney* or knees and *cir* bowl. Hmmm, no.' She looked at the other four cards. '*Dunden* or dance, *hep* happy, *tow* or toes and *finu* or delicate.'

Lan groaned. 'This should be embarrassing.'

Ake laughed. 'You wanted to play.'

Lan grinned. 'True. Okay, what do I have to do?'

'*Ge finu hep dunden tow fasta cir*,' commanded Ake in elvish.

Lan laughed and quietly exited the room and came back with a bowl. Ake laughed as he proceeded to attempt a ridiculous dance while smiling and dancing on his toes and carrying the bowl above his head.

Lan stopped very quickly and joined in her laughter. They drew a few more hands.

'*Dage*,' cried Lan.

'*Fele* feather, *fo* foot, *mate* spouse, *nove* hand.' Lan grinned. 'I demand you take your Anwyn form and give me a feather so that I may take it in my hand and use it to tickle the foot of my mate.'

Ake smiled and briefly took the form and plucked a feather. She tried to curb her laughter as Lan ran the feather over her sensitive feet.

'That's my ticklish mate.' He grinned and used his hands to tickle the rest of her.

'*Din*,' she cried out.

Lan relented and Ake sat up, her face red from the effort of laughing.

They played four more hilarious rounds until they fell asleep in each other's arms.

CHAPTER FOUR

The evil goddess Drianna slammed her fist into the wall nearby and smirked as it cracked. She sensed the elf Lan had his power back. *I hate Dane and his bloodline. I vow to destroy it before it destroys me. I still have a plan up my sleeve.* Drianna watched the druid council meeting through her crystal ball.

―――

Sweat beaded down Dane's face, his ancient heart beat rapidly from fear and uncertainty. The head of the druid elven council was being stripped of his powers by a unanimous vote. Orilan, the vampyr, had been accused of killing someone and they had blamed him for taking a murderer as his apprentice. Dane had hoped to redeem his grandson's past actions by getting him to serve others as a druid.

He understood the council's reasoning behind his punishment and when he was younger, he would have agreed. Dane had tried to argue that the sons of Telewanake or Trebrelan were pivotal players in the prophecy of the child of the stars. While Telewanake was important, Trebrelan was her husband. Orilan was his child and probably had a crucial part to play as well.

The druids had argued that Orilan was an ill-gained mistake, a pawn of Drianna, the dark goddess. He was not one of the two children of Ake and Lan destined to bring about Drianna's demise.

Dane had offered a counter argument, stating that interpretation of prophecies could always lead to fatal errors. By removing his powers and Orilan from the apprenticeship they could be endangering them all.

Dane now stood in front of the head of all druids his head bowed. No longer entitled to wear his green robes, Dane was dressed in a simple white gown. His long white hair dishevelled. He awaited his punishment.

'Dane, former head of the elven druids, you are accused of harbouring a murderer. Do you agree that your grandson and apprentice Orilan, son of Trebrelan, knowingly murdered Franbaya the Druidess in cold blood?' asked the shapeshifter.

'It would appear as if that's the case,' said Dane.

Oh, Orilan, my dear grandchild, how could you have done this? I fought for you to become a druid. Dane sighed sadly.

'Then you agree that both of you should suffer the consequences?'

'I have little choice; my fellow druids have voted against me. Yes, he was my apprentice. But apparently, I am responsible for his adult choices too.' Dane lifted his head to look at his former comrades defiantly.

All but Borrush, son of Dormalin of the Rock Fell dwarves, refused to meet his gaze. He was a burly druid seventy-one years of age, redheaded, tawny and stout, standing at four foot two. Borrush had always voted against Dane when it came to Orilan.

The head of the druids began to cast a spell from an unusual scroll. Rain began to pelt down fiercely against the walls of the ancient academy. Thunder clapped nearby making several people jump. The words sounded harsh and guttural and struck fear into all who heard them.

'*Garthas, grall, morte insidious Drianna,*' he growled suddenly.

A roaring wind slammed opened the shuttered windows and a cackling voice answered.

'You are finished, Dane. Your fellow druids all betrayed you for gold and jewels. All but one.'

Shadows seeped in through the cracks in the floor taking on the silhouettes of humans. He was held in place by the spell. Pain tore through him as his magic drained from him, leaving him weak. He gasped and clutched his hand to his chest before he finally collapsed on the ground. Dane rose slowly. His eyes scanned the room. *The situation is dire, all I can do is prevent the loss of life.*

Borrush cast protection spells over Dane and himself to protect them from the onslaught of shades who were slaughtering the other druids and apprentices. A shade reached into the chest cavity of a druid and squeezed the life from their beating heart. The victim collapsed holding their chest in surprise, blood oozed from their mouth. As they fell, gold and jewels spilled from their robe. Dane shuddered and turned to look at Borrush.

'Why are you protecting me, Borrush? Didn't you vote with them?'

Borrush shook his head. 'Nay, old elf, we were not friends, but I would not betray a fellow druid for the choices another made. I believe ye teaching Orilan was a mistake, but I do not believe ye deserve this.'

Dane rose to his feet. 'She's stolen everything, Borrush. I don't have long, I'm old. I need to get to Ake and Lan. Can you get us there?'

The stoic Borrush nodded.

Orilan teleported into the room and cast *Shadow Gate* on himself. A vortex of shadows surrounded the young druid, protecting him from physical attacks. The spectres turned on him. With a hiss they flew into the vortex and were destroyed. The smell of spilled blood drew the vampyr in him to the surface. His eyes turned red.

Dane shuddered as the head druid doppelganger took its true form. Four foot tall, it had thick grey skin. The monster, a spawn of Drianna's dark magic, had a squat square nose and a gaping hole full of fangs where a mouth would normally be. Its two puny white eyes were watching Orilan coldly.

'I fooled you all. Now you will all pay the price for complacency and greed.' It rushed towards him, its maw wide and fangs ready for the bite.

Orilan laughed. 'Pathetic.'

He grabbed the creature by the throat and plunged his own fangs in, drawing in the hideous magic. He felt the blood run threw his veins and growled in pleasure as he drew in its strength.

Orilan could acquire knowledge and some skills from his victims. He felt the magic alter his mass and eyes widened in surprised as his hand shifted to that of a doppelganger claw before switching back. *I wonder if I have gained the doppelganger's ability to shift and see through webs of lies.* Drunk on new power, he ripped the creature in two with his bare hands and flung it away from him. Grey blood dripped down his hand and Orilan licked it, savouring the new delicacy.

Borrush gasped. 'Dane, I know he is kin defending ye, but how can you not be terrified of him?'

'He is in love with Ake and respects his father. I don't think he will harm them; he is very loyal to blood.' Dane fell to his knees.

That is true. I guess I can see through lies. Orilan grinned.

'I can see that,' said Borrush.

Borrush teleported himself and Dane to the outskirts of an island. Orilan growled and followed.

Borrush glared at Orilan. 'Make sure he gets to them, demon.'

Borrush turned to Dane and bowed. 'Goodbye Dane, we had our clashes but I always respected ye, I wish we could have been friends.'

Dane smiled weakly, stood and bowed back. 'Thank you, goodbye and same.'

Orilan grabbed Dane before he fell. Borrush nodded and teleported away. Orilan cradled the beloved dying man in his arms and trudged lightly over the snow to reach the cabin. The stars in the night sky lit the way.

CHAPTER FIVE

Lan drawled in Ake's ear. 'I have a history of sons. I can't guarantee you a daughter. I am willing to try and make one with you, now I can protect you.'

It was the middle of the night, and he was spooning her. She sighed and her eyes fluttered open. She trembled against him. He turned her towards him.

'Look at me, sweetheart,' he said.

She looked in his eyes briefly then quickly cast them down when she saw the concern there. Lan waited silently until she looked at him again. When she did, he grabbed her face and kissed her sweetly. She yielded to him, and he smiled against her mouth.

'Better,' he said.

Lan knew he would have to take charge of their love life for now. As much as she tried to initiate it, she seemed lost. *Hopefully by leading her I can help her heal. I hope this is what she wants.* Ake turned away from him again in embarrassment but snuggled her hips into him. Lan slipped his hands between her legs and caressed her until she was ready to welcome him.

'Do you want this sweetheart?'

'Yes,' she whispered.

Lan pulled her against him, when someone or something pounded heavily on the front door of the cabin.

Lan cursed and rolled away from her and threw on his clothes. Ake got up and dressed as well but wouldn't look at him.

'Ake, you have to stop thinking you are soiled.' He smiled at her sadly.

He left the room and lit the candles in the main room with a thought. The others all sat up and rubbed sleep from their eyes. Lan slid his mystic knives from the holders at his wrists. Hau stood ready to remove the slide bolt from the door. *Why would anyone turn up here in the middle of winter?* pondered Lan.

'What do you want?' Lan asked.

Dane called weakly. 'Lan, it's your father, I have some urgent news.'

Lan nodded at Hau who slid the bolt and pulled back the door. Orilan stood there with Dane in his arms and grinned menacingly at his father.

'Hello, Father.' His gaze met Ake's and his eyes were filled with tenderness. 'Hello, Stepmother.'

Ake's face drained of all colour.

Chapter Six

Ake refused to leave Dane's side. She had changed the sheets and had made the old elf comfortable. He sat leaning against the pillows, a cup of tea held to his lips with a shaking hand. His face was lined with exhaustion and Ake placed a hand on his to steady him. Ake thought back to the encounter with Orilan and Lan and shivered.

Hau had grabbed Dane hastily and Lan had struck out at Orilan, his knives catching the light of the candles briefly. Orilan had easily stepped back.

'Rusty, aren't you!' Orilan smirked.

Lan lunged forward effortlessly, grazing Orilan's cheek with his other blade.

Orilan jumped back and whistled. 'Ha, finally a challenge. You might be capable.'

'Shut up,' Lan said.

Orilan heard the blood pounding in Lan's chest and the vampyr rose in him. He pushed it away.

'Your father is dying, and you're worried about killing me.' Orilan stepped back as Lan nearly delivered a blow to his groin.

'Always, after what you did to my wife,' said Lan.

'Lan,' Ake whispered as Dane groaned in Hau's arms.

Lan looked at Dane and slammed the door shut and drove the bolt home.

Ake turned her head in the direction of the open bedroom door, Lan paced about the main room, continuously checking the windows and front door.

'Dane, why are you here in the middle of winter?' asked Ake.

Dane briefly explained what had happened at the academy and how Orilan and Borrush were the last of the druids.

'Why is he here?' Ake shivered.

'No choice, he saved me, and I had to come tell you that with no druids, mages and mystics left, you lot are on your own. Borrush went home to the land of the Galli. I am sorry, Ake, that Orilan is here,' said Dane sadly.

'You know Lan may kill him.'

Dane nodded. 'Maybe that's for the best.'

Ake turned as Lan stormed into the room.

'Ake, you are safe. Hau is on watch. I need to talk to the druid alone!' He gestured to the other room.

Lan waited until Ake had left the room and his steely resolve softened when he looked at the ancient elf.

'Dane, why are you here?' he asked.

Dane briefly explained what had happened.

'I know you tricked Ake into giving me back my magic,' Lan said.

Dane went to apologise but Lan stayed him with a hand. 'I get it, it was necessary for me to keep my wedding vows. I promised to take care of her my whole life with all my magic and skills at her disposal.'

'Lan, I am proud of you. You must realise that? I know I interfered in your life. I was trying to be a father to you. I wish Regona had told me of you earlier.' Dane smiled weakly.

'You left her and my sisters. I was no more important than they were. She would not have told you after that,' said Lan.

'I regret leaving, Lan. I was called back by the druids to search for Ake. I had no choice in the matter. I was beholden to their rules. It was my duty as a druid. Surely you understand the meaning of duty,' said Dane.

Lan nodded. 'Yes, I do. I have forgiven you. I do love you.'

Lan was overcome with emotion and Dane patted his hand kindly. Ake, who had stood near the entryway, came back into the room and sat with Dane, holding his hand.

'Look out for him, Ake, he needs you.' Dane smiled.

Ake began to cry. Dane wiped away her tears with a trembling hand.

'You need to be strong, beloved girl. Give the children my love. Lan, I love you my s ...' Dane trailed off as his eyes closed and he slipped away.

Tears coursed down Ake's face as Lan left the room, that chapter of his life now closed.

—⁓—

Lan beat at the tree with the axe, making small, useless dents as tears streamed down his face. *How could he just die like that? Orilan got the best of him.* He threw the axe down on the ground in frustration. *This pile will be enough.*

Lan began to pick up wood and hauled them over to the pyre he was making. He wiped his tears on the corner of his sleeve. *I have to be strong for them.* He began adding the wood to the pyre, taking incredible care as this would be the final act he would ever do for his father.

As he finished, Ake came out of the woods, her hands full of winter flowers, grasses and herbs. *Hell, I hope she didn't see my weakness.* She had wanted to wander further into the woods to find prettier flowers, but he had insisted she stay nearby.

Her eyes were puffy from crying. She wiped her tears with the back of her hand and left a small smudge of dirt on her cheek. Her tears began again, and they made a path as they trickled down her cheeks and through the dirt. Ake wandered over and began lovingly placing the herbs and flowers on the pyre. He heard her sobs. When she had finished, he drew her into his arms.

'He is at peace now, sweetheart. Reunited with my mother.'

Ake looked up at him. 'You don't know that Lan. The gods stuff elves in stone circles where they have to wait a thousand years for their lover.' Lan took a shuddering breath.

'Oh, gods, Lan, I am so sorry. I shouldn't have opened my mouth.'

'Seems he would have been better off not having a lover, then Bel would have taken him to the heavens.' Lan glared up at the sky. 'So cruel.'

Ake clung to him, and Lan pulled her against him in a crushing embrace. 'Don't worry about it. And before you let those intrusive thoughts in, I don't regret loving you, Ake.' He sighed. 'If I was a god of death, I would never have loved ones separated.'

Is that a promise? A strange voice whispered in his ears. *Blasted Orilan messing with my mind. He is probably around here somewhere.*

'Cousin,' said a young voice behind them.

Lan released Ake and turned to see Hau, Carolina and Amities walking towards them. Hau gave him a twisted smile.

'You okay, Hau?' asked Lan.

Hau nodded. 'Sure. It's just another death.'

The boy is struggling. 'Hau, do you want to talk about it?'

Hau laughed. 'No, death is part of life. I am nearly grown. Elves do not show their pain.'

'Lan and I are here if you want to talk.' Ake walked over and drew Hau into a hug. Hau accepted.

Lan lifted the body wrapped in a blanket off the ground and set it down it on the pyre. He placed his hand on his father's shoulder. *Goodbye, Father. I cherish the few happy moments we were close. I hope Ma finds you.* Stepping back, Lan conjured fire, and watched on as flames licked at the shroud, consuming his father and separating them once again.

CHAPTER SEVEN

Orilan retired to the barn. He might be a vampyr, but he still felt the cold. He lit a small pile of wood with magic. The rooster cackled at him and gave him a look of disdain. Orilan laughed and captured the animal who pecked at him and gouged at his arms with its spurs, the blood trickled down from Orilan's cuts. Orilan swiftly dispatched his foe and prepared him for the flames. He consumed his meal then vaulted to the loft and slept in the hay.

Dane had passed a week ago and Orilan had been hiding in the loft since. As the snow melted a little, he had watched Hau feed the animals a few times. Orilan had snuck out to watch his family build a pyre of winter wood and dried herbs and burn the body of the great druid Dane. He had wept bitter tears for the man who had treated him like he mattered.

Orilan wanted to end the animosity between himself and his father. There was no need for it. The doppelganger's blood had unveiled the web of lies he had created to protect himself against Drianna's wrath, when it had mattered. Orilan had never attacked Ake and yet she would still believe it had happened as only he could undo the lie.

The barn door creaked open and Ake came in with a bowl of scraps. She began calling to the animals. 'Here, chook chook. Come goats.'

The animals raced towards the fresh feed.

Orilan saw an opportunity. He slipped passed her to the door, closed it quietly and stood in front of it. Orilan cast a spell to block sound coming from inside the barn.

'Ake,' he said quietly.

She turned and dropped the metal bowl in fear. Before it could crash on the stone floor and startle her further, he had already retrieved it.

'I'm not here to hurt you. I just want to talk,' he said.

An arc of *Mystic Fire* went whizzing towards him and set his clothes on fire. He put them out with a druid stifling spell.

'The barn is full of dry hay and is made of wood. That's not wise.'

'Shut up. Leave,' she cried.

'Not until I have said what I need to.'

'*Facstym mentys.*' Ake uttered a spell in the language of the Daione Sidhe.

A buzzing began in Orilan's head, and he put up a druid ward to block the mind-killing spell that would have left him unresponsive and barely alive.

'I did not trick you into sleeping with me when I was forced into pretending to be my father. I just made you think you had. Drianna would have killed me if I hadn't made us believe it happened.' He growled and moved out the way, barely avoiding another arc of *Mystic Fire*.

He was angry now. He let the vampyr take over.

'Lying demon.' She scowled at him.

Orilan knew her moves. Ake's eyes began to turn golden. He had moments before she called upon the blood of Dee to destroy him in molten lava. Thinking fast, and moving with unnatural speed, he grabbed her by the back of the head. She cried out in anger. Orilan bit his mouth and crashed his lips down on hers. Her mouth was still partially open, and she gagged on his blood. *Damn, she is beautiful. I need more.* He was enjoying himself and forced the kiss longer than was necessary. Ake jammed him in the solar plexus with a knife-handed strike and Orilan grunted and let her go.

Ake grabbed her throat and glared at him. Orilan had given her vampyr blood filled with death and dark magic and her body wasn't prepared for the deadly intrusion. What would have poisoned a mere human just gave her some insight. She scowled at him, her eyes blazing with fury. 'How could you make me believe that?'

Orilan shrugged. 'Mere survival. But I did enjoy that kiss. I can awaken so much more if you let me do that again.'

Ake blushed, showing her humiliation.

'Disgusting demon,' she yelled at him.

'You are predictable. You should really do something about that if you are going to take down Drianna. As you can see, you can let go of that hate towards me.' He grinned at her.

'Why can't you leave me alone? I belong to Lan.' She stared at him, her eyes filling with tears.

'Drianna made me to kill Lan and make you mine so our son would be a powerful pawn for her. I glean the history of someone when I bite them. You have forgotten that you are courageous, forgiving and full of love. Something Drianna tried to destroy in me. It was my first real taste of that, and it shocked me. I will not forget that.' He smiled affectionately at her. 'If I had the chance, I would possess you.'

'That's sick,' she said.

'Of course, it is.' He shrugged. 'At least you can look me in the eyes after I've kissed you.'

'Scoundrel, you profess your feelings and then sting people with barbs based on terrible trauma.' Ake wept.

'The truth hurts and it's how I make people see what they are unwilling to notice themselves.' He laughed softly.

Ake felt trapped. She had wanted to kill him for what he had done to her but now she knew that it wasn't true, she was wavering. The manipulation had been cruel and had affected her. But his barbs about her not even being able to look her husband in the eyes hurt more.

'You can leave now if you like. I've said what I needed to say.' Orilan gave her an exaggerated bow.

'Lan will have you for that kiss.'

Orilan shrugged. 'I look forward to the conversation.'

Ake hurled another arc of *Mystic Fire* at him as she rushed past and out of the barn. He dodged it.

Orilan laughed. *The goading worked.* Lan and Ake were immensely proud and indignant people. When they thought they had been bettered or pushed, that survival instinct in them fought back. Ake might be angry and humiliated, but she could do something with that. *Lan is in for an interesting night.*

Chapter Eight

Ake had stomped her way through dinner and the bedtime routine, muttering to herself and glaring at him, challenging him for some reason. She now sat brushing her medium blonde hair in front of a small hand mirror, dropping angry words at intervals.

He laughed and she poked her tongue out at him. He threw up his hands in exasperation.

'What is it?' he asked.

'I'm fine.' She snuffed out the lantern with a quick incantation.

'You are obviously not,' he muttered and relit the lantern with a thought.

Using a spell, she dimmed the light and crawled under the covers. He undressed and crawled in beside her. Mumbling to herself, Ake turned to stare at him, he'd had enough. Lan met her glares with his own and realised she was looking him directly in the eyes. He smiled.

—∿—

Ake was warring within herself. Orilan's bitter words had stung and made her want to prove him wrong. She wasn't frightened of Lan. Cephas took something from her, and Ake was determined Lan was going to be the one to give it back to her.

Lan had turned that charming smile on her. Ake glared at him.

She was going to do this. Lan shrugged, rolled over and closed his eyes. Ake sat up, psyching herself up, then snuffed out the lights. Beside her Lan was fast asleep, exhausted from the relentless martial arts exercises he had been putting himself through to regain his old skills.

She moved closer to him and caressed him under the covers. Ake felt him harden at her touch. He mumbled in his sleep and rolled onto his back. His eyes opened and he stared up into her grey-blue ones. She had straddled him her gaze fixed on him.

'You were going to wake me?' he asked.

She nodded; she had been running her hands through his hair.

'Good,' he said. His eyes smouldered with desire.

He deftly flipped her onto her back and pushed her down into the bed. She shoved him where it mattered, Lan winced and moved off her slightly.

'What the hell?' he demanded.

Ake responded by dipping her head and taking him in her mouth, he groaned and surrendered to his desire.

She released him and lifted her haunted eyes to him. 'I'm not frightened of you. Cephas beat me every time I looked at him or denied him. I was guarded day and night and couldn't have fought back if I wanted to. He had my magic contained in that anti-magic bracelet; the one Ori removed. I was made to believe you were dead and he threatened Amities' life. In the end, it was better to not fight him. The guilt!'

'You kept the both of you alive. Anyone would have given in after being treated like that. You fought for so long. There should be no guilt,' he said quietly.

He drew her against him and gave her a tender kiss. He smiled at her sweetly and kissed her again, his tongue tentatively touching hers. She responded and his kisses deepened into a passionate declaration of his love. Ake sighed and he drew back.

He slipped his hand between her thighs and Ake lay back, enjoying the sensations. Lan left a trail of kisses across her belly, kissing the slight stretchmarks, a testament to the children she had carried. Her eyes were flushed with desire.

'I want you,' she whispered.

'There's the passionate woman I married,' he growled in her ear and leant down to plant kisses between her breasts.

Ake closed her eyes, contented. Lan took her mouth with his, relentlessly. When she was out of breath, he moved her legs apart and became one with her. Ake whimpered and opened her eyes, which were filled with worry.

'Do you want me to stop?' asked Lan.

Ake began to tremble. She wiped a tear away with a hand. 'No. I won't let him take this from us.'

Ake averted her eyes. He set a gentle rhythm, and she began to respond. He kissed her and she looked up at him.

'It's me, honey. Keep your eyes on mine, that way you will know it's not him.' He gave her a gentle smile.

Ake stared at him. Proud, defiant, and beautiful. She rose to meet each thrust and their souls were together again at last.

———

It was nearly dawn and Ake lay in the crook of Lan's arms, content. He was fast asleep. Ake shivered and anxiety gripped her heart. *I have to tell him. It will break his heart.*

'Lan.'

'Yes, honey.' Lan's eyes fluttered open and he smiled at her.

'I encountered Orilan in the barn yesterday. He never attacked me all those years ago.'

Lan's eyes widened in shock, and he sat up suddenly. 'What?'

'He is innocent of the act. Although, he made me believe it, planting dreadful visions and emotions in my mind and heart.' She began to sob. 'Why do men do this to me?'

Lan saw the hopelessness in her eyes, and he reached out and caressed her face. 'There are good and bad people in this world, my darling, and you were targeted for your power and your looks. I will do what I can to prevent that from ever happening again.'

Ake gave him a smile of absolute trust.

'Remember, I love you. Will you be okay for a little, while I go see to Orilan?' He squeezed her hand.

Ake nodded, then her eyes filled with anger. 'He also confessed he wants to possess me.'

Lan got out of the bed and began to dress. 'Anything else?'

Lan saw her eyes fill with fear. 'He kissed me. I swallowed some of his blood and that is how I was able to tell he wasn't lying.'

'Stay in bed and rest. I will deal with this.' He sighed and gave her a sad smile, his brows furrowed with concern.

'Lan, let me help.'

Lan shook his head. 'You are emotionally fragile at the moment.' He leant down and kissed her on the top of her head, then turned and rushed through the door.

CHAPTER NINE

Lan entered the barn, unsure of how he would react. *You may have only tricked her into believing a facade but the impact on her was enormous. How dare you kiss her after all she has been through.* Lan ground his teeth in frustration and scowled. *At times it appears as if you are trying to help and then you ruin it. My son, you are an enraging enigma.*

Lan surveyed the barn and his eyes alighted on his son in the loft. Orilan stood looking down at him.

'Nice perfume you're wearing. I can smell her all over you.' Orilan grinned, baring his fangs.

'That's as close as you will ever get to that satisfaction,' Lan retorted.

Orilan laughed heartily and jumped from the loft, landing softly on the hay-covered floor.

'Good, it worked out for you and her then, can't have a submissive goddess, can we? Or did you?' leered Orilan.

'Why are you still here?'

'Dane's dead. There's nowhere else I can go.'

'So, you're a lost puppy then! Are you looking for a new master?' goaded Lan.

Lan knew how this must play out, gaining the advantage he pushed.

'Here boy.' He whistled at Orilan.

'Shut up.' Orilan glared at him.

'Always someone's pet, never his own master!' Lan smirked.

'I'm not an animal,' yelled Orilan, his bravado faltering.

'You sure? Sniffing around another man's mate is pretty base level behaviour,' said Lan.

'I came here to sort out her hate for me.' Orilan let out a long sigh.

'And you did that by flirting with and kissing another man's wife? Not a very moral thing to do.' Lan's eyes flashed with anger.

'I was made for her. Drianna ensured that!'

'So, an evil goddess mistreated you and designed you for her plan, and you somehow feel you're still entitled to the woman who chose me? The woman I would defy a prophecy for. Or is it more likely she was destined for me from the start?' Lan walked towards his son.

Orilan rushed at him. Lan sidestepped him.

'I'll close that yap of yours,' yelled Orilan.

'How dare you defy your master.' Lan laughed.

Orilan growled and started to cast *Shadow Gate*.

'Sit, boy.' Lan grinned and quickly cast a command spell in his mind.

Orilan sat and gnashed his teeth at Lan, who laughed hysterically at the ridiculous situation Orilan was in.

'That was predictable. As your father, this is how it's going to go down.'

'I did enjoy kissing your wife. Even if it was unintentional.' Orilan smirked.

Lan delivered a light slap to the back of his head. Orilan hissed.

'You are going to stop having any design on my wife. If you so much as breathe wrong in her direction you will contend with me. After what she has been through I will never let anyone force his affection on her again.' Lan glared at Orilan and slapped him again.

—⁓—

I am a disgusting lecher. Poor Ake. Orilan felt his heart constrict with pain and tensed up. *I still want her though.* 'I shouldn't have kissed her like that.'

'No, you shouldn't have.' Lan sighed. 'You are free to stay in this barn without fear of death from me, if you follow those rules. You can train with me and the boys out here. But you are never to go up to the house.'

'Fine.'

'I am sorry that you were born the way you were, believe me I am. I spent years away from my school looking for you. That allowed for Caelestis's downfall as I wasn't there to weed out the fiends of Drianna. I fought through many islands to find you,' said Lan.

'Bull,' yelled Orilan.

Lan released the hold spell and bared his wrist. 'You can glean the truth if you wish.'

Orilan leapt up. He already knew Lan wasn't lying but wanted to gain his dignity back. He bit into Lan's offered wrist and tried to drain him rapidly. Lan, aware of this, belted him with his other hand. Orilan released his bite and stumbled back.

'What will it take for you to listen?' hissed Lan.

'You have your magic back then. Let's spar. You win and I'll agree to your terms.'

'And if you win?' asked Lan.

'You let me help you train Amities, my brother,' said Orilan.

'No magic,' said Lan.

'Done.' Orilan smiled gleefully.

'You are going to learn not to bite, Orilan. Something you should have learnt as a child. I will not overlook your weaknesses like my father did. I am fighting to redeem you.' Lan smiled.

Orilan laughed at him and lunged, trying to grab Lan by the throat. Lan delivered a quick blow to the offending arm and Orilan hissed, drawing his arm back. Orilan moved swiftly behind Lan and tried to grab him in a bear hug. Lan sidestepped him and swept his feet out from under him. Orilan growled, rose and rushed Lan, trying to take him down with brute force. He barrelled into Lan, winding him. Orilan was much stronger due to his demon blood.

Lan stepped to the side to gather his breath. Orilan snuck up behind him, yanked his head back and bit down. Lan slid his mystic knives into his hands and lightly dragged them across the vampyr's face. Orilan hissed and released him.

'You bare your fangs and so will I,' said Lan.

Orilan, awake with fresh blood, rushed Lan, full of renewed vigour. His face began to burn and he grabbed at his burning flesh.

'What did you do to me?' he howled.

Lan sheathed his new silver knives as Orilan fell to his knees in roiling pain. He had never felt pain like this before. He cried like a wounded animal, baring his teeth. Lan made to leave but before he did, he turned and looked at his son.

'Remember your place,' he said.

Orilan felt weird. Now he had a place in a pack, rules he had to abide by, or the alpha would take him down. He was tamed a little.

CHAPTER TEN

Ake felt bored as she and Carolina had spent most of their time up at the house while Lan trained the boys in the barn. Bees hummed nearby and Carolina bent down to pick up a new unfurled bloom that signified the onset of spring. Ake hoisted the picnic basket in her hand and closed her eyes as a cool, flower-scented breeze caressed her cheeks. They took the picnic basket and sat down on the bank by the river, the gentle water bubbled softly over stones and frogs croaked and splashed playfully in the water. Ake taught her foster daughter how to make daisy chains as they enjoyed their repast.

'Hello.' A young boy approached them, carrying a fishing rod in one arm. He tipped his straw hat towards them with the other.

'Hello, who are you?' asked Ake.

'I'm Viktor. I live in the hamlet an hour walk through the woodlands. You taken over the Fredericks' farm? Haven't seen 'em in over a year.' Viktor shrugged.

Ake nodded and made excuses to leave. Viktor waved and left.

Ake was ecstatic and laughed. 'Other people on this island.'

She bounded around, dancing happily with Carolina who giggled with her. Ake and Carolina ran back to the farm. Ake placed the picnic basket hastily inside, then she and Carolina went towards the barn.

Ake called out happily. 'Lan, I have news.'

Lan heard her calling and came out to meet her. She was

glowing with excitement.

'What would that be?' He smiled.

She briefly told him of the encounter with Viktor.

'I'm aware,' he mumbled. Lan's eyes shifted away from her direct gaze and dropped to the floor, and he blushed.

'You kept this from us?'

'You need to be kept safe. I had no magic to protect you. I found it six months ago while hunting. That's where I was able to pick up my new weapons and winter supplies,' he explained.

'Well, I'm going to check it out tomorrow with Amities, Hau and Carolina.'

'It's not safe,' chided Lan.

'Rubbish. No less safe than anywhere on this island, us with a demon in the barn.' Ake scoffed.

Lan grinned at her. 'You are right. Tell you what, let us all go tomorrow and have a grand time of it.'

Ake ran up and hugged him.

'Do we have any money?'

'Yes, we have some,' he said.

Ake couldn't contain her excitement and squeezed him hard. He laughed and loosened her grip.

'I'll go prepare baths,' she said.

Amities walked out of the barn to stand next to his mother, with Hau in tow.

'Do I have to, Mother?' he complained.

'Yes, and you will wash behind your ears too.' Ake grinned, then ran off to complete her task.

CHAPTER ELEVEN

It was a stunning spring morning. Ake and her family had left after an early breakfast so they could arrive in good time at the little hamlet. Dawn had just broken, and the sun rose over the woodlands they were walking through. The rays streaked down and broke through the dense undergrowth. Ake caught glimpses of small flowers and plants that unfurled their foliage to catch this rare visitor in their usually dark little world. Little songbirds sang to each other, greeting the dawn. Ake smiled as they flittered about joyously on the branches of nearby trees.

Amities and Carolina chattered excitedly about what they may see and do.

'Carolina, I am going to buy toffees, you will love them.' Amities grabbed the little girl's hand.

'Okay, Amities.' Carolina giggled.

Hau discussed supply lists with Lan.

'We need more flour and grain for the sheep and goats,' Lan read from his list and sighed. 'We also need a new rooster thanks to Orilan.'

'You forgot rope, uncle,' said Hau.

Ake almost skipped along the crude path made from people making their way to the river. *I wonder if there will be a store filled with soaps, accessories and clothes. I would love to have a nice dress.* Ake thought to herself.

Ake let out a wistful sigh and turned to wait for her husband to catch up. Lan took her hand and continued his conversation with Hau. They were talking excitedly about experiments they were going to perform, and she heard words of explosions and items they would need.

They exited the woodland and came to a slight rise. They all looked down to see a peaceful hamlet. There were several cottages made with wattle and daub and thatched roofs. In the centre of the hamlet was a well and just in front of that, a small stone chapel. The rhythmic pounding of hammer hitting iron identified a small outdoor forge to their left. The large building opposite it served as an inn and general store.

Lan tugged on Ake's hand and led her down the hill. The children and Hau followed. People came out to stare at them. A couple of men nodded to Lan and spoke in a language she almost recognised. Ake was used to speaking Eriu, Galli and Regian. Lan explained that common Breteyne was a derivative of four languages, including the Galli tongues.

'You will be able to understand enough to purchase what you want,' said Lan.

He handed her some common copper coins used throughout the Regian empire. She saw a likeness to the man who had paraded her as his wife, Emperor Cephas. Lan realised what he had done and grabbed the coins back hastily. Ake visibly shook herself and let go of his hand.

Ake was shaken but she regulated her breathing and walked a little ahead of her family to compose herself. She was determined that horrid memory was not going to ruin their day.

Lan began communicating with the locals as she moved closer to him, it appeared as if the friendly conversation had become intense and was building into an argument. Carolina and Amities stood next to him.

An older woman came over and tried to grab Carolina, sobbing violently. The men with her pushed Lan slightly. An elderly man dressed in a simple tunic strode over to them and settled the fight.

Lan sprinted over to Ake, Carolina in his arms.

'Ake, that woman over there professes to be Carolina's maternal grandmother. She named the child's parents, and even guessed Carolina's age. Apparently, she had a falling out with her daughter a couple of summers back and Carolina's dad forbade her from coming to the farm. The priest says he has a record of her birth and baptism in his holy books in the chapel over there.' Lan pointed in the chapel's direction.

Ake took Carolina from Lan's arms and spoke to her. 'Carolina, do you want to live with us or people who knew your parents?'

Carolina looked at Ake and hid her face in her shoulder. The townsfolk insisted on them going to look at the records in the chapel. The discussion turned to the disappearance of the Fredericks. Lan told them briefly how they had come upon the house and seen the blood and lonely child. He stated they had been there a year, and no one turned up, so they assumed the child abandoned or her parents must have had an accident.

The townspeople looked at them like they were telling fairy stories. It was decided that Carolina should stay with them for a few weeks and visit with her supposed grandmother every couple of days until an arrangement could be met.

The townspeople then left them to it. With their spirits slightly crushed they decided to leave the visit to another day and headed home.

Chapter Twelve

Lan had taken Carolina for her last town visit and the child now lived with her grandmother. Three months had passed, and summer had arrived. The town council had ordered them to leave the farm as the property did not belong to them. They were making final preparations to vacate. Orilan had gone to town on one of the visits and had hidden in the shadows and witnessed the discussion between Lan, Ake and Carolina's grandmother and discerned the woman was telling the truth. Carolina had decided to go home to her family.

Ake felt tears pool in her eyes as she thought about Carolina. *I want another baby. We never had trouble conceiving before.* Lan had told her it was probably for the best as they were soon to be homeless. They had bitterly fought about the precarious kind of life they were living. *We are drifters caught on the sea of destiny.*

Lan sat in the inn sipping some local brew. He was deep in his cups and couldn't remember if he was on drink seven or eight. Lan hiccupped, bile rising in his throat. He threw a couple of coins on the table and grabbed up his bag of shopping and tried to set a steady pace home. His head pounded, and he vomited thrice on the way.

Orilan had followed Lan back and forth on his journey, making sure he was safe. He was aware why Ake couldn't conceive. The blood he had given her had rendered her unable to. Orilan could fix that, but he wanted permission to bite her again. He enjoyed that thought immensely.

Orilan had been supping on the local wildlife to meet his vampyric needs. It wasn't as exciting, but it kept Lan off his back. Orilan knew now was the best time to try to manipulate Lan to do his bidding.

Orilan stepped up to his father. 'Lan, you look unwell.'

'What do you want?' mumbled Lan, a little incoherently.

'I can help. Ake can't give you more children as I gave her my blood, rendering her unable to conceive.'

'Oh, that's probably for the best. Do you know we are not in a good place?' Lan rambled.

'If I bite her again, I can fix that.'

Lan glared at him. 'Don't you touch her.'

'What about what Ake wants?' Orilan asked.

Lan steadied himself as another wave of nausea threatened to engulf him and stopped walking suddenly. 'I don't care at the moment ... whatever.' He turned to hurl again.

Lan sat for a bit and fell asleep under a tree. Orilan grinned. *I will take that as permission.* He left Lan to rest.

Orilan reached the house quickly and knocked on the door, Ake answered and glared at him.

'You know you are not allowed up here,' she said angrily.

'Lan's asleep in the woods, drunk. He doesn't want more children at the moment. I told him you cannot have any because of the blood I gave you. I can fix that if you let me bite you.'

Ake turned white.

'He doesn't want more children with me?'

'Something about timing and me not being allowed to touch

you. He said he didn't care etc.' Orilan grinned.

'You said he was drunk.'

'Yep,' said Orilan.

Ake pushed past him to check on Lan, he followed. As they neared the tree she sighed.

'This is becoming all too common.' Ake shook Lan awake and helped him stand.

'Ah, Ake, I'm sorry we fought,' Lan grumbled.

Lan went to hurl, and Ake stopped him from falling over as she helped him in the direction of home.

Annoyed, Orilan went for a long walk. The sound of someone cheering caught his attention. Music and other strains of revelry erupted from the nearby hamlet. He moved closer.

Peering through a window he encountered a room full of merry people. The sound of blood rushing through veins and arteries pounded in his ears as saliva pooled in his mouth. He licked his lips in hunger.

There was a little squeal behind him, and he turned and bared his fangs. Carolina stood staring at him with tears in her eyes. Carolina's grandmother held her hand and glared at him.

'Grandmother, he did it, he killed them,' Carolina said.

Orilan smiled graciously. 'You must have mistaken me for someone else.'

'Help,' screamed the elderly woman.

The blacksmith and priest came running.

Orilan began to walk away, the priest muttered a prayer and stood in his way. Orilan glared at him. 'Get out of my way. You don't need to call out to your god to protect you from a demon. I am not one.'

'He bit my parents and they died.' Carolina pointed at Orilan.

Orilan turned and smiled sadly at Carolina. 'Stop this child, it won't bring them back.'

Before Orilan could defend himself, the blacksmith swung his hammer and hit him on the back of the head. Orilan lost consciousness.

CHAPTER THIRTEEN

Orilan gnashed his teeth at the villagers as they pelted fruit at him. *I've had enough of this ridiculous charade. I have been in these horrid stocks for a week.*

With just the hearsay of a small child they couldn't hang him. Carolina had returned to her farm with her grandmother and his family now lived in her old cottage. It wasn't much but it was better than nothing. Carolina had protested Ake and Lan's innocence and they seemed safe for now. He hadn't tried to escape from fear of his family being hurt in their beds.

The town priest and a few villagers were still deciding what to do with him. Their god encouraged forgiveness and they were trying to come to a compromise. He was so weak from lack of sustenance he couldn't escape if he wanted to. Lan was currently debating his punishment.

'Blinding,' said the priest. 'Then he will not be able to hunt more innocent god-fearing villagers.'

'Amputation.' The blacksmith glared at Orilan.

'Hobbling,' said a villager.

'Wait.' Lan held up his hand. 'I can offer the village a large amount of gold.'

'God has supplied our island with a rich abundance of wildlife and fertile soils. We have little need of your coin.' The priest gave Lan a kind smile.

'Then why not exile?' Lan looked at Orilan with concern.

'How about a hand?' asked the blacksmith.

Orilan didn't like what he heard. *I won't let that happen. I have had enough of these peasants.* He began to reach into his inner reserves trying to cast a teleport spell. He thought he almost had it when a large fisherman walked over to him. Before Orilan could finish the incantation, the man lopped off his left hand with a sharpened axe. Orilan collapsed to his knees in shock. Sweat poured down his face as the pain deepened and he began to shiver with an unnatural cold. His breathing became shallow and he felt the nausea build. He hissed at the villagers and a few backed off.

The priest unlocked the huge chains keeping the two boards of the stocks in place. Orilan rose weakly and glared at the fisherman, blood gushing from the point of amputation. Lan looked impressed with his endurance and gave him a rag to bind his limb and ushered him to their cottage as people booed and cursed them. Lan quickly shut the door. Amities screamed and hid behind Hau and Ake looked at the men in shock.

'How barbaric,' whispered Ake.

'No more barbaric than murder. Someone was going to catch him eventually,' said Lan.

Ake frowned.

Orilan began to falter and leant his back against the wall. Ake rushed over, cut her hand and was about to heal him with her blood when Lan shook his head.

'You do that, they will take his life instead. Ori must endure this,' Lan said.

Lan took out a non-silver blade and heated it in *Mystic Fire*. He went over to a shelf and got a stoppered bottle and uncapped it. Taking a swig, he offered it to him. He swallowed the contents quickly and coughed as the booze began to dull his pain.

Orilan held out the stump. The smell of burning flesh assaulted his nostrils as Lan cauterised the amputated limb. Orilan held in his screams as the bleeding stopped. Dizziness washed over him, and closing his eyes, the darkness overwhelmed him.

—―⁓―—

Drianna smiled. She had raised Orilan so she could track him whenever she felt the need. She grinned as she witnessed Orilan lose his hand. *Couldn't go to a more deserving traitor.*

There was an insistent knocking at her room. A slave entered and told her the Shadow Masters had arrived to plan Amities' and Ake's demise. Drianna grinned cruelly and went to meet them.

CHAPTER FOURTEEN

Ake walked over to her husband, tears in her eyes. He pulled her into his arms.

'Couldn't you have fought them, Lan?' asked Ake sadly.

'Why would I do that? Ori is guilty of the crime. I would have murdered innocent people. I wish they had exiled him though.' Lan squeezed her hand.

Ake sighed and nodded. 'I suppose we cannot stay here anymore.'

'I agree it would be awkward and there isn't much here for us. No friends and family. I suggest we leave as soon as we can. Well, as soon as Ori is able.'

'If he feeds, Lan, we can leave quicker. You said you were willing to try to give me a daughter. You say we have no family and friends and I want to build a family. I'm a mage, you are a mystic and Ori is a druid. Maybe we could go home, back to Caelestis and create a loyal following to help us against Drianna?' Ake's eyes were full of hope.

Lan looked at her thoughtfully. 'You want his fangs in you after what he has done?'

'Do we have another choice?' Ake shrugged.

'There is always another choice, Ake. I am sure I know of countless spells and potions that can probably counteract the taint in your blood. I will not allow him to lay a hand on you.' Lan glared at Orilan.

'How will he regain his strength, Lan?'

'I sired him. I am responsible for the lost demon. He can feed from me,' said Lan.

Lan went over to Orilan who was slumped on the floor. He had lain there all night, shivering. Ake had placed a blanket on him. Lan and Ake had both taken turns watching over him, waking him at intervals to make sure he sipped on pain-relieving willow bark tea. Lan sliced his wrist and put it near Orilan's mouth. Orilan's nostrils flared, and he opened his eyes. He stared up at Lan in torment.

Ori shook his head. 'What is it, Father, to bite or not to bite? Also, not after this.' He held up the amputated hand.

Lan shrugged and bandaged his arm.

'Then you will have to heal the ordinary way: food, rest, medicine. Ake, can you and Hau go foraging? I need more willow bark, evening primrose, feverfew and rosemary. I've seen them around. I believe we are close to Breteyne. Amities, you can get water from the well to boil and strip clean linen for bandages,' ordered Lan.

'There is a quicker way, Lan,' said Ake.

'He is not getting your blood, Ake. I'm getting annoyed with how fixated on this you are.' Lan sighed in exasperation.

Orilan glared at him. 'She can't help it, Lan. She will always try to fix people. That is a way she knows works. Go easy on her.'

'How do we know Orilan is not still linked to Drianna somehow? Without him even knowing,' said Lan.

Ake was lost in thought for a moment and nodded. She left the little cottage with Hau in tow.

CHAPTER FIFTEEN

It was evening and Hau had gone with Ake while she gathered a large basket of the required herbs. They were walking the half an hour back to town. They set a quick pace to try and get the vital herbs back to the stricken Orilan.

Ake breathed in the flower-scented air and wondered what the next course of action would be for her little family. Caelestis held fond memories for her, tinged with tragic ones. For her husband, Lan, they were lonely memories filled with terror and destruction of his elven heritage. She hoped he could overcome the darkness to set about rebuilding his legacy.

Ake was terrified of Amities' future. Her beloved son was supposed to be Drianna's downfall. *What does that mean for my child?* She wondered if this was Lan's concern too and that's why he didn't want another child, a pawn against Drianna.

They entered the cottage, and she handed the herbs to Lan who began to crush them up to make healing cordials and poultices. After Orilan was resting a little more peacefully, she approached the subject with Lan.

'Lan,' she said.

Lan turned to look at her. 'Yes?' He had been cleaning his tools and the crude table he was using as a preparation area.

'Are you worried about Amities' future? Is that why you don't want more children?' Ake asked quietly.

'Why have more if they are destined to die?' he asked.

Orilan groaned and his eyes fluttered open.

'Where in the prophecy does it say Amities will die?' asked Orilan.

Lan turned to his eldest and grumbled. 'This is our matter.'

'The prophecy says we were supposed to have two,' bartered Ake.

Orilan rolled over and tried to rest.

'This needs to stop, Ake. We tried and I will continue to help in that matter but why is it so all-consuming with you?' Lan sighed.

'Everyone I have ever loved dies. I had an unhappy early childhood, and our family life has been limited. I want to build us a big loving family.' She smiled.

'I get it, Ake. I haven't said we wouldn't.' Lan looked worried. 'Do you really think here is a good place to raise a large family?'

'What is our next step then, Lan? Do we leave here, go to the mainland?' she asked.

'Yes. I believe when he is well enough we get off this isle as soon as we can,' said Lan.

'I would also like to start training Amities in the arcane arts,' Ake suggested.

'That is a good idea.' Lan smiled. 'He does not have an aptitude for unarmed combat.'

Ake laughed. 'I didn't either. It took me a lot of extra effort.'

'I'm well aware. I need to test your combat skills myself, Ake. When was the last time you sparred with someone?' he asked.

Ake shrugged. 'Years.'

Ake laughed at the forlorn expression on Lan's face.

'Ake, how can you be so blasé? What if there is a threat on your life?' Lan muttered.

'Lan, you looked so cute with that expression.' Ake giggled.

Hau rolled his eyes at the mushy talk. Amities made a gagging noise.

'No time like the present to test your skills, Ake. Would you even be able to defend yourself from Drianna's minions?' asked Lan.

'I have some powerful bloodline spells.' Ake shrugged.

'I remember.' Lan shivered.

Ake's spell had once opened great vents in the earth. Fire had erupted from them and scarred him dreadfully. Ake had healed him but not before the damage had caused him to sink into despair, even attempting unsuccessfully to take his own life.

'*Magna crono*,' he said harshly.

Ake cringed at the harsh tone.

'Injured party trying to heal here. Take it outside you two. It's about time you two tested out your mettle on each other.' Orilan yawned.

'You want me to fight a woman, let alone my wife?' asked Lan. Orilan sat up.

'Didn't you suggest sparring, Father?' Orilan grinned.

'Sparring. Not actual fighting.' Lan blushed.

'Unlikely Drianna, another woman, is going to care and take it easy on Ake.' Orilan laughed.

Ake looked at the men. She was annoyed at both. One suggesting he was going to take it easy on her and the other for being right despite her dislike of him.

'I will let you test my mettle, Lan. Bet you still think you're in charge of your little woman,' she said.

'I don't think that way anymore, Ake. I was immature then. I'll win based on technique and thinking before I act.' Lan stared at her proudly.

Ake became flustered, her cheeks burned. 'You're on, Lan.' She stormed outside. Lan shrugged and followed, picking up her short sword on the way out.

CHAPTER SIXTEEN

This will be a learning moment for Ake, Lan thought. He watched as she walked to a space a few feet away and turned to face him. He held up the short sword.

'Forgetting something in a heated moment?'

Ake strolled over and held out her hand for the weapon. Lan gave it to her. She walked back over to where she had previously positioned herself.

'Magic and fighting but no Anwyn magic,' said Ake.

Lan thought about her goddess form, a gift from her celestial father, Gepatok. It allowed her to use divine magic and turned her blue eyes and fair skin golden. When Ake used her Anwyn abilities, golden wings sprouted from her back and gave her the ability to glide. He considered winking at her as a wave of desire washed over him and he blushed. *That would not be appropriate, considering how Cephas kidnapped her after witnessing that manifestation.*

'Shall we start with simple sparring?' Lan asked.

Lan was not prepared as Ake charged him; sword drawn to strike. He slipped under her raised weapon and turned to face her.

'That was unfair,' he said.

Ake began to charge him again.

Lan released his weapons into his hands from his wrist guards, just in time to deflect an overhead blow.

Ake laughed. 'Drianna wouldn't give me time to be prepared, Lan, and you wanted to see how I respond in battle.'

Lan nodded and went into battle mode. *She is correct.*

Lan leapt up and startled Ake as his knives arced down towards the top of her head. Ake raised the blade of her weapon over her head. Using the flat of the blade she blocked his attack and protected herself. Lan's knives glanced off the blade from the dual attack. Lan landed on his feet a few metres back.

'Are you sure you can handle and counter my spells, honey?' Lan grinned, his adrenaline pumping.

'Easily,' said Ake.

Doors began to open as villagers heard the clash of weapon on weapon.

Hau came outside with Amities to see what the fuss was.

Hau sighed. 'It would be kinder to the residents if you take this elsewhere. I will stay with Ori.'

Lan teleported himself, Ake and Amities to the rocky beach where they had arrived on this island. The hard terrain would test both their skills. Amities was made to stay out the way but in sight. They repositioned themselves and commenced their fight.

Lan hurled *Mystic Fire* at Ake. Lan held his breath, ready to extinguish it if necessary. Just as it was about to engulf her, Ake spoke a spell.

'*Waterius*,' she whispered.

She was suddenly engulfed in a bubble of water. The flames hit it and were put out in mere seconds.

'*Waterius moldis manas.*' Ake laughed.

The water shield gracefully unfolded from her in droplets and wrapped Lan up in a bubble full of water. Lan was impressed. He held his breath longer than was necessary to frighten her. Ake looked at him worried and was about to dissolve the spell when Lan teleported out of it. He grinned. Amities watched on fascinated.

Lan pulled a throwing dagger from his boot. 'Think fast,' he said, hurling the dagger at her.

Ake swung the blade of her sword across her chest and deflected the knife. The dagger made a sharp noise as it hit a rock nearby. Using a simple telekinesis spell, Ake flung some nearby stones at Lan. Wanting to be dramatic, Lan called down lightning to explode them. Ake rolled her eyes as he grinned at her.

'What is it with men and exploding things?' she asked.

Lan shrugged. 'For fun.'

While she was distracted, he moved effortlessly up to her, delivering a punch to her chest. She blocked his arm with a crescent block and changed her stance. Pivoting on one foot, Ake tried to deliver a side kick. Lan grabbed her foot, her arms flailed as she was held off the ground with little effort.

'Do you know how cute you are right now?'

'How are you doing that?' She crossed her arms, and he hoisted her higher.

Lan laughed. 'I am trained to distribute a larger male opponent's weight throughout my body using stances to ground myself and draw on my core strength. And you, my adorable wife, are a slight weight.'

'I'm not cute.' She pouted and a jet of water burst past his ear. Lan released her foot and guided her fall with his arm, she landed on her bottom.

'Distracted.' He laughed and offered her a hand up, thinking the fight was won.

She accepted but grabbed his arm and used a one-handed move to flip him away from her onto his back, her sword to his chest.

'Distracted.' Ake grinned down at him.

Lan grabbed the blade in his hand and heated it in magical fire. Ake wouldn't let the blade drop and held it stubbornly as it heated to almost unbearable levels. He pulled the blade out of her hand.

'Ouch.' She gasped.

He grasped her hand and kissed it.

'Why wouldn't you fling the blade away in that situation?' Lan gave her an impressed look while he got up and dusted himself off.

'And have no weapon?' she asked.

'Silly girl. How can you wield a blade with a burnt hand?'

He handed her the weapon back, but she had to swap to her left as her other one pained her when she tried to wield the weapon. She altered her stance and came at him. Unprepared for an ambidextrous attack Lan stumbled over a rock and her sword arced up diagonally from the left. Just as Ake was about to make contact, Lan picked up a large stone and used it to block the attack. Ake swapped hands and grimaced. Using the hilt of her weapon she hit Lan forcefully on the hand. He dropped the stone, and she dropped her weapon from the pain.

'Draw,' they both whispered.

They shared a brief kiss, then with Amities, they walked back to the village to treat Ake's hand and check on the others.

CHAPTER SEVENTEEN

Lan and Hau pulled the little rowboat up onto the rocky shore. It was quite heavy due to being overpacked with things the family would need on their journey. They had repaired the original lifeboat that they had used to escape the sinking elven ship *Syl*. It had carried them safely to the island. They now hoped it had brought them to a place where they could build a future.

With Lan and Hau rowing they had covered the eight-kilometre journey in an hour. The men slumped down in the sand to rest while Amities and Ake unpacked the boats and handed out food and water.

Ake sat down next to Lan and unrolled a map hastily drawn by the local elder who was all too happy to see this odd family leave their quiet isle. The map showed their next destination, an imperial settlement known as Moriconium. It was an approximate two kilometres away and even with their heavy gear it wouldn't take more than forty-five minutes to reach.

Ake shouldered her pack and looked at her clothing, she hated it. It reminded her of her days in Regis. While she wasn't wearing the sleeveless, long, pleated robe Regian noble women wore, her tunic was still a terrible reminder of those days and she shuddered involuntarily. The grey linen garment was shapeless and sewn almost to the top. Pins and a mix of brooches could be used to close the material along the shoulder and arm line. Lan had selected some simple bronze pins for her. Ake had tied up her hair and donned the common woollen mantle, as no respectable married woman would leave the house in just a tunic. It was now autumn and getting colder so she was grateful for the mantle at least.

Everyone wore Regian sandals. The leather sandals had hob-nailed soles which produced a very sturdy shoe. It was all they could purchase but it was perfect for their trek. The men and Amities wore long-sleeved tunics that came to the knees. Each wore a leather belt around the waist with a waterskin on one side and a coin purse on the other. Lan hid his mystic knives under his sleeves and Hau hid a dagger under his.

It would be suspicious if Ake, a woman, entered a Regian set-tlement carrying weapons or money when her husband was with her. So, she carried neither.

Without a living male family member or guardian, by Regian law, Ake had married in manu. This meant she was under her husband's control including everything she owned. She seethed at her knowledge of Regian law. *Lucky I am married to a good man.*

They came across a small road that led from the beach where they had landed. There was a small barracks on a hill near the shoreline a little further on. They took the path and proceeded to mingle with the crowd that was walking the road past the wooden barracks. Soldiers were garrisoned in pairs along the path, watch-ing the travellers and chattering among themselves.

Ake could understand what they were saying. During her time in Regis, she had learnt Regian. Dane, a master of languages, had known many tongues and had taught Orilan the language.

'Est Sidhe.' One of the soldiers pointed at the ears on the elven men.

'Father, they asked if we were elves,' said Orilan quietly.

Orilan promptly shape-changed his ears thanks to the blood of the doppelganger he had consumed. Lan untied his long hair to cover his ears and Hau walked to the other side of him. Ake shielded her son's face with the corner of her mantle under the pretence of having him walk close to her.

The soldiers shrugged and continued their conversation with each other.

Ake listened to the conversation and shuddered. She almost stumbled but Orilan steadied her as he was taking up the rear.

'Don't react. I heard it too,' he whispered.

When they were a little further Lan stopped to see if she was okay.

'Is being this close to Regian influence too much for you?' He placed a hand on her shoulder.

'Yes, and because of what they said.' Tears started in her eyes.

'Father,' said Orilan.

'Yes?' asked Lan.

'Come over here away from them.' He gestured towards Ake and the children. The two men wandered a short way off.

'What is it, Ori? We need to get as far away from this barracks as possible. I think the soldiers are a grim reminder for Ake,' Lan said.

'They said that there must have been a mistake as the emperor had the rest of the elves destroyed looking for Ake.' Orilan translated.

Lan sighed and his eyes alighted on Ake. 'She's going to blame herself you know.'

'Lan, you must be prepared for that. An Anwyn is a goddess of love and compassion. She will try to help anyone who hurts, even if they are at fault.' Orilan shrugged.

'Great. I'll need to protect her from herself.' Lan shoulders slumped dejectedly.

'That's why the lost and tortured soul in us is drawn to her, Lan, why we love her seeking something we lost. We will all protect her,' said Orilan stoically.

'No, I love her for her kindness, her stubbornness, her integrity and perseverance against all odds. She is brave and makes me laugh. Standard mundane things couples like about each other,' said Lan.

'They are hardly mundane qualities. They are what make life worth living. Qualities you both share in equal amounts. The fact you see past her innate power to love her for the person she is makes you meant for her. Dane and Het knew this. I see it now,' said Orilan.

Lan smiled at him.

———⟪⟫———

Ake shook herself and raised her head. A group of people had been staring at the newcomers talking in an unusual tongue and it was drawing attention to them.

She went and stood nearer to Hau who was glaring proudly at the people. Hau had always been timid but lately, while training under Lan, he was becoming more confident. At nearly sixteen he looked more and more like his deceased human father, Het. He had brown curly hair which he kept short.

Hau was tall and becoming quite muscled, His ears were barely elven. Hau's older twin, Falcon, had eventually looked like a miniature version of their elven mother, Elder Flower. Elves' appearances could change drastically as they grew. Hau looked human apart from his shimmering hazel eyes, their unnatural quality a gift from his people.

'Hau, don't try anything.' Ake gave him a meaningful look.

'I have elven hearing, cousin Ake. I heard Orilan's translation.

I know of the genocide. My people and our kingdom are dead because of humans.' Hau turned to stare at her, eyes full of hurt and rage. 'I will kill their emperor and his bloodline.'

Lan saw what was happening and ushered them along. Orilan went over to talk to the group of onlookers.

Orilan smiled.

The group laughed and replied.

The group of onlookers went about their tasks once more.

'What did you say to them and what was their reply?' asked Amities.

Orilan gave Amities a grin and ruffled his hair. 'I told them she was a stubborn wife fighting with her husband. They replied there is always drama between couples.'

The group kept walking and came across what looked like a line of businesses. Eight circular buildings had been built in what looked like a market area. They were made of wood and painted in reds and browns. Regian descriptions were engraved on signs above every store. Ditches had been dug behind each shop. The ditches were used for drainage and to catch refuse so it would not contaminate the area.

Ake heard laughter and loud conversations filtering out of the biggest building. Some men sat outside at tables and were drinking while wenches served them. Ake assumed this was the tavern.

'We should go inside and get a drink. If we mingle, we might be able to gather more information,' said Ake.

'That is a wise idea.' Orilan smiled.

'I agree but let's at least keep a low presence,' said Lan.

They entered the tavern.

CHAPTER EIGHTEEN

Mandami felt the anxiety claw its way up from the pit of his stomach and settle as a tightness in his chest. He didn't know whether to keep his worry to himself or tell his father. They were currently touring Breteyne to get away from Regis after the death of his little brother Sia. The Loit plague had devastated the great city of Regis centuries ago, but pockets of the disease still flared up. Mandami had suffered through the disease for two weeks with symptoms of diarrhoea, skin lesions and a sore throat. Now he was immune to it. Mandami was an unnaturally resilient child. Sia seemed to be okay for the first week but then died.

Mandami missed his tiny sibling and his baby giggles as they ran around chasing each other. Mandami was lonely and not allowed to play with peasant children. He shed a few tears, angry at his fate. The sickness had woken a terrible sin in him, magic. He could conjure a flame in a hand and snuff it with a thought. A demon was now walking with him, unable to fend it off while weak with illness.

Mandami's father, Emperor Cephas was in the Moriconium tavern celebrating his victory against the elves. He recently had destroyed the last elven kingdom, the forest elves of Caley. A few of the citizens had survived and scattered. Mandami was pleased with his noble father's actions. They deserved it. They needed to suffer retribution after his mother had chosen her elven child over her two Regian sons. She had humiliated his father.

Mandami had made a vow that he would seek out his elven twin and kill him. *Why should he have our mother's love? I've always been a good son. Why couldn't she love me?*

A guard knocked and entered. At nearly seven, Mandami was old enough to accompany his father. The guard had come to collect him. Mandami's tutor, Gaston, was to accompany them as well for added protection. Mandami explained to the guard he could defend himself and had been training this past year. Mandami was so skilled he no longer used a wooden training sword and had even been given a dagger which he wore on a belt.

A slave came in and made sure he was properly attired in a short-sleeved, ruffled, white silk tunic, belted at the waist. He slipped his dagger into the belt, it shone and was beautifully crafted. Wolves baying at the moon were etched into the silver hilt. Blue sapphires worked into the sharp steel blade spelled out the elvish word for honour and duty, *Osen*. It was a gift from his father's campaign. *I will kill my brother with the blade of his elven people.*

The slave lowered a leather breastplate over him. It was carved with Regian serpents and various scenes of Regian history. Sandals graced his feet. A beautiful warm purple cloak, the Regian colour of royalty, was placed around him and pinned across one shoulder. He was deemed acceptable, and they left the villa to meet his father.

CHAPTER NINETEEN

Ake ran her hands over the rough table and shivered as she heard people talking in the Regian tongue, an ancient common language made up of Regian, Breteyne and Galli words when the ancient tribes had once shared territories before the Regian's conquered them. The language brought back all the times Cephas had whispered in her ear in Regian, 'I can take you anytime.' *Try to forget,* she willed herself.

They were seated at the back of the tavern, trying to be inconspicuous and listening out for information. Lan had ordered Breteyne ale and was enjoying the local brew. Lan enjoyed drinking a little more than the others and was a little less tense, four cups later. Orilan had found the taste awful and stuck to the imported Regian wine. Ake opted for a mead and the children had watered-down ale as the local water was almost undrinkable unaltered, full of bacteria and pollution.

Lan looked around and saw Ake's top lip quiver and she slid down in her seat, paled. He grabbed Ake's hand quickly. The others turned to see what the fuss was and saw a noble child, guard and chaperone enter and look around. The child smiled and headed to the opposite corner where an elderly general sat among wenches, guards and local men regaling them with various stories.

Is this one of the generals or guards that kept Ake under imprisonment? Lan wondered. The noble child was presented to the rest of the general's party. The general turned and lifted him up in his arms and kissed his cheeks. *The child looks like someone I knew, what was her name? Ah Kenra, Ake's grandmother. That must be Ake's son, Mandami.*

While Kenra's daughter, Melowy, had been born with her father's fair elven skin, Kenra had been like her tribesmen, brown hair, brown eyes and lightly tanned skin. *If this is one of Ake's sons, that means that brute is Emperor Cephas.*

Lan stood quietly and pulled Ake up with him. Orilan got the drift and ushered Amities to come with him. Hau followed. They moved towards the door when Mandami turned and looked straight at Ake.

'Mater, it's me, Mandami.'

The emperor turned and stared straight at Ake. He stood quickly with Mandami in his arms sneering at her and saying something in Regian.

Ake shook as she realised what Cephas had said, 'Welcome home, wife.'

Lan ushered them out of the tavern and teleported them some distance away. There was a commotion behind them, and a guard grabbed Amities. Cephas had warned the guards and the message spread rapidly until it reached the guards closest to them.

Lan turned and sliced the guard's throat open as he slid his knives into his hands. The guard stumbled back grabbing at his throat. He briefly made a gurgling noise as he drowned in his own blood and collapsed. Hau drew his blade. Other guards approached a little more cautiously. Lan destroyed them with barrages of *Mystic Fire* and Orilan put others to sleep with less-weaponised druid incantations.

'Get up, Ake,' yelled Lan.

Ake sat with her knees drawn up to her face, shaking in despair while carnage occurred around her. Mandami and Cephas arrived with more guards.

Lan called down lightning bolts directly at Cephas who pushed his son out of the way. The old general was struck with one and collapsed. Mandami saw Amities, drew his dagger and charged the frightened elven boy.

Ake scrambled to her feet when she saw what was happening and grabbed Mandami as he rushed at Amities. Mandami slashed at her and struck her on the arm. She yelped and pulled the dagger from his hand.

Lan took down more guards in a complicated combat display. They slashed at him with their swords. Most of the strikes missed but two made contact, slicing through his tunic and grazing his skin. He moved away from them with unnatural grace and ended up taking their lives as he countered and struck back, dancing just out of reach.

Hau realised who the general was and moved towards him, dagger out. He killed two guards as he neared them but was rendered immobile with a blow to the head, when the other guards nearby struck him. Two guards helped Cephas up, he was barely alive.

'Enough bloodshed over me.' Ake ran, trying to flee out of fear and guilt.

Orilan cast a sleep spell on her, and she drooped to the ground with Mandami in her arms. Lan killed the guards detaining Hau by throwing his knives at them without remorse. After he retrieved his blades, Lan teleported the rest of them to the other end of the island.

Chapter Twenty

Ake was startled awake as Mandami tried to push her arms off him. Lan briefly checked his wounds to see if they were life-threatening before he turned his indignation on Ake.

'What the hell was that, Ake? We were all in danger and you just sat there!' He stared at her in shock.

'Lan, don't.' Orilan shook his head at Lan and went over to check on Hau.

Lan sighed. 'I get it, you were scared. He is not a god, Ake. He can't hurt you anymore.'

'That's not quite true, is it? Look at the elves. He has the numbers. I think she is sick of all the death. Aren't you, Father?' asked Orilan.

Mandami began to struggle in Ake's arms. He conjured a small flame and tried to hurl it at Amities who moved out the way. Lan noticed and came over to the child and hauled him out of Ake's arms.

'How old are you, boy?' he asked.

In fluent Eriu, Mandami spat vehemently, 'Ask that woman. She would know I'm almost seven.'

Lan grabbed Mandami's face in his hands and scrutinised it.

'Ake, the boy, is he Amities' twin?' Lan asked.

Ake nodded.

'And you didn't think to take him with you?' he asked gently.

Ake scowled at him. 'Why would I take that man's son with me?'

Lan sighed and grumbled some curse words to himself.

'What is the likelihood of twins having two fathers, Ake? Are you really that innocent?' Lan gave her a sidelong glance followed by a coy smile before turning his attention back to Mandami.

'Look at him, he looks human, and I am fair,' she said.

'Ake, you look human. I am hardly fair, look at his dark hair and eyes.' Lan turned the struggling boy's face to his mother.

'Your skin is fairer than his, as is mine,' she said.

'Do you remember your grandmother and her people, Ake?' asked Lan.

'Vaguely … Oh.' She began to weep as she finally understood.

'Lan, that's a little cruel, blaming her for something she was unaware of,' said Orilan.

Mandami booted Lan in the shin. Lan laughed and released the temperamental child, who tried to hurl a flame at him. Lan snuffed it out with a thought.

'He's got your spirit, honey.' Lan smiled at her sweetly. He turned to Orilan. 'I never blamed her for not taking the child. I simply asked why.'

Ake ignored Lan and turned to Orilan.

'Cephas will still come after us. He will want what he thinks he owns,' she muttered.

Orilan nodded his agreement.

Hau spluttered awake and yelled. 'I'll kill him.'

The shocked teen settled when he realised the current fight was over.

'Ori, is it true? Is Mandami Lan's?' she asked quietly.

'No doubt,' Orilan said.

'I'm sorry, I had a brief window of escape and thought to save the child I knew to be yours.' Ake glared at Lan.

'Don't be. That was awful of me to say those things and I'm sorry,' said Lan sadly.

'If I give myself up, do you think he will let you and the boys be?' she asked.

'That's ridiculous, Ake, he's a cruel man who takes what he wants. He will not give up you or that boy he thinks is his. You are my lawful wife and those are my sons. I will not give you or them up to anyone, not even to an emperor.' Lan's eyes bored into hers and his mouth was set in hard frown, as if he was determined never to let her go.

'Lan, what is happening to you? You used to be so gentle. Are you not bothered by all those dead people?' Ake began to sob.

'I've learnt death is inevitable. I've stopped feeling sorry for the ones who revel in it and even for those who are instrumental participants in its fruition. Like those dead soldiers who knowingly followed their evil warlord blindly into genocide. When it comes to you and our children, rules go out the window.' His eyes filled with anger, and he stepped towards her.

'Our people are dead, Ake, at the hands of this man and his vast numbers. He stole my last chance at happiness and abused her and you believe I would hand you over to cease bloodshed when he cared so little for the lives of the elves and his own guards. Because of his lust and pride he can't give you your freedom,' said Lan passionately.

He closed the gap and scooped her up and she sobbed into his chest.

'I may have a solution,' said Orilan.

'I will hear you out,' said Lan.

Orilan smiled. 'Let's go find somewhere to rest.'

Mandami tried to make a run for it and Hau grabbed the child.

'Are you okay to make sure he follows?' asked Lan.

'Concentrate on your wife.' Hau smiled.

They followed Lan as he led them to take shelter under some trees. Orilan took out parchment, ink and a quill from his backpack and began to write as he discussed his plan with Lan.

'As you know, Regian's are proud of their laws and try not to break them,' said Orilan.

'Go on,' said Lan.

CHAPTER TWENTY-ONE

Orilan had paid for a messenger to deliver a letter to Cephas at the tavern. Cephas was weak from Lan's lightning attack and shook at regular intervals. His pride stopped him from collapsing completely and he unfurled the scroll.

To Emperor Cephas,

You have been accused of knowingly partaking in raptus, abducting a free imperial noble woman and forcing her into adultery. Under imperial law this can be punished by death as decided by the head of the household. In this case Trebrelan.

Telewanake was married in manu to Trebrelan in 335 CE. Their marriage was consummated before and after the ceremony. She gave birth to so-called premature twins eight months after her illegal wedding to Cephas. The first born was incredibly fit for a human child that was declared premature. The elven child, Amities, being more fragile than a human infant, was in appropriate condition for a full-elf child.

We can prove beyond all doubt that the husband of Telwanake, Trebrelan was never recognised as an elf. Telewanake is beholden to her husband under imperial law, being born in the Regian empire. You knowingly kidnapped his pregnant, lawful wife, abused her and stole his children. Including mistreating the youngest twin.

The child, Mandami, is comparable in features to his father and his mother's tribal people. Like his mystic father, he can cast magic.

You have boasted of your destruction of the elvish people for imagined slights against your name when a free Regian citizen fled. Telewanake was born into a Brythonic tribe on the Isle of Man'hannon under Regian rule. Her parents were killed young. She became a student of Caelestis at her mother's behest. You do not recognise elvish law. Ake is the last remaining human heir to the seat of the elves through her uncle Serenade, as their women rule. As she is married in manu to Trebrelan, he is now the heir to the noble seat through his wife.

Hau, the grandson of King Serenade is under Trebrelan and Telewanake's care, they would be recognised as regents in his stead.

We are hoping to come to some civil agreement to cease further bloodshed. Meet with Trebrelan and myself tomorrow at dawn in the tavern.

Signed, Orilan, druid of Relequis.

Summer 342 AD

Cephas growled and wrote a hasty reply, agreeing to their meeting.

Chapter Twenty-Two

The server stepped back as the table groaned under Cephas's weight as he leaned over to glare at Lan, accompanied by one of his soldier's. The dawn light cautiously entered the tavern through small windows as the three men were caught up in their volatile discussion.

'The Regian empire doesn't recognise the elves under imperial law. Either she is an elven noble or a human commoner,' yelled Cephas slamming down the cup of ale on the table.

'She's a human noble as she married Lan. Hanton, a Breteyne noble, adopted Lan. Upon Hanton's death he inherited Caelestis and the title,' said Orilan.

'So, the elf is a human noble, and the human woman is an elven lady?' asked Cephas.

'Yes, and according to the law, you are to compensate the head of her household for forcing her into adultery against her will,' said Orilan.

Lan seethed. *I hate this. I want to kill this man but then the entire Regian empire might come against us. I could handle that if it wasn't for Ake and my children.* He glared at Cephas and dug his nails into the table to stop himself from reaching across the table to strangle the man with his bare hands.

Cephas was tired. His hope of an heir was gone. He didn't want to be emperor anymore. He was too old for this. He wanted to retire and hand over the reins to someone. 'I need an heir. I love

Mandami and would adopt the child as my own. It is cruel for you to take him from the only father he has known.'

Lan swore and went to throw himself at Cephas. Orilan hauled him back.

'You abused my wife and mistreated my son. You would dare ask to adopt our child?' Lan pushed Orilan's hands away. 'You murdered my people searching for her. You deserve nothing.' Lan slammed his fist down on the table his eyes blazed with hatred.

'I would counter with compensation for the death of my guards, but we will call it even with the unnecessary conquering of your people. I want proof of their marriage.' Cephas smirked.

Lan begrudgingly produced a beautiful piece of needlework on red linen. A white leopard in full sprint was accompanied by a black stallion running at her side. Elven runes encircled the animals. An outer border of flames finished the piece. These were the two symbols of the elves of Relequis and the mystics of Caelestis. His and Ake's legacy.

Lan had taken up needlework in the ten years he was separated from Ake by the elves. Lan unwrapped the cloth and pulled out near pristine pieces of vellum. He had kept the certificates on him, a reminder of the happiest times in his life. There were two certificates, one from Relequis, the other from the town of Mencrey. He had registered their marriage several days after Elder Flower had taken Ake to Relequis. He had hoped to use the law to get her home but had descended into madness soon after. *I wish I had been strong enough to go to her earlier. It was as if the madness was unnatural.* His eyes filled with shock at the sudden realisation. *Drianna sent the madness to keep me from her. I can sometimes be so clueless.* Lan was interrupted from his thoughts.

'Why are there two? This one is registered in Mencrey years before this wedding certificate in Relequis.' asked Cephas.

'Mystic tradition. I approve of all weddings after the students graduate. I make the final decision,' he said.

Did Ake approve it? Orilan signed to Lan.

Lan had learnt to sign when he had lost the ability to talk after a terrible injury. He had been caught up in Ake's Anwyn flames during the battle when Cephas had left Lan for dead and kidnapped her. Dane had taught Orilan this language as well. Lan shook his head.

'I am kind of impressed you had the guts to fight for what you wanted. But it is a little disturbing you didn't ask her. That is something you wouldn't normally do.' Orilan's eyes widened in shock.

Cephas laughed. 'So, you also took what you wanted.'

'No, by law she was already in manu to me. Under mystic tradition I approve the weddings and partners. By my upbringing and heritage, I broke no traditional law. Morally, it may be a grey area for registering our marriage without her knowledge. But she agreed to be my lover. That, under both human and elven law, is agreement to betrothal these days.

'As head of our household and the order of the mystics I had the right to register my marriage when I saw fit, after her agreement. Never once did I take her by force. She came to my bed freely without coercion, beatings or fear of her child being killed. Why am I explaining myself to a lecher like you?' Lan scowled at Cephas.

'I will recognise the human one. I am too old to chase her anymore. What do you want in compensation?' asked Cephas.

'You agree to let us leave freely. You will never come near my children and wife again and you will document all this within your Regian administration. The Isle of Man'hannon and the village of Mencrey and Axeton are under mine and Ake's rule into perpetuity. No one must enter the island without a writ. Relequis, or what is left of that, and Caley will belong to Hau. And I will duel you, not necessarily to death but until one of us is so bloodied I feel you may have felt half of what she went through.' Lan glared at Cephas.

'I agree on one condition. When Mandami comes of age he can choose to be my heir as well. I have raised him. He may be your birth son, but he calls me Pater,' bargained Cephas.

'I agree I cannot force the boy to see me as his father. That was taken from me nearly seven agonising years ago,' said Lan resentfully.

'I agree then,' said Cephas.

They drew up the documents and had them witnessed and signed. Two copies were made for each of them. The duel was planned for noon.

As they were leaving the tavern, Cephas saw the others seated outside. Mandami's eyes looked at his former father hopefully. He had given up trying to run only to have Hau catch him.

'Just so you know, watch her with those children. She was never a mother to them, they all probably died of heartache. Your wife was good at one thing though, especially when she fought me.' Cephas turned, stared at Ake and grinned.

Lan went to rush him; Orilan reminded him of his agreement for noon. Lan backed off; his eyes smouldered with rage.

Cephas sauntered away, his head held high. Mandami's little chest heaved with sobs. Ake reached out her hand to him and the boy slapped it away.

'Mater, let's go home to Pater and we can be a family again.'

'This is your family, Mandami.' Ake gave him a sad smile. 'I am sorry for all the times I pushed you away. That was wrong of me.'

'You only care for me now because you think that horrid elf is my Pater.' Mandami pointed at Lan.

Ake gave him a wounded look. 'That is not true, Mandami. I couldn't get close to you as that meant getting close to Cephas. That made it hard to bond with you. Please don't call your father a horrid elf. The elves were benevolent people.'

The boy began to sob. 'No, they were evil beings who enchanted women away from their rightful husbands. My Pater told me so.'

'Ake, I think this is too much for him to hear this early on.'

'You are right.' Ake stood up and picked up Mandami. The child looked surprised before he struggled. 'I have always cared for you. I can show it from now on.' She gave him a brief hug before putting him down.

Mandami drew his blade and rushed Lan. 'You will die, elf, and I will rescue my Mater from your evil influence.'

The child reached Lan and he grabbed the dagger out of the child's grip. 'You can have this back when you stop threatening us with it.'

Mandami began to kick him. Lan grabbed the child and lifted him into his arms. Mandami tried to punch him, and Lan grabbed his fist and looked down at him. 'Hello, Mandami, I am pleased to officially meet you. You are very brave, my son.'

'I have his eyes. It must be true.' Mandami muttered and began to cry.

Lan cradled the child to his chest briefly before Mandami struggled.

'Put me down,' said Mandami.

Lan placed the child down and he marched over to glare at Amities. 'What games do elves play?'

Orilan laughed. 'Cute boy. He is more like Lan in personality than you, Ake.'

Ake smiled. 'True.'

'We should get something to eat. Then I need to warm up before this fight.'

'Fight?' Ake gave Orilan a stern expression.

'Let me explain.' Orilan gave her a warm smile.

Lan grabbed a handful of coins from his pocket and ran into the tavern.

CHAPTER TWENTY-THREE

Orilan relayed the conversation to the rest of the group while Lan practiced his combat skills nearby. The remnants from their sandwiches were left on the bench.

'Don't you think I should have had a say?' asked Ake.

Hau's mouth was set in a hard frown. 'It was my mother's kingdom that fell. I am old enough to speak on behalf of my kingdom. Now Lan is the heir through his wife until I turn eighteen and produce a child of my own? I would have just killed Cephas and been done with it.'

Ake glared at her husband's back. *I can't believe he registered our marriage without even a single letter to let me know.* She sighed. *I get it, Serenade never goes against the laws of his people and if I married under human law, elven laws became secondary as I wasn't a full elf.* She stood up. *I wish he had overcome the madness earlier and tried to get me. Things might have been different.*

'Ori, can you watch the children?' asked Ake.

Orilan nodded.

'I'll be back.' Ake turned and hurried over to Lan.

'Lan, we need to talk.'

He stopped mid-exercise and stood a few moments, breathing heavily, sweat beading down his face.

'Sure, I should probably rest now anyway,' he said.

They wandered off a little and Lan picked some wildflowers,

handing them to her. Ake knew it was a peace offering but it was still sweet.

'Lan, you need to stop making decisions for me.'

'I am aware of that. I can't change all the Regian laws. We have our own isle, Ake, free of their empire and their cruel laws regarding women. We can make a legacy together that will continue on through our bloodline forever. I may live centuries, but I am not immortal. I have tried to provide a home for you, for as long as our legacy remains. I'm sick of how much choice has been taken from you and yes, I am aware I am at fault in the past too. Both with my words and actions. This is how I try to make amends.' Lan smiled at her.

Ake was stumped for words for a few moments.

'I thank you for the gift. You know, I've never really given you one. I was never creative or persistent in learning. You have given me magic writing pads and songs and now an island kingdom. I never gave real gifts to others either, a regret.'

'You are so wrong, Ake. You saved my life when I was poisoned, gave me back my powers and steered me in the right direction. You gave your heart to your friends as they did with you. That is better than a physical gift.'

'I should have been less centred on pranks and messing about and done more for them.'

'You did, it's the little everyday things that matter. From joking around, offering sound advice, nursing others when unwell and bravely standing up to the darkness in others even when we are small and weak. We remember the fun and comfort others gave us in times of need. With all that divine power in you, you could be an all-powerful, awe-inspiring creature of the gods. But it's your humanity that touches people and will be told down through the ages.'

Ake dwelt on Lan's poignant words.

'I miss them all, Lan, and this duel and reclaiming what was already yours seems such little justice when they gave their lives for ours. Caelestis has been regained through bargaining and mere slips of paper. But I consider the purchase paid in full, with their blood.'

'Drianna will pay, Ake, and it won't be Amities who will take her down. Amities is too gentle. He will be our legacy. I believe it will be our fiery Mandami that makes her pay.'

'I never hated the boy, Lan. I couldn't hate my own child. Cephas controlled that boy and if I had given into mothering him it would have felt like I'd given into Cephas. I was never unkind to Mandami.' Her gaze dropped to the ground and she sighed and blinked back tears.

'No one who knows you would believe that you would be unkind to him, Ake. You really are far too gentle.' Lan smiled at her.

They walked hand in hand back towards the others. Lan was ready to bring Cephas to heel for the pain he had caused his demure goddess.

CHAPTER TWENTY-FOUR

The midday sun reached its zenith as the small town of Moriconium had gathered around to watch their emperor defeat one of the last elven lords. They had heard that this evil creature could even cast magic, truly a sign that it was a kinsman of demons. The fight was to take place in the sandy training yard of the barracks. The area was surrounded by seven levels of circular marble steps. It was packed with attendees and local vendors served bread and ale.

Amities and Mandami were squabbling. Mandami was goading Amities with how he got to live with their mother for five years while Amities was a slave.

'She chose me,' said Amities.

Mandami went to slap Amities and Lan caught his hand.

'Do not hit your brother,' he warned.

'That creature, that elf is no brother of mine,' Mandami cried vehemently.

'Then are you also a creature, boy? You have an elven father, and you can cast magic. If anything, he may look like an elf, but you have their tendencies,' said Lan.

'I hate the fact you sired me. She may be my lousy Mater, but you will never be my Pater,' yelled Mandami.

People stared at them and Mandami cowered slightly.

'Say what you want about me, Mandami, but the truth is your mother is my wife. Your so-called Pater took her and left me for dead. You are both my sons, and I would have raised you both if it were not for your Pater. I know you are hurting but your hate is misdirected. Was your mother ever cruel to you?' Lan looked at the boy sadly.

'No. But I hate you, I hate how she chose you. I hate how she taught me your stupid language. She even left Sia, my real brother and he died,' yelled Mandami.

'I'm sorry you lost your brother. But that is hardly Amities' or your mother's fault. How did he die?' asked Lan.

Mandami was surprised someone thought to ask after his beloved baby brother.

'Plague killed him. But that is because of you evil elves and your magic,' said Mandami.

'Well, that doesn't make any sense. Those forest elves your so-called Pater murdered are healers and could have saved him,' said Lan.

'You are a lying devil. I hope Pater kills you,' yelled the boy.

'So be it.' Lan shrugged.

Lan hugged Amities who took his hand. He offered his other hand to Mandami who bit it. A guard nearby laughed. When Lan didn't react Mandami let go. Lan picked him up by the back of his tunic and hauled him over to Ake who was seated nearby. Hau was with her. The feisty child shrieked and fought.

'Mandami, stop that. It is unbecoming of a Regian prince, my child,' hollered Cephas entering the barracks.

Mandami stopped fighting and Lan handed him to Ake. Amities sat down quietly next to her.

Lan reached his hand out and wiped away the tears that were welling in her eyes. 'I intend to win, honey.'

'We could just leave. We have the boys,' Ake whispered.

Lan shook his head. 'You know he must pay.' He leant down and kissed her briefly.

Mandami turned and whispered to her. 'I hope your husband dies then we can be a family again.'

Ake hugged him tightly. 'I understand that you are hurting.' Mandami eventually returned the hug.

Satisfied, Lan walked down the steps and his feet met the sand that would soak up Cephas's blood. Cephas and Lan were introduced to the crowd. Cephas's list of crimes was not read out so his reputation would not be tarnished. No one cared, they just wanted to see the fight.

Two slaves came over and offered them a choice of weapons. Lan ran his hand over the weapons and scowled as he noticed their poor quality. He looked up at Cephas who had chosen a spear and Regian short sword. Lan grabbed a staff.

'I will use my knives as the daggers offered to me seem to be of the poorest quality.'

'The weapons of women.' Cephas laughed.

Lan examined him. Cephas was very well built for an older human. Scars crossed his muscular arms and chest. He wore only a pleated leather skirt.

'That sword you wield isn't in proportion to your size. Most warriors wield bigger swords.' Lan smirked at Cephas.

Cephas laughed. 'There is nothing wrong with my sword. It conquered your wife and your people.'

Lan's eyes flashed with anger and it took all his willpower to prevent him from disobeying the rules of honour and killing Cephas. *I can't fight with anger or I will lose like last time.*

Lan was dressed in leather breeches and wrist guards, which concealed his weapons. He had cut off his long black hair and now wore it short in the Regian style. He wouldn't have that as a liability if Cephas decided to fight dirty. Lan's elven ears stood out prominently.

The officiate yelled out a command.

Lan looked about, confused.

'It translates to "your positions, gentlemen", said Cephas.

The men faced each other.

'Proceed,' cried the officiate.

Lan stood back waiting for Cephas to charge. Cephas stared back. The crowd cheered.

'They are urging us to fight,' said Cephas.

Cephas was a cautious warrior and Lan relied heavily on judging his enemy's weaknesses such as poor defence and unsteady stances. Both men stood back waiting for the other to make the first move. The crowd booed.

'She was a reasonable lay.' Cephas laughed.

Lan scowled at him.

'You think that will cause me to lose myself and falter?' asked Lan.

'What if I relay the details? Man to man and we can compare who got more use out of her. How many children did she give you? Two. I got four,' said Cephas cruelly.

'Your seed is doomed. I have three healthy sons. You couldn't keep your children alive,' said Lan.

'I have three daughters still alive,' said Cephas.

'Then why would you want my children?' asked Lan.

The crowd booed and threw bread at them.

'Because what use are daughters? Mandami is hers and I love her in my own way. If you die here, you think I will keep my word?' Cephas grinned at him.

'Evil devil.' Enraged Lan rushed at Cephas. 'You will not have her. You could never truly love anyone.'

Cephas brought up the shaft of the spear in his hand to block Lan's overhead strike. As their weapons interlocked, Lan was pushed back on his defensive stance to defend against the onslaught. Lan drew the staff back and tried to swing at Cephas's now open side. Cephas dropped his spear and picked up his sword. Lan's staff broke in two as the sword crashed down.

Lan cursed and threw the pieces to the side. Cephas picked up the spear and hurled it at Lan who easily stepped out of the way. Almost a blur, Lan retrieved the spear and launched it at Cephas, it pierced his left thigh. Cephas grunted and pulled the weapon from his leg. Blood gushed from the wound. Cephas stood up proudly, and rushed Lan. Knowing he was likely to die, he gave it all he had left.

Lan used his knives to counter the overhead blow. He struck out, grazing Cephas's hand. Cephas used his strength to counter another of Lan's attacks and metal shrieked against metal. The blades slid against each other as each man used their strength to try to overcome their opponent. Lan was thrust back, his stance faltering under Cephas's enormous strength.

The crowd cheered and clapped.

Cephas punched Lan in the face with his free hand. Lan stumbled.

'Shall I beat you like I did her?' Cephas laughed.

'What skill, a large brute beating a tiny woman. She could not fight you because you could kill her child and had restrained her magic,' growled Lan.

Cephas charged him repeatedly, striking in all directions. Lan stumbled on one blow and the sword sliced through his arm. Lan gasped at the pain. He heard a small cry above the chanting crowd and turned to look.

Cephas kicked him in the chest while he was distracted and brought the blade down across Lan's shoulder. Lan heard Orilan shouting something in Regian but had to concentrate on the fight.

'You really thought you could threaten me. I am Regis, I am the law. I will die but I will take something down of yours in return.' Cephas grinned cruelly.

Lan somersaulted over Cephas, dragged him by the back of his throat and whispered. 'Was Regis, you're dead now.'

Lan drove his blade through Cephas's back and into his heart. The man gasped and fell forward, his face in the dirt.

Lan had little time to enjoy his victory, he looked around. The cheering crowd stood and bustled about obstructing his view. He heard the whizz of arrows and turned in their direction. Orilan was slinging protective spells to stop the barrage of arrows aimed at Hau and Amities. Cephas had given the guards strict instructions to not injure Mandami or Ake.

Ake was immobilising guards with paralysis and sleep spells. Hau was fighting swarms of guards, his dagger taking life after life. Lan cried out and sent a barrage of lightning bolts hammering into the overwhelming numbers of guards. Hau was struck down and murdered before his eyes.

A dark rage broke in Lan and the sky turned dark. Rain hammered into the ground. A maelstrom of shadows began to form and draw anything living into it. Ake countered with a barrier of water between her family and Lan's dark creation. Regian citizens shrieked and fled. Many were killed in the trampling that ensued. Lan's eyes turned blood-red and he used the vortex to hurl guards in every direction, killing them as they landed. The remaining guards fled but Lan pursued them. Death at his beck and call.

Lan turned his attention to his family. His chest was streaked with blood, some of it his own. He hurled the last of the guards away from him. Blood ran down his face, arms and chest and pooled at his feet. *Maybe we all should die then it will be over.*

Orilan grabbed the boys. 'Run, Ake.'

'Don't be a coward,' Ake yelled over the tempest.

'I am not a god, Ake, I can't defeat that,' said Orilan.

'I can. I can't let that darkness destroy him,' said Ake.

'Find us when you can, Ake. We will be at Caelestis.' Orilan shouted over the ever-increasing noise.

Orilan teleported himself and the boys away. Ake turned to face her awakened lover.

CHAPTER TWENTY-FIVE

Ake's eyes fixed on Lan as he walked towards her, his face contorted in a weird mix of insanity and pride. He halted the vortex. The world fell silent, waiting on bated breath. Lan raised his hand to beckon her.

'Come here, my little goddess.' He laughed insanely.

The wind began to howl and dark shadows burst from him straight towards her.

'*Waterius*,' Ake wrapped herself in her water shield.

Lan laughed. 'Water won't put out this rage.'

The rain began to pelt down again, the temperature dropped to below freezing. Ake's water shield began to freeze. She shattered it. Ake cast paralysis spells on him with no effect.

'I told you to come here,' growled Lan.

He wrapped her in tendrils of shadow and dragged her towards him. She struggled and broke through in her Anwyn form. Rays of sunlight erupted from her. Lan covered his eyes briefly then sent his shadows born of despair hammering into her light shield. They both jostled for control. Their power sparking and flaring as it crashed into each other in waves of power.

'Lan, stop this. This isn't you,' she yelled over the din.

'You created this. If you hadn't healed me with your blood, I wouldn't have this amazing divine power.' Lan grinned at her.

'I didn't make you this.'

'Actually, all these battles, all these deaths are because others are afraid of you or want you,' he said cruelly.

'Then you should have killed me, Lan.' She tore her gaze from his as she blinked back tears.

'I intend to do that. Then this will all be over,' he said.

'Fine, Lan. What of love?' Ake wept.

Ake pulled back her light shield. Lan's shadows engulfed her and dragged her to him.

He pulled her face up to look at him and whispered in her ear. 'It's out of love I intend to kill us both. We won't suffer anymore.'

'You won't hurt me, Lan, I love you. I trust you,' she said.

'Really? I'll hurt anyone who causes me this much rage.' He snarled.

'It's not rage, Lan, it's despair born of those you love and lost,' said Ake.

He plucked one of her golden feathers and traced it over her lips.

'Your love and sweet words over the years caused me to fight for your honour. Now look at all this betrayal and death.' Lan scowled.

'I never asked you to. You chose to, Lan.' Ake gave him a defiant stare.

Lan pulled her face up inches from his. 'Like I ever have a choice when it comes to you.' He laughed.

She watched as he conjured up a dagger of shadows.

'Any last requests?' Lan asked, almost calmly.

Ake shook her head.

Lan was annoyed. *She won't even fight back. It's ridiculous, all that power and no will to destroy me with it and end this suffering. I am sick of it and need to end her control over me,* he thought madly.

He destroyed the dagger.

'I think I will see what all the fuss was,' he whispered sensually in her ear.

'No one has ever done anything to me in this form. It's danger-ous for a mortal.'

'I'm not mortal anymore, you saw to that by fusing your blood, body and soul with mine.' Lan laughed softly.

'You married me to you and courted me!' She struggled in his grip.

'True,' he said coldly.

'Maybe we were wrong for each other.' Ake sobbed.

Her tears and words bothered him.

'I'm not the devil, Ake, I won't ever force that on you.' Lan scowled at her.

'You're acting like one,' she said.

Lan shrugged. 'I just want to try it once in this form before I kill us. Why shouldn't I want that? Why should I always act like the good guy? It's not like I haven't known you before!'

Ake freed her hand and slapped him, hard.

'Good, stop acting so demure all the time. Do you think Drianna would even stop to talk with you before killing you?' he raged.

'You want me here, among the blood of innocent people?' She shrank back in disgust.

'When will you get it through your head? They were not inno-cent. The guards fought with Cephas, wishing for our deaths.' Lan gave her a smile, his eyes full of overwhelming desire. 'You are beautiful. I wouldn't have taken you here, there's a field over there.'

He picked her up, still wrapped in the shadows, and took her away from all the carnage.

'I will kill you with my bare hands, not cowardly with magic. The sin will be mine alone. But you will die among flowers not over there.' He walked towards the place he had picked the flow-ers for her.

Ake began to sob. 'I don't want to die. I want to see wonderful things in the world and raise my children. I didn't ask to be this.

But I don't want to die because of who I am.'

'I don't want you or I to suffer anymore.'

'Who are you to decide who lives or dies, Lan?'

'I am now Lord Bás or quickly becoming him. I never asked for that either, Ake. How do I contain that without killing you or me? I can't die if you don't too.'

Ake shivered as Lan used the name of the former Lord of Death. 'Do you want to die and leave us, Lan?'

'I can't bear another loss, Ake.' Lan scowled and looked away.

Ake glanced up at him, eyes full of love and compassion.

'Don't you dare! You think that is enough to make me overcome this hate of these humans?' He groaned.

'One last request. At least kill me at home. I don't want to die here. Not when my best memories are there.' She gave him an imploring look.

He nodded. They were caught up in a swirling golden light. When it cleared, they were home. The white fortress of Caelestis shone against a brilliant blue sky.

—⁂—

Drianna screamed. She felt her reach weaken on Lan and fuelled all her power into a ball of rage. It surged through Lan.

'You must kill her, elf. Kings will rise and fall, and they will want a powerful queen. You will spend the next centuries giving your life for hers as they seek her out.'

'I would gladly give my life for hers again and again.' Lan struggled against Drianna's influence.

'And when you fail again as you have done before. They will take her to their bed, and she will suffer again.'

—⁂—

Lan gritted his teeth and his red eyes glistened deeper. He dropped Ake and grabbed at his head.

'No one will put her through that again. Death will prevent that.'

Lan drew his mystic knives and charged Ake. She yelped and clambered to her feet. Ake cast her sun shield at him, and Lan staggered back.

Lan sent a vortex of shadows crashing into her shield, shattering it. Drianna was an older more powerful force than Ake. He charged her again and nearly struck her when he was surrounded in a druid ward. Orilan stood next to Ake.

'Do I have to do what you vowed to do?' asked Orilan.

Lan bristled, then laughed. 'You dare defy me, little demon?'

'Those are Drianna's words,' cried Orilan.

Lan, under Drianna's influence, clicked his fingers and the druid ward exploded. Lan pointed at Orilan and he was flung like a rag doll. Lan charged Ake again and she hammered him with her sunlight shield. Lan faltered and pretended to catch his breath.

'Ake?' Lan called softly, pretending to weaken.

He felt Drianna reach in and draw more of his powers and screamed and clawed at his face. 'Get away from me, you foul goddess.'

Ake walked over to him wearily. She wrapped her arms around him. Drianna felt the link break, but she had damaged him.

Lan felt Ake's arms wrap around him. He grinned and gazed down at her. Her eyes fixated on his, full of love. He grabbed and shook her. Ake kicked him and Lan laughed and released her.

'Fine, you want me dead,' she said softly.

Using her thieving skills, she took one of his knives. Ake hoped she could call his bluff. Orilan got up and groaned.

'Go keep the children safe,' said Ake.

Orilan nodded and rushed off.

Lan saw Ake draw the knife across her wrist. The blood poured out.

'What the hell are you doing?'

Lan sent the knife flying in a vortex of shadows.

'You wanted me dead. Which means you will have your death too,' said Ake.

He dragged her towards him without lifting a finger. She fought back weakly, then fell to her knees. Lan soon felt ill. The dark power began to recede, and he saw Ake fall and grabbed her up. He teleported them to the infirmary and set about suturing and bandaging her wrist.

Her eyes spluttered open. 'See, Lan, I knew you wouldn't hurt me.'

He slammed his hand down on a table nearby, shattering it.

'How could you have known that?' he asked.

The red in his eyes disappeared.

'You promised to protect me.' Ake gave Lan a radiant smile.

'But I did try, Ake. Don't you realise that? You defended yourself.' Lan looked at her, despair in his eyes.

'That was Drianna using you. Now I can't hide, Lan. We need to destroy her,' she said with conviction.

'I need to leave you,' said Lan.

'Don't you dare do that. Sit down, now. You made all my decisions for me and played the damn hero. Now when I realise I need to fight with you, you think you can leave? Hell no,' she yelled.

'But I—' Lan was interrupted.

'Now who is acting naïve, Lan? You were not at fault. Thank you for killing Cephas. I am sorry I questioned you over those deaths. You had every right to try and protect us.' Ake smiled.

He looked at her in anger. 'What if I refuse to stay?'

Ake flexed her wrist and unbandaged it. She cast healing magic on it, and it became almost like new. Ake turned to smile at her husband.

'I'm going now.' Lan turned to leave.

'Sure, for now. I'll come find you when I want you.'

Lan turned his head to look at her one last time, tears in his eyes. Then he walked away.

'He always comes back.'

Chapter Twenty-Six

Orilan had teleported them back to the town of Moriconium. *It's been two days since he left.* Ake walked into the bakery and lined up among other women getting bread for the day's meals. She wrapped her cloak around herself, trying to appear as a commoner. Several women whispered behind her.

'Isn't that the former empress?'

'Don't be ridiculous, as if she would be unaccompanied. I know that word has been sent to the emperor's mother to look for Mandami.'

Another woman rushed forward eager to add to the gossip. 'She won't want Mandami. That boy was sired by the demonic elf that killed the emperor.'

'How do you know this?'

'My husband was the guard picked to accompany the emperor when the contract for the fight was drawn up. Our former empress is an elven noble. Cephas took her against his will.'

The women made noises of disgust.

'Well, I kind of feel sorry for her. I can't feel sorry for that elf though, we are still burying the dead.'

The women grabbed their bread and left. Ake's heart began to beat rapidly, and her eyes darted around the room as she cautiously approached the counter.

'Excuse me. Do you know of anyone who helped bury the dead after the fight?'

'I did,' said the baker.

Thank goodness, this is the sixth person I have asked. 'I am looking for information on a teenager. He had green eyes and chestnut hair. Did you bury anyone like that?' Ake stared up at him.

'I am sorry, there were so many, I didn't check. Most of the bodies were mangled. We are still burying the last of them.'

Maybe I can still find his body and bury him near Relequis. There is no shield after the death of the mages who maintained it.

'Thank you for the information. Can I have that cake over there?' Ake handed over the gold coin that she had taken from the Caelestis vault. *The boys will love this.*

The man looked at her then smiled. 'This kind of money is reserved for elven nobles. Welcome home Empress.'

Ake turned and ran. She heard heavy footprints behind her as the man followed her on to the street.

'That is the Empress,' yelled the baker.

Ake watched Mismanam rise from where he was seated nearby. He had been Cephas's most trusted general and appeared to be giving orders. Another regiment of fifty soldiers had been ordered to Moriconium to help keep order and had arrived that morning. Ake trembled with fear and her eyes scanned her surroundings, looking for an escape.

Mismanam motioned to several other guards to cut her off. 'Poor woman, she is quaking with fear after being stolen from her loving husband. We can't let that demon elf come back for her,' yelled Mismanam.

'How dare he claim Mandami as his,' cried another.

'Cephas was a good man. He would never have hurt her,' said a citizen.

'See how she returns to the place of the Emperor's death. She clearly loved him,' said Mismanam.

To the Regian empire, Cephas had appeared as a brilliant

warlord and builder of cities. When they saw Ake, she had looked beautiful, dressed in the latest fashions, borne on a litter to dinner parties. When she had given birth to a son, the Regians believed their god had smiled upon the union.

Very few knew of the cruel things Cephas practiced behind closed doors. Cephas had told his people the elves had kidnapped Ake and had avenged her by ridding the world of their evil presence. After that he had focused on raising his son.

On the anniversary of Ake's disappearance Cephas held a feast in her honour. Little did the Regians know this was to save face at having a mere woman elude him. To the Regians it appeared that Cephas had cared for his bride.

Mismanam approached Ake gently. 'Hello, your highness. I have you surrounded. It is unsafe here. That elf could be anywhere.'

'I wonder if she can still call on that evil magic. Hopefully that was due to that elf's influence, and she is no longer tainted,' said Mismanam as three guards closed in on her.

'Leave me alone,' Ake screamed.

———~~~———

Orilan jabbed the shovel into the ground and shivered as he heard a woman scream. *I have had enough of the screaming of women and children.* He had slowly been filling in the graves. With only one hand he couldn't dig them, but he could push the soil into the ground with his good hand.

The children sat nearby, and he saw Amities cover his ears.

'What is it?' asked Orilan.

'That's Mother.' Amities stood up and stared in the direction.

Mandami unsheathed his dagger and without a second thought ran towards the noise.

'Stay here and hide, Amities.' Orilan turned and sprinted after Mandami as Amities went and hid behind a stack of wood.

'Come on, Empress, we mean you no harm. You need to tell me where Mandami is. He is in danger. If spies hear he is missing, they may try to kill him to weaken the empire.' Mismanam gave her a gentle smile. 'I know as a lone woman you must be very frightened.'

Ake glared at him. 'Let me go or you will suffer.'

'She's not willing to listen. Use force to capture but don't injure her if it can be helped.' Mismanam darted towards her, no weapons drawn.

He stumbled as a sharp blade was pushed into his leg. Mismanam grunted and turned to see Mandami glaring at him.

'Get away from my Mater. Pater would hate you for this.'

Mismanam bowed. 'Of course, my Emperor.' He withdrew the dagger and handed it to Mandami. Mandami reached out for the dagger and was captured by the general.

He began to squirm. 'Put me down.'

'No, little master, we must see you safely home.'

Ake began to sob. *Not more death.* She conjured fire and burned the guards as they came close to her. They screamed. Mismanam put Mandami down and charged her, sword drawn.

A whirling vortex of shadows appeared in front of Ake and the general was forced backwards. The noise that accompanied it deafened those that got close to it.

'Do not give in to the demon, Empress,' cried Mismanam.

'Get out of here, Mandami,' yelled a voice full of darkness.

Mandami turned and ran. The shadows swelled as if they were losing control. Ake screamed as she was caught up in them. She could not see in front of her. *This must be Orilan's Shadow Gate spell.*

―――⁓―――

Orilan saw Mandami running away from a large general. The general had his back towards him and was retreating from a massive vortex of shadows. The general turned and ran. *That general helped capture Ake when Caelestis was defeated.* Orilan growled. His eyes turned red, and he grabbed the general.

'Hello, lunch.' He sank his teeth into the man's neck and took his fill.

Orilan threw the body away from him. He picked up Mandami's dagger and approached the vortex.

'Ake, are you okay in there?' He thought he heard her voice.

―――⁓―――

'Ori, I need to make sure Mandami is okay.'

Ake felt someone caress her cheek and drew back. 'How dare you touch me after all I have been through.'

The person made a noise of anguish and the shadows retreated. Ake blinked in the sunlight and saw Orilan grinning at her.

'I am glad you came to help me but no more of your games.'

Orilan had his fangs bared and quickly closed his mouth. He blinked and his eyes returned to normal. 'Sorry, I had to help you.'

'There is no sign of Hau. Let's get the boys and get out of here.'

Orilan nodded and they both ran in the direction Mandami had taken.

CHAPTER TWENTY-SEVEN

Lan teleported himself back to Caelestis and ran until his lungs couldn't give anymore. He found himself on the beach. He sat down and closed his eyes. *I need to learn how to control this thing until she is no longer frightened of me.* Lan's stomach gurgled and he opened his eyes. *It must be later than I thought.* He looked up and the stars shimmered, softening the black depths of the moonless sky.

He stood up and began to walk along the beach. He walked for what seemed like a few hours and saw a cave. He blinked and looked up and saw the sun high in the sky. *I have lost track of time in my grief.* His shoulders slumped with exhaustion, and he walked into the cave and lay down as the weariness washed over him and he fell asleep.

Lan opened his eyes and Caelestis materialised in front of him. He shivered in the cool of dusk. *She is expecting me.* A horrid chanting captured his attention and his gaze settled on Orilan dancing naked under a full moon, incense burned steadily in holders set in nearby stone. The smell was awful and Lan wrinkled his nose.

'*Exitus morte kultes, exitus Drianna,*' cried Orilan.

Lan smiled and sprinted past. Sneaking into Caelestis, he ran into his office, threw back the trapdoor and ran down the steps.

His eyes darted about the room and settled on Ake. She shifted in her sleep. He sighed and his robe caught on the music box he had made her. His heart filled with joy as he remembered the night he sang to her. The room began to spin and he closed his eyes. *'Exitos morte kultes,'* pierced his eardrums and he covered them trying to block out the sound. As the noise faded, he opened his eyes and realised it was morning and he was in the village of Axeton. He shoved the music box into his pocket. He rushed over to the town well and drew up a pail of water and began gulping it down. After his thirst was quenched, he dropped the pail and it made a clunking noise as it hit the insides of the stone well, the handle spun rapidly, aiding the pail's descent.

Wandering around the market square, Lan paid for some food. Glancing up, someone familiar began to approach. The darkness swelled around him. *Time for Het's mother to confront you.* Closing his eyes, Lan took a deep breath, ready to face her wrath.

Lan's eyes fluttered open. Kathy had disappeared. It was dusk again. He turned and his eyes skimmed over a familiar house. The roof had collapsed, and the once carefully tended herb and flower garden was overrun. Tears welled in his eyes as he remembered the fight that took his mother's life. *My poor mother. I need to get home.*

He teleported himself back to Caelestis and saw his sons throwing a ball to each other.

'Amities that was a weak throw.' Mandami grinned.

Amities scrambled towards the ball and picked it up. He threw it again and it didn't make it to Mandami. Mandami rolled his eyes, picked up the ball and strode over to his brother. He shoved the ball in his brother's arm and lifted Amities other arm and held it straight.

'Throw with the other, keep this one straight as a guide. It will help you throw straight.'

Amities followed the instruction and was able to throw the ball further.

'Good job Amities,' said Mandami.

'I love you Mandami,' cried Amities.

'Love you too brother,' mumbled Mandami.

Lan picked up the ball and cleared his throat.

'Father,' yelled Amities.

Lan thew the ball and Mandami caught it. Amities rushed over sobbing and threw himself in to his father's arms. Lan hugged him before gently placing him down.

A whispering began in his ears as both boy's took his hands and they walked towards the fortress. 'Exitos Morte Kultes.'

Lan felt dizzy and closed his eyes, when he opened them he was in his room. He threw open his wardrobe and began rummaging around. *I have to let her know this is happening.* He pulled out an ink vial and quill and shoved them in his pockets. Then he continued to search the wardrobe when his hands brushed a small black box. The smell of dried rose petals wafted on the air as he opened it and pulled out a wad of letters. The room began to spin, and he groaned as he heard three little words, *exitos morte kultes.*

⁓⁓⁓

Ake sat at the tavern in Axeton, the smaller of the two villages on the island of Man'hannon. It had been several weeks since they had returned from Moriconium. She had heard from some villagers in Mencrey that they had spotted an elf wandering aimlessly around the market square. When a citizen had approached, the elf had disappeared as if he had never been there. She placed her drink down on the table and looked around. The Braying Burro had been renovated, no longer resembling a shack. The floors were made of polished wood and the foundation was made of interlocking stone walls. Masons had chosen stones of similar size and shaped them with a chisel and hammer to make sure they fit snuggly against each other. This process was known as a dry stone wall. A trench would have been dug to support the foundation.

Almost every farmer and villager knew how to make a simple wall this way and Ake was aware of the process having seen farmers repair simple walls in her trek to find Lan. The other half of the walls were made of split timbers that interlocked and the roof was thatched.

She took out the hastily scrawled note from her pocket and read it again.

Ake,

Sorry I didn't wake you. I know you are angry with me for saying I needed to leave you and that is understandable. I could never do that. I am going for a walk to clear my head. I will be back at dusk. You must realise the danger I could put you and our children in. I took so many lives at Moriconium. Please forgive me for what I said and remember you and our children are my whole world.

I love you all,

Lan

Ake slipped the letter back into her pocket and scowled. *You never returned. We could have worked through this together, you stubborn elf.* She stood up and went to order another drink. Some middle-aged men were enjoying their beverages. An older, familiar man sat with them. A woman entered the tavern and stared at her in shock.

'It can't be.' The woman rushed over to her and enveloped her in a hug.

Ake gently pulled back. 'Kathy?'

'It is you, Ake. I didn't think you survived the fall of Caelestis. I heard rumours that Lan had, and I saw him a few days ago. I called out to him, but he disappeared.'

Ake gave her a huge smile and hugged her. 'It is good to see you again. Thank you for the information on Lan.'

'I am sorry you never got to marry Het.' Kathy frowned.

'I am sorry you lost a son, Kathy. It was horrible that a good man lost his life.' Ake's eyes brimmed with tears. 'He was brave to the end.'

Kathy wiped a tear from her eye. 'Come join us.'

Ake followed Kathy over to her family and sat down.

'Do you remember Ake?' asked Kathy.

'How could we forget Het's beau?' said Het's father.

Ake shifted on the spot. *Should I tell them about Flo and the twins she bore?*

'Do you at least still wear the ring?' asked Het's oldest brother.

'What do you mean?' asked Ake.

'Het intended to propose to you the night he died. Didn't he get the chance?' asked Kathy.

Ake blushed. 'No, he didn't. I am sorry.'

'Oh, I am sorry, Ake. We shouldn't have mentioned it. It must hurt you that he never got to ask you.' Kathy put her hand on her shoulder. 'You will always be a welcome member of this family.'

Ake stood up and the chair screeched across the wood in protest. 'Let me buy a round to celebrate Het.'

Before they could refuse, she ordered a round. They raised their glasses in a toast. 'To a good son, brave warrior and a man that was like a brother to me. We raise this toast.'

'Hear hear,' said the Gingers and a handful of other people in the bar.

Ake sipped her drink slowly and listened to the conversation that focused on the pranks Het and Ake had got up to in their youth. Ake stood and wandered over to the bar and ordered a sarsaparilla. She asked for a piece of paper and a writing implement. The barkeep handed her some rough paper and a stick of charcoal used for writing down drink orders. *It is not my place to deprive her of information regarding her son.* Ake hastily scribbled out a note.

Het loved the elven empress Elder Fower. She bore him twin sons Falcon and Hau. Unfortunately, Falcon died young, and Hau passed away recently. I am so sorry, Kathy, to tell you this way.

Kathy approached her, out of earshot of her family, and gently grabbed her left hand. Ake watched as Kathy's eyes settled on her engagement ring. The exquisite silver ring had a moonstone carved in the shape of a star set into it.

'Did my son make his feelings known at least?'

Ake nodded. 'Yes. I told him I loved him like a brother years earlier. He was aware.'

Kathy sighed. 'I am sorry if we made you uncomfortable. Het talked constantly of you. We were not aware you had chosen another. I believe he figured you would choose him in the end.'

'I am sorry, Kathy, I should go.'

Kathy smiled. 'I am sorry about all this. May I ask a question before you go?'

Ake wiped her eyes. 'Of course.'

'Did you choose Lan in the end?'

Ake looked shocked. 'What do you know of that choice?'

'I am a cleric of Dee. It was either Het or Lan.' Kathy squeezed her hand.

Ake stared at her in shock. 'Did you encourage Het in any way?'

Kathy let her hand go. 'No. Het came home from school one day and said he found the girl of his dreams. When he told us your name, I didn't discourage him. Hoping I could help protect you from Drianna and others who would use you, I put a block on your powers hoping to throw off Drianna. I intended to protect both of you and linked you to Het.'

'I cast a spell on you that if either of you ever kissed your beloved the spell would be broken. This would unleash the floodgates on both of you, causing your powers to grow. You wouldn't be alone with your intended at your side.'

Kathy squeezed her hand. 'After you were wed, and the marriage bed was consummated your souls would have been bound. If your husband was ever put in danger your father's gifts would awaken. I had hoped to keep both you and Het safe.'

Ake took a step back. 'That is why I failed school in the earlier years. I could barely cast the most basic of spells. I thought I had dreamt my village going up in flames as I wished those that would harm my mother pain. I could have learnt to control that power rather than Lan being nearly killed. Het did kiss me when I was sixteen and my powers started to awaken. But he was never my beloved.'

Kathy gave her a look of warmth. 'It seemed Het believed you were his beloved. His love for you was enough to awaken the first stirrings of your returning magic.' Kathy smiled. 'I am glad the spell protected you from the Shadow Masters and their scouts for many years.'

'I suppose it did.' Ake sighed. 'I must go. Take care of yourselves.'

The women gave each other a brief hug and Ake pushed the note into Kathy's hand and left.

—⁂—

Orilan shivered as a demon's horrendous cries rent the air. He snuck out of Caelestis and ran towards the beast. He stared transfixed as a hideous apparition clawed at his invisible wards.

'I will counteract you at every turn Drianna! Do you hear me? You will not lay a hand on Ake or my brothers.'

He scrutinised the creature and his eyes brimmed with hot, angry tears. *How could she do that to her own daughter?* Fate, Drianna's only child, had once been his lover. He had killed her when he was weak and drained her of her powers to escape his cell when she had tried to tempt him into overthrowing her mother. The monster had Fate's hauntingly beautiful face, attached to the neck of a giraffe. It was absent of human limbs and chest, and instead sported the thorax of a blue beetle, bat wings and scaly reptilian-like appendages had been attached in place of arms or legs. Jagged scars at the point of attachment almost suggested they had been laboriously sewn on. The foul monster moaned, its tongue lolled outwards as it tilted its eyes and fixed its gaze on Orilan.

'Come, lover boy.' Its eyes rolled back into its head. 'Let me in.'

Orilan looked about and rubbed his shoulders in the cold night air. There was little light as the moon was covered by rolling clouds.

'Be gone, hideous demon. You cannot break my wards.' Orilan swivelled and took a step towards the fortress.

The creature screeched and began throwing itself at the invisible barrier. 'I smell a fellow demon, you inbred wretch.'

Orilan's shoulders slumped, and he sighed before turning to face the monster.

'I am an inbred and often callous wretch. But at least I am my own man now and I have something Drianna doesn't. Ake and Mandami.' Orilan laughed as the beast howled and scratched at the barrier before turning its own appendages on itself, clawing at its body.

'Free me from this body, Mother,' it yelled.

'You obviously can't get in.' Orilan ran back towards Caelestis as the moon peaked out from behind the clouds, a cacophony of howls, screeches and roars assaulted his ears. He slowly turned to face the onslaughts as thousands of sets of eyes blinked at him from the ancient oaken forest. He trembled and closed his eyes. The sounds faded and he risked a peek, the eyes had vanished. *They can't get in yet. But they are getting stronger and bolder. Mandami just has to reach adulthood and when Drianna is defeated, I can live a life free of her taint and prove myself a good man.* Orilan walked towards Caelestis, his held high and smiled, hope filling his soul with joy.

CHAPTER TWENTY-EIGHT

Galloping hooves pounded the earth and a tingling of bells filled the air as Ake and Borrush appeared at the location a messenger had relayed to them. Ake saw an elf run past, chased by men on galloping horses, the elf wheezed with the effort of prolonged running.

'That's our elf,' cried a booming voice behind him. A spear whizzed past the elf, and he ran towards them.

'Help me,' cried the elf.

Ake threw flames at the two horsemen, the horses reared up, unseating their masters.

'Come with us now, you will be safe,' said Ake.

'No, I travel to find my lord,' said the elf.

'There are no elven kings,' cried Ake.

'Liar!' The elf rushed past Ake into the woods.

Ake chased him, searching everywhere for him. The horsemen followed them. Ake turned as the sword came crashing down upon her head. There was a tingling of bells and she stood outside Caelestis.

Ake jolted awake and rubbed her eyes, exhausted from the morning's search that had just haunted her sleep. *I only closed my eyes for a moment.* Ake sighed, picked up her quill and signed the letter with her name. This was the thirtieth one she had written. Orilan's research had yielded promising results. He had reached out to Borrush, the last dwarven druid, by letter.

Borrush had written several crude replies telling Orilan to stop contacting him. Orilan had given it one more go, telling him that Ake was trying to re-establish the mystic order and hoped to work with druids and mages as well. Borrush had arrived a few days later.

Ake began stuffing the letters into addressed envelopes. Her tongue was dry, and she realised she had missed the evening meal. *I can't believe it's been over a year since Lan ran.* She ran her hands over the manifesto that she and Borrush had compiled of sightings of survivors from Caley and Relequis. While she had managed to offer sanctuary in Caelestis to some, others had refused, taking their chances on the road. Strangely, several had arrived rescued by a presence surrounded by a vortex of shadows. *So, Ori does care. He is helping too.* She looked at the crossed-out names of the deceased on the page in front of her. The words became bleary as her eyes watered. She sniffled and fought back tears. *Poor things.* There was a gentle knock on the door.

'Come in.'

The door opened and Orilan struggled with the tray. Ake rushed over and took it from him as he balanced it against the door while he pushed it open.

His skin sagged and had taken on an ashen hue and his hair was unkempt. She knew he was eating well but he appeared to be wasting away.

'Are you okay, Ori?'

Orilan smiled. 'Why wouldn't I be?'

'Have you been hunting?'

Orilan stared at her, bewildered. 'You told me not to play any more games.'

'That's not what I meant. You seem to have misunderstood.' Ake placed down the tray. 'Thank you for the meal.'

'I didn't cook it. Borrush hired a servant from Mencrey.' Orilan laughed. 'Beats your cooking.'

Ake smirked then joined in. 'Have you ever cooked before belittling mine?'

'I like my prey rare.' Orilan gave her an eerie smile and his eyes flashed red briefly as he tried to hold her gaze.

Ake pried her eyes away, clearing her throat, uncomfortable. She pushed the food around on her plate before noticing the slice of chocolate cake. 'What's with the cake? Not that I am complaining.'

'It's yours and my birthday. I have never had a birthday cake before. I know it's not an elvish tradition to celebrate other than our hundredth birthday, but I wanted to try it anyway.'

'That's right, you were born on my ninth birthday. I am sorry you never had a birthday before. Wait a second.' She smiled. 'I can rectify that.'

Ake pulled open the draw in the desk and drew out a candle. She walked over to the torch on the wall and lit the candle. 'Come here, Ori.'

Orilan stepped forward, curious. 'What do I do now? I thought we just ate the cake.'

'No, you are supposed to make a wish with eyes closed then blow out the candle and hope it comes true. Then people embarrass you by singing a song.'

Orilan laughed. 'What a strange tradition. But you must do it too as it is your birthday as well.'

Ake smiled. 'Okay.' She closed her eyes. 'I hope Lan comes home.' Ake opened her eyes, and he tore his gaze away. She frowned as his eyes had drifted down her form.

'Your turn. Make your wish.'

Orilan closed his eyes.

Ake watched Orilan scowl. 'Ori, are you okay?'

Orilan opened his eyes and smiled coldly. 'Of course.'

'On the count of three we blow out the candle.'

Orilan nodded.

'One, two—'

Orilan blew out the candle. 'We make our own wishes.' He grabbed Ake and embraced her. He released her quickly. 'Happy birthday to me.' He grinned.

Ake stomped on his foot and he yelped.

'What was that for?'

'You don't hug people without consent.' Ake placed the candle down on the desk.

Orilan tilted his head, feeling confused. 'I see you hug people all the time without asking.'

'I know these people, Ori. They also don't harbour romantic feelings towards me.' Ake sighed. 'I forget you were raised with Drianna. Did Dane ever teach you anything on social norms?'

'You mean how to charm people to do your bidding by being tactful?'

'That's diplomacy, Ori. I mean how to greet others, what forms of touch are acceptable between friends and how it differs between family and spouses. Did Dane teach you any of that?'

Orilan shook his head.

Ake stared at his pointed ears. 'Right, you are only twenty-eight.'

'What of it?'

'Starting tomorrow you are going to do some reading. As an elfling you are very far behind.'

'No, I do not wish to learn your human ways.' Orilan turned and walked from the room.

'You will have to Ori if you expect to stay here,' she called after him.

Mandami listened at the keyhole. *That dirty demon is after my mother. Thank goodness she sorted him.* Orilan pulled open the door suddenly and Mandami fell against him.

'Hello, little brother.'

'How many times do I have to warn you not to call me brother?' Mandami glared at him.

'Are you here to wish your mother a happy birthday?' Orilan gave him a smug smile.

'I am now.'

Amities rushed towards them and ran through the door. 'Happy birthday, dear Mother.' The little boy hugged Ake.

'He always gets in first.' Mandami glared at Amities.

'He remembered, you did not,' said Orilan.

'True.' Mandami turned and gave Orilan a warning glance. 'You better not touch my mother again. As much as I detest your father—'

Orilan grinned. 'Our father.'

Mandami tried to shove Ori. 'Keep your hands off her. She belongs to your father.'

Ake looked up. 'I would prefer you didn't enter my office alone, Ori, if you are going to try and hug me.'

Orilan sighed and closed his eyes briefly. 'Okay, I was just feeling down.'

Amities winced. He ran over to Orilan and offered his arms to him. Orilan picked up his brother and the boy gave him a big squeeze. He placed the boy back on the ground. 'Thank you for that.'

Orilan strode from the room.

'Mother, Ori is sick,' said Amities.

'I agree.'

Lan watched Ake from a distance, hiding in the shadows like some criminal with ill intent. He checked in on her, what felt like weekly, hoping she was safe. He had followed her from Caelestis to Axeton, she didn't make this trip often and he was curious.

'Hey, are you that mistress from Caelestis?'

Ake looked up from checking the contents in her basket.

'Yes, I am.' Ake smiled.

'That whorish husband of yours has been frequenting the bawdy house and seducing as many men and women as possible.'

Ake's eyes drew wide with shock. 'You must be mistaken.'

'Elf, dark hair and unusually tall for one of those creatures.'

Ake gulped and her eyes filled with tears. 'He wouldn't do that.' She glared through her tears. 'Elves aren't creatures.'

The woman laughed. 'Rumour has it, he fled Caelestis and his frigid bride and slakes his needs elsewhere.'

Lan moved closer and drew his hood tighter around his scowling face, a shelter against his anger and the icy cold draught.

'And where did you see this so-called elf?' Ake sniffled.

The woman turned and pointed to a small shack. 'Madam Benedict owns the joint, cheap booze and lovers. Free diseases too.' The woman smirked and wandered off.

Ake approached the door and slowly opened it. Lan could hear the raucous laughter. He watched billows of smoke hit her as she entered. She coughed and was the victim of cat calls and indecent comments. He ground his teeth and used the shadows to conceal himself, following a step behind.

'Hey, Benedict, is this a new wench of yours?'

'Pretty wee thing. Bit too skinny though.'

'Hey, Arnold, buy her a meal and fatten her up.'

Another whistled and made a thrusting motion at Ake. 'I'd tumble her.'

Lan saw Ake shiver and went to touch her then withdrew his

hand. Ake ignored the comments and approached the bar. A buxom woman greeted her. 'I am Madam Benedict, what are you wanting?'

'I am looking for a male elf, dark hair, dark eyes, about this tall.' Ake indicated a little taller than herself.

The madam pointed to a room. 'He's getting it for free now.'

Ake blushed as laughter followed her. Lan watched as she entered the room and closed the door. He picked up the drink of the guy who had thrust himself at Ake and dumped it on him. The man looked taken aback and backed away, tripping and falling into the lap of his mate, who laughed.

Orilan looked startled as Ake opened the door and entered. He blushed as he saw her face fill with relief.

'So, it's just you then, Orilan.'

Orilan jabbed the man in the nearby bed in the ribs. 'Get out of here.'

The man grumbled, dressed and rushed towards the door. The man tapped his foot, annoyed at her and she scrambled out the way.

'He was willing, Ake.'

Ake shrugged. 'He's not dead so I guess it's your life, Orilan.' She gave him a brief smile and looked distressed.

Orilan sauntered towards her, naked and without shame. 'You thought it was Lan up to these sorts of antics. You know he wouldn't do that.'

Ake began to sob. 'I know but I miss him. Who knows what Drianna's influence has made him capable of.'

Orilan sighed. 'You know he would harm himself before he did something that would make you hate him.'

'He's been gone too long.' Ake covered her face with her hands and wept.

She squealed when he wrapped her in his arms. She began to fight, and he held her firmly against him. 'I'm here with you.'

Orilan slid the bolt across the door and Ake kicked him and struggled. Orilan laughed and drew away. She looked down at his obvious desire for her and blushed before scrambling for the bolt. She drew it but not before her eyes widened in fear as he turned her towards him and kissed her, she struggled, and his hands slipped under her dress.

'So, you are all natural under here.'

She belted him across the face, and he pushed her gently away. Her face was bright red, and her eyes shone with anger.

'Damn, you're beautiful when you're angry. I'll be honest, I want you. I have no qualms about sharing you with him and deferring to my father when he returns.'

Ake yelled at him. 'I am your father's wife. Do you have any shred of decency? You will stay away from Caelestis. I don't want to see you again, you disgusting person!'

Orilan laughed. 'I will not. Someone must look out for you while Lan's gone.'

'What has gotten into you, Orilan?' Ake opened the door.

'Please, wait,' he pleaded.

She sighed and turned to look at him. 'Be quick about it.'

Orilan looked away, as feelings of despair washed over him. 'It's begun to overwhelm me. Vampyrs who are away from their masters too long eventually become rabid and primal. I feel lost and I need hel—' Orilan smiled. 'You have enough to worry about. Leave me alone, Ake, it really isn't any of your concern, unless you care to join me. I can ease both our loneliness.' Orilan took a step towards the bed and gestured to it as he threw on a nightgown.

Lan heard Ake weep then yell in distress. He saw her open the door and turn to stare at Orilan naked. He rushed into the room.

Orilan grinned and caught the nearby vase she threw at him. 'Don't you touch me like that ever again or I'll—'

Lan felt the rage build. *I have warned him about touching her against her will.* He slipped past Ake and delivered Orilan a kick to his tender regions.

Orilan's smile soon vanished as he yelped and slid to the floor in pain, clutching his groin. 'S— that hurt.'

Ake laughed. 'Befitting.'

'Wow, thanks,' grumbled Orilan.

Lan turned to stare at Ake and his love for her overwhelmed him, the shadows disappeared for the briefest of moments. He smiled at her and reached out a hand. *Kill her, you have the power make her your bride in the underworld.*

'No,' Lan groaned.

Ake rushed towards him, a look of desperation on her face. 'Please, come home.'

'I tried.' He gave her a sad smile. He felt time pressing in on him. The room spun and then it was morning, and he was near the beach. He yelled out in frustration before falling to his knees and sobbing.

Ake returned to Caelestis and began to pace the room. She wrung her hands in frustration. *I hate Ori at the moment, but he clearly needs help.* Ake sighed. *I need rest. I will talk to Borrush tomorrow evening when he returns from his current task.* She sighed again and her thoughts turned to her absent husband. Her lip trembled and tears ran down her face. *I can't believe Lan would rather stay away than let me try and help him. Am I really that helpless?* She scrambled beneath her blankets and fell into a fitful sleep dotted with past terrors, hugging her knees to her chest.

———∿∿∿———

Borrush sat in the cafeteria dipping a drinking horn into a barrel of ale. He drew it to his lips and drained the vessel. *Nothing better than a drink or two after a challenging day.* He had spent the day teleporting to sixteen places to deliver Ake's letters. *Why did I give her so many names?* He smiled to himself. *Five replies. We will have four retired elven mystics and a half-elven mage.*

Ake walked into the room. 'How are you, Lord Borrush?' Ake dipped her head.

Borrush scrambled up. 'Well met, Lady of Caelestis.'

After the formalities were over, the conversation became less formal.

'I have news. Four elven mystics and a half-elven mage will be arriving with the dawn. The mystics used to teach here before they retired fifty years ago.'

Ake smiled. 'That is fantastic news. I can't thank you enough for all your help.'

Borrush smiled. 'I thank ye for the compliment, lass. My king has given me three weeks of leave a year. I would like to teach druidcraft at Caelestis every summer.'

'I would appreciate it but that would mean taking you away from your family.'

'They are fine with it, lass.'

'Then at least let me pay you.'

Borrush snorted. 'After Dane's awful passing I made a promise to look out for you and his boy. I will not take your gold, lass.'

'Okay, Borrush.' Ake held out her hand.

Borrush clasped her hand. 'It's a deal now.'

Ake released his hand and sighed.

'You worried about that demon lad too?'

'He isn't hunting.'

'That would explain his ill look. I think it's time we rid him of the vampyr within.'

Ake stared at him in shock. 'He can be rid of it?'

Borrush nodded. 'Fairly simple ceremony. Lad's done most of it himself by resisting the temptation. Dane tried before but gave into the lad's pleas. Had a real soft spot for him.'

'What do we need?'

'Patience, silver, faith and a whole lot of sturdy rope.'

Ake grinned. 'When do we start?'

'Your boys asleep?'

Ake nodded.

'Then let's go deal with the lad.'

They proceeded out of the cafeteria.

———

She had that awful nightmare again last night. Something about an old man and rivers of blood. Her cries had chilled him to the bone. He shivered. *I will wake her and confront her if it happens tonight. Expressing it to another may rid her of it.* He saw Mandami peek out from behind a half-closed door.

I wish that child would stop following me. I am not going to kiss his mother without her permission. He smiled at that thought. *Now, if she insisted …* The door creaked open further.

'Mandami, stop following me.' Orilan strode over to the door and pushed it open.

Mandami drew his dagger. 'Why are you by my mother's door?'

'None of your business.'

'It is my business. That is my Mater.'

Amities yawned and rolled over. 'She prefers Mother.'

'Are you attempting to court her, Ori?' Mandami glared at him.

'How can you say something so crude? Your father is missing, and I am looking out for his wife.' Orilan gave the child a disarming smile. *It's not entirely a lie. I am looking out for her. I don't believe in drawn out romantic gestures. I would never court a lover.*

'Why didn't you say anything? We are both trying to look out for her.' Mandami gave him a fake smile.

They heard the sound of Ake and Borrush talking as they walked down the hallway. Orilan stepped out of the boys' room and into the hall.

'Your children aren't asleep yet,' said Orilan.

Ake turned and looked at the dagger in Mandami's hand. 'Go to bed, Mandami. And give me that dagger, you can have it in the morning.'

Mandami glared at her. 'No, a soldier is never separated from their weapon.'

Ake strode towards him, and the boy slammed the door shut and locked it.

'Fine, just stay in your room, boys.' Ake sighed and turned back to Orilan. 'Would you be rid of that vampyr within you?'

Orilan tilted his head. 'Of course, but Dane tried and failed.'

'That's because Dane was an oversentimental sort when it came to you.' Borrush grinned.

'Better than a callous dwarf.' Orilan grinned at Borrush.

Borrush scowled. 'Why you little ba—'

'Please don't swear near my children,' admonished Ake.

'Sorry, lass.' Borrush pulled a bracelet from his pocket. He reached out and pulled Orilan over to him and slipped the item over Orilan's one hand and onto his wrist.

'Is this a dwarven marriage proposal?' Orilan grinned.

A wave of dizziness overcame Orilan and he reached out against the doorjamb to steady himself. His wrist began to burn, and he opened his eyes, now a blazing red.

'Silver,' Orilan hissed.

Orilan reached out to strike the druid, Ake put herself between him and Borrush. Orilan lowered his hand. Ake took out a rope and began to bind his upper arms.

'I didn't think you were into those kinds of games.'

Ake glared at him.

Orilan's eyes became serious. 'Why are you doing this?'

'I will rid you of Drianna's curse. We will set you free, Ori,' said Ake.

'And if I refuse?' asked Orilan.

'Then I will kick you out myself,' said Borrush.

'Fine, let's see if you are indeed a powerful druid,' Orilan teased.

Orilan gritted his teeth as the bracelet burned his wrist. He followed Ake as she pulled the rope. They exited Caelestis and the warm air caressed their faces. Orilan looked up to see a full moon. 'Beautiful night.'

They stopped a short distance away.

'Lay down, Ori. I am going to bind your legs,' said Ake.

Orilan lay down. 'So, that is how it goes down.'

Borrush booted him. 'Show some respect for a lady.'

Orilan grinned at Borrush. 'I meant you, druid.' Orilan battered his eyes at Borrush. 'I am not opposed to either.'

'Lecherous elf, isn't he?' Borush glared at Orilan.

Ake knelt down next to Orilan. 'Believe it or not, it's not uncommon among their nobles to have countless lovers. It wouldn't surprise me if other elves do the same.' Ake finished binding Orilan's legs.

'I don't believe that, lass. Dane only had eyes for his wife. And

Lan, he has only ever pined after you.' Borrush tested the knots.'

'Lan is extremely faithful, but he is not the pining type.' Ake stood up.

Borrush gave a hearty laugh, and it echoed in the dark. Ake jumped.

'I caught him writing a cheesy love ballad once. I had been ordered by my king to deliver a missive to Serenade on trade negotiations and decided to visit Lan. I always liked the boy,' said Borrush.

Ake blushed.

Borrush continued. 'The elf was pacing and talking to himself.'

'What did he say?' asked Orilan.

Ake sighed. 'This situation is serious, Ori. You could lose your life, so please focus.'

Orilan eyes took on a determined glare. 'I will not die before I see you reunited with Lan. I owe you that much.'

'You should never interrupt a dwarf in the middle of his tale, it is rude,' said Borrush.

Ake turned to her friend. 'Forgive me, Borrush, that was rude, please finish.'

'As I was saying, Lan was singing the song as I looked in through the open door. He was fiddling with a tiny music box. Winding it up and singing along to it.' Borrush laughed. 'Then he threw the thing down on the bench and grumbled that you would hate it and he doubted it would impress you enough to accept that he loves you.'

Borrush turned and gave Ake a gentle smile. 'This will make you swoon, lass, as most girlies are known to do. The lad pulled out a pile of letters from a box of rose petals. The boy whispered some of the contents to himself. It was a collection of poems and'—Borrush cleared his throat—'Romantic innuendos with your name in mind. I backed out of the room and gave the lad space. He was clearly pining for you.'

Ake began to sob. 'Why didn't he show me these things?'

Borrush patted her back. 'It would have been hard for the lad. Elves don't usually display their emotions.'

Ake nodded and sniffled. 'True. We best get this over with.'

'Can you two hurry up? I am getting eaten by mosquitos.'

'Oh, the irony.' Ake laughed through her tears.

'But they die instantly from my tainted blood. Revenge is sweet.' Orilan bared his fangs and laughed.

Ake shivered. 'Orilan, we are going to tempt you. You need to resist it. The urges will get stronger and threaten to overwhelm you. You must fight it until it no longer tempts you.'

'Is Borrush going to attempt a sultry dance? I can't wait.' Orilan gave her a wicked smile.

Ake rolled her eyes and turned her face away from them both to hide her smile.

Borrush pulled a small knife from his bag and stood over the prone Orilan. He cut his hand and squeezed his palm together and let the blood drip down. Orilan's nostrils flared. They heard him make an animalistic growl. Orilan's eyes widened and turned red. 'Let me go, I must have that.'

Ake could make out the pain in Orilan's eyes. Orilan whimpered pathetically.

'Fight it, Ori,' said Ake.

'I will kill the druid for that blood,' cried Orilan.

Orilan summoned a gust of wind and knocked Borrush from his feet. Borrush grunted and tried to sit up. Ake saw the bracelet shimmer and she watched as Orilan's skin sizzled. The smell of burning flesh assaulted her nose and she turned her head. Orilan snapped one of the ropes binding his arm and shook his hand free and dragged the winded druid towards him and latched onto Borrush's hand. The dwarf booted him off. Ake ran over and began dragging Orilan back.

Orilan turned and grabbed her and held her down on the ground his fangs close to her throat. She struggled against his vampyric strength. He ran his tongue up her skin, his mouth lingering near hers. She felt his breath against her lips.

'Get off me.'

'You insisted on this. I am starving.' His hand caressed her soft neck, and he grazed her skin with his fangs. 'I can't do it.' He cried out as Ake slapped him across the face, adding power behind her strike with magic. He turned away from her whimpering.

Ake stood up and walked away to compose herself, her eyes blazed with anger. She conjured *Mystic Fire* in her hands and went to fling it at Orilan.

Borrush stopped her. 'Calm yourself, lassie. He is not himself. A year of starvation and then we tempt the lad.'

'I can see why Dane gave in.' Ake waved her hand and the flame disappeared.

'He didn't bite you, lassie, I saw him hold back. There was affection in his eyes. You are going to have to be the one to tempt him. I just don't do it for him.' Borrush grinned at her.

Ake laughed.

'That's it, lass. We will get through this.' He squeezed her shoulder.

Borrush walked over and retied the ropes. Orilan refused to look at him and grunted as Borrush held him down, applying his full strength to his shoulders.

Ake walked over to Orilan. She saw his eyes fill with fear as she knelt down and drew the knife across her palm. She gave him a look of pity as she saw his eyes burn with an overwhelming hunger.

Orilan began to struggle. That small amount of blood had awakened the vampyr within him. 'Get off me, you horrid dwarf. I will have her blood.'

Ake stood up. 'Let him go.'

'I can't do that, lassie, he is dangerous.'

'Trust me, Borrush. I am trusting your word that you saw him hold back.'

'Okay, lassie.' Borrush stood up.

Orilan hissed and stretched the ropes until they broke. He grabbed Borrush by the throat and threw him an incredible distance.

'*Waterius.*' The dwarf was enclosed it a bubble of water which broke his fall. Ake dodged out the way as Orilan ran towards her.

Ake turned sharply to face him. 'Stop, Orilan.'

He stopped and whimpered, looking like a starving animal. His pitiful cries softened her anger. 'You can resist this.'

'If Dane couldn't help what makes you think you can? I have tried your blood before.' Orilan strode towards her.

I believe he is strong enough to fight it. He has done so for over a year, that takes courage.

She felt herself roughly pulled against him. His hot breath was on her neck.

'Why do you want to save me?' he whispered.

Ake's mouth trembled. Her heart beat in fear as a man other than her husband dared get this close after all Cephas had put her through. She began to sob. 'Lan always wanted to save you.'

'So, you do this for him. I can respect that,' said Orilan.

Ake opened her eyes and tried to pull away. He laughed softly. Ake put her hand behind her back and the sudden movement made the blood splatter in the air near them.

'Get away from her, demon.' Borrush panted running towards them.

'Stay back, Borrush,' said Ake.

Borrush stopped in his tracks. 'Okay, lassie, but this is looking very dangerous for you.'

Orilan's eyes pleaded with her. 'I can't take your blood against your will for some reason. Yield to me, Ake.'

'No.' Ake stared at him with utter defiance.

Orilan lifted her chin. He laughed as she struggled.

'Stop. I don't want to hurt you.' Ake's eyes blazed with anger.

'You will give in.' His mouth brushed her neck in a gentle kiss, his fangs pressed against the tender flesh. 'The women always do.'

Ake reached out and channelled holy magic into the silver bracelet. Orilan thrust her away and bit at the bracelet trying to pry it off. He howled in rage and chased Borrush. The dwarf teleported himself out the way.

Ake squeezed her hand and the blood enraged Orilan further. He moved swifter than she could and began dragging her away. Ake applied steam to his arm, and he released her as the skin began to blister. She got up and tried to run, throwing flames at him. He teleported behind her just as Borrush began slinging sleep and paralysis spells at him. 'Weak, non-combative druid spells. Enough, I am hungry.'

'Fight it, Orilan.' Ake's eyes pleaded with him.

Ake cried out as his fangs bit into her neck. He raised his head and stared into her eyes as they began to turn golden. They were filled with despair.

'You really did believe I could fight this. Now it appears you have given up and would destroy me instead, hoping to prevent the deaths of others.'

Ake held his gaze. 'Yes.'

He held her hand to his chest, his heart began to beat rapidly as the blood pooled on her neck. 'This beats for you.' Orilan gave a cry of anguish as if something had broken in him. Tears streaked down his face, and he thrust her away.

Ake calmed herself and applied pressure to her wound to stop the bleeding. 'It is done. He is free of it. Lan will be happy when he returns.'

Ake watched Orilan disappear into the distance.

'Bloomin heck, lassie, you were as cold as ice.'

'Not inside, Borrush. I was very afraid.'

They turned and headed back to Caelestis.

CHAPTER TWENTY-NINE

Orilan had returned with the dawn and refused to look at her. The new staff had sat down to a few meetings with Ake and come up with an education plan.

'I will begin to recruit from the local villages. I don't want the Regians to become aware of our presence. They have appointed Cephas's cousin as regent until Mandami returns. They must not find him,' said Ake.

'I agree, we must build up our forces to protect him so he can live to adulthood and defeat Drianna,' said one of the new teachers.

'I guess it's time to start training him. We start on Monday.' Ake stood up and stretched.

'That only gives us three days,' said the teacher.

'Is it enough time? Caelestis has an extensive library and I have restocked the ink, vellum, herbs and alchemy stores,' said Ake.

'Well, that should be easy if you have done that already,' said one of the mystics.

Ake smiled. 'Thank you for this.'

'Our pleasure,' said another.

The staff headed out of Lan's office. Borrush stood and smiled. I will return in a few weeks. I am off to recruit dwarves for your cause. Will you be okay, lassie, with that moping elf around?'

'Orilan is of little threat, Borrush. Thank you.' She hugged the dwarf.

Borrush smiled. 'Good luck to you then.' Borrush disappeared.

Ake knocked on another door. She had just walked from Axeton to the larger village of Mencrey. No one had accepted her invitation of checking out Caelestis as a schooling option for their children. No one believed she had the skill to protect their children, despite Kathy's glowing recommendations regarding her character. Ake shivered, the hairs on the nape of her neck prickled as if someone was watching her, she looked around.

Lan saw Ake shiver. *For some reason I know that it is around her birthday. Has it only been a month? Or is it two? Are we in summer?* His days had begun to meld into one as the Lord of Death's influence delved deeper within his mind. *Why is she knocking on doors?* He saw her shiver. *She can't know I am watching over her until I cure myself of this rancid thing.*

Lan slipped closer to her as another door slammed in her face. He slipped something into her pocket and retreated. He saw her reach into her pocket and retrieve the letters.

Her eyes widened and she walked over to a bench and sat down. He heard her laugh as she read the second one and he smiled. He watched as she began to sob as she read the fourth one and he didn't hold back tears of his own.

Afraid a thief had relieved her of her money her hand slipped into her pocket and she drew out the vellum. She unfurled it and anxiety gripped her heart as she recognised the writing. She began to read.

Dear Ake,

I know I have been gone for a long time. I hope you are well, and Falcon is taking care of you like I asked. I hope you and him are both safe.

I found Orilan after traversing many islands. Each island contained cultists wrapped in hideous robes the colour of blood. They used human bones to build their structures. I shudder remembering their evil faces. They made me truly afraid.

I could not leave the islands using teleportation magic. Prior to my journey I discovered only members of Drianna's cult could enter or leave the islands under her domain using dark magic. This made kidnapping victims easier and made my escape harder.

Orilan's guards gave me a dreadful injury. I can't believe I failed my son. I wish I could have saved him from Drianna. No child deserves his fate. I fear for my child and his future.

I recovered from my injury with the aid of a delightful griffin named Cory. You would have loved him. He was comical, friendly and sweet. Unfortunately, Drianna turned her sights on him, and I lost my new friend. I am cut up with grief and I relive his death in my dreams.

I wish you were here to brighten my day with your antics. I know you have just celebrated your eighteenth birthday. Happy belated birthday.

I believe I had a dream where you rescued me from poisoning. It felt so real and, if it was so, did you feel a connection between us? I am finding myself missing you lately.

Regards,

Lan.

Ake pulled out another one and began to read she realised they were inconsistent. *There must be a few missing.*

Dear Ake,

How are you? This is our seventh letter so far. I wonder how your last year of school is going. I am holed up here with Dane. Did you know he is a stickler for rules? I walked the grounds of the druid academy and entered the training rooms without his permission, interrupting a class he was giving. I believe the students will forgive me because his voice was monotonous, and he repeated things several times. I wonder if my classes were ever that boring? Not that you were ever my student.

Dane caught me and ordered me from the room saying he would punish me later. He even attempted to try to get me to do chores for entering the classrooms without a student clearance. I laughed at him and refused, and he became flustered.

Ake, do you miss me? I miss you. I will be home the night of your graduation. I would never miss something so important to you. Especially now I am ... Forget that.

Regards,
Lan

To my dearest Ake,

I hope this letter finds you well. This letter will be embarrassing and may change the way you look at me. I am ashamed and my cheeks burn as I admit my sin to paper.

Father says I am an elf. Obviously, I rolled my eyes just now. I do not like to admit I am an elf because my father abandoned me. I am also wary of other elves. The royal ones appear to be polygamous and not invested in their spouses.

They apparently marry their own cousins. I am not okay with that. I have learnt the priestess of Ea I requested check in on you is my niece by marriage. What a small world.

I have gone off on a tangent. The elven part may relieve my conscious. I have questioned our age difference of nearly fourteen years. I am sure you are wondering why. I can't stop thinking about you. I woke up last night burning from desire. I had pictured you in my bed. You were beneath me, your long hair was dishevelled as you were caught up in my passion. Your lips swollen from my kisses. I know this is wrong. But part of me believes it may not be.

I understand if I have embarrassed you and you may not reply.

From someone whose heart burns for you,

Lan.

To my sweet Ake,

I hope this letter finds you well. I can't believe I have penned over fourteen to you. It fills my heart with joy that I have been able to share my feelings with you.

I cannot sit still due to my excitement. Father won't stop telling me to control my emotions, declaring that I will put you off if I am too excitable. It is only a few days before I come home. I would have returned home sooner if I had not had lingering side effects from that Shadow Scout. I have tried to approach my father about these thoughts that sometimes make me say terrible things when I am stressed.

Father dismissed me saying that it was the side effects of basilisk poison and could take over a decade for it to filter out of my body. I hope it won't make me say awful things to you. I couldn't stand to be the cause of distress to you.

I am a fool and have written you a poem. I know it is

ridiculous but there is something I would like to confess to you. I know I am probably too late, and that wonderful boy Falcon has made his feelings known to you. If you have accepted, then I hope you are both happy. I wonder if that's why you have never replied. But I must give it a shot, or I will never forgive myself. Here goes.

It crept up softly and filled my mind with honeyed thoughts.
I tremble at its delightful touch as it fills my mind with pictures of you.
I cannot eat, I cannot sleep as I long to kiss you.
My love for you consumes me.

I apologise for that awful poem, but I am in love with you, Ake. I hope with all my soul the feelings are mutual. I intend to make you my bride.
Love,
Lan.
PS and hopefully your future husband.

Ake looked around; tears had made her eyes puffy. 'You should have sent them to me all those years ago Lan,' she whispered.

She stood up and took a step forward as she saw the shadows shift momentarily. *It's almost like I can sense him. I am imagining things.* She turned and began to walk away.

Happy birthday, my darling. I have nearly learnt to control these powers. We will be together soon. The strong emotions caused Lan to lose control and he closed his eyes. When he opened them again it had snowed. Frustrated, he swore and entered the tavern.

Lan slammed his cup down on the bar. 'I recommend you recon-sider.' He threw a gold coin down on the table.

'Don't you think you have drunk enough? You can barely stand,' said the barkeep.

Lan wobbled on his feet. 'Just give me the drink. I can't bear to have the company of my brain …' Lan sat down on the stool and the barkeep pushed the drink towards him. 'My mind is filled with thoughts of her and my boys.'

'Is she alive?' asked the barkeep.

Lan nodded. 'Very much so and ravishing.'

'Then why are you here?'

'I am a dangerous man.'

'I wouldn't be announcing that.' The barkeep gestured his head towards some cloaked figures in the corner.

Lan finished his drink and stood up, holding onto the bar to prevent himself taking a fall. He left the tavern. Out of the corner of his eye he saw three hooded figures following him. It was sum-mer again. A warm breeze caressed his face.

He heard footsteps approach him and a hand was placed on his shoulder. 'Empty your pockets.'

Lan grabbed his assailant's hand. With a flick of his wrist, the man landed on his back, gasping for air. Lan booted him. 'I am an elf, I can see in minimal light. My hearing is unsurpassed. As if I didn't realise you were following me.'

Lan felt the dark blood dissolving the effects of drunkenness. *I hate that. I occasionally drink to get away from my thoughts of them.* He turned and strode towards the other hooded figures. One drew a dagger, the other held a club.

'A blasted elf is more valuable alive. The people at that tower are looking for one that fits the description.'

'I hear the attractive missus takes them to her bed.'

'Wouldn't put it past these noble sorts laying with all sorts of creatures.'

Lan laughed and his eyes glinted red. He strode towards them.

'That is not your standard elf. Let's get out of here.'

His friend nodded.

'Leaving already?' Lan grinned. 'That missuses you are referring to indeed takes elvish creatures to her bed. Particularly this one. I sired her sons.'

The man on the ground scrambled up and Lan turned to face him.

'I've heard of this one. He's known as Trebrelan. I believe it's her husband.' The man reached out and punched Lan in the face. 'Disgusting elves, taking our women for themselves. Especially the pretty ones.'

Lan smiled. He rammed his own fist into the man's chest and the man stumbled back.

'Take him down but don't kill him, boys,' said their leader.

Lan felt a blow to the back of his drunken skull and reacted. He turned and grabbed his assailant by the scruff of the neck and threw him into the man with the dagger. Another lunged at him with a club, he dropped into the splits and punched the man in the groin. The man swore and held his injured appendage.

Lan rolled out the way as the club crashed down. 'I am really enjoying getting to know you three. It has taken my mind off my pain. But I must say goodbye.'

Lan leapt up and the air was suddenly static with electricity. It made the men's beards frizzle and his own hair responded.

'It has magic,' cried one of the hooligans.

Lan laughed and he summoned lightning bolts to strike the ground in front of the men, intending to scare them. They turned and ran. Lan noticed the damp patches on the back of their trousers and grinned.

His ears pricked up as a gentle sobbing came from the bushes. He carefully approached. 'It is safe, they are gone.'

The bushes parted and a small elven child approached him. Lan held out his hand. 'Where are your parents?'

The child pointed to the trees nearby. Lan jogged silently over to the trees with caution as the child held his hand. He shuddered and pulled the child away as he saw the bloodied bodies of an elven man and woman. He recognised the father, having purchased goods from him in the village of Axeton. He hadn't believed the rumours that the villagers were hunting down elves to be rewarded by Regian bounty hunters. An arrow whizzed past his ear.

He picked up the child and teleported away to Caelestis. He saw Orilan walking back from town. 'Go with him to that building up there. A golden-haired princess will take care of you.' The child smiled through watery tears and ran towards a startled Orilan.

Lan looked at Caelestis, his heart yearning to go home. The darkness overwhelmed him, and he sobbed as he knew that he would forget himself.

Chapter Thirty

Ake waved to her boys as they entered the classroom with two dwarven children and a child from the village of Mencrey. It was her children's first day of school. Amities gave her a huge grin and Mandami gave her a brief wave before hurrying after his brother.

I am not going to cry. Her body betrayed her, and she began to weep. Ake shifted the books under her arms and walked towards the exit. She wandered some distance away and sat down. *You are being silly. The boys are fine.* She brushed her tears away with the back of her hand and began to read, paying special attention to the labelled pictures. The techniques were simple, quick and affective.

Ake rose and began to practice the unarmed combat techniques from the manuals she had discovered in the library. She was caught up in her practice and didn't realise hours had passed.

'Hey, Ake, the gardener and mason are here to meet you,' Orilan called out.

She turned and saw him walking towards her. She stared in shock at the elven child in his arms.

'Where did that child come from?'

'From the forest. The child was shouting that the golden-haired princess would take care of him.'

Orilan handed the very young child to Ake.

'Where are the parents?'

'They were found deceased in the forest. Bounty hunters.'

Ake's eyes filled with tears. 'We have to do something!'

Orilan shrugged. 'Not our problem. We have enough to handle.'

Ake glared at him. 'These are your people.'

Orilan's eyes flashed with rage. 'The elves never accepted me, despite Dane's effort to include me. I was declared a monster.'

'Ori, it is the right thing to do.' Ake gave him a gentle smile.

She turned and walked into Caelestis, the child in her arms.

—◆—

Over three years and he still hasn't returned. I guess we are over. Ake was kneeling on the ground digging holes for the flowers she was planting. The first half of her memorial garden had been built. She turned and admired the statues. *I will be able to paint them soon.* Ake had taken up painting under the tuition of one of the elven mystics. She had begun to excel with watercolours.

Her boys, now ten, were chasing and wrestling each other on the lawn, and she stood up and stretched. She wandered over to a bucket and began washing her hands then dried them on a towel. Orilan walked through the arch that gave access to the circular garden surrounded by flowered borders. He looked determined as he strode towards her.

'Amities tells me you have stopped looking for him.'

Ake nodded.

'Why?'

'He doesn't want us.'

Orilan gave her a gentle smile. 'You know that's not true. He is staying away to protect you and the boys.'

'What if he has decided to give us up?' Her eyes were full of despair.

Orilan reached out to caress her face but settled it on her shoulder instead. 'That would never happen.' He removed his hand and turned to watch his brothers arguing.

'I won that one,' declared Mandami.

'Nope, you jumped me from behind. How is that fair?' Amities asked.

'In a battle all is fair.' Mandami grinned. 'I can't help that you aren't strong.'

Amities began to walk away, ignoring his brother's insult.

'Hey, wait up,' cried Mandami.

The two boys rushed past them on their way back to class.

Orilan turned back to Ake who had grabbed her painting things and was testing a variety of paint on a stone bench.

'I know you almost caught him the last time he was in Mencrey.'

Ake didn't look up from her project. 'I always manage to just miss him.'

'I think it's time you hired a professional.'

Ake stood up and smiled at him. 'That is a good suggestion.'

'The cook is planning a special meal for the boys' birthday tonight. Borrush couldn't make it. Will you join us?'

'I would love to.'

Orilan turned on his heel and rushed from the garden as Ake began to paint some of the statues.

―ᴡᴡ―

Sweat beaded down his forehead as he shivered with fever. Lan lay on the floor in his cave. The cold floor was relief on his burning flesh. He screamed as pain swept through him. He placed his hand to his face as he felt the sweat thicken. A clear thick fluid poured out of him. Shadows wrapped around him as the legacy of the god of death removed the basilisk taint in his blood. The god of death was highly resistant to toxins that would kill a mere mortal.

Few people ever survived one draught of basilisk poison and Lan had consumed many. Lan's quick healing ability had kept him alive after Ake had rescued him. But the taint in his blood had often made him say terrible things when overcome with emotion and it had impacted their relationship.

Lan turned and vomited as the rest of the poison left his body. He recognised the addictive taste as residue was left in his mouth. He reached for a bottle of water, but the taste remained. He grabbed a bottle of liquor and drank a mouthful. It removed the taste for a while. When it returned, he drank the alcohol with gusto.

Father said it would take decades for the poison to leave my body. I will never be addicted to that stuff again and if alcohol prevents that so be it.

Lan gagged as the taste returned. He took another swig of alcohol and lay back down, closing his eyes. His body was wracked with pain and exhaustion. *It also dulls the emotional pain. Why is Caelestis preventing my access?* He yawned and drifted into a restless sleep.

Mandami shoved the large boy against the wall of the white fortress. It was mid-afternoon and the sun beat down on his bare back. He had been practicing with his dagger when he saw a boy wrestle Amities to the ground and steal his books. Amities had wept. *My poor, weak, little brother. I guess it's my job to look out for him.* 'You will lay off Amities.'

The boy laughed. 'Why do you care? You are always wrestling and belittling him.'

'That's what older brothers do. Now lay off him.' Mandami released the boy and turned away.

'Related to a nearly extinct weak and cursed race. You must be proud.' The boy shoved him in the back and he stumbled.

Mandami rounded on him and punched the boy in the stomach. The boy clutched his abdomen and grunted.

'Where did you learn to hit like that?'

'From the books written by a weak and cursed elf, as you would put it.'

Amities brushed the dirt off his robes and picked up his books and wandered over.

'Here comes the weakling now.' The bully jabbed out his leg and Amities tripped.

Amities' eyes filled with tears and Mandami sighed. 'Stand up for yourself. I can't fight all your battles for you.'

'Nah, he will just sit on his butt crying like the pathetic elfling he is,' said the bully.

Amities exchanged looks with his brother and they grinned.

Mandami grabbed a tome from his brother's arms and launched it at the bully.

'Wait not that—' The hardcover book fell open as it vaulted over their heads, loose pages of the old tome got caught up in a draft. '—one,' Amities screamed. There was a thunk as the book collided with the jaw of the bully, whose pupils dilated in shock. Mandami smiled briefly. Amities scrambled to his feet and clawed at the pages as they were swept away from him.

Mandami grabbed the collar of the bully. 'Help him.'

'You must really care for him.' The bully struggled.

'He's my twin. I am responsible for him,' said Mandami.

'I love you too, Mandami,' cried Amities, awkwardly jogging past him, pages clutched in his hand, the tome in the other.

Mandami blushed. 'We don't say that in front of others.'

The bully shrugged off Mandami and sprinted towards the classroom. 'I am telling the teacher on you two.'

'Who cares,' shouted Mandami.

Amities began to hyperventilate. Mandami patted him on the back. 'Breathe, little brother.'

Amities counted backwards and took in gulps of air. After a few minutes he stuffed the pages back into the tome. 'I wasn't supposed to take that book.'

The bully came back with a teacher. Mandami took the book off Amities and handed it to the teacher.

'I took it and threw it at him.' Mandami pointed at the bully. 'He was picking on Amities.'

'What do you have to say for yourself, Amities?' asked the teacher.

'I took the book. The others had nothing to do with any of this.' Amities stood in front of Mandami and the bully.

'Come with me, Amities. You will spend the rest of the day copying lines from that tome you took,' said the teacher.

'Urggh,' said the bully.

Mandami squeezed Amities' shoulder. 'Very brave, what a tedious task.'

Amities winked. 'I wasn't supposed to read it. Now I get to write out whole passages,' he whispered.

Mandami laughed as Amities followed the teacher.

'Your brother is smart,' said the bully.

'Yep.' Mandami held his head high. 'He is.'

—◦◦◦—

Mandami pushed Amities' hands out the way as they both reached for the jug of cordial. Amities stole his cup and Mandami put the jug down and grinned at his little brother.

'Do you not have any respect for your older brother?'

'A few minutes is hardly an older brother. Ori is far older than you and you don't respect him.'

'He wants to kiss our mother.'

Amities laughed. 'I highly doubt that. Our mother only has eyes for our father.'

'I never said she would kiss him back.'

The door was pushed open, and Ake entered the room with two small boxes and placed them on the table. The boys dove for them and Ake pulled them away.

'A little patience, boys. Your brother is joining us. Borrush gives his apologies as his daughter is unwell and he needs to tend to her,' said Ake.

'I don't think that's a good ide—' Mandami stopped himself as Orilan entered the doorway with gifts of his own.

Amities rushed over to Orilan and held out his arms for the gift. The child was shaking with excitement. Orilan handed him a book.

Amities' eyes widened. 'Thank you, Ori, this is the latest science on the possibility of electroplating without magic. This book is from a foreign land and is a treasure.'

Curious, Mandami came over as Amities turned the page. He saw a diagram of a terracotta pot. One half showed the outside and the other the inside, where a metal rod descended through the middle surrounded by liquid. Amities closed the book and went over to his mother, waiting patiently. She laughed and handed him the box and he ran over and sat down at the cafeteria table.

Like the rest of Caelestis, the walls were made of white stone. The floors of the cafeteria had been renovated in red slate and murals graced the walls of feasting elves and maidens dancing the may pole as lads chased them. The cafeteria held twenty picnic-style tables made of oak. To the back of the room stood the large ancient marble bench that separated the huge hearth that was used for cooking from the rest of the room. Utensils and pots lined shelves that were built into the stone wall.

The cook had a large pot of Eriu stew bubbling over the hearth and was filling bowls ready to serve them. The tantalising aroma wafted towards Ake and her mouth watered in anticipation.

'I like this,' said Mandami.

Ake turned back to watch Mandami hefting a small leather buckler in his hands.

'It is well made. Thank you,' said Mandami.

Orilan smiled and went over to the marble bench as the cook placed down bowls of stew. Ake pushed her gift towards the boys.

'Mother, I am sorry to ask, but what is it?' Amities had pulled one of the toys out of the box.

Ake smiled at him. 'Press the button on the back.'

There was a click as Amities did as instructed and the round wooden container sprang open revealing a crude looking chicken that sprang out and flapped its disproportionate wings. Amities smiled.

'I know it doesn't look right, but happy birthday, boys.'

'A gift is a gift.' Orilan placed a bowl down in front of each of the boys and went back for the other two.

Mandami followed Ake's instructions and one of his toys opened with a click and a tiny bow appeared. The bow was drawn back, and a tiny arrow attached to a piece of string flew past his face until it reached the end of its string and was wound back into the toy. Mandami smiled and put the toy down and began to eat his stew.

After a few mouthfuls Mandami looked up at his mother. 'That is a toy for small children, but it is amusing. Thank you for your effort.'

Orilan placed the bowls down. Ake smiled at her son with the adoration of a mother and sighed.

'I wish I had been shown that kind of love as a child,' said Orilan.

Ake gave him a sad smile. 'I am sorry, Ori, that you never experienced that.'

Orilan shrugged and pulled out a chair. She gasped as he pushed her down onto the chair with a firm grip on her shoulder.

'What was that about?' she asked.

'I've been reading through those books you suggested,' said Orilan.

Ake laughed. 'You pull out the chair for a lady and let her sit down. You don't force her down yourself.'

'That makes more sense, that looked very awkward.' Orilan touched her shoulder. 'You aren't hurt?'

'I am not fragile, Ori,' said Ake.

Mandami looked up. 'Hand off my mother.'

Orilan removed his hand from Ake's shoulder. 'Nothing was meant by it, Mandami.'

Ake pushed her chair in and began to eat her stew. Orilan walked around the table and sat down next to Mandami and began to concentrate on his meal.

The cook came over and plonked a poorly decorated cake down on the table. The cook had already sliced it into portions.

'Mother, did you make that?' asked Mandami.

'Of course.' Ake smiled.

'I am finished, Mother. I excuse myself.' Mandami went to rise and Orilan pulled him back down by his tunic.

'I said I was done, Ori.' Mandami shrugged him off.

Orilan reached for a piece of cake and plopped it into Mandami's bowl. 'Eat it or you get to deal with me.'

Ake laughed. 'It's okay, I am a terrible cook. But I am practicing every day.'

'Try it, Mandami, before you reject it.' Orilan grabbed a piece for himself and ate it without complaint.

Ake laughed at Amities who was on his second piece.

Mandami tried it. 'It is fine, but I care little for cake.'

'You are like our father.' Orilan stood up and pushed his chair away. 'Thank you for inviting me.' Orilan held out his hand to Ake. 'I believe you are expected to shake it.'

Ake nodded and held out her hand and he shook it.

'I am going into town to practice some of these social cues.' Orilan turned and left the cafeteria.

'He is really odd,' mumbled Mandami.

Ake stood up. 'It is time for you two to be in bed.'

'Aww, Mother,' whined Amities.

They followed her from the cafeteria as the cook collected their dishes.

Chapter Thirty-One

Ake had just applied the last of the paint to the statue. She sighed and turned away as the emotion of staring into her mother's eyes caught her off guard. She put the brush down and stood back to admire her handiwork. *It is good.* Ake looked towards the entranceway. *She is late.* Kathy walked quickly into view carrying a large plant. She reached Ake and put the plant down and drew Ake into a hug.

'How are you, Ake?'

'I am well and you?'

Kathy smiled. 'I am good. Sorry I was late.'

Ake returned the smile. 'Bring that beautiful plant with me.'

Kathy followed her towards a collection of painted statues.

Ake pointed to four in the corner. 'I will give you your space. Feel free to plant that wherever you wish.'

Kathy began to sob, walked over to her and thrust the plant at her. 'The statues are too lifelike. I can't do this, I am sorry.'

Ake pulled her into her arms and began to cry as well. 'I am sorry, Kathy, if this has upset you. I miss them too.'

Kathy pulled herself away from Ake. 'I have yet to see Lan around. Where he is?'

I can't lie to her. 'I don't know. He left us.'

Kathy stared at her in shock. 'Really?'

Ake nodded. 'Yes, he is fighting a darkness within and refuses to come home.'

'Would you be willing to hire help?'

'Ori suggested the same thing?'

'There is a bar Lan frequents in Mencrey. It is an unsavoury place. Ask for Freidan at the Topless Tipple. It's not a place I thought I would see your husband, Ake.'

'How do you know all this, Kathy?'

'I have been following him for several days. He had been drinking himself into oblivion but rejecting every advance made towards him so I don't think you have to worry about him making a mistake. Make sure you take someone with you.' Kathy reached out and squeezed Ake's hand. 'Take care, Ake.'

'You too, Kathy. Are you sure you won't stay for lunch?'

'No, I thought I could handle this place, but it is a reminder of the happy days my son spent with you before it became his final resting place.'

Ake sighed. 'I understand. Goodbye, Kathy.'

Kathy hurried away and Ake noticed age had crept up on her; her steps were not as quick and she seemed shorter. Ake strode towards Orilan's room and knocked on the door. He opened it and smiled at her.

'You look determined.'

'Can you join me in town?'

'Are you asking me on a date?' Orilan grinned.

'What have I told you about the flirting, Ori?'

'That it is inappropriate with my father's wife.'

Ake sighed. 'Have a good night, Ori.'

Ake turned and began to walk away.

'Wait. Why did you ask?'

Ake turned. 'I am going to get information on Lan from Freidan at the Topless Tipple.'

Orilan walked through the door and closed it. 'Right, let's go.'

'Wait, I have to ask one of the staff to keep an eye on the boys.'

Orilan headed outside as she made the arrangements. Ake's light footsteps barely made a sound as Orilan turned his gaze, settling on her gown. The twilight air was frigid, and she shivered.

'I love this time of day.' Orilan took a deep breath and closed his eyes, appearing to enjoy the fresh air. He turned and followed her as she took the familiar path to Mencrey.

Lan lay his head down on his arms as he fell into a drunken stupor. Someone ran their hands across his shoulder and leant down to whisper in his ear.

'Come on, let's get you home to bed.'

'Ake?' He opened his bleary eyes and saw a pair of green eyes staring at him. 'Get away from me, I don't want your company.'

The woman smiled. 'Probably couldn't do the deed anyway.'

One of the patrons laughed and Lan sat up.

'How many times do I have to tell you to back off? This is the second time tonight you have bothered me.'

'Typical elf, can't satisfy a woman,' said a man.

'That's why there aren't too a lot of your kind left.' One of the wenches laughed.

Lan covered his ears at the intrusive laughter. His vison cleared as the alcohol began to leave his body. He swore as Orilan entered the bar and ran into one of the curtained-off areas.

Ake entered the inn. She turned and glared at several patrons as some men and women whistled at her.

'Hey, Ori, how did you get one like that?' The barkeep nodded his head towards Ake.

'She's my father's wife,' said Orilan.

The barkeep laughed. 'You really do like to push the boundaries.'

A woman walked over to Ake. 'Aren't you a pretty wee thing.'

Orilan grabbed Ake's hand and dragged her over to the bar. 'Stay away from Rochelle.'

Ake looked up at him innocently. 'She was just giving me a kind compliment.'

The barkeep laughed. 'That's how it starts. Then a drink and then you are in their bed.'

Ake drew her cloak close about her, covering her blue velvet dress that was parted along the sides. She made sure her silk stockings were pulled up and that the cloak covered the low-cut bust. Orilan had manipulated his ears to appear human.

Rochelle sat down on the stool next to her. 'A drink for these two and myself, Friedan.'

Ake smiled. 'Freidan, is it?'

The barkeep nodded.

'We are looking for information on the whereabout of a dark-haired elf,' said Ake.

Friedan poured three drinks and put them on the bar in front of Rochelle.

Friedan stared at Ake intently. 'It will cost you.'

'Name your price,' said Ake too quickly.'

Friedan smiled at Orilan. 'I demand a kiss from Orilan.'

There were cheers from the bar and Ake looked apologetically at Orilan. 'Let's go, Ori.'

'You forgot your drinks.'

'I am sorry.' Ake smiled at the woman and drank half of the drink. 'It's quite bitter.'

Rochelle smiled. 'It's very quick acting.'

Orilan shrugged and leant over the bar and gave Freidan a chaste kiss. 'Now answer her.'

'Ori,' Ake whispered.

He turned as her eyes glazed over. 'You should have been wise enough not to accept a drink from a stranger, Ake.' Orilan glared at Rochelle. 'What have I told you about interfering with my things?'

Rochelle gave him a flirtatious smile. 'Look at her, she is gorgeous. She could be very fun between the two of us.'

Orilan locked eyes with Friedan. 'The information. Now.'

'Elf is in one of the curtained-off alcoves.' Friedan pointed to the alcove Lan had run into.

'Do you know where he lives?' asked Orilan.

'No, but I can find out.' Friedan held out his hand.

Orilan nodded and took some money from the pocket of Ake's cloak and put it in the open palm. 'Send word to Caelestis.'

'Keep your hands off her, Rochelle.' Orilan strode over to the curtained-off area. 'Come out, Lan.'

Orilan turned as he heard Ake giggle. 'That tickles.'

Rochelle was tickling her. Orilan marched over to Rochelle. 'Get off her.'

'Ake, come here now.' He held out his hand.

Ake pouted. 'You're no fun.' Ake walked over to him, suddenly fascinated by her hands. She conjured a ball of water in one and flame in the other. She blew into them and a gust of air danced around them. 'Look Ori, magic.' Ake pouted. 'I am missing earth.' She bent down and grabbed a pile of dust and added it to her creation.

'Come on, Ori, let's have fun with her.' Rochelle winked.

Several other degenerates encouraged them.

'Yes, let's have fun, Ori.' Ake smiled. 'Add some magic to this thing I am making.'

'Hey, Ori, she wants you to show her a night of magic,' hollered a guest.

The crowd whistled and cheered.

'Lan, your wife is out of control, come deal with her,' yelled Orilan.

———ᨆᨆ———

Ake is here? I am done with this monster in me, I am going home and she is coming with me. Lan used the shadows to conceal himself and slipped past Orilan.

He watched as the green-eyed woman tried to cuddle up to his son. He grabbed Ake and pulled her into the shadows that concealed him.

———ᨆᨆ———

'She is gone, Orilan.' Rochelle frowned.

Orilan looked around suddenly. 'Ake?' He got up and walked to the door.

Rochelle followed him as he stepped outside.

'Ake, are you out here?' Orilan turned his anger on Rochelle. 'I can't believe you drugged her. That's not like you. I thought we had something.'

Rochelle grinned. Orilan looked on, fascinated as bubbles appeared under her skin as it began to stretch. The creature that had possessed Rochelle growled and stripped off the skin. Large, hyper-extended legs and arms stretched forth connected to a black shaggy body. The neck was incredibly long and attached to a tiny nightmarish face. 'You only knew the wench a few weeks.' The creature walked on all fours towards him. 'Drianna sends her regards.'

I am going to die against a Tintuhade with only druid spells at my disposal. The monster's name was almost comical when translated from elvish. The monster known as *tiny head* looked ridiculous, but it was powerful and without his vampyr strength Orilan would struggle.

Ake looked around joyfully as the shadows twisted and turned 'So pretty.' She giggled. Lan smiled indulgently at her. He heard villagers screaming and grabbed her hand and pulled her towards the noise. 'Hey, what have I told you about touching me.'

Lan stared at her, pain in his eyes and he pulled back the shadows. Anger clouded his mind when he realised she was drugged. *How dare someone drug her.* He continued walking and she stumbled behind him. 'Let me go.'

There was a hideous scrapping as large claws dragged over the ground. Lan watched Orilan cast ineffective spells on the hideous monster. *What is that thing?* Ake escaped his grip and ran towards the monster.

So, it is immune to paralysis and sleep spells. Orilan charged the evil beast. He muttered a spell, and his hand burned a vibrant green as he placed it on the monster's pelt. The monster hissed and its head bobbled on its long neck. The head began to weave back and forth and Orilan closed his eyes. *So, it's immune to poison too. I can't let it hypnotise me.*

He felt a thick, sticky ooze pool around his legs and opened his eyes. The monster had begun to dissolve into thick grey sludge. Orilan tried to move his feet and realised he was stuck. The monster's neck detached from its body, and it slithered towards him and began to wrap itself around him. Orilan heard the screams of villagers. Five archers fired at the monster with little effect against the thick shaggy fur that doubled as armour.

Orilan gagged as the monster's head kissed him, forcing his mouth open. Its giant tongue slid down his oesophagus hoping to devour his organs. He used his sharp canines to bite the tongue in half. The creature howled and retracted its tongue. Orilan realised the blood that pooled in his mouth no longer tasted delightful and spat it out.

He grinned and teleported himself out of the monster's muck. He turned as he heard shouting. Ake ran towards the monster.

'Get away from—' She suddenly looked confused. 'If you're here, Ori, who is back there?'

The monster hissed and beams of black light shot out from its eyes towards Ake. She leapt out the way and jolted her ankle. Wincing, she steadied herself. The beams shot out towards her, and the monster was enveloped in a vortex of shadows. The creature began to howl. Black blood spurted out of the vortex and sprayed Ake and Orilan in the face.

Ake brushed the blood out of her eyes with her hands. She saw Orilan blink. His eyes looked sore, and he couldn't seem to focus. 'The blood feels like it is burning my eyes. I can't see.'

Ake turned and saw the monster claw at Lan as he leapt onto its back. It howled as he began ripping out clumps of its hair. He saw the skin beneath and plunged one of his knives into the beast. Black blood spurted into his face, and he jumped off the monster. He watched in fascination as the wound began to close. 'The wound needs to stay open,' said Lan.

The creature turned and its large claw clasped him and pulled him towards its face. He laughed and teleported onto its back and drove his knife into the closing wound. He briefly retracted the shadows as the beast's neck detached itself and slithered over its body. It extended its tongue and wrapped it around the knife and tried to pull it out.

'Lan?' Ake called out to him.

'Ake, concentrate on killing the monster.' Lan smiled.

Ake closed her eyes and drew on her mage powers. *What is its weakness? I can't think.* Her mind was still hazy. The monster rolled and grabbed Lan and threw him to the ground. He appeared winded as his back slammed against solid earth. He summoned lightning and the bolts crashed into the monster. Lan gagged as the revolting smell of singed hair and hide assaulted his nostrils. The creature looked injured.

'Ake, help me kill this thing.' He teleported out the way and summoned hail and the huge balls of ice slammed into the creature with no effect.

Ake opened her eyes and stalked towards the creature and the earth opened up. The creature tried to scramble away but Ake created multiple openings and it became trapped as it backed into one of the vents. It screeched as its innards were slowly crushed when the pit began to close. In a last ploy to survive, it detached its neck and launched it at her.

Ake gasped as she was teleported into her husband's arms. The shadows swirled around them once more. His eyes glowed red and something deep responded within her.

'Your eyes are now golden,' said Lan.

She watched as the beast's form began to regrow from its head, directly behind Lan. A leg reached out for him, and she was suddenly filled with fear. Ake screamed.

Ake saw Lan's eyes fill with pain. Ake stumbled backwards as he closed his eyes and disappeared. The beast reached for her. She conjured up molten lava. It wrapped itself around the monster who howled in pain as it disintegrated. *So, molten earth is your weakness.* Ake looked around. The use of divine magic had cleared her body of the last of effects from the drug in her drink.

'Lan?' She began to weep. 'Come back here, I wasn't frightened of you.'

―~~―

I terrify her. It is not time to go home no matter how hard I try. But first let's deal with this thing. He opened his eyes, and it was morning. The frustration overwhelmed him, and he realised he was on the beach carrying a bag. *No. I was fighting a monster.* Panic set in and his heart beat rapidly, his breath came in shallow gulps. *I hope she is okay.* He turned to look at his den and saw Ake in front of him. *It is over, I can't be with her. I lack control.*

CHAPTER THIRTY-TWO

Friedan's note had arrived yesterday, months after the battle with the Tintuhade. Ake withdrew it from her pocket and read it again. Her tears ran down her face and stained the paper. *I can't believe he has been found.*

> To the mistress of Caelestis,
>   I have discovered an elven hermit living on the beach in a cave near Caelestis. We believe him to be your husband Trebrelan as he fits the description of a dark-haired, dark-eyed elf.
>   Freidan.

Ake pocketed the note and went to the cafeteria. It was almost empty as the students had returned to their class after the early morning meal. After the battle with the Tintuhade, the villagers were awestruck with Ake's ability to handle monsters and had willingly sent their children to the school in hopes they could learn to defend themselves. Caelestis now had eighteen students and more would be arriving soon.

She looked around, hoping to find Orilan as she knew he usually had his breakfast at this time. She saw him eating toast and thumbing through a book. He looked up as she walked over to him.

'Good morning, Ori.' Ake held out the note.

Orilan read it and smiled. 'This is wonderful news. When are you going to speak to him?'

Ake sighed. 'I don't think that is a good idea. He obviously wants to be left alone.'

'This will sound harsh, Ake.' Orilan grabbed her hand. 'You are extremely naïve. As if Lan would ever leave you alone if it wasn't necessary. Obviously, he feels he is dangerous and is staying away to protect you and his children. How many times must I mention that? You are a fool if you think otherwise.' Orilan released her hand and stood up. 'You are going to retrieve him.'

Ake sighed. 'I want to, Ori, but I am terrified he will reject me.'

'So, you have decided it is over?'

'I don't know what to do,' whispered Ake.

'You are going to make him a gift. I know you have been giving your boys your unusual contraptions and they have improved.' Orilan smiled. 'Then you are going to go down to that beach and seduce him.'

Ake blushed. 'That is crude.'

Orilan grinned and showed his fangs. 'I am crude. You could always appeal to his intellect.'

'I guess I could try.' Ake smiled. 'Thank you for your help, Ori.'

'We are friends, Ake. I am here to help.'

'I am glad we have put our differences aside and become friends.'

Orilan pulled her into a hug, startling her then he pushed her away before she could protest.

'Please don't hug me.' Her eyes flashed with anger. 'We may be friends but your past actions make that kind of display forfeit.' She sighed. 'I know you are still learning. Sorry for my outburst. Well, I best go draw up plans for that gift. If he rejects me, so be it.'

Orilan smiled. 'Well, off you go.'

Ake waved and strode away.

—⁓—

Ake looked out her bedroom window. It was the small room she had lived in when she was a senior student at the school. She could not sleep in their marriage bed; it reminded her too much of her husband. *Lan has missed so much. Our boys' first day of school, their birthdays and the solstice celebrations.* She dug her fingers into her hand and scowled. *How dare he, damn him!* Hot tears of anger ran down her face.

It was now the winter holidays and her beautiful boys were eleven and thriving under the routine of Caelestis. Amities could not wield magic but was incredibly smart. He had decided to branch into inventing, research and science. The fiery Mandami was a natural when it came to the arcane and was already ahead in the mystic arts. He was still emotionally distant to them but did take his meals with them and discuss his day. That was enough for her.

Ake had been trying many different creative arts and believed she had succeeded in the perfect gift for Lan. She hoped he would want to come home. *Can I forgive him?* Ake knew she always would, but the pain of his constant absences had begun to affect her, and she no longer allowed others to influence her decisions. There was a gaping wound in her soul. Every time she loved someone, they eventually left her. She wiped away her tears. *Enough, you silly woman. Don't waste bitter tears on him.*

She left Caelestis with her backpack and headed towards the beach. Friedan had sent another note telling her Lan had just been seen in town. Ake strode towards the shore where she knew there was a cave.

'Hello. Anyone there?'

—⁓—

Lan wondered if he should answer her or walk away. She was beautiful and his heart contracted with pain and longing. He fought back tears and sighed. She was turned away from him looking at the entrance of the cave.

What do I do? I miss her so much, but I am dangerous. I need her to realise it's over, I will never be safe to be around. The thought of it being over filled him with rage and he knew he must make her leave before his resolve melted and he swept her up into his arms. The shadows threatened to overwhelm him.

'Go away, Ake!' he yelled.

She turned and smiled at him. 'No.'

'I am not safe to be around.'

'I've had enough of waiting for you, Lan. You need to come home.'

Walking ahead of her into the cave, he put his things down. Ake followed him and put her bag down.

He turned to stare at her. 'You shouldn't be here. I would prefer it if you left.'

'No. You are coming home whether you like it or not.'

'Don't you think that is my decision? I can't come home. When I realised you are frightened of me I decided it is probably for the best.' Wisps of shadow wove their way around her and she looked surprised.

'It was you that day?' Ake looked at him, horrified. 'I pushed you away, I am so sorry.'

'You were terrified of my touch.'

'I thought you were Orilan.'

'And during the battle with that monster?'

'I don't remember much. Orilan said I was drugged. He said he never saw you but did witness the vortex.'

Lan's eyes flashed red. 'You baulked at my touch. I knew then I had to stay away and learn to control this thing.' Lan took a shuddering breath. 'During the battle with that monster I thought I had learnt to control it, but it was a lie. Please leave.'

'And what if you never learn to control it?'

'Then you should move on and try to find some happiness.'

Ake gripped his shoulder. 'I will never marry anyone else. I love you.'

Lan's heart beat faster and he reached for her hand then withdrew it suddenly. 'Please leave. It is over and I won't change my mind.'

Ake began rummaging for her bag and pulled out a small wooden box and a pile of scrolls. 'I am willing to make a deal. If you pass, I will stay away indefinitely.'

Curiosity got the better of him and Lan walked over and grabbed a scroll from her and went to unfurl it.

Ake snatched it back. 'Not yet. Give me a moment.'

'Okay, I am thirsty anyway.' Lan pulled out a bottle of booze, took the cap off and drank the contents greedily.

'Want some?' he asked.

'Sure,' said Ake.

Ake took the flask and downed the harsh liquor. It burned and she spluttered. Ake wiped her mouth on the sleeve of her dress. Lan analysed her from head to toe, noting it accentuated her curves. Ake had filled out; her hips and buttocks were womanlier. The dress was of red velvet and slits ran up the sides, from her ankles to the tops of her thighs, showing the skin below. The sleeves were long and the bust dipped to the top of her breasts. She wore silk stockings and knee-high boots for a sense of modesty.

'So, you're here to seduce me and bring me back.' He laughed.

'No, I came to appeal to your intellect,' she said.

'Dressed like that? Sure.' He grinned at her.

'I always dress like this.'

Lan let his eyes wander, admiring her form. Ake blushed and

looked away. Ake unfurled the scrolls, trying to ignore his observations. Lan walked over to look at them. The scrolls contained riddles and diagrams of intrinsic runes and graphs. Ake placed a puzzle box on a nearby table.

'What is it for?' he asked.

'Solve it and I will leave you alone indefinitely.' Ake's eyes filled with sadness and welled with tears. 'I have Mandami. This is enough to defeat Drianna, according to the prophecy. I will give you your peace. The condition is I stay with you while you work it out.'

'You give me your word?'

Ake nodded.

He turned away from her. His eyes burned with the threat of tears. *If it means her and the boys are safe from me, it must be done.*

'I agree.'

Ake placed the items on the table and stepped back.

Lan sat down at his crude table and began pouring over the documents. He picked up the box and turned it in his hands, looking for any hidden switches. It was handcrafted and a little crude-looking. Lan looked for any key holes and saw a small hole in the bottom. Lan peered inside; a kaleidoscope of colours greeted him. He stuck his finger in the opening and a pin jabbed him. Lan winced and put the finger in his mouth.

'I like this one.' Lan smiled at Ake.

He turned back to the puzzles.

Day turned into evening and Lan forgot to drink the liquor. Ake lit two candles and cooked a simple soup on his fireplace and handed Lan a bowl.

Lan drank it. 'You've gotten better.'

Lan went back to his puzzles. Ake lay down on his wooden settee covered in furs and blankets and fell asleep out of boredom. Lan stayed up late solving the first few pages before he became frustrated. *I need her to be rid of me, so she will be safe.* Lan swore and threw a writing quill.

Ake mumbled in her sleep and rolled over onto the floor and jolted awake. Lan laughed.

'There's a bed back there.' Lan pointed deeper into the dark cave.

Ake got up. 'I cannot sleep alone in dark caves.'

'I am not going to share a bed with you, Ake. I can see through your ploy.' Lan smirked.

Ake glared at him.

'No ploy, I have a blanket. I'll sleep outside.' She pushed past him.

Lan dragged the settee to the entrance and sat down on it to watch her. Ake put the thick blanket on the ground, lay down and wrapped herself up in it and fell asleep. He turned away from her and drifted off.

Lan woke up with the dawn and heard Ake muttering in her sleep about how he was acting like a cad by handing her love letters then avoiding her all these years. He laughed playfully and called down rain on her. She yelped and woke, angry and drenched. Ake stood up and stomped into the cave.

'You look like a drowned rat.' Lan laughed. He got up and stretched, grinning at her. 'I am a cad after all.'

Ake scattered his clothes, looking for a towel. He tossed her one and she spluttered as it landed in her face. Ake took off her dress and began to dry herself. She was dressed only in a see-through chemise. Lan controlled the urge to take her to his bed and went back to his puzzles.

—⁓—

Lan swore. The puzzles were getting extremely complicated, and he was finding them harder to solve. They had branched into science, and he was struggling with the chemical names and genus for biological species. It was now late afternoon of the second day, and he pushed the table back in anger. Ake had fallen asleep on the settee next to him. He involuntary put his hand on her thigh and hissed at his weakness. Lan pulled his hand back and stood up.

'Get up, I'm hungry,' he said hoarsely.

She scrambled up, rubbing her eyes.

'We're going to town.' Lan threw her a rough-spun woollen robe.

'My dress is dry,' said Ake.

He shook his head. 'No way a wife of mine is going to the inn in that. Do you know what men get up to with the wenches there?'

'You said I'm not your wife, Lan.'

'Suit yourself. It was just a suggestion.'

Ake put her dress on and tidied herself. He walked ahead of her for the two hour journey. They entered the bustling town of Mencrey. Several smiths and inns graced the main street. Vendors plied their wares and the streets buzzed with laughter and merriment.

Lan had forgotten to wear his hooded cloak and people stared at him.

'Look, an elf,' stated someone.

'I thought that boy up at the tower was the last one,' said another.

'Yes, the little engineer child,' said one proudly.

A few people noticed Ake and bowed. 'Hello, Mistress.'

'This is my husband, Trebrelan, Amities and Mandami's father,' Ake announced shrewdly.

'The Trebrelan of old Caelestis?' they asked.

'The very same,' she said proudly.

'We heard stories of his prowess over Emperor Cephas after the death of our ancient friends, the elves,' stated another.

'Extraordinary for a single elven youth,' cried another.

'Yes, he has just returned from a long journey.'

Lan grabbed her hand and pulled her along. 'Enough.'

They entered the Topless Tipple and he took her into one of the curtained-off alcoves and pushed her gently against the wall.

'Stop telling people we are married. I am not returning to Caelestis.'

She ran a hand through his short hair and pushed her hips against him.

'I will not lay with you. No matter how much you try.'

'Liar. I can prove it. This is as good a place as any.' Ake gave him a sultry smile as she rolled down her stockings.

He looked around and saw some people glance at them through a gap and turn back to their business. *What the hell is she doing? Ake has always shunned this kind of behaviour in public. Has she really changed that much in a few months?*

Her hands trailed down his chest and rested on his belt. His heart beat quicker and he was tempted to take her as the darkness welled up in him. He pushed it down, annoyed. *God, I hate this thing inside me.*

Ake could see the desire in his eyes and reached out and pulled the curtain shut.

'Well, go on,' she whispered.

Wisps of shadows whirled around them.

Lan's eyes shined red in the darkened alcove. 'You seriously want me to believe that you would sleep with me here? All right, we can play your little game.'

Lan pushed her into the wall with his body. He used one hand to hold both her hands above her head, the other slipped under her gown and stroked her inner thigh. His head dropped to her neck and his mouth left his mark. *I could so easily take her here. I've become a monster.* She began to struggle as they heard footsteps approaching. He stopped, unwilling to satisfy his primitive need for her and let go of her hands.

She gasped, pushed him away and turned her head in shame. Ake raised her hand to his love mark.

Lan grinned as the skin began to discolour.

'I thought as much. You have more class than me. Stop with these ridiculous games. Now stay here.' Lan drew the curtains apart and went to order food.

Ake rearranged her clothing. While she was doing so, a man walked over and asked her what the going rate was. Another offered her a drink. Another said they had something strong and mighty to show her. Ake punched several in the mouth as they tried to grab her hand and pull her towards them. They called her a crude word and wandered off.

Lan turned at the commotion and was filled with rage. *I should have known better than to bring her here.*

His food was ready, and he grabbed the bag and headed towards her. A large man came over and tried to grab her chest, she kicked him in the groin. The man grunted and went to slap her. Lan caught his hand. His eyes glinted red, and he began to crush the man's hand. Shadows wafted around them.

'I'm sorry, didn't know she was your mistress,' he blathered.

'She is my wife, you stupid lout,' said Lan.

He released the man. Lan put his hand on the curve of Ake's back, glared meaningfully at the man and led her over to a table. She sniffled and he pulled out a chair for her.

'Sit. Eat,' said Lan.

She sat down and wiped her tears on her sleeves.

Lan winced. *My behaviour and that of the other men has probably brought back some terrible memories.* The shame caused his cheeks to burn.

'I shouldn't have left you alone in a place like this. Can't you see

I am not a good man. Please let me go,' he said.

She smiled at him. 'I refuse to believe that.'

'Stop tempting me, Ake. It is unfair.'

'No. I want you back and will do whatever it takes. You are mine,' she said.

Lan blinked at her in shock. He fumbled with the bag and took out bowls of boiled meats and vegetables.

'Yuck,' said Ake.

'It's simple fair, Ake. Good enough for me,' he said.

'Really, Lan?' She stared at him.

'I'm not a posh man anymore, Ake.' Lan laughed.

'There are no forks. How do we eat it?' asked Ake.

'Open your mouth,' said Lan.

Ake watched as Lan scooped food up with his hands and placed a boiled potato in her mouth. She chewed it, horrified.

'It isn't even seasoned.'

He pushed the bowl towards her.

'Eat it,' Lan commanded.

Ake ate it begrudgingly.

'Time to go,' said Lan.

They left the inn and trekked home in the dark, silently.

—◦◦◦—

Orilan sat up suddenly in bed and cursed to himself. *I will have to alter the wards to let Lan back in. That means Drianna's monsters may attempt to come in. We are not ready to face her yet.* Orilan threw back the covers and drew on a shirt. He grabbed a knife, pulled open his door and slunk down the hallway. He saw light seeping under a doorway and pulled it open. Amities was seated in a classroom, his head on his books, tools and materials strewn about. Orilan took off his shirt and placed it over Amities before backing out of the room.

He made a quick turn and exited the fortress. The dawn sky was streaked with red. Orilan knelt, closed his eyes and took several deep breaths before he began to hum. The humming rose to a crescendo before cutting off sharply as Orilan was showered in blue light. 'Exitos morte kultes nano Trebrelan,' he cried.

There was a loud ripping noise as if someone had torn material right next to him and he shuddered. *Father can get in, but so can Drianna's monsters.* The air was warm, but Orilan shivered anyway.

Chapter Thirty-Three

Lan sighed as he picked up Ake and moved her to his bed. The nights were starting to get colder and she had stubbornly slept outside again. It was now the morning of the third day and Lan had just solved the last riddle. He grinned with satisfaction. Picking up the puzzle box he ran his fingers along the wood. There were some very faint etchings. They were clearly Elvish, and he sounded out the letters.

'Terrors lurked in the dark, you alone had become my bright spark. So corny,' he mumbled to himself.

Where have I heard that? Of course. Lan drew out the little silver box he kept close to his heart. He had given this to Ake on her nineteenth birthday. Lan had taken it along with the letters to remember her by. He opened it up and let it play next to the puzzle box. The other box opened slowly, and a kaleidoscope of coloured gemstones flickered in response to the song. Lan slammed the music box shut and sighed.

Impressive and extremely sweet. I guess I'll get my wish, he thought sadly. Lan's eyes glinted red in anger. Shadows began to swell around him in response to his dark emotions. He entered his bedroom at the back of the cave. Lan clung to the darkness, a mirror of his own feelings of despair. A soft glow came from under the worn blanket.

Lan pulled the blanket back and saw Ake in her Anwyn form. She looked so innocent curled up in a ball. He had taken off her dress and her wings had ripped through the sheer chemise. His body responded and he tried to curb it.

Ake opened her eyes. 'Your eyes are like embers.' She shivered.

'They turn red when this thing threatens to overwhelm me.' The shadows clung to him, and he stared at her intensely. 'I couldn't solve the wooden puzzle.'

'Really?'

'I won't come back with you.' He shrugged.

'You gave your word, and those boys need you,' she cried.

'Better off without me.'

'So, the fatherless cycle continues again.' Ake smirked at him.

'How dare you! I'm nothing like Dane. He chose to go for duty's sake.' Lan glared at her. The shadows deepened.

'You left to fulfil your duty to protect us, like his duty to his druids. Cephas was finally dead. We had the chance to be a family. Our sons are now eleven. You spent little over a year with Amities. You went off at me for leaving Mandami behind. But at least I have shown up for the last four and a half years.'

'Four and a half years? No, it's only been a few long months trying to control this thing inside me, Ake.'

'No, Lan. It's been four and a half years. They are growing up fast. Especially Mandami, he will be a teenager soon.'

'You're lying. Trying to force me home!' Lan wrung his hands in frustration.

Ake shook her head. 'I'm going home today, Lan. To my sons. Stay if you wish. I release you.'

'You can't release me. Only death can do that.'

'Or distance. You didn't want us anymore.'

'Don't be so apathetic about this whole situation, like I didn't care. That is unfair.' Lan looked at her, shocked.

She stared at him defiantly. 'How else am I supposed to take it?'

'You wanted this creature for a husband?' Lan felt distressed and the shadows swirled around him in response to his emotions.

'Yes, because it was you.'

'It's dangerous, Ake!' He stared down at her, a fierce look in his eyes.

'And this ridiculous form is not? When I became crazed with power and nearly took your life did you not fight for me? Here I am fighting for you and all you want to do is hide.' She wept.

She is right. I have lost all this time with them believing only a few months had passed. My pride and fear of hurting them kept me from reaching out.

Lan reached out and wiped away a tear. Ake held his hand to her cheek. She smiled up at him, her eyes full of love.

'I've been a fool. And you are not ridiculous.' He pulled her towards him, unbuckling his breeches as he did so.

She tried to switch out of Anwyn form, but he used his dark powers and would not let her.

'Lan, not in this hateful form.' She lashed out, kicking him.

'You say I need to accept whatever this is, but you won't except this beautiful one. The one that shows your true soul. Kind of hypocritical.' Lan smirked.

'Cephas took me because of it,' she yelled.

'No, he did it because he was an evil man. I'm sure he lay with other unwilling women.'

Ake nodded. Lan pulled her to the end of the bed and stood between her legs. He leant down and kissed her harshly. She bit his tongue. Lan laughed.

'What are you playing at?' she spluttered.

'Sometimes it's a little coarse and urgent with couples.' Lan shrugged.

'I've overheard many a time while listening to the servants that there are different ways.' Ake looked up at him, trying to appear confident.

'It's bound to be very different with me now, Ake. I was trying to tell you that. This thing literally wants to consume that form of yours or something like that and I don't know how to control it. I'm not sure if I want to even if I could.'

'Lan.'

'I can walk away now if you want.'

Her eyes glowed in response to his.

'Try and defeat me.' Ake stared at him, her face flushed with desire.

'Are you sure?' He growled and lifted her chin, searching her eyes with his own for any doubt.

'Bet you can't,' Ake charmed.

'I need a direct confirmation, Ake, before I put you through this ordeal.'

'Yes, I consent.'

Lan removed his shirt and pants and threw them hastily on the floor. He kissed her, slipping his tongue into her mouth. Lan drew back, Ake sighed.

He was holding back, trying to not let the darkness overwhelm him. Ake gave him an encouraging smile. Lan reached down and removed her chemise.

'I love you. Do you realise what you do to me?' He groaned and looked away.

'You don't think it's the same for me? I love you so much a little piece of me died every time we were separated.' She gave him a heart wrenching look full of grief.

'I am sorry, sweetheart. Time moved differently for me.' Lan looked away unable to face her grief. 'I know you probably find it hard to believe that I tried to get back to you on several occasions. Every time I entered Caelestis I would here three awful words.'

'What do you mean you tried to return and heard three strange words?'

'Orilan was dancing naked under the moon and incanting something. Every time I entered Caelestis I could only stay momentarily before hearing *exitos morte kultes*. The room then span and I would appear elsewhere. I know that when I was emotionally charged, time would change but this felt different.'

Ake's eyes filled with tears and she clung to him, she shuddered as tears racked her body.

'What is it?' He squeezed her to him.

'Ori said he put up wards against Drianna and her death cult. Those wards—'

'Prevent a god of death from lingering in the home.' Lan made a sound of anguish and Ake shivered.

'I don't think Orilan knew it would affect you.'

Ake's gaze locked on his and he frowned.

'You never know with him.'

Ake caressed his face. 'I should have figured it out.'

'Hardly your fault. Druids trained him. He should have known.'

Ake trailed her hand across his chest and lower. Lan closed his eyes, enjoying the touch. When he opened his eyes again, her gaze was full of ardent desire.

'So, there are different ways, my sweet.' He gave her a flirtatious grin.

He flipped her onto her stomach, and she cried out briefly in surprise when he took her in earnest. The darkness in him rose and she was almost overwhelmed with his need for her. She began to wear out and he slowed his pace, giving her a moment's reprieve. Ake rolled onto her back. She could see he was still ready and refused to give into weariness. Ake grabbed his face and kissed him.

'That thing can't ever win,' she panted.

The creature was successfully goaded, and he crushed her into the bed. His mouth trailed down and he roused her to a suitable level and entered her again. The shadows engulfed the pair, but Ake countered him with her own light. She pushed him onto his back, straddled him and set her own rhythm.

She has never had the confidence to be assertive in our bed. I could get used to this. His eyes flashed with pride. He reached up, pulled her face to his and brushed her lips with his own.

'You should try that often,' he whispered.

Her cheeks turned red, and he laughed softly.

Sparks, golden and black, danced around them as they both continued to try to subdue the other.

CHAPTER THIRTY-FOUR

Ake's body was deliciously sore. She yawned and rose, no longer in her Anwyn form. Lan was sleeping peacefully now. In the end she had subdued him. When he was finally spent, the darkness was absorbed by her light and his eyes were no longer red. She went into the outer cave and saw the puzzle box open and laughed. *Clever devil, playing me at my own games.*

Lan snuck up behind her, fully dressed, and embraced her from behind.

'Who came up with the puzzles?' he breathed in her ear.

She giggled. 'Amities. The puzzle box I designed and made myself. I know it's a little crude and wonky.'

'Clever boy. And clever wife.' He nuzzled her neck.

'Lan, why did you never send those letters?' She turned in his arms to stare up at him.

Lan looked genuinely surprised. 'I did. Tok was in charge of the post, and I never saw a single reply.' Lan swore. 'He was a traitor. You never got them, did you?'

'No,' she said sadly.

'Tok gave them to my father, and he returned them to me. They were opened so I assumed you had read them.' Tears suddenly welled in his eyes, and she brushed them away. 'Tok must have read them and knew I was returning to you on your graduation night. That's how Drianna's minions were able to raise an army in time.' He sighed. 'Again, I put you and the others in danger thinking of my own desires.'

Ake drew back and grabbed his face in her hands. 'That wasn't your fault. You were allowed to fall in love and want to be with me.'

Lan gave her a sad smile. 'Do you think the letters would have helped?'

'Of course. I hadn't seen you in years and then you suddenly declared your love for me.'

'That explains your why you looked embarrassed. I am sorry if it was traumatic.'

'It's fine.' She gave him a sweet smile. 'I want to discuss something with you. Elves and half-elves often arrive unannounced on our doorstep. We give them sanctuary until they choose to leave. They mentioned they were saved by a sorcerer surrounded by shadows. I thought it was Ori. Was that you?'

Lan nodded.

'See, you are a good man.' She reached up and kissed him.

His eyes filled with happiness. 'I had to help when I could.'

'Are you coming home?' she asked forlornly.

'Don't do that. Or we may never leave that bed,' Lan whispered in her ear.

She trembled.

He drew back, laughing softly. 'If you and Caelestis will have me.'

'Lan, when will you realise that I only ever feel at home in your arms?'

'It is the same for me.' Lan gave her a dazzling smile and pulled her against his chest and kissed the top of her head. 'I'm a little nervous to see our children. They are going to hate me.'

'I can't deny they will be angry with you. Mainly Amities. Mandami is hard to read.'

Lan sighed. 'I know we must train Mandami. But don't you think he and Amities deserve a better childhood than either of us? Maybe we should travel a bit.'

She kissed him passionately in response. When she looked up, his eyes glinted red.

'I thought it was gone.' She shivered.

He shook his head.

'I believe it responds to you. Or rather I respond to you. I think it's part of me now. But I believe when I'm making love to you it's satisfied for a while,' he flirted.

'You were relentless.' She blushed.

'You matched me, so it matters not.' Lan shrugged.

Ake stared at him possessively. 'Did you look at the wenches in those inns? With that kind of drive, I assume you were tempted.'

He laughed at her. 'First time you've shown any jealousy. No, of course not. For me it's been a few bad months, and I would never take another lover, Ake. I'm not attracted to anyone else. I am not an amorous mage elf, Ake. I'm of the Sidhe. Hill folk, we mate for life. After we are wedded I cannot physically bed anyone else. That's why when a mate dies, we do not remarry. I guess that's why they had so very few children and died out.'

'Wasn't your father from Relequis?' she asked.

Lan shook his head. 'No, he came to the druid council from the Sidhe lands and decided to become a citizen of Relequis. Now, it felt like four and a half years for you. You seem to be asking me all sorts of insulting questions about infidelity. Did your eyes alight on attractive men as the loneliness consumed you?' He growled, his eyes turned red, and he pulled her closer to him in a crushing embrace. Ake tried to push him away.

'Don't be horrid, Lan, I would never.' She gave him a glare.

He laughed and kissed her.

'I am aware of that, Ake. But it hurt when you insinuated that of me.' He released her and she took a step back.

'Fair call. Do you think there are any of the Sidhe left?' she asked.

'Hmm. I very much doubt it. But we could try travelling there first. I would have to do some research though,' said Lan.

'Another thing, you won't be able to be handsy with me all the time when we return, Lan, there are people everywhere.'

'I will try, Ake.' He grinned at her and pulled her towards him, his hands cupping her rear.

'I was serious, Lan!' She pulled a ridiculous attempt at an angry face and pushed him away.

Lan laughed as Ake stomped away to pack his belongings. She shoved things away hastily. He proceeded to help her pack. Lan gave his lair one more look and shivered, glad to be rid of his cave of despair.

—⁓—

Lan teleported them to Caelestis and before Ake could protest, he grabbed the bags and slung her over his shoulder.

'What the hell are you doing?'

'I can't return to my school without my pride, Ake. What did you tell them? That I slunk away, and you were going to retrieve me?' He laughed.

They entered Caelestis.

'What is wrong with you, Lan? I told them you were on a research mission, and we needed help to rebuild.' She pummelled him angrily.

Servants and maids adverted their smiles, and the elven mystics acknowledged them with heads simply bowed. A hearty laugh rang out over the courtyard and Borrush looked at them approvingly and walked over to them.

'Good to see someone can keep her in line. Ha, these human women! That one, while smart, doesn't generally follow the rules and is often pushing our traditional boundaries.' He winked at them.

Ake hid her blazing face. She had little understanding of dwarven humour. While crude and outlandish, it was meant well. Lan was aware of Borrush's approval of couples being close. So, he decided to play along.

'If you can't keep the little woman in line, what kind of husband are you?' He laughed, dropped the bags and patted her on the rump.

She squirmed and kicked him in the face.

'Feisty wives are the best, aren't they?' said Borrush.

'Put her down,' hissed Mandami, walking through the main doors.

Borrush rolled his eyes. 'Stuck up little boy.'

Lan placed Ake down and looked at his son. He looked like Ake's grandmother, Kenra. Now around five feet, he was strongly built. His features were human but his dark eyes, now obsidian, were elven.

'Fancy bringing the lady of the keep back like that,' said Mandami.

Mandami had grown up under the strict rules of Regian nobility. Reputation in public, especially modesty for noble women, was strictly upheld. Lan shrugged and Ake stormed off testily. Mandami followed. Everyone went back about their business.

'Where you been, boy? Your wife and that weird grandson of Dane's has done a great justice to you. Classes are restored and mystics and druids are learning skills across the board with a little magery thrown in for good measure,' said Borrush.

'I will have to thank them. Why is Dane's grandson weird?' Lan asked.

'Dane expressed it was his real grandson but in all our studies we know nothing of him. At one time I hated him. But I have come to respect him,' said Borrush.

'Why?' asked Lan.

'Apart from helping rebuild, he defended your father against a doppelganger and several shades and even went on to defeat the vampyr within. That shows great fortitude, worthy of dwarven respect.'

'Hmm, seems like my son helped greatly,' said Lan proudly.

'Your son. He can't be your wife's. She's too young,' said Borrush.

Lan explained the awful nature of Orilan's birth and kidnapping.

Borrush's mouth hung open for a few seconds before he cleared his throat. 'Ah, well then. I better let you go check out the school.'

'Thank you, Borrush, for all that you've done. I'll see to it that I can help you with something,' said Lan gallantly.

'Well said, man. I may take you up on that at some point,' said Borrush.

They shook hands. Lan picked up his bags and entered his home.

Chapter Thirty-Five

Amities rushed along the halls. His black robes almost tripping him up. He was a small boy for his age at only four feet. *Mother is home.* Amities stopped to catch his breath and looked at the hallway covered in portraits of the deceased. All their accomplishments were listed on gold memorial plates under their portrait. He waved at Hau and ran towards the main doors.

Ake stormed through them followed by the devoted and quiet Mandami who bowed his head at his brother. Amities waved and rushed into his mother's arms.

'Baby,' Mandami mouthed at him.

Amities stuck out his tongue. Ake hugged him tightly and smiled down at him.

Orilan came out of the office and smiled at Ake. 'You look angry. He wouldn't even come home for you?'

Orilan looked at the mark on her neck and Ake covered it with her hand and blushed. 'Well, he's claimed you, that is progress. Hopefully he will come home soon.'

'Oh, the cowardly elf is here,' said Mandami quietly.

'What is wrong then?' asked Orilan.

Ake explained the humiliating entrance.

'He's always been ridiculously proud. You know he is flawed like that, Ake. He was also playing around with the dwarven humour. Believe it or not you were both complimented,' said Orilan.

'Why? He abandoned his wife.' Mandami glared.

'Mandami, your father is being haunted to become the god of death. He has never abandoned her. He could easily have killed us all. He chose to protect you three. The problem with the god of death is that time is different to him. It's to protect him from experiencing every day of eternity with only the dead for company,' explained Orilan.

'Whatever.' The preteen shrugged.

'Father's here, Mother? I will have words with him for you,' said Amities sweetly.

'Bluurgh. Suck up.' Mandami proceeded to make retching noises.

Amities stepped back and poked his tongue at Mandami.

'At least I'm not a small boy pretending to be a stalwart soldier,' he quipped back.

Mandami grinned at the brotherly banter.

Ake smiled. 'You two are very silly.'

The doors swung open and Lan looked around at the gleaming halls. The furniture had been updated and was more lavish. Caelestis had always had trappings of luxury but now it abounded in every corner, from exquisite art to vases full of flowers and fine rugs on the floors. Lan rubbed his chin thoughtfully. *Yep, Ake has taken over.* He laughed quietly to himself.

Lan went up to Orilan and shook his hand and thanked him.

'Please show me the rest,' said Lan.

Orilan guided him to the modern classrooms equipped with the latest books and graphs on science and engineering. The walls were pleasantly decorated with simple scenes from elven folklore.

'You did good,' said Lan.

'We did good, Father. I didn't paint those watercolours, she did,' said Orilan.

'Simple yet elegant. I will thank her when she's a little calmer.' Lan laughed.

'Why did you humiliate her, Lan? She has never mentioned where you went. I didn't know either until a few days ago. It was petty. You can't keep letting your pride best you and treat her like that,' Orilan admonished.

'Yeah, it was wrong of me. But it was very funny,' said Lan.

Orilan laughed. 'Yeah, it was.'

Orilan became serious. 'Please don't do it again. Not in front of others. She is quite proud herself. Now, are you okay?'

Ake walked into the room and looked around.

'I'm sorry, Ake, for humiliating you,' said Lan.

The door opened and the faculty members came in to meet Lan.

They were introduced and classes were discussed at length for more than an hour. Lan liked the curriculum. Ake ordered tea and everyone partook. As the teachers were leaving, Ake cast a paralysis spell on Lan when he wasn't looking and tried to throw him over her shoulder, almost dropping the scowling Lan, but succeeded and turned to the group.

'I have to deal with my mischievous husband.' Ake carried him from the room.

No one could keep a straight face. Not even Orilan.

Borrush's hearty laughter was contagious. 'He is well matched.'

Ake ended the spell and dropped him. Lan landed on his rear. He leapt up and dusted himself off.

'You win this one.' Lan grinned at her.

She started giggling. 'I know I do, Lan. You may be smart, but I will always find a way to counteract your little games.'

'It's great, Ake. All of it. The paintings are wonderful, well done. Thank you,' he said sincerely.

She nodded and everyone began to leave the room.

Borrush came and gave Lan a hearty blow on the back. He pinched Ake's cheek. 'Well done, girl. I am off to the cafeteria for ale.'

The other faculty members followed suit. Orilan went to tell his brothers of the comical scene.

Ake took Lan's hand, and he followed her around looking at the rest of the upgrades, including the memorial garden that had grown around the graves of the dead. Ake had ordered statues made of all their loved ones. His eyes filled with tears as his hands ran along the gravestones. He began to bow at each one, paying his respect.

'I am so sorry I never showed you my grief. Hanton always taught me a man must be strong and never divulge his emotions in a passionate display. He was wrong. I miss you all every day.'

Lan sighed and walked over to a statue in the likeness of Het and Flo. Flo leant against Het's chest and the valiant warrior had a trident in the other hand, a fierce look in his eyes. Lan placed his hand on Het's shoulder. A likeness of the couples' twin sons, Falcon and Hau, in their childhood sat at their feet.

'I am so sorry you died defending stone walls.' Lan knelt at the base of the statue. 'Please forgive me, Het.' Lan touched Flo's hands. 'Thank you for trying to save Ake when I could not. I will strive to be a better husband for her. I am so sorry I failed your son.' Lan reached out and brushed a leaf off Hau's head.

Ake walked over to her husband.

He turned, still kneeling, his head bowed. 'I am sorry for all the dreadful things I ever said to you. I will not make excuses for the basilisk poison that is no longer in my blood. I beg for your forgiveness and vow to be a better man and husband to you.'

Ake knelt down and lifted his head to look at her. 'Did you go through the ordeal of the poison leaving your body alone?'

'Yes.'

'How many days did you suffer?'

'That was the only time I didn't lose time. The sun rose four times before the fever and taint left my blood. The taste remained and alcohol dulled the taste for a while, but I could never stay drunk for long as the god of death's legacy sees alcohol as a taint as well. I soon came to rely on the brief relief of alcohol. I am ashamed for my weakness. I vow not to overindulge in it too often.'

He stood and pulled her up into his arms. He lay his head on her shoulder, and she felt his tears moisten her shirt as he sobbed quietly.

'All is long forgiven.' Ake kissed the top of his head, and they stayed that way long after Lan's sobs no longer wracked his body.

CHAPTER THIRTY-SIX

Lan looked over his shoulder to make sure no one was watching then pulled back the tapestry and slid into a hidden alcove. *I haven't been down here in over a decade. She has funded the school on brilliant investments alone. Now I want to do something special for her.* Lan pressed the cold stone in several places, there was an audible click and a rope ladder fell from a crack in the roof as a slab of stone slid backwards. Lan stifled the urge to cough as dust showered down on him. He tested his weight on the ladder, and it held his mass. He climbed and pulled himself up into the secret room.

Lan felt for the torch sconces nearby. He felt the oily rag and with a thought, the torch flared and he blinked in the sudden brightness. He looked around at the piles of gold coins and gemstones before his gaze settled on a simple chest. He drew in a deep breath before pressing the latch. The lid sprang open and he gently pulled back the yellowing linen. His nose was assaulted by a variety of dried herbs including lavender, bay, cloves and rosemary in an attempt to keep moths from attacking the garments within. Lan withdrew Ake's wedding gown. Some of the embroidery was fraying and the garment was no longer completely white.

After Cephas had stolen Ake, Dane returned to Caelestis when Lan was stable. He had tried to find the two magical spears used in the battle that destroyed Caelestis over twenty-two years ago, just after Ake's graduation. Mbel Daione could be wielded by anyone.

The weapon could unleash an unlimited barrage of *Mystic Fire* on its victims. The sister spear could only be wielded by a woman of divine blood mixed with elven heritage. The name Empon Searto meant to wield water, and they had discovered its atrocious power when Ake had turned it on an army of cutthroats. It manipulated the water of life, blood. The once-human men had taken on hideous forms, as flesh peeled from their bodies and was replaced with hideous forms from vampyrs to ghouls. Diseases ravaged the once-human forms and the air had been rent with hideous screams and obnoxious smells. Lan shuddered and lifted his head to stare at the place where he had hidden the spears. *I am sorry, Father. I couldn't let them fall into the wrong hands. They could come in useful in the fight against Drianna.*

Lan placed the dress within a sack he had brought and closed the chest. He strode over to the pile of treasure and took a few handfuls of gems and coins and let them fall in the open sack he placed on the ground. He began kicking away piles of gold until he spotted a small indent in the ground. He withdrew a faded and fraying red ribbon from his pocket. He ran his hands over the golden embroidery before placing the cloth in the indent and whispering. '*Ea ley.* My beloved.'

A hazy light appeared with the outline of two spears hovering in the air, he clasped the spears as the light faded. He bent down and retrieved the ribbon and gently placed in his pocket. The ribbon had been used to tie his and Ake's hands together at their wedding ceremony; it had indicated their matrimonial bonds. He retrieved the sack and left the vault.

Lan stuck his head out from behind the tapestry and saw no one in the hallway, he slipped out from behind the furnishing and headed to a small classroom. He took out a small embroidery kit and began to make his alterations to the dress. *I hope she doesn't hate it.*

———∿∿∿———

Ake yawned and reached for her husband; bolting upright when she realised he was missing. She clamoured out of bed and rushed for the stairs that led to Lan's office. *Please don't let the darkness come for him now, we have only had a few months.* Her breath came in gasps as she lost her footing and nearly twisted her ankle. She threw open the trapdoor and climbed out into the office. Her eyes fixated on Lan. He gave her a lazy smile as his eyes fluttered open. He was resting in a large armchair, his legs on the table. She watched his eyes fill with concern and he slid his legs to the floor and rose.

'What's wrong?'

'You are still here.' Ake felt her lips tremble and she braced herself against the wall and glared at Lan. 'You are not to leave our bed without telling me.' She sniffled as hot tears traced their way down her cheeks. 'How can I trust that you won't be taken from me again? The gods seem bent on tearing us apart.'

'I can't plan a surprise with you present.' Lan winked at her.

'Stop acting so nonchalant.' Ake let the tears overwhelm her.

She was drawn against his warm chest, her whole body shaking with the onslaught of her heart-wrenching sobs.

'I am not going anywhere if I can help it, honey.' He tilted her head to look at him. 'You're stuck with me.'

'You can't make that promise. The gods hate us.'

He withdrew something from his pocket, turned her away from him and ran his fingers through her hair. She let out a noise of annoyance as he tied up her hair.

She turned on him in fury. 'What the hell! I am serious and you're worried about my hair?'

'You and I are bound by destiny, just like that ribbon in your hair bound our hands in matrimony over twelve and a half years ago. I pledge myself to you again and I will fight to stay with you.'

Ake willed her anger away and just stared at him.

'You seem distracted.'

Ake nodded and looked away before composing herself. 'Sorry. I have had other things on my mind.'

Lan shrugged and took a parcel from the desk. 'I wanted to cheer you up.'

Ake smiled and opened the package. She gasped and withdrew her wedding dress. The dress had once cascaded down to the floor but had been altered to just above her knees. The lace bodice once encrusted with diamonds, now had an array of rainbow-coloured gemstones that twinkled in the dawn light filtering in through a window. The pink silk roses that had formerly graced the hem were now replaced with red blooms including peonies, orchids and carnations. Ake ran her hands over the blooms and stared at Lan in astonishment.

'The changes you made to the dress are magnificent.' Her voice took on a husky tone. 'I can't wear this outside of Caelestis with these flowers. They represent—'

Lan pulled her towards him and unlaced her nightgown and it slid to the floor. 'Desire, passion, love and that you are taken. All the amorous stuff. I am aware.' He buried his face in her neck. 'I have another surprise. I am taking you to lunch in that gown.'

'But what will people think?'

Ake gasped as his hands found their way between her legs. 'That you aren't alone up here anymore and someone is loving you.'

Ake closed her eyes and sighed as his deft hands invoked her passion. She moaned and heard him laugh. 'Lunch can wait. I want breakfast.'

She opened her eyes as he lifted her onto the desk. 'Wait, this is your office. We can't do that here.'

'You tried to get me to take you in a tavern.' Lan pushed her down and clambered onto the desk. 'Here is just fine.'

His mouth took hers and she gasped for air in between his intense kisses. He winked before he ducked his head between her legs and she cried out. 'Where did you learn that?'

Lan looked up at her his face flushed with passion. 'Instinct. We have a lot to learn together. After so many years apart I intend for us to both be apt scholars. We never really had a chance to have a real marriage and I am still learning new things I adore about you each day.'

He pressed himself against her, as his mouth claimed ownership of hers.

Ake felt the love for him well up within her and she wrapped her legs around his waist, pressing her trembling body against him.

'So, I guess here is fine then?' He pulled away from her and undressed. As he did so, an ink pot clattered to the floor and bunches of scrolls followed. He bent to pick them up, slowly, grinning at Ake while he did so.

'Stop drawing it out.'

'Oh no, I will take my time.'

'No hurry ... in case—'

'Don't worry, honey. I'm in control. I am not going to disappear suddenly.'

Ake felt the anxiety build and grabbed for him. 'You don't know that. Please don't draw it out.'

His face softened with worry. 'If you're sure.'

Ake nodded.

Lan shifted his body so that he was positioned between her thighs. With a thrust of his hips, they were joined. She felt her body keep time with his gentle rhythm. As the passion built between them, she watched his eyes glaze over, lost in their mutual pleasure.

'I don't forgive you for leaving me. How can I trust you won't disappear again?'

Lan gazed down at her, his expression one of desire and annoyance. 'I said I am in control of the darkness and therefore myself.'

'How do I know that?'

'So, I need to ask for constant forgiveness, do I? I fought ceaselessly to try and get back to you, thinking multiple times I had conquered it. I have already apologised.' Lan shifted his weight as he pinned her firmly against the desk, burying himself deeper inside. Ake cried out.

'What will it take?' Lan set an intense pace and Ake felt waves of pleasure wash over her again and again.

'Time. We need to build trust again,' she cried out.

Lan growled. 'Fine, if that's what it takes. For what it's worth, I trust you with my life.'

Ake stared at him. 'I trust you with my life. Giving up my heart wholeheartedly again is a different matter.'

Lan smiled fondly. 'I can understand a guarded heart. I thought you didn't trust me in other areas.'

'You silly elf.' Ake laughed. 'I know you didn't mean to hurt me. Just give me time. And please don't leave without telling me.'

'That I can do.' Lan groaned as his ardour was satisfied. He collapsed against her, wrapping his arms under her and nuzzling her neck. He yawned and closed his eyes.

'I am exhausted.'

'Were you up all night?' Ake brushed the hair out of his face as he lifted his head to stare at her.

'Most of it.' Lan pushed himself off her. 'Let us go bathe and then we will head into town.'

Ake nodded and he led her back down the stairs to their bedroom that contained the hot springs.

—⁓—

Lan's mouth watered as the scent of cooking reached his nostrils. They had entered the outskirts of Axeton and a group of travelling merchants were set up on a field nearby selling various wares including exotic foods that were being prepared and cooked on open fires. He recognised some of the herbs and spices used and several he didn't know.

Ake blushed as sets of eyes from both men and women appraised her. The outfit complimented her figure. Lan's gaze dropped to her feet. She wore white boots that looked like they were well past use. *They were a present from Het, I remember her telling me. I miss Het, and Flo too, sweetheart.* Lan approached a cobbler and saw a new pair of red boots about Ake's size.

'Can I get those, please?'

The vendor ignored him and served someone else. Lan waited, When the vendor had finished, he placed two coins down on the table.

'Can I get those, please?'

The vendor turned and sneered at him. 'Be gone, elf. Your type brings trouble. Look at what happened to the Regians. May their souls be at rest.'

Lan stared at him in astonishment. 'Excuse me?'

A familiar voice reached Lan's ears as Kathy approached the vendor. 'We aren't Regians. While there are some horrid persons among the isle, most people here like elves. You would be wise not to gain the disdain of the Lord of Caelestis, ruler of most of this isle, barring several villages.'

The vendor glared at Kathy. 'So, you will force me to sell to a creature I distrust by using their nobility against me?' The vendor gave Lan a mocking bow. 'Oh, worthy lord, take them free of charge.'

Lan sighed picked up his coins and strode away leaving the boots behind. He heard footsteps behind him. He turned and waited for Kathy to approach him. Her hair had begun to grey, and her posture was more stooped as if the years had caught up with her. *She must be at least sixty by now. Village life is harsh.*

'Hello, Kathy. Thank you for trying to help. I ignore biased sorts these days.'

'Apart from cutting your hair, you haven't aged since Caelestis fell.'

'As an elf that's to be expected. How are you and your family?'

Lan tensed, aware of the awkward conversation about to occur.

'We are well.'

Lan looked around, searching for Ake.

Kathy cleared her throat and Lan looked back at her.

'So, you returned after all. You look … good together.'

Lan shifted his feet anxiously at the sadness in Kathy's voice. 'I am really sorry about Het. He was a good man.' Lan bowed to Kathy.

Kathy smiled. 'You really have grown up.'

'I should never have made Het Ake's guardian. It put him in a dangerous position. I should have sent Ake to Serenade, at least she would have been safe there.'

Kathy sighed. 'Het would never have left her. He volunteered to be her guardian when Dane asked. Someone had to be until you and Ake were grown and ready to marry.'

'Het knew I was destined for her, yet he still wanted to marry her?'

'He loved her deeply—'

'And he died protecting her. I feel deep regret for that.'

'Do you love her, Lan? Not just as a protector, but with the passion of a husband?'

Lan blushed. 'Of course, I do.'

Kathy smiled. 'Then I am happy for you both. I have my own apologies to give.'

'Why would you need to apologise?'

Kathy sighed. 'Ake could never master magic at school as I kept her magic controlled until her marriage was consummated. The powers would awaken after her first heartfelt kiss.'

I wondered where her powers were after she blew up her village. Someone is always interfering in our lives.

'There is nothing to forgive. I am sure you meant well.'

Kathy looked at him sadly. 'This meant Drianna set her search on the other half of the prophecy. If she couldn't destroy Ake while young, she would torture and destroy her mate and put a corrupt one in his place still with the bloodline of the ancients. So, you endured pain while Ake thrived.'

'Well, that's all behind us now. I wish you well, Kathy.'

So, I had to be the decoy so she could live to adulthood. As horrible as it was, she is alive and that's all that matters. Lan turned and began to walk away. *Kathy means a lot to Ake.* Lan faced Kathy and held out his hand, Kathy shook it.

'You know where we are if you ever need anything.' Lan gave her a brief smile and his eyes darted to where Ake was buying cakes. He laughed and headed towards her. She wrinkled her nose as she passed a bubbling pot. He wandered over and placed an arm around her waist. She smiled and leant into his shoulder.

'What are you serving?' Lan pointed to the pot.

'Too spicy for the delicate mouths of elves.' The vendor stood and laughed.

'I'll take a bowl.' Lan handed over the coins and sat on a nearby haystack.

As Lan sipped the broth he watched Ake, his heart filled with joy as she enjoyed her fare. She pushed some cake towards him.

'No, thanks.'

She frowned. He grabbed her hand as she drew it back and took the small morsel with his mouth but then continued to kiss her hand.

'Hmm, I believe this hand is covered in sweetness.' He nibbled her hand.

Ake laughed. 'People are watching.'

Lan shrugged. 'Let them. I am going to go get some more spicy broth. I'll be right back, I promise.'

Ake nodded. 'Okay.'

Lan walked back over to the vendor.

'Back again.' The vendor laughed.

'That was nice.'

'Nice.' The man smirked. 'Most people can't handle that type of food.'

'Why are you offended? I wasn't mocking you.' Lan held out the coins. 'I'll have another bowl, please.'

The vendor smiled. 'You sure you wouldn't like something more flavoursome?'

'It won't be too spicy, will it?'

'It will be just right.' The vendor bent over another pot and ladled broth into a bowl and handed it to Lan.

Lan handed the coins over and walked back to Ake and sat down. The steam hit his face as he smelt the brew.

'Your eyes are watering maybe you shouldn't eat it.'

Lan grinned. 'Waste little, want for little.'

He drained the small bowl and felt the hot liquid rush down his throat and his tongue began to burn. Tears coursed down his face as he felt the heat rush through his body. 'I think I will pay for that.' He coughed and saliva burned his throat and he erupted into a coughing fit. Ake rushed off and came back with a cup of water. He drank until he felt his burning throat cool.

'I'm okay,' he said huskily from his tortured throat.

'You don't look okay. Can we go home?'

'If you want.' Lan stood and coughed again. 'I think we need to hurry though.' He pulled Ake to him and in a swirling light they appeared in front of Caelestis.

'Please excuse me.' Lan's stomach grumbled in anger and he rushed inside, knowing he would need to make use of the amenities quickly. Ake followed and stayed outside the room.

'Are you sure you're okay?'

'I am sorry about how the day ended but I need privacy.'

'I am worried about you.'

'Go get Ori to make a stomach reliver.'

'I'll do it myself,' said Ake, wariness in her voice.

'What transpired between you two?' Lan groaned in pain.

'I'll be back.'

He heard Ake's footsteps hurry away. *I shouldn't have had that second bowl. I will have to have a discussion with my son. If he touched her, I will kick him out myself.*

Lan knew they needed an advantage against Drianna and her minions. Several weeks had passed since his stomach illness. *I have to convince Ake to overcome her fear of Empon Seato and wield it against Drianna and her minions. But first I must do some research to make sure the weapon is safe in between preparing for this trip. Training may have to wait until we get back.* Lan sighed. He had taken all the books from the library shelves with any mention of the spears. He turned the pages and began to read, falling asleep near dawn. Lan opened his bleary eyes as someone knocked.

'Father, you missed breakfast again and school starts in an hour,' said Amities, entering the room.

'Thanks.' Lan groaned and stretched before standing and walking out of his office. He rushed towards class. Ake stopped him in the hallway and passed him a cup of tea. Grateful, he kissed her before entering the classroom.

—⁓—

Ake looked at her exhausted husband in the bed beside her. It had been four months since he returned, and this last month he had gotten caught up in a school project, increasing his workload. She stood up and crept from their room. Her nausea hadn't settled these last few days, and she picked up a bucket, prepared to use it if the nausea overwhelmed her. Her heart leapt with joy, and she smiled to herself. *I am late by four months. Oh no, we conceived it in that cave.* Her joy turned to worry and her throat felt suddenly dry. *Lan's got enough on his plate. I can't tell him about this. Who knows how he will react.* She looked in a mirror and lifted her nightgown, she was already showing. She crept back to their room and donned a heavy robe from the wardrobe and crawled back into their bed. *He is still afraid of the darkness within him and he may not want this baby. Is it even a baby? Could it be a demon?* Ake shivered and Lan eyes fluttered open.

'You okay?'

Ake gave him a charming smile.

He drew her towards him and kissed her. Their lovemaking was brief as exhaustion overcame him and he fell asleep, clinging to her.

—⁓—

Ake smiled to herself. *Lan is thriving running the school and developing wards around Caelestis.* Amities had warmed quickly to him, but Mandami still refused to forgive him.

Borrush had told them a few Sidhe remained among the Galli Isles likely on the island of Eriu, but their numbers were sparse. He said they should come see the great dwarven city of Rock Fell. They had added that destination to their trip list.

Ake felt the child kick and grinned. She was now six months pregnant. Ake had kept this a secret. Lan would cancel their plans if he knew. She was terrified of losing this baby. This would be her sixth pregnancy with only two children living.

Ake had named the baby Caoimhe which meant beautiful, gentle and precious. Lan's dark spirit had not reappeared in their bed since and she was fine with that. He was so caught up in his plans and school that he hadn't even noticed her growing belly. She had worn heavy, loose garments, even when they were intimate, and Lan was always busy and exhausted and didn't notice the changes to her wardrobe.

They were leaving today, and she had packed an extra bag for the baby. She had plotted their course well; they would arrive in Rock Fell when the baby was due. She knew there were midwives there.

She heard Lan coming down the stairs to their cavern room with the boys. Ake picked up her two bags. They burst into the room. Amities was discussing a new research discovery with Lan. He was full of excitement. They dumped their bags on the bed. Mandami came over and stood by his mother.

Lan looked at her bags.

'We decided one each, honey,' he said.

'I need this one or do I need to talk about womanly needs?' she asked.

'I'll put it in with my things. I'll take some stuff out,' he said.

Mandami, who carried little, grabbed it and put it in his half-empty bag.

'Mummy's boy,' said Amities.

'Says the one always clambering to get attention from her,' bantered Mandami.

Lan and Amities were dressed in black robes over long pants and wore sturdy boots. Mandami wore his tunic and Regian sandals. Lan had ordered two more sets of clothes for him including a cloak. Mandami didn't like to pack heavy. Amities bag was bulging. He had packed ink, quills, books and only one change of clothes.

'Are we ready?' asked Lan.

They all nodded, and he teleported them to the location, using the rough coordinates given to him by Borrush. They landed ankle deep in squelching mud. They had landed in one of the infamous bogs off the west coast of Eriu.

This is dangerous. Lan looked around for stable earth. The bog stretched miles in each direction. He balanced his weight and managed to step out on top of the mud. Mandami followed suit. Amities tried and kept falling in the mud. Ake wanted to use her wings to glide but that would mean revealing her pregnancy.

'No magic from here. We don't know how the locals may react,' said Lan.

Lan hauled Amities out of the mud and onto his back. He went to offer Ake a hand. Ake conjured a staff and started using it to guide her through the mud, taking the points that held her weight. She would show no sign of weakness in case Lan questioned this whole trip into unknown lands.

'Ake, no magic,' said Lan.

'My choice, Lan,' she said.

He shrugged. It was slow going but they finally made it to what appeared to be stable ground. They sat down to have a drink break.

'It has to be around here somewhere,' said Lan.

Lan saw a rock formation nearby and leapt onto it. He surveyed the area. *Bog as far as the eye can see.* Amities walked over and pulled a magnifying glass out of his bag. The child knelt down and began scrutinising the rock. Lan looked on amused.

'Father, this rock is odd. It's not natural to the region,' said Amities.

Curious, Lan jumped down, landing quietly next to Amities, spooking him. They both examined the rock. Ake laughed, as did Mandami.

'They are real rock heads.' She laughed and looked at them endearingly.

'They sure do like that geology study.' Mandami grinned.

'I'll help, watch this, Mother,' said Mandami.

Mandami ran over and started kicking the rock to the annoyance of Amities who tried swatting at him. Mandami poked his tongue out at Amities and continued to aim his blows wherever his brother examined the large stone.

The blow to the rock hit a small gem embedded in the surface. The gem began to tick. Lan heard it and hauled his boys back. He gave them a stern warning to stay away and then sat down to watch the strange rock.

Ake grinned and took the thieves kit which she always carried in case of an emergency out of her bag. The kit consisted of lock picks of varying size and shape, leverage tools, oil and a listening aid. She approached the rock to examine the noise. Lan put himself in front of the stone and blocked her path. Ake rolled her eyes and walked around him. He grabbed her hand.

'What are you doing? It could be dangerous,' he said.

'It doesn't sound like that,' said Ake.

'What do you mean?' he asked.

'Listen, the ticking is caused by the lock turning and jamming on something. If I can release it, it may be an entrance,' she said.

'Give me the tools, I'll try,' he demanded.

'Lan, you have to let me do things.' She sighed.

'I vowed to protect you.' Lan grinned.

She laughed. 'That is bordering on ridiculous.'

Lan gave her an apologetic smile. 'Ah, sorry. I am trying.'

'I'll let you know when I am in trouble.'

Lan nodded. 'Sure.'

Ake let go of his hand and knelt. Ake tapped around the area of the lock and felt a hollow section. She tapped it sharply and a hinge came loose. Ake pulled it back and found a tiny hole.

Ake looked at her tools. The small pick was made of thin metal and one tip was slightly curved. The other tool was slightly longer, and the metal was bent at one end, resulting in a hook. The second object was used as leverage for the first.

Ake inserted the bent end of the lever into the hole and turned it to one side and applied tension. She inserted the curved end of the pick into the hole above the lever. *This feels like a standard five-pin lock.* Using the pick, Ake fiddled around, trying to find a seized pin. She was able to find it and forced it up until she heard an audible click. Ake continued the process, applying tension at the bottom with the other tool. Using the pick, Ake tried to release each pin as another seized when one was freed. There were four more audible clicks as the lock opened. The rock began to slide back, and she stood up.

With a loud clanging, the rock rolled to one side and a spiral staircase could be seen going down into the earth. The group shouldered their packs and stared at it a while. After a few minutes the rock began to slide back. Ake grabbed her boys' hands and rushed down the spiral stairway. Lan cursed and followed. The door slammed shut and they were rendered in total darkness.

Amities and Lan's eyes adjusted quickly. Ake conjured some tiny stars of light above her head so she could see and released the boys' hands. Ake proceeded down the stairway. The rest followed.

CHAPTER THIRTY-SEVEN

There was a narrow stone passageway ahead of them that seemed to stretch on for miles. Ake walked straight ahead without looking down. Lan grabbed her as she almost stepped over the edge. She looked down into a cavernous drop. The other side was over thirty feet away. Lan pulled her back. She shuddered and he pulled her into his arms.

'Always in a rush to live life, my little wife,' he said.

Lan let her go when she was calm. He told the boys to stay back and leapt the gap easily. While he was looking about on the other side for something to tie a rope to, a jolt of fear passed through him.

'Lan!' Ake screamed.

He turned and saw Mandami take a flying leap. The boy almost cleared the distance and stumbled for footing on the other side. Lan grabbed the child and scolded him for his recklessness.

'You could have been killed,' said Lan, his eyes full of fear.

'That was impressive. I wanted to show you I could do it too.' Tears started in Mandami's eyes, and he began to sob softly.

'I only raised my voice because I thought I may lose you.' Lan gave him a reassuring smile.

Mandami nodded and brushed away his tears. 'Don't tell Amities and Mother I cried.'

'Of course not. Always keep your head about you. Literally look before you leap, Mandami. It will take you years to gain the dextrous skills most elves have naturally.'

Mandami nodded.

Lan turned away and let the boy calm himself. *I do not want to injure the child's self-confidence.* Lan pulled some rope from his bag. 'Let's look for a place to tie the rope.'

Mandami smiled.

They found broken chain links where a rope bridge used to be. Lan tested them to see if they were serviceable. He could ask Ake to glide across with Amities, but he thought he could teach his children a few skills. He tied a rope through a link, showing Mandami the right knots.

'Ake, when I throw the rope across tie it the other side. Show Amities the correct knots.' Lan threw the rope and Ake finished tying it to her link.

'Mandami, stay here.' Lan tested the rope, walking across to the other side without hindrance. 'Please wait here, sweetheart.' Lan smiled at Ake and carried Amities across.

Ake tied her dress into her garter belt, took her staff and started to balance herself across the tight rope. She took her time and made it as Lan turned to head back to get her. When they were all safe, he leapt back and untied the ends. He came back and did the same with the other end. Lan then rolled up the rope and put it back in his pack.

The hallway continued for another hour until it stopped suddenly at what appeared to be a dead end. Amities examined the walls. The others sat and rested for a minute, eating a little food. Amities munched on his bread and then dropped it. He rummaged through his pack and found a potion, which he threw against the wall. The glass smashed and the liquid dripped down the surface. Words appeared and quickly began to fade. Amities wrote them down.

We are of the hills, as old as time.
Answer ye if this riddle is right, or nay if it be wrong.

Be careful of impending doom, answer wrong and you will have earned your tomb.

Ake and Mandami were about to say something, and Lan held out his hand for silence. He took the quill and some paper and wrote. He showed them what he had written.

Don't talk. The answer is either ye or nay.

Ake glared at him.

'We aren't stupid,' she said in his mind.

'*Never said you were. Nice new skill, Ake*,' said Lan.

'*The answer is nay*,' said Ake.

'*How do you figure?*' asked Lan.

He knew the answer but was just seeing if she did. Ake was about to speak up when Mandami and Amities announced *nay* aloud. A drumming noise began and became increasingly louder. Everyone covered their ears and worried they had made a mistake. The noise stopped abruptly, and the wall slid open.

Ake smiled. 'The riddle is wrong, if the Sidhe were the first children of the gods and immortal—'

'They had no need to invent time as we know it. They can't be as old as time if they had no need for that construct,' said Mandami.

Amities gave his brother a warm smile.

Gloomy sunlight filtered into the passage. They walked through the doorway. The view was incredible. Intricate buildings were carved into the rockface. Earthen walkways connected the structures. Trees and flowers grew across the surfaces. An ivory bridge was built over a ravine, the only link between them and the other side.

Tiny elves tended the flowers and plants while others stood about chatting. A large white swan soared above them and landed on the bridge. A small person leapt off its back and unsheathed the sword at his waist. He wore only a loin skin and started to chatter in ancient Elvish.

Ake examined him. He was unusually tanned and solid for an elf. Like the elves of Relequis, Lan was leaner and extremely pale in comparison. The tiny elf had the same obsidian eyes and dark hair gifted to Lan by his father, Dane.

He branded his blade at Amities, Ake and Lan.

'*Ghast, Devala*,' he yelled. He sniffed the air and stared at Mandami.

'*Halfey*.' He grunted and rushed over to Mandami staring up at him. The strange little elf growled at the others. Mandami glared and growled back.

'I doubt these people are Dane's kin.' Lan gave Ake an awkward smile.

Ake giggled. 'I can't imagine Dane living here.'

The frightened elf rushed Ake, thinking she had insulted it. Lan caught him and the elf slashed at his hands with his weapon. Blood dripped down.

The tiny elf leapt back and smelt the air and cried out loudly in Eriu, '*Mórs teaghlach*.' The elf jumped up and down and put away his weapon.

'He just called us Big's family.' Ake laughed.

The elf ran across the bridge and shooed the swan away. He ran from one elf to the other, laughing and hugging them. Thirty excited little elves rushed over the bridge and stared at them. Ake wrapped Lan's hand in some clean cloth.

'I am Swan Rider of Anwyl, king of the Daione Sidhe,' said the little elf.

Lan bowed and introduced himself. 'I am Trebrelan, son of Dane of the Sidhe, and Regona. This is Telewanake, daughter of Gepatok and Melowy. These are our sons, Mandami and Amities.'

'You are Big's son,' cried Swan Rider.

'No, my father, Dane, was taller and fairer,' said Lan.

'Big was odd. Cute baby but he grew too tall for the houses. He felt alone and left. I was very sad. Where is he?' asked Swan Rider.

'He died,' said Lan sadly.

'Oh. How?' asked Swan Rider.

'Drianna,' Lan muttered.

'We hate her. She hates Dee and Sorendee,' said Swan Rider.

Swan Rider had the other elves bring cushions and refreshments. He sat and ate with them.

'You are Dane's father?' asked Lan.

'Yes, and his mother is over here.' He pointed to an elf woman that had just appeared on a cushion next to him.

'This is Deas. She cast a spell on our new baby in the wrong phase of the moon. Deas was trying to bless him. Our son became very powerful and strong. Dee later told us our son would need this strength for the journey ahead. He would one day sire a supernatural son, a mate for the goddess of mercy. The oldest mortal blood will flow through our great grandson. The magic in it will help him kill Drianna,' said Swan Rider.

'Wait a minute. The first Daione Sidhe were immortals who eventually founded Relequis,' said Ake.

'Humans often misinterpret sacred texts. We are mortals with very long lives. Countless lives were lost in the fight, trying to find Sorendee's granddaughter. Our family are the last. The humans still hunt us. They took over our sacred bogs and hills and now the magic that gives us extraordinary long lives is lost. We will stay here now and never leave. Soon the last of us will be gone. But I am happy I have a grandson and great grandsons,' said Swan Rider.

'Oh. You helped in that battle?' asked Ake.

'Yes,' said Swan Rider.

'I am so sorry.' Ake wiped a tear from her eye.

Amities was writing this all down and making sketches.

'Weirder and weirder family,' said Mandami.

A flower-scented draft blew in from a passage nearby. The smell was divine. Someone brushed past Ake and she felt at peace. Swan Rider's nostrils flared, and he stared at Mandami.

'Dee has spoken. Half-elf child you smell of the gods.' Swan Rider laughed with joy.

The little elf leapt up and rushed over to Ake and smelt her hair. He proceeded to run over and sniff Lan who backed off. Ake laughed.

'Creepy thing,' said Mandami.

'You are Lady Saol, Lord Bás and the Princes Cròga and Ceardaí,' Swan Rider smiled.

Lan seethed at the dark title accorded him. He ground his teeth in annoyance and looked away.

'I am not the Lord of Death. My sons will not be patrons for the gods of war and crafting. Enough.' Lan growled and stood up.

The little elf, Deas, stood and whispered soothingly to her mate and he looked suddenly apologetic.

'Forgive me, grandchild. I thought Big may have had many children including sons. I didn't realise you were the divine couple. You chose to wed a goddess of mercy and life. With life comes death and that shadow will always follow you until you embrace it. What did you think would happen?' asked the little elf.

'I won't be an evil pawn of Drianna,' yelled Lan.

Ake reached for his hand. He pushed it away. The little Deas tilted her head and stared at Ake's abdomen and smiled. Ake looked away quickly.

'Death is not evil, it's a part of life. A good man who becomes the god of death brings compassion to a sometimes-tragic passing. He heals the souls in the underworld before they can reunite with Dee and Sorendee. For a smart elfling you know so little. Did your father teach you nothing?' asked Swan Rider.

'I don't want the job,' said Lan.

Deas pulled on her mate's arm and muttered something in his ear.

'Women will now talk away from angry husbands. Men should not be angry in front of wives. Bás I will teach you more about the gift Dee has given you. I am glad I have found out. Hopefully, the information I give you will lessen your resistance towards it,' said Swan Rider.

Lan glared at him. He stood up and began to pace. Ake was suddenly levitated over to Deas. She looked odd floating cross-legged in the air. Lan smiled at her in amusement. Swan Rider cleared his throat and Lan sat back down.

'I could have told you that. We do not fight in front of women, they are inclined to passionate and wilful displays,' said Mandami.

'That is stupid, Mandami. Women are entitled to engage in heated discussions with men.' Lan laughed.

'You think they are equal?' asked Mandami.

'Gods, you have been raised wrong.' Lan gave Mandami a sad smile.

'Silly boys. Women are equal. You are both wrong. It is disrespectful to raise voices to mothers and sisters. I would not yell at Dee. Equal discussion is welcome. Heated displays boil the blood and cause heartache. Use the logic of words, never anger. Humans soon used angry words and would not discuss things in a logical manner. Then in fear they killed us,' said the wise Swan Rider.

Swan Rider began to tell Lan about Lord Bás and engage him in the principals of his people. Amities began taking notes.

'What do you know of Lord Bás?' asked Swan Rider.

Lan sighed. 'Drianna tricked him into giving up his position during a game of Din and Dage. Lord Bás became mortal.'

Swan Rider nodded. 'Correct. Then what happened?'

'Bás took his own life vowing to come back as a mortal and marry the goddess of mercy, helping Sorendee fulfil the prophecy.' Lan smirked. 'What has that got to do with me?'

'Do you know anything about his personality traits?' asked Swan Rider.

Amities looked up. 'Like Father, he is known for his pride, vanity and stubbornness. He is prone to mood swings and feels great empathy, resulting in bouts of mental anguish. He has a temper at times only outdone by his soulmate and breaks rules and traditions as he sees fit.' Amities gave his father a knowledgeable smile. 'He is one of three gods not born of Dee and Sorendee but born from the moon goddess in her darkest phase.'

Swan Rider smiled. 'Clever elfling. I will tell you the story of how the sun and moon came to be. When our world began Drianna was jealous of her older sister Dee and slapped her with great fervour. The gentle Dee refused to retaliate and was always bleeding her hot liquid blood upon the surface of our world. As time passed Sorendee grew bored. Dee and Drianna reached adulthood and began to fight less, and the world became less hostile, and Sorendee finally saw Dee and knew at once that this was his life partner. He wanted to impress his love, so he took two arrows and tied them with a lock of his hair.

'Sorendee lit the arrows with fire and threw it fast, way up in the air. It looked like a bright disc in the sky and it lit Dee's face. Sorendee's shot was so good it stayed up there and became the sun. Dee, not wanting to be outdone, plaited her brown hair and they became masses of trees, the forests. Then, crying with happiness, her tears became oceans and lakes. Now it came for the hand fasting and the sharing of gifts. Dee created animals, both pleasing and non-pleasing to look upon. But each had a use. Now these creatures were hungry and tried to devour each other. Seeing that they would all be consumed, Dee made the flowers, plants, grasses and her favourite was Sweet Grass.

'Sorendee made a man and woman to walk among the forests and beasts. To each of them he gave free will and the knowledge of tribal life. These first people were special for they were Daione Sidhe and lived within the breasts of Dee, the hills. They could see with night-eyes, hear every movement and draw of breath. They were made to have long lives and be helpers of the new people who were to come in twenty thousand years. These Sidhe bred and became many. Then two people, a man and his wife were made and were sent to live in the hot lands, they were the first. By this time Dee had conceived hundreds of sons. Her first was Bel, who became the keeper of flame. Then her others became the stars so bright they could not be seen for it was forever day.

'Sorendee thought his children beautiful, so he again cast two arrows tied with hair in the air, not lit so bright and this became the moon. The sun was a living being, as motion is the force of life. The sun fell in love with this new being and agreed to let her shine half the time. Thus, night and day was formed, and you could see the stars at night. The sun and moon were not children of Dee and Sorendee. In time, the moon gave birth to Lord Bás and the first mortals began to perish. Sorendee awarded the child the title of the Lord of Death. When he was grown, he would form the underworld and protect the souls of the righteous. He is also known as the brooding god as he is impacted by the callousness of others, causing him to suffer vast changes in moods.'

Swan Rider took a moments' rest and sipped some wine from his wooden cup.

Lan smiled at him. 'That is an interesting take on elven history. I love a good fae tale as much as the next person.'

Amities looked at his father in shock. 'Don't you think it's insulting to question their lore?'

Lan blushed, stood and bowed deeply. 'I am sorry.'

Swan Rider laughed. 'Elflings are expected to make mistakes. Sit and listen, I am not finished.'

Lan sat and waited.

'The royal sons and daughters of Anwyl are Arakaen, gifted with wings and dominion over various parts of nature such as fire, time and earth and so on. They can see in the dark as a cat can and are naturally agile in forests, bogs and woods. Lord Bás vowed to come back among the Anwyl, his favourite people. He believed their gentle and wise ways and equality among their men and women was paramount to his future development.'

'Women are not equal.' Mandami laughed. 'Pater once said they are like children and need a firm guiding hand.'

Lan stood up and walked over to his son. 'Just like men, women vary. Some are wise, others are not. You cannot categorise all of them with that ridiculous notion. Is your mother silly?'

Mandami blushed. 'Mother is different. Pater guided her well.'

Lan gave Mandami a gentle smile. 'You are young and naïve, Mandami. Cephas was a cruel and evil man and it's about time you learnt that. I once believed I should be in charge of my wife because that is the law among humankind. Over the years, as I matured, I saw how wrong that was.'

Mandami stood up. 'You have your views and I have mine. I will not stand here and listen to uneducated views from an elf of all things.'

Lan sighed. 'Fine, go. Your views are offensive, outdated and cruel. I will not discuss equality with a confused child.'

Mandami smirked and wandered away. Lan sat back down.

Swan Rider continued. 'Alas, Drianna heard of Bás's wishes before his death and vowed to corrupt his development, hoping Bás's less favourable traits would undermine the joyous nature of the Arakaen. Big, or Dane as you know him, once visited me for advice when he married a descendant of Dage. As the last prince of Anwyl he was concerned Lord Bás could be born from the union. I assured him he had no control over it if Lord Bás made his return but to be wary of Drianna's corruption among the druids. He laughed and told me no druid could be corrupted. He had too much faith in the goodness of others.'

Lan nodded. 'Yes, he believed all beings were capable of good as well as evil.'

'Deas read the omens. Lord Bás returned around fifty years ago, give or take a year or two. He was born on the island of Man'hannon or within close proximity to it.' Swan Rider stared at Lan intently.

Amities looked up from his writing. 'That is you, Father.'

Lan looked away. 'I won't accept that. I agree I am infected with a darkness born of my hate for Cephas. I highly doubt I am the Lord of Death.'

'Whether you believe it or not, I will educate you on his abilities. He has dominion over weather and can manipulate time and space without the usual limitations accorded to mystics. Mystics should only be allowed to teleport a few times a day. Unlimited use is usually reserved for druids and a few talented individuals.

'Toxins such as poisons and alcohol are purged from his body rapidly and his body will heal quickly. Bás can command others and will one day receive his wings as part of his Arakaen heritage. With that same legacy he will be beholden to his soulmate, never being attracted to anyone but them. Once he marries, just like him, his body is loyal. He will be overly passionate with his bride and his love will be bared by his very soul, terrifying to mortals.'

Lan wrung his hands nervously. 'That could be anyone.'

Swan Rider stood and stretched. 'Bás will be born first in order to protect the goddess of mercy in her formative years and serve as a distraction for Drianna's wrath. Stars Fallen will be of royal blood, her mother sired by an elf of Relequis.' Swan Rider smiled sadly at Lan. 'Bás will endure ordeals at the hands of Drianna, kept apart from his bride preparing for the eventual rift where in love he must sacrifice his time with his bride in order to take up the mantle after Drianna's destruction. Time will pass quickly for him but not for his lonesome bride. He must make a pact with Dee to become the Lord of Death by saving his bride from death due to the consequences of their passion. If he refuses, all the souls the evil goddess has stolen will perish once Drianna is defeated.'

Amities sharpened his feather quill and with a flourish wrote the last of his notes. He began to blow on the vellum hoping to expedite the drying process.

'I have told you all I know, grandson. Make of it what you will. Would you and your family like to join us in a feast?' Swan Rider gave Lan a kindly smile.

'I will ask Ake, but first I am weary and would take a walk.' Lan smiled at Swan Rider sadly and wandered over to stand near the bridge, staring down at the crevasse lost in thought.

Amities walked over to his great-grandfather. 'My poor father. He just wanted a quiet life of learning.'

Swan Rider laughed, and Amities stared at him confused.

'Bás chose this path. He wanted to defeat Drianna but most of all he wanted the love of the mercy goddess promised to him in his former life by Sorendee. Sorendee refused to bring that soul into the world. Dee went against her husband, a hopeless romantic and hatched the plan with Bás. He must sacrifice godhood in order to meet her, becoming mortal.' Swan Rider pointed to Lan. 'And he is the result of that.'

Amities stared at his father sadly. *I will learn all I can, Father, and somehow aid you and Mother in the future. I feel your confusion and pain.* Amities smiled. *I also feel your love for Mother. It is intense and beautiful. I am proud to be your son.* Amities began to draw up plans for several weapons in his book. Swan Rider went over and stood near Lan, watching him quietly.

CHAPTER THIRTY-EIGHT

Amities watched as Swan Rider struck up a conversation with his father on their travel plans. Swan Rider gave Lan the rough coordinates of the village and explained that while the village wasn't that far away in normal circumstances, the harsh terrain made the trek longer. Amities turned and saw his mother smiling among the women.

Mandami was hiding nearby, eavesdropping and Amities rolled his eyes. *My dear brother, when will you learn our father is not your enemy?* Amities sighed and stood up. *Maybe if I pretend I am frightened Mandami will come and look after me and give our parents a break.* Amities walked towards Mandami and conveniently tripped. He rubbed dirt into the graze and began to cry.

Ake was seated a fair distance away and other female elves had joined them. They had started to gift her pouches of teas and dried wreaths of unusual flowers.

'For the *Leanbh sióg*. She will need teas made of flower nectar. The baby will need to be around flowers for health. Do not nurse her more than six weeks or the child will become ill,' explained Deas.

'I'm having a fairy baby?' asked Ake.

'Two gods engaged in a great battle of love. You absorbed life and death essence, that is how fairies are created,' said Deas.

'Lan is a god?' Ake smiled. 'He would dispute that.'

'He isn't one yet. Do not concern yourself with that at the moment. Concentrate on the baby.' Deas patted her hand.

'Lan will not be pleased I'm having this baby. He is already struggling with an inner darkness,' she sighed.

'Fairies bring joy and laughter. You will need her. There are very few fairies left, you should be pleased. Be careful though. Fairies are always born from a hard birth, take no risks,' said Deas.

'Is it wrong I have not told him?' asked Ake.

'We never tell our men and just show them the new baby. They think it comes out magically. Secret women's business.' Deas laughed.

Mandami had wandered over, bored with his father's modern idea of women. He had overheard the conversation and was pleased he knew something his father did not. Mandami would keep his beloved mother's secret.

Lan had finished talking with Swan Rider. The women helped Ake pack away the gifts. Ake offered them sweets and honey. She too had done her research. The elves accepted them graciously and ran off to share them.

Lan walked over to Ake. 'If we cross the bridge there is a tunnel that bypasses the bogs. From there it is a day's journey to a village. King Swan Rider has suggested we stay the night and feast with them.' Lan smiled. 'Do you want to stay for the feast?'

Mandami rolled his eyes. 'You could have decided.'

'That's a great idea, Lan.' Ake ignored Mandami's quip.

An elven woman led her away to change. Mandami heard his brother sobbing and ran over to him.

CHAPTER THIRTY-NINE

Ake had been taken to a hot spring and was currently relaxing in the flower-scented water. There was a rustling behind her, and Deas slipped a small silver chain over her neck.

'Your husband comes to bathe the bog mud off. This jewellery is charmed. He won't be able to see or feel any change in your body that he doesn't remember.' Deas disappeared.

Lan slipped into the water next to Ake and smiled in desire at her.

Ake rolled her eyes and moved away, trying to relax her aching back muscles.

'Been a while since I've seen you completely without a stitch on,' he said.

Lan proceeded to scrub off the mud.

'Are you okay with all this information and new family members?' She turned and looked at him.

'I think it is odd. Sadly, as sweet as these people are, I am finding it hard to feel a connection. I believe them though,' said Lan.

Ake couldn't hold back her giggles. 'I'm imagining you trying to live here. Constantly hitting your head on buildings and having teeny elves worship you.'

Lan laughed at her description.

'They are sweet. But very wise and wholesome too, Ake,' he said.

'They will hail Lord Bás,' she said.

Lan smirked at her. His eyes turned red, and he drew her towards him in tendrils of shadow.

He gave her a sultry smile. 'I refute that title but are you welcoming the darkness again, my beloved?'

'Oh, cut it out. Not like I haven't seen it before,' said Ake.

She is afraid of me. She has been avoiding my touch lately and this confirms it. Lan released her. He got out and began to dress. *I don't want to frighten her further.*

'Lan, you are so silly sometimes. If you were trying to be scary, I was explaining I wasn't afraid of you. Nothing more was meant,' she said.

'I am relieved, Ake. I have not given you much attention lately. I have been distracted by the school and preparing for this journey. Elves tend to lose the regular urges of humans when caught up in other things. I'm sorry if that distance has made you back off me, Ake,' he mumbled.

'Don't be silly. That isn't it. I was distracted by my own projects. But here? Where are the boys?' Ake asked.

'They are taking a nap in one of the little houses. Mandami insisted he could take care of Amities. I decided to give way, showing I trust him. Deas said she will keep an eye on them.'

'That will make Mandami happy.' Ake smiled. 'I guess they are old enough.'

'It is safe here, Ake, but we are going to enter human villages soon. We will have to take care and keep those boys with us at all times. Especially Amities, as an elf he is still so very little. If the humans see elvish ancestry I think we will be targeted. This trip is my attempt at a honeymoon. Who knows, we may get that baby and finally raise it ourselves. If you become pregnant, I insist on going home to protect you and the baby. I lost so much time with you and my sons. There is no way I will let anything like that happen again.'

Lan could see she was worried. *I will comfort her.* Lan grabbed Ake and lifted her up against a nearby column. His eyes burned a brilliant red and his hands cupped her bottom. Ake blushed.

'Damn, you are adorable.' He kissed her earnestly then released her.

Lan leant down and withdrew something from under his robes. 'I know you didn't want me to get you a birthday present, but I couldn't help myself. I am sorry it arrived late.'

'You already baked me a cake. Sharing that with you, Orilan and the boys was enough.'

Lan took out a sheathed sword. The leather sheath was made of silver inlaid with golden elven runes for protection. Lan handed her the blade, and she withdrew it from its sheath. The silver blade was attached to a wooden hilt inlaid with three grey-blue tanzanite stones. Ake began to test the blade and made a fatal error.

He walked up behind her and steadied her hand. 'That would have left you dead.'

'Thank you for this beautiful weapon.' She turned into him and kissed him which such ardour it took his breath away.

'The stones match your eyes,' he said after he caught his breath.

Ake sheathed the sword and placed it on the ground.

'What do you say to a little sword play of our own?' Lan whispered in her ear as she stood up.

Ake looked around for any surprise guests.

'I told them to stay away,' said Lan.

'That line was cheesy yet strangely compelling. I have missed you.'

'Well, let's make up for it.'

'Yes.' She whispered, her eyes full of yearning.

He drew her down onto the ground with him and made love to her with gentle urgency.

CHAPTER FORTY

Deliciously comfortable after their long and leisurely swim and clad in fresh attire, Lan and Ake glanced around. Ake adjusted her weight on the thick cushion and winced as she bumped her knees on the low table her family and a few elves were seated at. The table was piled high with exotic fruits and vegetables. The elves offered them cups of milk laced with honey. Lan took out a bottle of wine and declined their drink. He noticed Swan Rider was drinking a flower wine and offered to share.

'Take that elfling's wine.' Swan Rider pointed at Lan. 'Even elf-lings nearing adulthood don't drink wine.'

Ake and the boys laughed heartily. Lan watched as a nearby elf pointed at the bottle. There was a popping noise and it appeared next to Swan Rider.

Swan Rider sniffed the bottle and poured himself a cup. 'What a delicate brew.'

Lan walked over, grabbed the bottle back and took a swig. Lan went to spit it out, but he swallowed and squeezed his eyes shut in protest as if he had eaten a lemon. The king stared boldly at him. He began to finish the bottle slowly in protest and his face paled.

'Yes, a delicate brew.' Lan gagged before returning to his seat and grinned at Swan Rider.

Ake sighed. *He always has to have the upper hand.*

Deas arranged for ethereal music to be played. They had never heard anything like it. It stirred them to tears, laughter and anger as Deas began to sing a haunting tale of love and betrayal.

Cakes were brought out and Ake and the boys devoured them happily. Lan tasted a few but wasn't particularly fond of desserts. He enjoyed watching his family enjoy themselves. Ake glowed with happiness.

The little elves rolled in drums and other percussion instruments and drummed up a rousing tune. Swan Rider led Deas out to dance and the other little elves joined in, dancing wildly to the percussion tunes. Amities sketched the little feast happily. Ake looked at Lan meaningfully.

'Sorry, Ake. This isn't my style of music.' He gave her an apologetic smile.

The truth was he hadn't been taught to dance, a skill almost all nobles had. Mandami loved the music. It reminded him of the music in Regis, made up of simple tunes with crude flutes and drums. He stood and bowed to his mother and offered her a hand.

'The *curadh*,' he ordered, puffing out his chest. It was common for the son of a Regian noble to lead his mother out to dance when the husband was detained. That way she kept her modesty in check.

The *curadh* was a soldier's dance thought to be created by Regis the founder of the Regian empire. With one hand behind his back, Mandami offered his other to Ake. She thought he was sweet and took it. He proceeded to take a double step forward and one leap backwards then guided her towards him.

'Mater, you need to perform the same steps,' said Mandami.

Ake tried to replicate him. Mandami tried to remain serious but even he ended up smiling as she failed multiple times. Eventually she got the hang of it.

Amities decided to join in by randomly jumping about and spinning. The child was enjoying himself. Soon the music ended, and the little elves wished them well on their journey and returned to their homes.

Swan Rider came over to Lan and handed him a book. 'I bless you in Dee's name.'

Lan bowed back and the little elf kissed him on the top of the head. Lan gave him an awkward stare.

'Take care, grandchild. My son would have been proud of you.'

Lan smiled. 'Thank you for sharing your wisdom with me.'

Swan Rider turned and walked away.

CHAPTER FORTY-ONE

They camped just before the tunnel, ready to leave in the morning. Ake went to sleep quickly. Amities wrote in his journal and Mandami stood watch like a good soldier. Lan sat perusing the book. *It doesn't look that complicated,* he thought and started memorising some of the instructions.

'Mandami, for goodness sake, relax,' murmured Lan.

'Someone has to watch out for them,' said Mandami.

'That is my job, Mandami. Not a little boy's,' said Lan.

'Humph, I've been doing it longer than you have. You were not there for years at a time,' the boy muttered.

'Rubbish, Mandami, your mother has taken care of you. You are a young child.' Lan laughed.

'Brother Ori's been her confidant more than you have,' said Mandami.

'What do you mean by that ridiculous statement?' asked Lan.

'Bringing her drinks late at night when she was stuck going through your books. Eating meals with us. Guarding her door from time to time.' Mandami smirked.

'Do you really despise me so much, Mandami, that you would try to break up your mother and me? You have an odd attachment to her.'

Mandami jumped on him and tried to punch him. Lan easily deflected him. They woke up Ake who was lying next to Lan. She grabbed Mandami and admonished him. The boy ran off just out of sight.

'I should go after him.' Ake sat up.

'No, Ake, he needs to deal with the fact I'm the adult here, not him. I don't expect him to see me as his father, but I insist on him not talking to me with such disrespect,' said Lan.

'Respect is earnt. It will take time,' said Ake.

Lan sighed. 'Yes, you are right I shouldn't have mentioned his unusual attachment to you.'

Ake smiled. 'You will get there, Lan.'

'Mandami told me Orilan used to guard your bedroom door and was very attentive to you. Can you trust him?' Lan stared at her.

'Not this rubbish again. Lan, I'm over your stupid jealousy. How did Mandami know all that if he wasn't present, Lan? He practically follows me everywhere. Why is it you are so smart and so dumb at the same time?' Ake glared at him.

Lan's brows furrowed in bewilderment. 'I wasn't trying to be jealous, Ake. I was looking out for you, considering the way Ori treated you in the past. Why are you so tense lately? Is there something I can do?'

Ake got up and grabbed her bedroll and threw it down next to Amities. The little boy jumped up surprised.

'Sleepover with Mother,' he cried.

Ake laughed. *I really need to control my emotions, or he will figure it out. That was wrong of me. I'm still annoyed at him though and I don't get it. I have never had mood swings with any of my other pregnancies.*

Mandami walked over to Lan and smirked. Ake grabbed him.

'Cut it out, Mandami. I love you but you will not try to come between us again. You are the child. One day you will grow and move on, and I will still be with him. It is time you stopped following me around. You are not going to lose my love, so stop stalking me.' Ake hugged him and he squirmed before returning the embrace.

'Okay, Mater.' Mandami lowered his eyes.

'You have been the perfect soldier, Mandami, but the general is now home. You need to listen to him,' said Ake.

'But, Mater,' he simpered.

'No, now go admit you're wrong.' Ake released him.

Mandami shuffled over to Lan. 'I'm sorry I tried to make you mad, sir.'

'It seems we are both in the proverbial pig pen tonight.' Lan laughed.

'Looks like it,' said Mandami.

They both pouted at Ake. The other two laughed at their ridiculous behaviour.

Lan dragged his and Mandami's bedrolls over. He grabbed his bag and pulled out a bunch of fruits and desserts he had put aside. They all cheered and helped themselves. Ake and Lan took turns telling spooky stories until the boys fell asleep. Lan kept watch until the early hours when Ake took over.

Chapter Forty-Two

Lan pocketed the small piece paper with the coordinates Swan Rider had given him. He had teleported them an hour away from the village. They continued the pleasant walk, tracking across the grassland. Vibrant green stalks rustled in the gentle breeze. Cattle lowed in the early morning light and wives and daughters rushed to milk them. Men could already be seen tending the fields and even the smallest children worked, drawing water and feeding animals.

Amities hated the small, itchy, woollen hat pulled down over his ears, as did Lan. The little elves had gifted it to them before they left. Mandami had laughed at them both and touched his own ears before crying, 'Isn't it great to appear human?' They had changed out of robes into long tunics and simple shoes.

'Hello,' Lan called out in Eriu.

'Hello,' the villagers cried back.

Visitors were a rare and welcome treat, often bringing news that was hard to come by. Children rushed over and began chattering to the boys. The children led them away to play simple games. Amities beamed and Mandami begrudgingly followed them. Ake and Lan headed towards the farmers to gather information on nearby towns.

The peasants explained that there was a hill fort a day's journey away owned by Clan Daingean. A high summer feast was being held there in the next three days. Almost everyone from the surrounding area would be attending.

Chief Cathal would supply a great feast with games and danc-ing. There would be competitions to test skills such as weaving, strategy and storytelling. Great warriors would test their prowess in skills of swimming, boxing, archery and spear throwing.

The villagers invited them to break bread with them and they enjoyed the simple repast. They explained they could not stay long as they wanted to get to the fair as quick as possible. Mandami and Amities wandered over.

'Have a safe journey,' said several of the kindly villagers.

'Take care,' said Ake.

Lan tilted his head in farewell and the boys waved before they all continued their journey.

Ake was excited, her face lit up with the brightest smile and she couldn't stop talking about all the things they would try. 'I will finally get to experience a great fair filled with all manner of exciting things.'

She ran over to Lan and grabbed his hand. He smiled down at her as she chatted away. They began to encounter other travel-lers on the dirt road. The atmosphere was one of excitement and joy. Ake struck up conversations with other women and Amities joined in a game of chase along the road with some smaller chil-dren. Mandami walked with his father in silence.

A vendor was selling bags of boiled sweets made from honey and flower extracts. Lan laughed as Ake made numerous pur-chases and came over to offer them to Mandami and Lan who both shook their heads and declined. Several hours passed and Lan heard Mandami's stomach gurgle.

'Are you hungry, Mandami?' asked Lan.

The boy nodded.

'Would you like to help me find dinner?'

Mandami smiled. 'I have never hunted before.'

'I never mentioned hunting, Mandami. As elves we forage first and if Dee presents us with the animal, then we accept with great reverence before taking an animal's life. Every elfling should know these skills to provide for his family one day.'

'I accept because it's a skill I must learn, not because of any elven blood I have.'

'Why do you still detest elves after all these years?'

'I dislike them less and less as I get to know you. As you know, I am not elven in any way.'

'You keep telling yourself that.' Lan grinned. 'At least I can be a father to you in some small way. Give me a moment.' Lan strode over to Ake and held a brief conversation before striding back over to Mandami.

Lan smiled at Mandami. 'Your mother will stay with Amities on the path. We have a few hours before nightfall. Follow me.'

Mandami stared at his mother before turning to his father. 'Will they be safe?'

Lan laughed and Mandami scowled.

'You are definitely my son. Always worrying about your family. The safety of your mother and my children occupies my thoughts all the time.'

Lan left the path and his pace quickened. Mandami could barely keep up. He ran after his father, stumbling over rocks and sticks as they entered the waist high grass that covered either side of the road. Lan moved gracefully without a sound. Mandami mumbled under his breath. 'Ruddy elves.'

Lan stopped and bent down suddenly and waited for Mandami to catch up. The boy stopped and caught his breath before watching Lan pick up a stick.

'See this plant that looks like a noxious weed?'

Mandami nodded.

'It is an elven staple known as *yelu rowts* or yellow root. It is similar to the starchy root vegetable humans call potato. The flowering part is bright orange and toxic so don't eat it. The leaves are brown and are great for relieving digestive issues. The edible parts are the yellow bulbous roots themselves. Tasty when boiled, seasoned and fried in butter.' Lan handed Mandami the stick. 'Dig for them.'

Mandami drove the stick into the ground and pulled the excess dirt away with his hands. Lan turned and walked a few feet away and picked a selection of herbs among the weeds and bushes and brought them over to Mandami who held up several tubers.

'Well done, Mandami.'

Mandami stood and gave Lan a reluctant smile. 'Thank you.'

Lan held out the herbs. 'Elves originated in Eriu. This herb is *sutu wed*, or salt weed. As you can see it is grey in colour with thorns and white leaves. When crushed into a fine powder it is a great substitute for salt.' Lan handed the plant to Mandami.

Mandami smelt it and looked at it closely. Lan held out another to Mandami.

'This one is *urun wed*, or orange weed. It is peppery and like *sutu wed* the whole plant can be consumed. It has an orange flower, thorns and green stem with no petals. Taste both.'

Mandami bit into each plant and chewed it. He coughed when he tasted the second one. 'Very peppery.'

Lan turned suddenly and looked into the distance. 'Look, Mandami, there is a stag.' Lan pointed.

Mandami grinned. 'Dinner, I assume.'

'No, Mandami, we never kill the head of a herd or pack. He is often the sole protector of his family. We also never take the life of pregnant female so that contingency is assured.'

'That makes sense. But how can you tell if the female is pregnant?'

'An elf can hear life within the womb after a few months,

depending on when its heart starts beating. Sometimes it is obvious if the animal is heavy with child.'

Lan turned as he heard a gentle scuttling. He pointed at a rabbit nearby and withdrew his knives. 'Dee has provided. Thank you, rabbit, for your sacrifice to feed my family.'

There was a brief squeal as Lan threw his knife. Lan walked over and gestured to Mandami. 'Let me show you how to prepare it.'

Mandami took his dagger and with Lan's gentle guidance learnt how to prepare the animal. They began to walk back to the group.

—⟋⟍—

As night fell, Ake and Lan set up camp a little way off the path. So did other families. Many herded together and shared meals, gossip and music. Lan had a small fire going and was showing Amities how to cook the rabbit on the hot coals. He used a variety of flat rocks as plates and another to ground down the herbs into a substitute for salt and pepper. Ake had wandered off and purchased butter and a small ceramic pot from several of the travelling merchants. Lan wrapped the rabbit in some aromatic leaves he had picked and covered it in cooled embers. After an hour he filled the pot with water from the nearby river, the tubers now boiled away on the fire. He had Amities drain off the water and add butter and the ground herbs to the pot. The buttery, salty smell caused Amities' mouth to water.

'The rabbit should be done now.'

Lan pushed away the embers with a stick and slowly pulled away the leaves. The aroma of roasted and seasoned meat wafted on the air. Ake and Mandami came over and sat down and the family consumed the meal.

'Well done, Amities and Lan, it tasted great.' Ake turned to

Mandami and smiled. 'Your efforts with foraging are also appreciated, Mandami.'

Mandami gave her a brief nod and concentrated on his food, smiling to himself.

Someone took out a lute; the simple bowed instrument was made from a turtle shell. The surface was covered in calf skin and the plectrum was made of animal horn. The instrument had a wooden neck and five strings. The musician began to play, and beautiful voices lifted in song.

Beware the wolf that lurks nearby,
hiding among the rye.
Do not dally in the moonlight,
be wary as to not catch his eye.

Beware the wolf that lurks nearby,
hiding amongst the rye.
His teeth be sharp,
and his hunger strong.
Hiding among the rye.

Many a life has been lost.
When his path they have crossed.
Dallying in the night.

So, heed my words.
When the grey wolf howls
Run in fright because there he is,
hiding among the rye.

What a catchy tune, thought Ake. Amities proceeded to write it down in his journal. Most of the families kept a small fire burning.

They were terribly afraid of wolves running off with their precious babes. Wolves were killed whenever they approached humans.

Ake heard stories being told of wolves that could change into men and lure away maidens to be food for their packs. The gossip continued. Young women and children had recently gone missing while out walking on their own.

With all I've seen, shape shifting wolves are a possibility. She shivered. 'Lan, what if a shifting wolf carries off our children in the middle of the night?'

Lan laughed. 'You have spooked yourself. The likelihood of wolves coming near such a large gathering would be unusual. I will tend the fire and stay up until you all fall asleep.'

'Will it be enough to deter such creatures?' asked Ake.

Lan shrugged. 'I sleep light.'

'Then the boys will sleep close to us.'

'I agree.'

Ake lay out their bedrolls and the boys. exhausted by the day's events. snuggled into their bedding. Ake's gaze fixed on Mandami as he slipped his dagger into the bedroll. *He is a little worried too.* Ake climbed into her bedding and Lan crawled in next to her. She giggled as he stole some goodnight kisses before she pushed him away. He went and sat by the fire. She turned away and closed her eyes.

—— ∼∾∼ ——

The fire burned low, and the creature crept towards the gathering with no fear. It was the size of a small pony and as black as the darkest night. It had the face of a jackal and layers of teeth like a shark. Its eyes were as red as the foxglove and its mouth frothed from the rabies it carried. The creature was skinny like a whippet as it was always hungry but was never satisfied or put on flesh.

The paws were on par with those of a large lion and its talons were as sharp as an eagle's. It moved closer, its paws padded soundlessly. A small child whimpered, and the creature hurried over to it. It passed fires, casting no shadows.

Mandami's eyes fluttered open as he smelt a stench that was of bodies long since decayed. He grabbed his dagger and leapt up. The creature turned and lunged at him. Its voice cried out like bones creaking continuously together. Mandami cast *Mystic Fire* at the creature, it leapt aside and turned and charged again.

Lan jumped up and pushed the boy out the way as the creature barely missed him. People woke up screaming, grabbed their children and began fleeing.

Mandami somersaulted onto the creature's back and drove his dagger into the bony flesh. The dagger stuck and he held on. The creature bucked and tried to throw him. Mandami bravely clung to the beast.

Ake held Amities. 'Get off that hell hound, Mandami,' she screamed.

Lan stayed her with his hand. 'Wait. I believe Mandami can defeat this.'

Amities was weeping. 'Please don't kill my brother.'

The hellhound rolled on to its back and tried to crush the child. Mandami crawled out from beneath and delivered a sharp kick to its underbelly. The creature leapt up and tried to bite the boy. Mandami punched it in the snout, barely missing its deadly fangs.

The creature charged him again and was engulfed in vents of steam, it writhed in pain. Mandami retrieved his dagger and drove it into the heart of the beast. The creature slumped down dead. Mandami wiped his blade, sheathed it and went back to bed without another thought. Ake rushed over.

'Are you injured?' She pulled back the blanket and grabbed his hands checking his limbs for any scratches or lacerations.

'Mater, lay off. I am fine.' Mandami rolled over and feigned sleep.

The family of the whimpering child came over and praised him.

'Oh, gracious Lord Conri, thank you for rescuing our child.'

'These are all the coins we have. Please accept them.'

Mandami sat up and pushed the hand away.

The musician began chanting. 'Conri, wolf king.'

The people began talking excitedly among themselves.

'His blade has wolves carved on the hilt. The boy is Lord Conri.'

'It's the boy, the one in the prophecy that kills the dark goddess.'

'Does that mean his mother is a star child?'

'Leave it be, go to your beds. I am just a soldier of Regis. Any good soldier can defeat that. I am not Conri or Cròga. I am Mandami and I order you to leave me be,' yelled Mandami.

The peasants bowed and shuffled away, still talking late into the night.

—◦◦◦—

Ake had fussed over him for too long. Mandami had told her to leave him alone. Amities and Ake were soon fast asleep when Lan said he would stay up and talk to the boy. Lan and Mandami sat near the fire.

'I see you are not a child anymore, Mandami. You were brave and fought well,' said Lan.

'I am a Regian prince. My duty is to the people. That creature would have eaten that child,' said Mandami chivalrously.

'Where did you learn to fight like that?' asked Lan.

'Pater and my teachers have taught me a bit. Mater tutored me from books. Most is instinct.' He shrugged.

'So, your mother found the books I wrote. I am proud of you, Mandami.' Lan smiled at him.

'Athair, thank you for letting me test myself,' muttered Mandami.

Mandami had just acknowledged Lan as his father. *Using a different tongue doesn't feel like a betrayal to Pater.*

Lan stood and bowed to him. Mandami rose and bowed back. They both sat in silence for a bit, neither needing to say another word.

CHAPTER FORTY-THREE

They had camped near the fair the night the meet was due to start and had spent the day watching the area around the fort getting prepared. The hill fort was simple in design. The clansmen had created a manmade rise and fenced it with a wooden palisade. Rudimentary huts served as dwellings and service areas. A large wooden lodge, engraved with Galli symbols stood in the centre. This was the great hall and lodgings of Chief Cathal of Clan Daingean.

On a level field, archery targets had been set up. Areas were cordoned off for boxing and spear throwing competitions. People were dragging nets through the river, trying to clear the swimming area of debris.

Locals laid out wares on tables to be sold. A crude wooden stage was lifted by well-built men and placed nearby for dancing and other artistic displays. Women sat weaving and preparing needlework to be sold or entered into competitions. Poets and musicians shared songs and poetry, adding new songs to their repertoires.

Six ale wives pushed barrels alongside simple tables, ready to ply their wares. Bakers prepared bread in underground ovens and butchers sliced cold meats. Live animals were being sold as pets and livestock. Seeds, fruit and vegetables were available to stock up on. A corral nearby held prize bulls ready to be hired out to service milch cows.

Jewellery smiths checked over their finery, making sure they would not be stolen. Countless stalls were selling farming tools, ropes, buckets and bags. And half a dozen stalls held a variety of syrups, teas, jams, flour and cheeses.

The once-empty field had now turned into a bustling market of valuable trade, important to the people of the area. Young single people would soon socialise to try and make a good match. They had travelled from small rural communities where almost everyone was related.

Ake was excited and kept walking back and forth among the stalls. She could not wait for tomorrow. Lan had signed up for the boxing tournament. Mandami had entered himself in the youth swimming competition. Like most boys raised in Regis he had learnt to swim early, a favourite past time.

——⁓——

Amities sat listening to the musicians and poets practice their arts. A blacksmith was laying out small axes and daggers. His assistant, a bowyer, laid out six of the favoured Eriu longbows in varying lengths between four and five feet. The flint-tipped arrows were lined up in quivers. Amities saw the bowyer test one of the smaller bows. It was a little unusual, being only two feet in length. The man sighed and seemed unsure whether to place the bow down on the table.

Amities felt drawn towards the stall. He stood watching the man battle an inner turmoil before he put the bow down on the table. Amities drew out a handful of coins and purchased the bow and seven arrows.

'I am glad to see another little boy buy the bow. My seven-year-old son passed a year ago of an unknown fever. I made it for him as a training bow.'

'Sorry for your loss.' Amities ran off with the bow to practice where no one could see him.

—w—

Amities nursed several welts to the face and wrist from the string. He managed to hit a target he had made of cloth tied around a tree. His elvish vision gave him an unnatural sight and his ancestry gave him a natural affinity to ranged weapons. He wandered over to the archery targets and approached one of the attendants.

'I would like to enter the youth competition please.'

The attendant laughed. 'I will put you with the other children.'

'I am eleven. I belong with the youth,' said Amities.

'You are a liar. Either come back for the children's competition tomorrow or get out of here.'

'Fine, my name is Amities.'

'See you tomorrow after the swimming competition.' The attendant waved him away.

Amities sighed and wandered off.

—w—

It was a couple of hours after dusk. The air was pregnant with expectation. The sky was clear and stars twinkled overhead. A small crowd was seated near the stage, awaiting the grand opening ceremony. Chief Cathal stood on the stage dressed in expensive furs and a tunic made of red linen. A great axe was slung across his back. He was burly with a grey beard and long hair. His green eyes sparkled as he raised a cup of ale to welcome them all. Musicians were invited to play rousing jigs as Cathal declared the taverns open.

Cathal walked among the stalls, praising his people. He invited nobles to join him in the great hall for a feast. As they left, the locals began to relax and enjoy the meet.

Lan took Ake by the hand to watch the performers on the stage. They were seated nearby at a local ale wife's establishment. Lan was eight cups in and keenly watching the dancing. They had told the boys to stay together. Lan felt Mandami could look after himself and Amities. Amities had stowed away his bow and arrows.

A performer got up and began to sing, accompanied by a slow and haunting melody. They recognised the lute player from the night Mandami had defeated the hellhound.

Beware the wolf that lurks nearby,
hiding among the rye.
Do not dally in the moonlight,
be wary as to not catch his eye.

Beware the wolf that lurks nearby,
hiding amongst the rye.
His teeth be sharp, and his hunger strong.
Hiding among the rye.

Many a life has been lost.
When his path they have crossed.
Dallying in the night.

So, heed my words.
When the grey wolf howls
Run in fright because there he is,
hiding among the rye.

But bested the wolf be,
by little Lord Conri.

He took up his fairy blade and drove it into the shade.
The beast tormented, bucked and flailed.

The little boy is a god veiled.
He called upon the fires of heaven.
A child of just eleven.
He smote the demon dead,
where others would dare not tread.

The musician bowed and stood back for dramatic flair. Someone threw the carcass of the beast onto the stage. The motion caused it to roll over, its tongue hung off the edge of the platform. Some women screamed and men swore. People clapped and the performance continued.

'The devil doth come upon the land to eat of our children. Drianna sets her sights upon us once more. Conri is among us and his mother Lady Saol too. They may even walk this meet. But be wary, Lord Bás, her lover follows not far behind. Death a constant reminder in our lives.' The musician knelt by the beast and wept.

People began to cheer and threw fruit, flowers and coins onto the stage. The beast was bought by one of Cathal's men and taken to the great hall as a trophy. The musician picked up his prizes and paid his friend who had carried the beast.

Lan slammed his cup down. He pulled his hat down over his face, his eyes glinted red. Ake tried to hold his hand, but Lan rose and pushed her hand away.

The musician walked past them and recognised Mandami looking at the axes near the stage. He rushed over to him and lifted the boy onto the stage.

'This is the boy who killed the beast. This is little Lord Conri,' shouted the musician.

Mandami left the stage to cheers and various comments.

'Those eyes, they are not human.'

'It can't be, he's just a lad.'

'Where is his father? Will there be deaths at this meet?'

Lan marched over and took his son's hand.

'What nonsense. My son is trained in combat. What he did was brave and talented. He is no god but flesh and blood,' said Lan.

Lan took his knife and pricked his own finger. He let it drip and held it up.

'See, his blood is my blood. We are men of flesh, as is the performer.' Lan gestured to the musician.

The crowd laughed and there was a collective sigh of relief. Everyone thought it was a great show staged by them all. The musician glared at Lan for upstaging him.

'He lies. I vow to continue spreading Lord Conri's tale throughout the country. The truth must be told.' The musician bowed to Mandami and walked away.

Lan walked with Mandami back to their camp. Ake followed, collecting Amities as she left.

CHAPTER FORTY-FOUR

Ake pushed Lan's hand away as he tried to clasp hers.

'Lan, we can't drop everything every time a problem arises.'

'I am worried for our safety.'

Ake smiled. 'You handled it well. We are staying whether you like it or not.'

'I will teleport us home if there are any more disturbances.'

Ake laughed. 'You do that and I will have Ori teleport us back. I am going to bed.'

Ake crawled into her bed-roll; the boys were already asleep. She rolled over and watched Lan storm away to a tavern and sit and order a few drinks. She closed her eyes and drifted off.

―᚜᚜᚜―

Ake mumbled in her sleep and felt someone climb in next to her. She was startled awake as Lan pulled her against him.

'I am … sorry … honey. You and the boys are the most precious thang ta me,' mumbled Lan a little incoherently. 'You are the sun and encompass all the light … in my world. I am the da-rk side of the moon, bitt-er and … cold. Please … don't shut me out.'

Ake smiled as he whispered sweet words of atonement. He leant in to kiss her and his breath reeked of alcohol.

'You need to sleep that off.' Ake laughed as she felt his head lean against her shoulder and his breathing slowed. He cuddled into her and mumbled in his sleep. She sighed with contentment, the fight forgotten, and closed her eyes.

Dawn broke and Ake let Lan sleep in. She took the boys among the stalls which were now plying their trades. Ake, well known for her sweet tooth, bought jams, syrups and sweets. She stocked up their preserves of meats, fruit and tea. They sat and ate slices of bread and fruit for breakfast. Ake was fascinated by the sight of tiny canaries in little wooden cages. *I love birds.* She stood and wandered over to the stall, followed by her sons.

The yellow birds leapt about gracefully chattering to their kind. Amities purchased a little brown mouse and put it in his belt pouch. He dropped bread and fruit in for it to eat. Mandami petted the wolfhound pups and smiled when they licked his hands.

Ake wandered over to another stall. She saw some new wrist guards in red leather and purchased them for Lan. His other ones were well past replacing. Ake smiled. They were engraved with Galli shield knots, used to ward off evil and protect the wearer in battle. *Elegant and practical. I believe Lan will like it.*

Lan awoke with a slight headache. He began to recover fast thanks to his unnaturally quick healing ability. He saw his family returning to their camp to drop off their purchases. The air was warm with the promise of a sunny day. Lan looked up at the sky, the sun was nearly at its zenith and the sky was a brilliant blue.

He looked at them full of guilt. 'I am sorry for my drunkenness.'

Amities came over and showed him the little rodent.

'It is very cute.' Lan smiled.

Ake backed away from the rodent. 'Keep it away from me.'

Lan laughed and she pouted.

'There were these gorgeous canaries. I want to get one when we return home.'

Lan smiled. 'Sure.'

Mandami held up a new axe. 'What do you think, Athair?'

'Very nice, Mandami.' Lan listened contently while they spoke. *They are all quite adorable.*

Ake pulled out the wrist guards and handed them to Lan. He smiled and replaced his current ones. Then he drew Ake into a hug. He whispered in her ear. 'Thank you. I am delighted. They are useful and elegant.'

Ake smiled up at him.

Lan joined them for another walk among the stalls. An extra stall had been set up near where Lan had gotten drunk. The prizes were simple dolls and bears.

'Come have a toss. Thow a ball through the various hoops and win a prize,' cried the stall operator.

Lan watched each member of his family win a small prize after many unlucky attempts. He tried the game twice and failed.

The man at the stall laughed. 'Better luck next time.'

Lan became flustered. *I am sure this game is deceptive.*

'It is okay, I will share my toy with you,' said Ake.

'That is sweet. I thank you,' said Lan.

Lan made a few math calculations. *This game is slightly skewed.*

Lan handed over a single coin. There were a couple of cheers as he threw each ball through the hoops successfully. The man running the game grumbled and handed him over a large fluffy unicorn.

Lan handed it to Ake. As she went to grab it, he cheekily

dipped her at an angle and kissed her. Amities laughed and several people cheered. He set her down. Ake blushed. When she had recovered, they headed to the river.

—⁓—

It was time for the swimming competition. Mandami stood with six other lads between the ages of twelve and fifteen.

'Jump, gentlemen,' called the attendant.

Mandami dove into the water. He was off to a strong start. He kicked hard and swam past two of the boys. The older boys were stronger and no matter how hard he tried he couldn't surpass them. They rushed ashore to adulations from the crowd and were handed coins for their efforts.

The warm air began to dry him quickly and he stalked towards his parents and brother.

'Well done, Mandami,' said Ake and embraced him.

Mandami pushed her away. 'I should have tried harder.'

'You will get stronger, Mandami. You were the youngest in that competition by the looks of it.' Lan smiled at Mandami.

'I vow to get stronger.' Mandami smiled back.

'Good effort, brother.' Amities patted him on the back. 'Now, if you will follow me please.'

Amities turned and walked away. The others followed.

—⁓—

Amities approached the archery targets. Ake and Lan's eyes widened with surprise, and they exchanged smiles when Amities took his position among the other beginners.

'The child who hits the centre the most times out of three, wins.' The attendant stepped to the side. 'Begin.'

A girl of about eight years stepped forward. She missed her first shot before hitting the centre twice. The girl's parents and siblings cheered. She turned and smiled at them and stepped back.

A boy of about seven took a step forward. He hit the centre and an older man nearby cheered. The boy hit just off centre and people clapped politely. The boy missed the next time, and the arrow pierced a hay bale nearby.

Amities stepped forward, drew back the string and nearly dropped the bow. The other children laughed. The other competitors were younger but, being human children, were stronger.

Amities drew the bow, checked his sight and hit the centre. Several people clapped, thinking it was a fluke. He hit the target in the centre on his second and third attempt and won first prize. The crowd cheered.

Amities put his bow on his back and collected his arrows before climbing over the ropes and joining his family.

Ake rushed over and hugged him. 'Well done, Amities.'

'You did well, son.' Lan placed his hand on his son's shoulder.

The archery attendant approached Amities. 'Congratulations, here is your prize.' Amities was handed a small stuffed dragon with outstretched wings.

Amities smiled and pretended it was flying towards Lan. 'Roar. It will destroy you, Father.'

Lan laughed. 'Oh no, I succumb.'

Amities grinned. 'The mighty dragon, Amities, defeated the great Trebrelan.'

Mandami clapped Amities on the back, interrupting his game. 'So, you do have some fighting skills. I am pleased with you, brother.'

'Thank you, Mandami,' said Amities.

They heard someone call out. 'Boxing will start soon.'

Lan's eyes filled with anticipation as he turned to Ake.

Ake laughed. 'Go enjoy being beaten up. We will join you soon.'
Lan grinned and ran off.

Ake grabbed her unicorn and began to chase a giggling Amities. 'The queen of the unicorns vows to avenge Trebrelan.'

Mandami rolled his eyes. 'Even my own mother is immature.'

Ake shrugged and began to chase Mandami who ran towards the boxing area.

—— ◆ ——

Lan watched as men crashed their fists into each other's faces. He eyed-up the competition. Even among the youth, the humans were built stronger than him. Like the other boxers he was dressed only in a woollen kilt.

He was matched against a twenty-year-old man who stood over him at six feet. The boxing officials had looked Lan over and declared him to be of the same age. His rival waved his huge fists in his face, trying to goad him. Someone blew a horn and the fight began.

The lad swung straight at Lan's face with a left and right hook. Lan dodged and drove his fist up into the man's nose. His opponent stumbled back. They were pulled apart and made to touch fists before starting again. The man pummelled Lan in the chest, winding him. Lan recovered and delivered a quick punch to each ear hypnotically fast. His opponent forfeited.

After seven more wins, Lan reached the final and wasn't prepared to face Cathal. Lan stared up at him, trying to ascertain his opponent's weaknesses. *He is huge. Must be at least six foot five. I'm impressed their chief fights commoners.* Lan watched the man stare at him then over at his family.

'Why are you staring at my family?' asked Lan.

Cathal shrugged. 'That hellhound was real. I have heard rumours that your son killed it. Quite impressive for a lad that appears to be eleven or twelve, don't you think?'

'My son is a trained fighter.'

'You don't look old enough to have sired a twelve-year-old nor does your bride. You look between twenty and twenty-five as does your wife. Lord Bás is immortal and descended from ancient elves. I am wondering if he is hiding among my people.'

'Everyone knows there aren't many elves left.'

'Then remove the hat.'

'No.'

'What have you got to hide, lad?' asked Cathal.

'My hair looks like it has been tortured. I would not subject your people to the sight of it.'

'Suit yourself.' Cathal grinned.

The horn sounded and they moved into position. Cathal swung a double punch at Lan who assumed the large man would move slowly. Lan took a blow to the jaw and cheek bone. He grinned in surprise. They touched fists again and Lan ducked under a left and right hook to deliver a double upper cut to Cathal's nose and jaw. Cathal hit him in the stomach twice and Lan stumbled back, wincing. The crowd cheered. Lan delivered punches in quick blows to Cathal's upper and lower torso. Again, they were made to part and touch fists.

They reigned blow after blow upon each other. Lan took a punch to the left eye, and it started to close over. Lan's elven youth gave him the stamina to counter with a flurry of punches.

Cathal took a step back and tried to catch his breath. He knew he was defeated and declared Lan the winner. As the referee held Lan's hand in the air, Cathal swiped his hat. The crowd gasped when they saw Lan's elven ears.

Cathal broke out in contagious laughter.

'Bested by a faery. I have never had a better opponent. Give the lad his prize. Well done, elf.'

'I'm hardly a fae.' Lan blushed but held his head up proudly.

A man came up and gave him a bag of silver coins. Lan walked quickly over to his family to the sound of well-meaning cheers and laughter. His eye was swollen shut, his jaw ached and his stomach and chest sported patches of red, beginning to bruise. Ake looked around, wondering if she should fuss over him.

Lan gave her a pleading look. He had been declared a faery, a delicate creature of the woodlands and he was trying not to let his pride best him. He blinked in surprise when she kissed him passionately. The crowd cheered and went off to see the other exhibits.

Cathal wandered over, sporting his own injuries.

'Well done, lad. Join us at my feast hall after dusk. Dress in your best.' Cathal turned and walked away.

'Well done, Athair,' said Mandami.

Lan gave him a smile.

'Are you okay, Father?' asked Amities.

'I am fine, boys. Why don't you go look at the displays.' Lan swept Ake up in his arms and she giggled as he kissed her.

'We are in public you two.' Mandami turned and strode away.

Amities laughed and ran after his brother.

Lan placed Ake down gently. 'Was that too much?'

She caressed his cheek. 'It is fine. We should really go find formal attire.'

Lan took her hand and they proceeded to walk among the stalls.

CHAPTER FORTY-FIVE

They had painstakingly browsed the various wares on offer by seamstress's and tailors looking for formal attire, until Ake had finally settled on a green shift. She stood still as it was altered to fit her curves.

'You look slim, but the fabric width suggests otherwise. I have let it out, but it looks too wide and unbecoming with your looks. You will need a belt,' said the seamstress.

'Looks can be deceiving,' said Ake.

The seamstress found a gold belt, placed it around her waist and did it up.

'It's not perfect but it will do.'

Ake handed over some coins and picked up her other purchases. 'Thank you.'

She left the tent and wandered over to her family. Amities was dressed in a long-sleeved shirt and simple kilt.

'Why aren't you dressed yet, Mandami?'

'The clothing is unsuitable.'

'Put in on, Mandami.'

'No.'

Mandami began to sprint for it and Ake chased him, garments in hand.

'Who is being a baby now, Mandami? Amities laughed.

'Fine.' Mandami took the garments and went into the seamstress tent to change.

Lan refused to wear the attire and it was nearing dusk when he settled on a red shirt and black trousers. His eye had healed and the bruises to his face were receding fast. He entered the tent after Mandami left and quickly changed.

They walked to the fort and were greeted by the guards and a servant who asked their names.

'I am Lan of Mencrey, this is my wife, Ake. These are our sons Mandami and Amities,' said Lan.

They entered the great hall and were introduced among many guests who paid them little heed.

Ake looked around. A large fire burned in a stone pit in the floor. Meats and other delicacies were being cooked in the fire. A large, circular, stone table surrounded the pit and wooden stools with padding were placed at intervals. Everyone sat and chatted among themselves. Everyone stood to bow when Cathal entered.

'Be seated, please,' bellowed Cathal.

Cathal addressed the closer of his nobles. They spoke of family and trade deals. Everyone was offered unlimited ale until simple roasted meats such as boar and venison were sliced and served. A selection of gravies and sauces were offered.

Ake tapped her fingers on the table and yawned with boredom. A few nobles recognised Lan from the match, and they were discussing techniques. The boys chattered among themselves about how great the day had been.

After the table was cleared, they were escorted through to a large empty room. Noble women who were not at dinner were now introduced. Musicians flooded in and began to strike up a rousing jig. The men began to caper before escorting their partners onto the dance floor.

Each couple stood apart, men on one side and women on the other. The music slowed and the couples would walk forward, one hand behind their back. When they reached their partner they would raise clasped hands, turn and change sides. This was repeated a number of times. Each man would then change to the partner left of them. The dance ended when each man returned to their original partner.

Cathal joined in the next round, grinned at Lan and escorted Ake onto the dance floor. Ake laughed and her eyes sparkled with joy. The dance finished and Cathal guided Ake over to Lan.

'Lad, you should join in, the next one's slower. Live a little,' said Cathal.

The music slowed to a soft ancient ballad and Cathal led one of the older ladies onto the floor. Other couples followed suit. Lan recognised the tempo as one of the songs in the dance manual Swan Rider had given him. Bells rang out mystically, a flute lilted and a steady ancient drumbeat began to play. Ake stood; her wistful gaze transfixed on the couples caught up in the moment.

Lan grabbed her hand. 'We may as well try it.'

He walked her over to the dance floor. They turned and faced each other. The dance was more complicated than the first one. Ake watched the other dancing couples, unsure of what to do.

'Follow my lead,' said Lan.

Lan put one hand on her waist, put his other hand across her back and drew up her other hand. He led her forward then guided his hand up over her shoulder and spun her away from him. Lan leapt backwards on steady feet then danced a step forward before lifting Ake up by the waist and putting her down.

While other couples laughed and exchanged dance partners Lan refused to hand over Ake. His eyes filled with determination. *I must finish this dance with her. It is the only one I know, and I will not falter.*

Lan appeared more confident as they repeated the steps. His gaze dropped to meet hers. She smiled up at him in utter adoration and he gave her a tender smile. Lan drew her close and kissed her.

———〜〜〜———

Amities sketched the scene and wrote in his journal, capturing the genuine love that flowed between his parents. Underneath the drawing he scrawled a detailed account, summarising the nights events. Mandami watched his parents peacefully. They were caught up in their own little world full of sweet smiles and tender glances. His Pater had never treated his mother with such gentleness, always forceful and commanding. Lan led with kindness but yielded as necessary. *Maybe Pater was a cruel man.* He shook himself. *I vow to never treat a woman like Pater treated my mother.*

———〜〜〜———

The music finished and Lan escorted Ake off the dance floor.

'As for any more dances, Ake, that is the only one I know and a poor attempt at it,' said Lan.

Ake embraced him. 'You were as good as anyone there. I never learnt to dance either.'

'Not even in Relequis?' asked Lan.

'Nope. Too busy studying,' said Ake.

'So, you just thought you would give it a go?' Lan laughed.

'Of course. Why not? It was fun, wasn't it?' she asked.

'Better than I thought,' he said.

They joined the other couples for a few drinks before returning to their camp with their sons. Walking hand in hand they only had eyes for each other. Mandami and Amities rolled their eyes and laughed at their lovestruck parents.

CHAPTER FORTY-SIX

The little band of four travelled on for another three months, visiting small villages and learning about the land. They spent many a happy day bonding as a family. It was not long before Ake was due, and they had just reached the outskirts of the dwarven city of Rock Fell.

It was noon and the boys had been discussing what they would see in Rock Fell. Ake had fallen behind; the last few weeks of her pregnancy had drained her and she felt exhausted and anxious. Lan walked ahead of their little party looking for any signs or landmarks that would show them where the hidden entrance to Rock Fell was. Lan stopped suddenly and gestured them to be quiet. He tilted his head and listened. Lan withdrew his knives and slowly backed up towards them.

'Arm yourselves, quickly,' he said.

Amities fumbled with his bow and knocked an arrow. Mandami grabbed his dagger and grinned at his father, itching for a fight. Ake grabbed her short sword and trembled, worried a fight could harm her baby.

'Look over at those bushes.' Lan tilted his head towards the bushes, there was no wind but the leaves rustled slightly.

Lan turned and pulled Ake behind him. A large figure stepped out from behind a tree. It had the bearing of a human but appeared to be an unholy mix of monster and man. It wore heavy, red, plate armour decorated with explicit scenes of death and destruction. Its serrated tail slapped the ground impatiently. Its goat-like horns jutted through holes in a helmet that barely disguised its misshapen head. Its white eyes burned with malice through small slits in the helmet.

'Father. They are behind us too,' whispered Amities.

Ake turned to see several men in ragged clothing armed with an assortment of weapons leave the cover of the bushes and surround them.

'Give us the woman and the elven child,' said the figure in a booming voice.

'Hey, what about their money too?' said one of the vagabonds guarding the rear.

Amities couldn't keep the bow drawn. He turned, hoping to shoot the arrow into the dirt. The arrow was released as Amities dropped the string. There was a yelp as the vagabond who spoke found an arrow in his foot. Amities blew on his hand as the bow string caught his hand.

'You scoundrel. Get 'em.' The vagabond growled, removed the arrow and charged; his comrades followed.

Ake turned and her sword clashed against a pitchfork. The noise rang in her ears. Mandami rushed into the fray, his dagger an extension of himself. One of the vagabonds clubbed him on the back of the legs and the boy fell down. Mandami rolled out of the way as the club thudded into the ground where he had been.

Mandami grinned. As the man pulled back his weapon, he leapt and slashed the man across the face with his dagger. Ake hurled the pitchfork away from her with her sword, then cast a paralysis spell on her assailant and he grunted and fell down. Amities fired his bow and a man dropped with an arrow in his eye. Amities shook with fear and dropped the bow.

The large, armoured creature reached for Lan who cast *Mystic Fire* at it.

The monster laughed. 'Fire is my weapon,' it boomed.

Lan ducked under its legs and called lightning down upon it. The beast turned and laughed. 'Drianna has blessed me with resistance to you, elf.'

Lan closed his eyes as he heard an inner voice reach out to him. *'The Lord of Death commands others.'*

'I command you to cease.'

Lan opened his eyes to see the figure stop and look confused. Then its eyes burned with hate as it overcame the command spell easily. It charged Lan, who took a steady stance as the figure crashed into him, his knives arched upwards, blocking the huge gauntlets. A hideous laugh escaped its mouth, showing serrated teeth. Lan felt his weapons heat. The hideous hybrid channelled fire through its gauntlets and they caught alight. The tips of the gauntlets burned like dying embers.

Lan shivered, remembering the injury to his face. It caught him off guard. *I can't deal with that again.* Lan teleported out the way and the figure turned and rushed his family. He swore. *I guess I will have to.* Lan teleported back in front of the figure, and it crashed into him, sending him reeling.

Ake sent another vagabond to sleep, Mandami leapt on him and rammed his dagger in between his ribs.

'There was no need to kill him, Mandami,' Ake cried.

'He would have killed me without a second thought.' Mandami rushed under the last assailant's weapon as Amities shot the rogue in the derriere. The man yelped and collapsed as he was overcome with Ake's paralysis spell.

Ake's hair caught alight and she patted it out. She turned and saw Lan barely managing to dodge another one of his attacker's onslaughts. '*Waterius,*' she screamed.

Lan was covered in a shield of water as the figure raised its arms at him and jets of fire spewed forth from its gauntlets. Lan

sat there, stunned remembering the anguish from his disfigure-
ment and how vulnerable it had left him. He took a shuddering
breath, forgetting for a moment he was surrounded by water. He
spluttered and teleported out of the shield. He stood and coughed
up the water as the figure reached Ake.

'*Magna Crono.*' Ake's eyes turned golden and wings ripped
through her dress. She held the front of it up to maintain her
modesty.

A vent opened up in front of the figure and it stumbled into
it. Steam spewed forth and the figure covered its eyes. The steam
subsided and the figure uncovered its face and its eyes burned
with pure malice. 'Fire and steam have little effect on me.'

It grabbed for Ake. Lan leapt onto its back and drove his knife
into its torso, looking for any weakness. The metal shrieked as his
knives glanced off the plate armour. Lan screamed as the figure
heated the whole of its armour and burned through Lan's boots.
Lan somersaulted off the figure and landed heavily. The figure
turned and charged him. Ake tried to cast sleep and paralysis
spells over it with no affect. Their attacker reached Lan and fire
streamed forth from its magic gauntlets. Lan shivered. Ake sent a
jet of water to block the fire from reaching him.

The sky began to darken. Lan's heart beat fast as the fear of losing his life and not being able to prevent his wife and son's capture
threatened to overwhelm him. The temperature dropped and a
cold wind ripped through everyone. Ake took a sharp breath,
suddenly numb. Ake's water jet froze and cracked into large fragments of ice that shattered. The creature backed off. Lan's face
darkened with anger as shadows swirled around him.

'It is frightened by the cold,' he yelled.

I wonder if I can combine my spells. He drew on the bitter wind
and began to manipulate it and combine it with a simple telekinesis spell.

The wind began to howl. Large boulders of hail formed in front of Lan, and he hammered them into the armoured creature. The figure stumbled and fell. It rose and tried to run. As it did so, it tried to grab Amities. The boy shrieked, grabbed his bow and ran. The assailant was slammed into the ground as Lan continued to hammer it with hail. It rose and fire streamed from its gauntlets at Amities. The boy dodged the spell, aimed his bow and fired. The figure stumbled back and fell down, an arrow in its eye. Amities dropped his bow and ran to his mother. The sky lightened as Lan withdrew the shadows.

Amities sobbed in his mother's arms and Lan strode over and embraced them both.

'Shh, Amities, well done,' comforted Ake.

Ake released the child and Lan kneeled and looked the boy in the eyes.

'Sometimes we must defend ourselves, Amities, and that may mean doing something we hate. I am proud of you.' He gave Amities a kind smile.

The boy wiped his eyes with the sleeve of his robe and nodded.

Mandami wandered over and grinned. 'Well, that was fun.'

'Mandami, we fight to defend ourselves not because it's fun. But you fought well,' said Ake.

They tied up the highway men and hid their weapons. Ake left them with a few coins.

Lan rolled his eyes. 'Ake, they attacked us. Why leave them money?'

Ake sighed. 'They attacked us due to poverty and hunger, Lan. I can't say the same for the armoured brute. Hopefully, they will feed themselves and, without their weapons, choose a less violent path.'

Lan gave her a gentle smile. 'I am not as good or as merciful as you. It is unlikely they will become law-abiding citizens, but I love the fact you try to see the possibility of good in the worst of humanity.'

There was a rustling behind them, and a dwarf poked its head up out of a hole in a rock. It pointed to a gap in the sandstone and then disappeared. Ake and Lan grabbed their boys' hands and hurried over to the hidden entranceway. They followed the dwarf, squeezing into the small gap. The small cave slowly became bigger and opened up into large cavern. Everyone gasped in awe as they saw a subterranean path that led down into a ravine where a huge underground city sprawled out in front of them.

Two gigantic dwarven statues stood either side of the subterranean path, their huge axes clashing in a long-forgotten battle. They walked under the impressive design, entering the city.

Small stone buildings sprawled out from a large keep. Torches hung outside the haphazard buildings while the poorly planned sandstone roads often ended in small dark alleys; a breeding ground for cut throats and nocturnal monsters.

They looked around and saw armed dwarves including women and children. Most of the men were barrel-chested and sported long coarse beards in earthy tones. The women had paler hair but were no less stocky. Dwarven women decorated their hair in precious gems and metals. Their stalwart husbands, deft at mining, willingly took the large lifts down into the earth to dig for them. Lan rushed over with Amities to examine a lift; they stared into oblivion.

A miner carrying a pickaxe and lantern entered a large metal cage that served as a lift. It was attached to a large steel pillar by a collection of cogs and chains. A dwarf shovelled coal into a nearby furnace. He shut the access panel and pulled a lever. Steam bellowed out and the cage began to lower. Amities made a quick sketch before they found an inn and settled down for the night.

CHAPTER FORTY-SEVEN

Lan's eyes fluttered open and he sat up suddenly and covered his ears. The noise assaulted his senses, growing louder. 'Sounds like one hundred men blowing into war horns,' he muttered.

Mandami snorted in his sleep. An insistent scratching of quill on vellum caught Lan's attention. Amities sat in a chair scribbling in his journal and Lan watched his son sketch.

'It's the alarm that signals the dawn. Only dwarves and elves can hear it.' Amities held up the picture; an outline of Lan covering his ears while war horns floated around his head.

Lan laughed as the sounds faded away. 'That's funny.' Lan slipped out from beneath the covers before he tucked Ake in. 'I'll be back Amities.'

Amities nodded to him as he slipped out the door and closed it behind himself. Lan padded down the steps and into the tap room of the hotel. A large dwarf was drying metal steins, another was wiping down the brass stalls that were lined up against the steel bar. Lan's feet were silent on the cold sandstone floor and he hurried onto a bearskin rug.

'What ya want, elf?'

Lan smiled at the barkeep. 'What do you have in the way of breakfast?'

'Ale, beer, whiskey or coffee.'

'Ah, what about food?'

'Meat and flatbreads. How many serves?'

'Four please.'

The bartender began slapping down cast iron plates and the sound made Lan's ear tingle as metal hitting metal rang out loudly. The dwarf threw a selection of course flatbreads and grey-coloured meat onto the plate.

'What kind of meat is that?' asked Lan.

The dwarf glared at him. 'Picky elf. It's rock foul, a small, blind, featherless bird that lives in cracks in rocks eating insects. About the size of a dwarfling's fist. Great tucker.' The dwarf smacked his lips and placed a jug of coffee on the tray. 'I assume you have elflings, we don't serve ale to elves under a hundred.'

Lan laughed. 'And what of dwarflings?'

The dwarf grinned. 'As soon as they are weaned. Six coins.'

Lan counted out the coins, placing them on the bar and grabbed the tray. He ascended the stairs and Amities opened the door. Ake was pacing the room, fully dressed. Mandami was pulling on his shoes.

Ake smiled at him when he placed down the tray and handed her a cup of coffee. 'You came back.'

Lan kissed her. 'Of course.'

'Gross,' said Mandami.

Lan laughed. 'I say we go shopping after breakfast.'

Ake nodded and screwed her eyes up as she sipped the bitter brew. 'Yuck. No sugar.'

———

The boys found a toy shop and stared at the gold and silver clockwork animals walking about in the window display. Little monkeys clanged cymbals and a clerk was showing excited children jack in the boxes. The boys rushed inside with strict instructions that they stay there.

Ake found a dressmaker's store that doubled as a midwife. Elegant designs were displayed on mannequins near the door.

'I will be a while, Lan.'

'Okay, I will be in that jewellery store across the road.' Lan crossed the road.

Ake entered the dressmaker's and bought a beautiful, off-the-shoulder dress in blue. It was sleeveless and flowed down to her knees. Gems studded the hem. The bodice was decorated with a Galli love knot; two interweaving hearts sewn in gold and silver thread. She changed and removed her necklace and went to talk to the midwife.

A dwarven woman walked over and showed her to another room. The midwife asked Ake to sit down. She listened to Ake's distended stomach and looked worried. Ake winced when the woman pushed down on her abdomen.

'The child is in the wrong position, lassie. How many months?' asked the midwife.

'Eight and a half,' said Ake.

'Come back here tonight, I will try to turn the child,' she said.

Ake nodded and offered her some coins.

The dwarfess shook her head. 'I take payment upon delivery.'

Ake replaced her necklace and left the store. *I hope my baby will be okay. I will tell Lan about the baby after it is turned.*

Ake saw her boys chattering away with arms full of toys. Lan looked at her in awe.

'You are stunning.'

She blushed. 'Thank you.'

'I am hungry,' said Amities.

'Let's have lunch at the inn,' said Lan.

'I'm not hungry. I will take a nap,' said Ake.

They reached the inn and Ake proceeded up the stairs. Lan handed the boys a handful of coins and followed Ake.

—∿—

Ake pushed open the door and lay down, exhausted. She turned her head to the door as Lan entered.

'Are you okay?'

'I need to rest.'

'Is that all?' Lan walked over and checked her forehead for a temperature.

'No. I have something to discuss later.'

'Why not—'

The boys entered the room, talking loudly.

'Father prefers the vegetable dishes,' cried Amities.

'Well, I ordered meat. It makes a man strong,' said Mandami.

Amities rushed over to his father and handed him the change.

'Let's go, boys, and let your mother rest,' said Lan.

The boys followed him out of the room and he closed the door.

Ake closed her eyes and drifted off.

—∿—

At dusk, Lan entered the room and shook her gently awake. Ake opened her eyes and blinked before focusing on his worried face.

'I am going to take the boys for a twilight walk to get dinner. Will you join us?'

'I would prefer to rest. I am not hungry.'

'I should stay and look after you.'

Ake shook her head. 'I am fine, go enjoy yourselves.'

'I will try to keep them amused for a few hours so you can rest. When I get back, we will have that discussion.' He kissed her and left.

Ake stood up and dressed. She waited for ten minutes before leaving the inn and returning to the midwife's shop and entering the back room. Several women in white robes waited with steaming bowls of water for hand washing. Incense burned sweetly. Ropes now hung from the ceiling. *That is strange.* The midwife directed her to a stone table covered in layers of linen.

'Please lie down.'

Ake climbed onto the table and groaned as her aching back refused to give her any reprieve.

'Drink this.' The midwife gave her a sweet-smelling tea. Ake began to drift and she couldn't hold her eyes open and yawned.

Ake's eyes darted open. The light assaulted her eyes, and she blinked before the midwife's face swam into focus.

'You were out for an hour.'

The midwife helped her sit up.

'I could not turn the baby. I can bring on labour early and try and turn your baby as you deliver.'

Ake nodded. Someone gave her another herbal tea. Ake winced as she drank the bitter concoction.

'Come back when your waters break, or your pains become too strong.'

Ake nodded and left the shop. As she walked down the road towards the inn, she winced as the baby kicked her harshly and she felt a minor contraction.

Ake returned to the inn and lay down.

—⁓—

Ake woke to Lan removing her necklace and replacing it with his own. Ake sat up. The necklace was a gold chain with a simple heart charm made of a star stone. Pain ripped through her, and she yelped. Her hands rushed to her distended belly, and she turned to stare at her husband.

'This is what I wanted to discuss.'

Lan threw back the blankets. 'What the hell!'

Amities looked shocked and Mandami appeared indifferent.

'Did you know, Mandami?' Lan paled and clenched his fists.

Mandami shrugged.

Lan turned back to Ake and his eyes filled with tears. 'How could you not tell me?'

'You are so possessive and always making decisions for me. I was so excited to go on this journey. You would have cancelled our plans if you knew,' she said.

'Get out, boys!' Lan pointed to the door.

The boys left.

'Calm down.' Another pain ripped through her and she winced.

'Due date?' asked Lan.

'Supposed to be a few weeks,' said Ake.

'So, conceived that night.' He gritted his teeth.

'Yes.'

Lan's eyes burned red, and his face was a mask of pain. 'Who knows what you will deliver. I was not there with those boys when they were born, Ake. And now this! You couldn't let me share this one thing? Do you think so little of me?'

'In Regis it was women's business.'

'Fine, have it your way.' He glared at her before leaving the room.

'Wait,' said Ake.

Pain tore through her, and blood pooled between her legs. She cried out. Mandami came rushing into the room.

'Where is your father?' Ake grunted.

'He ran off. Amities chased him,' said Mandami.

'I need you to help me to that dress store, Mandami. This baby isn't right.' She yelped as another wave of pain coursed through her.

Mandami slipped under her arm and she leant on him heavily. They slowly made their way to the midwife's shop.

Lan ran through the city in an angry storm of shadows, invisible to those around him. *How dare she keep this from me. Of course, I will forgive her. But she can wallow for a bit.* Lan began to weep bitter tears. He teleported himself onto the roof of a nearby building.

He heard a little voice cry out to him. He looked down to see Amities looking up at him.

'Father, I think the baby is coming and something is wrong. When I returned to Mother there was blood everywhere. I came to get you as quickly as I could,' yelled Amities.

Lan disappeared and reappeared in front of his son.

'Let's go deliver a baby then.'

Amities took a step back and fear pooled in his eyes. Lan shivered as he saw a terrifying face reflected in the window behind his son, his red eyes filled with anger and his mouth distorted in a dreadful smirk. *No wonder he's terrified.* Lan closed his eyes and took calming breaths and opened his eyes. He blinked and the red drained from his pupils.

Lan gave his son a sad smile. 'I am sorry, Amities.'

He placed his hand tentatively on the child's shoulder and Amities patted his hand. Lan turned and began to walk away. He heard his son's gentle foot falls on the road behind him.

Ake had insisted Mandami wait outside. They had felt for the position of the baby and said it was a little way off. Ake grunted with each contraction, pulling down on the birthing ropes with each new wave. She sat on the stool at the midwife's suggestion, hoping gravity would aid her.

Pain ripped through her, and blood ran down her legs in rivulets. The midwives exchanged looks charged with sadness and helped her over to the bed. One placed their hands on her abdomen, feeling for the baby's position and shook her head.

'I may need to cut you. Is there someone other than that boy out there who can take the baby if something happens?' asked the midwife sadly.

'Tell my son to find his father.'

One of the attendants left to give Mandami the message. The midwife began to sterilise sinew, knives and cloth.

What do they mean by cut me? Do they mean down there? They put a cloth covered in a strong chemical over her face and she was instructed to breathe deeply. Ake began to feel lightheaded and strange. She felt pressure on her abdomen and winced as something stung her. She was too giddy to care.

—ww—

Mandami rushed from the building and out into the street.

'Athair,' he yelled.

Lan and Amities found him.

'Father, she is dying, the baby is killing her,' said Mandami.

Mandami rushed off in the direction of Ake. Lan stormed after him in a tempest of shadows. He felt the tendrils of death reaching out to him and it drew him closer.

The door crashed open as Lan burst through in a vortex of shadow, eyes glowing like red coals. The midwives drew back in shock. They had opened Ake up and were about to draw the baby out. Blood ran down the sides of the wound.

'What have you done?' Lan asked.

'If we don't get the child out, they will both die,' said the midwife.

'Do it,' he commanded.

Lan felt death encroaching on both Ake and his baby. *I demand they live.*

'Succumb to the Lord of Death then. You want the power to decide. There will come a time when we demand payment from you,' projected a gentle voice in his mind.

'I am Lord Bás. I accept it for their lives against my own,' said Lan.

'No.' Ake's eyes fluttered open.

The midwife reached in and drew out the tiny baby. With it came Ake's injured womb, beyond repair. They hastily sewed up Ake as they handed the tiny child to Lan. She was curled up in the foetal position, tiny translucent wings curled around her body. Her little eyes were closed.

Lan felt her tremble and whispered in her ear. 'I order you to live.'

The fairy baby unfurled her wings and yawned, blue eyes blinking up at her supernatural father. She cooed and smiled. Lan felt his heart warm and retracted the shadows. He got up.

'Leave, I am a healer,' said Lan.

The midwife and her attendants left the room.

Lan checked to see if Ake was breathing and placed the baby on her chest while he inspected the wound. *They have made a terrible mess of it.* He ground his teeth in annoyance and placed her under a sleep spell.

Lan grabbed a blade and slowly unpicked the stitches. He picked up the needle and nearby thread and sutured the wound closed with incredible speed and skill. He walked over to a table and found a selection of linen cloth and herbs. He grabbed some larger leaves and bandages and returned to Ake. He placed the slippery leaves on the wound before applying the bandages. *Hopefully that will prevent the stitches from sticking to the dressing.*

Lan cleaned up as best as he could. He opened the door to his sons' worried faces.

'Amities, go fetch coins from the inn.'

Amities ran off and Lan turned and went back over to Ake, followed by the midwife and an attendant.

'Is she okay?' asked the midwife.

Lan turned and stared at her. 'I hope so.'

Amities returned. He handed his father the coins and began to gulp in huge amounts of air.

'Remain calm, Amities. Count backwards in your mind.'

Amities' breathing soon returned to normal and Lan paid the midwife. 'Are you okay, Amities?'

The child gave him a weak smile and nodded.

'This is too much,' said the midwife.

'Keep quiet about this whole incident,' ordered Lan.

'On my honour, I will not tell a soul.' The midwife turned and strode from the room.

Lan handed Mandami the baby swaddled in a cloth and picked up his wife gently.

One of the scared attendants had already left and was spreading the story as quickly as she could in terror and awe. Lan growled to himself as he heard her yelling in the street.

'A demon king and his human bride have produced a fairy. The wife is now dead.'

Lan surrounded his family in a veil of shadows rendering them invisible. *A teleport spell might kill her in her fragile condition.* He walked the short distance to the inn with Ake in his arms. The noise from the inn goers covered their footsteps as they climbed the set of stairs to their room.

—⁓—

Mandami looked at the strange baby. The baby smiled and cooed. He rubbed her blonde downy hair, and the baby closed her eyes.

He felt very protective of her. She reminded him of the times he had held Sia as a baby, a fragile, trusting life looking up at him in complete innocence.

Amities and Mandami took the little baby over to the big bed they shared. Mandami rummaged through his bag and took out the second bag Ake had packed. He opened it and found a padded, round bed and placed the baby in it. Ake had lovingly packed a sling, tiny blankets and gowns.

Mandami sat watching the baby while their father gently tucked Ake into the other bed.

Lan paced back and forth. *I may still lose her.* She whispered something and he leant down to listen.

'I am sorry I didn't say anything. I was afraid you would try to get rid of her thinking she would be a demon.' Ake sobbed.

I probably would have reacted that way before I had a chance to talk to Swan Rider.

'Don't worry about it. The baby is fine. Rest for now,' said Lan.

Ake smiled weakly and drifted off. She seemed to be resting easier and he went to check on his daughter.

He picked the baby up, unwrapped her and checked for any injury from her dangerous entry into the world. They had nicked her feet and he seethed. The child was dainty and without deformity. She measured two of his hands. He sat down with her and placed her across his lap.

Lan gazed in wonder at her gossamer wings. *How the hell did our blood make a fairy baby?* Lan sighed and covered his face with his hands. The baby suddenly cried. He didn't know what to do with a fairy child.

Mandami retrieved the powdered flower nectar and gave it to

Lan. He relayed the instructions given to Ake. They boiled some water and added the powder. They let it cool and tried to feed the baby from a little cup. The baby drank small amounts of the brew and seemed to settle.

Lan went through Ake's gear and found the flowers. He wrapped the sleeping baby up and placed the purple flowers in her crib with her. Her wings turned a glittering purple, glowing through the swaddle. *Trust me to sire unusual children.*

He turned to his boys. 'Thank you for your help.'

They yawned and climbed into their bed and soon fell asleep, exhausted by the whole ordeal. Lan put the baby bed on the side table next to him and sat up next to Ake. *I wonder what price we will pay for my oath.* He soon drifted into a fitful sleep.

Chapter Forty-Eight

Ake had woken from bouts of fever muttering incoherently to herself. Lan bathed her sweat-soaked body with cloths soaked in lavender tinctures to reduce her fever. He had packed her wound with strips of cloth and a herbal paste made of goldenseal, thyme and fenugreek to reduce inflammation and prevent infection and forced her to sip water and pain relief brews when she was semi-conscious. Ake woke up two days later, as her fever broke.

Lan and the boys had been trying to keep the fairy baby settled but she was now needing more than nectar tea. Ake tried to sit up and Lan rushed over to help her ease up. He checked her wound and she winced. Lan gave her some willow bark tea for the pain.

The baby cried and Ake's breasts ached in response.

'Give her to me.'

'You should leave, boys.'

The boys left. With past experience, Ake nursed the tiny baby. After she had finished, Lan brought over soup and began to feed her with a spoon. He placed the bowl down and lifted a cup to her lips.

'It's a vitamin tea, it will aid your healing.'

Ake took a sip. 'It tastes foul.'

'Drink it.'

Ake drank the horrid brew. She gave Lan a weak smile and looked down at their baby nestled on her chest. 'Caoimhe.'

'The second name should be Elona. A mixture of our mother's names and Elder Flower's. It means strong as the oak tree, in remembrance of my druid father,' said Lan.

Ake nodded.

'I'm sorry, Lan. I'm sorry you had to make that deal.' She began to sob.

'It's okay. Better I made it out of love than hate. It was coming for me anyway,' he said gently.

'I'm sorry I hid her from you.'

'I scare you sometimes, when I am in that form, don't I?' he asked.

'You did during that fight where you attacked me.'

'And that first time together after four years. Ake, be honest.'

'I wasn't scared of you that night. I was afraid when I became pregnant because of it.'

'I need you to confide in me no matter what. No more making big decisions separately anymore.'

She nodded weakly. He carried her to relieve herself in the water closet. Lan left her to complete her absolutions. Afterwards, he lay her back on the bed, and gave her tea to help her relax and reduce her pain. Ake quickly fell asleep.

I am satisfied she will be okay. He opened the door and gestured for his boys to come back in. They sat quietly discussing the whole ordeal and playing cards.

—⁓—

The family spent the next week helping Ake heal. She began to sit up by herself and take small steps back and forth to the water closet. She inspected the scar as Lan changed the dressing.

'How extensive is the damage?

'You are healing well.' Lan looked away.

'Tell me.'

Lan replaced the dressing and stood up. 'You were injured internally. You cannot have any more children.'

He sat down next to her and held her as she sobbed. 'I am sorry, my darling.'

'At least you got to see this one be born.'

'I am grateful for that.'

Ake looked around. 'I need to get out of this room.'

Lan helped her stand. 'I believe you can have a meal downstairs. The boys are already down there.' He placed the sling across his chest and swaddled his daughter, securing her in the sling. Ake took his hand and they left the room and descended the stairs. Ake sat down; her eyes fixed on nothing. She sighed as if lost in thought. Lan ordered her a meal. When the meal arrived, she smiled at the array of sweet things plated next to a selection of savouries and began to eat.

'Ake, I am going to go out for a few moments. I will be back.'

'Okay.' Ake nodded.

Lan turned to Mandami. 'Stay and look out for your mother. I will be back soon.'

'Fine.' Mandami went and stood behind his mother. Lan turned and left.

—◦—

Lan pushed open the door to the jewellers; a tiny bell rang above the door and he saw glass cases lined with breathtaking pieces of jewellery. His eyes skimmed over them. *These are better quality pieces than those of the other jewellers.* The shopkeeper approached him.

'How can I help?'

Lan held up the necklace. 'I need this altered to fit this child. It needs to be adjustable as she grows. It is enchanted so you should use all due care.'

'It will take a few days. I deal with enchantments every day. This is a minor task and will cost you fifteen gold coins.'

Lan handed over the necklace and coins and left. As he started walking back, he heard a commotion at the inn. Lan ran, the baby cooed against his chest. He slowed down a little so he would not distress her.

A line of dwarven guards with axes strung against their backs had surrounded the inn. Lan lowered his hood over his eyes and wrapped his cloak across his chest. He walked inside and saw one of the midwives with a poster. She was showing a guard and pointing at Ake. Mandami stood near Ake with his dagger in his hand. Amities stood back his bow aimed at the guard. *My wonderful sons, I am proud of you.*

The dwarven guard handed the greedy assistant midwife a big gem and she took it into a corner and examined it. Lan snuck up behind the guard. He drew a knife and held it against the guard's throat.

'What do you want with us?' asked Lan.

The man gulped, his laryngeal prominence bobbing up and down.

'We heard there is a Trebrelan and Telewanake staying here. On behalf of Lord Borrush, you have cordially been invited to attend the keep. We are here to escort you for your own protection. Some odd rumours about a death king,' said the guard.

Lan stepped back. He put his knife away and smiled. 'No harm done. What is with the posters?'

The dwarf rubbed his neck and glared at Lan. 'Someone spread rumours about a demon murdering his wife. We put up posters offering a reward for any information as we were concerned for the safety of our citizens. We relayed this to our master. Lord

Borrush assured us that you were in fact the divine couple and told us to use any information to find you.'

Lan went over to his family and the boys lowered their weapons.

'They want us to accompany them and meet Borrush.'

He handed the sling to Amities. The boy put it on and began to coo at the sweet little face smiling up at him.

Lan looked Mandami squarely in the eye, his mouth set in a determined frown. 'I need you to be my eyes and ears. Keep that dagger close.'

Lan picked Ake up and she wrapped her arms around his neck. She was still too weak to walk the twenty minutes to the keep.

The embarrassed guard composed himself. 'Go to their rooms and collect all their things.'

Several guards ran off to retrieve the items.

'Who said we won't be coming back here?' asked Lan.

'It is not the place for the children of gods. You will attend our lord at his insistence,' said the guard.

Inn patrons talked in hushed whispers.

'I'm sick of the gossiping,' said Ake.

'Let them talk.' Lan smiled. *So much emphasis is placed on our supposed titles, and I am going to have a little fun.* 'I am Lord Bás, the god of death. I am angry that no accommodations were made for my wife, Lady Saol. I am feeling quite vengeful.' His eyes turned red.

He stared meaningfully at the dwarven midwife who dropped her gem. She glared at Lan.

'Lan, they healed me with what they knew,' whispered Ake.

'I agree, but why spread gossip around? Healers have a duty of privacy,' he yelled.

The midwife picked up her gem and raced from the inn, terrified. Lan laughed gleefully and Ake rolled her eyes and tried to hide a smirk.

'You are as bad as me.' Lan grinned.

CHAPTER FORTY-NINE

The guards escorted them out of the inn and down a main street. Dwarves stopped to watch the unusual display. Lan held his head up, his eyes glowed red as he called on the dark magic.

This is quite fun. Hopefully, I can draw out any enemies as well. Lan saw a street musician and threw him a handful of coins.

'Why not spin us a yarn about the Lord of Death and his divine bride,' said Lan.

The musician nodded. 'Give me a moment.'

'Ake, look at this,' said Lan.

Ake looked up, worried at the sudden rise in his voice. Her eyes turned golden in response to his use of dark magic. Lan laughed and the crowd cheered. Ake tried to make herself disappear by hiding her blazing face in his chest. He folded half his cloak over her. The dwarven bard took out a simple tambourine. *Nothing memorable will come of simple street music.* Lan grinned to himself.

The crowd cheered. Lan turned his head towards some patrons who were having a discussion.

'The great Dananzo is going to perform.'

'He can compose hits in minutes.'

'We are in for a treat.'

Lan's gaze settled back on the wizened dwarf who had deep brown eyes and an ochre beard. A deep rumble came out of his mouth as old as the stone. He began to play the tambourine and hum, producing multiple gravelly tones at the same time. The dwarf locked eyes with him and gave him a sad smile.

The humming died down into silence. The dwarf's voice rose, accompanied by other sound effects like birds calling and water bubbling over brooks. He set the scene for his earthy lament. His voice was a rich, baritone.

Time is endless for the god of death.
While dwarves and humans yearn for more.
Time is endless for the god of death.

He chased a divine bride of golden eyes.
In is arms she should always reside.
Counting down the dreary days,
Time is endless for the god of death.

Their son will conquer the devil queen.
He will hear death's bell keen.
Duty will split them apart, breaking his heart.
Time is endless for the god of death.

As she wanders the earth, he will reside in hell.
Where forever he shall dwell.
Time is endless for the god of death.

The crowd began to sing along. The earthy voices had a haunting affect as the dwarven bard began to hum sadly. They reached the keep and were ushered inside the gates. Angry tears rolled down Lan's face. His purchase had backfired, and he keenly felt his pact to save Ake and the baby's life.

He placed Ake down as Borrush came out to meet them in

plain green druid robes. The singing could be heard outside the gate and Lan covered his ears. He drew back the darkness and as the shadows receded his eyes returned to normal. Slowly the citizens moved away, and the unearthly lament petered off.

'I'll make sure we aren't separated,' he yelled at the retreating dwarves.

'Well, that was quite a dramatic entrance, my lad.' Borrush crushed Lan in a bear hug.

Ake began to swoon in exhaustion and Borrush released Lan, offering his arm to Ake, and she leant on it gratefully.

'What is wrong with the lassie?' asked Borrush.

Amities came forward at Lan's gesture and Lan pointed to the baby.

'My daughter is a week old. Ake hid her pregnancy from me. I found Ake dying. She was cut open and about to have my baby in a dress store,' said Lan.

'Don't you have two already?' asked Borrush.

'I'm assuming the prophecy means two pregnancies,' said Lan.

'No, lad, it was very clear. Twin boys. Only another god could have produced that baby,' said Borrush.

'Separated four and a half years until the day of her conception, Borrush. Don't go there, fellow,' said Lan.

Lan's eyes glinted red and shadows began to sweep around them.

'Shite, young fellow. When did dark divine blood seep into you?' asked Borrush.

'It was always there. I was destined to be her husband. Where there is life there is death. A traumatic event awakened it. When I thought I might lose them I made a pact with the gods. One day I will become the god of death,' said Lan.

'But you both had to be in divine form to produce another child. Dark blood would have tried to devour a mercy goddess.

You could have stripped her of her powers and sired a demon,' said Borrush.

Borrush's brow furrowed, and his mouth was set in a grim line. 'Are you okay, lass? Were you willing?'

'I'll pretend you didn't just insinuate forced intimacy. I stayed away out of fear of hurting her. She sought me out, Borrush,' Lan warned.

Ake glared at Borrush. 'I thank you for your concern, Borrush. Lan would never. And our daughter is not a demon. Why have you summoned us?'

'We have found hot spots of Shadow Scout activity. If we start destroying the hives, we greatly reduce Drianna's influence.' Borrush grinned.

'That is excellent news, Borrush,' said Lan.

Reducing Drianna's influence means less death on our plane. This may mean more time with my family, thought Lan.

'Come in and discuss it, please. I am sorry I insinuated anything, laddie. We know very little of the god of death and even less about your control of him,' said Borrush.

Lan and Ake nodded and followed their friend into the keep.

CHAPTER FIFTY

Borrush took them down a large hall. Servants flurried about tending lesser nobles, and guards stood sentry. The walls were plainly decorated with pictures of the royal family. Large glass displays held various gems, metals and interesting contraptions. Amities rushed over and stared at them, fascinated. Mandami retrieved him.

They headed to a small study. The walls were lined with stone shelves and stocked with books and scrolls. A large sandstone table and chairs filled the rest of the room. Ake slumped down into a chair. Borrush ordered furs to be brought in and placed under her.

'She should really be abed,' said Borrush.

'You ordered us here, Borrush,' said Lan.

'Less of an order and more of an insistent invitation.' Borrush grinned. 'I swore to myself to look after you and your wife after your father's death.'

Lan laughed. 'Insistent invitation. I might use that when I ask my children to do something, and they try to get out of it.'

The baby began to cry. Amities took her out of the sling and removed her swaddling without thinking. The baby unfurled her wings, her little limbs flailing in hunger.

'By our king's axe. A blooming fairy,' shouted Borrush in surprise.

'Keep it down,' said Lan.

Borrush stood and rushed over to the baby. He picked her up and examined her.

'Hand her to her mother, Borrush,' ordered Lan.

'It's a fairy, laddie. Do you even know what you have here? They are rare and bring immense joy to those around them. People with a fairy gain vast wealth and build empires, laddie.' Borrush smiled.

The baby squalled louder.

One of the servants knocked on the door and came in with tea. She dropped the tray in shock. The servant picked up the tray and backed out of the room. Lan stood up and walked over to Borrush. He retrieved the infant and handed her to her mother.

'Let's give them some privacy,' said Lan.

Borrush nodded.

The males left and waited outside while Ake tended the child. Lan calculated their quickest escape route. Trumpets sounded and someone of note came marching down the corridor, surrounded by guards and courtiers. Lan's eyes fastened on Borrush's.

'I won't say anything, laddie. Blessings on you and your family,' he said sincerely.

Lan's brow creased with worry. 'The servant.'

They scattered and began searching the corridor. Courtiers were talking around the noble, discussing mining and economic details. The servant was skilled at being inconspicuous and reached the noble. The noble bellowed when he was interrupted by the lowly servant.

'Lord King, there's a fairy baby in the keep.' The servant bowed.

'Is this some kind of prank by one of you courtiers?' The king laughed.

'Over there, in Borrush's study, my king.' The servant stood and pointed.

Lan teleported into the room with the boys. Ake had just

finished nursing when the door was thrown open. Borrush tried to distract the king who pushed his way inside.

'Lord King, these are my guests. Please my lord, hospitality dictates courtesy,' said Borrush.

'Out the way, lad, I know what hospitality dictates. I'm your bloody king,' the king roared.

The king pushed Borrush aside. Lan cast a sleep spell on the king. Borrush blocked it with a druid ward.

'I can't let you hurt my king, laddie.' Borrush frowned and his sad eyes fixed on Lan's.

The king grabbed the baby out of Ake's arms. She stood too quickly, and winced as pain tore through her wound. A guard rushed forward and grabbed her. Ake lunged at the king. Her eyes turned golden, and wings tore through the back of her clothes.

The king held the fairy baby up and she cooed at him sweetly.

'What a beautiful mother you have. That explains how you came about.' He smiled at the baby.

He ordered the guard to release Ake and handed her the baby.

'My king, you can't take their child,' said Borrush.

'Where there is light there is darkness. What manner of devil is the father?' asked the king.

Ake tried to catch his eye, but he refused to meet her stern gaze. Lan growled, and the darkness reacted to his rage. His eyes burned crimson. Shadows seeped in from the wall around the king.

'Lan don't harm him,' yelled Ake.

The king was pushed out the room in a whirlpool of shadows. Lan hurried towards him with hatred in his eyes. Ake ran to Lan, struggling in pain. She stood in front of him and threw her arms around him, cradling the baby between them.

Lan ignored her and growled at the king. 'You think you can rip a child from its mother's arms and expect the father not to react? I don't care how unique my child is, you still don't man-handle a baby.'

The waiting guards hefted their axes.

'I could kill you for that display. And I may have if it wasn't for your wife putting herself in the way. Back off, elf. It seems I startled you when I got caught up in my joy. I wouldn't have taken your baby,' said the king.

'Please, stop,' whispered Ake.

Lan swore and backed off. Ake trembled against him, and he forgot his feud.

'Leave us to compose ourselves.' Lan gave the king a disarming smile.

The king turned and walked through the door.

'Lan, the king won't easily overlook this, laddie. This may affect me helping Caelestis,' said Borrush.

'Borrush, get your arse out here and follow me to my quarters,' yelled the king.

Borrush sighed and followed his king.

Lan grabbed the baby from Ake and handed her to Mandami.

'Get ready to leave, boys.'

Ake had already changed back into her human form and was unconscious from the effort. *I can't teleport her in this condition.* He lay her on the floor and placed a fur under her head and covered her with another.

Lan paced. *How can I overcome druid and dwarven law?* He grinned. *I can counter with my own druid.* He mind-linked with Orilan who appeared quickly into the chaos of the room.

'What is going on here?' asked Orilan.

Orilan looked at Ake then at the chirping baby in Mandami's arms. Lan took the baby off the boy and handed her to the druid. Orilan's eyes grew wide with awe. Lan quickly explained their journey so far.

'What is it with you changing prophecies? Now we must placate an offended dwarf king just so we can keep our friend Borrush out of trouble. Hopefully, he will still want to help us. Then there is the matter of your strange condition.' Orilan sighed.

Orilan decided to sit at the desk and brainstorm ideas.

Borrush knocked on the door and called out. 'Lan, the king needs to see you immediately and bring the little one.'

Borrush poked his head in and saw their new visitor.

'Great. That's all we need,' muttered Borrush.

'Well met, Lord Borrush. I hear your stately king wishes to meet with our Lord Trebrelan of Caelestis. I believe his lady wife, Telewanake, was slighted when her child was taken from her arms without permission. I believe my lord father behaved passionately as any husband may. We should be able to come to an agreement.' Orilan gave Borrush a charming smile.

'A lot of fancy words from a smarmy elf. It won't be useful against my more earthy king.' Borrush laughed.

Orilan grinned. 'I'll stay with Ake. Father, go and sort this out.'

Lan stopped pacing, picked up his baby and followed Borrush.

—⟿—

They entered a small, circular room. The king was seated on a steel throne set upon a stone dais.

'Approach, elf,' roared the king.

Lan approached and bowed his head briefly before raising his eyes to stare at the king defiantly. 'You summoned me, your highness.'

'Hand me the baby.'

Lan ground his teeth.

'Lan, he won't harm her.' Borrush took the baby from Lan's arms and handed her to the king.

The king pointed to a guard. 'He has dishonoured me by

threatening my safety. Administer the punishment to him.'

The guard approached Lan. 'Do you accept your punishment.'

'Depends on what it is.' Lan kept his eyes on the king.

Lan's eyes widened in shock, and he stumbled back as the guard delivered a heavy punch to the side of his face, followed by another to his eye.

Lan took a defensive stance and blocked another blow.

'Enough.' The king stood up and descended the steps. 'I apologise for taking your child from her lovely mother. I will not lay a hand on your baby again. Now I will accept justice.' The king handed Lan his daughter.

The guard turned and delivered two blows to the king's face.

The king grinned. 'This matter is resolved. You are welcome in Rock Fell, Lord Bás. You and your delightful family will join me for breakfast.'

Borrush bowed and strode from the room. Lan bowed to the king and hurried after his friend.

—◊◊◊—

Lan walked back into the study with a black eye. Orilan noticed Lan appeared utterly bewildered as his father scratched his head and shrugged his shoulders.

'How goes the dwarven justice, Father?' Orilan laughed.

Lan stared at his son. 'The king ordered himself beaten as well.'

Borrush grinned. 'Even a dwarven king is punished when he makes a mistake.'

Ake whimpered in her sleep and Lan rushed over to her.

'She is okay, Father. I haven't left her side.' Orilan stood up and stretched.

There was a gentle knocking on the door, Orilan opened it. A servant entered the room.

'If you follow me, I will guide you to your quarters.'

Orilan took the baby from his father. Lan picked up Ake and his boys followed him. They stopped at a doorway and the servant opened the door.

'This room is yours, master druid. A servant will come collect you in the morning to attend breakfast with the king.'

Orilan handed the baby to Mandami and stepped into the room and closed the door.

The others followed the servant down the hallway. The servant bowed deeply and pushed open the door. 'My lord, here are your chambers.'

Lan watched the servant scurry away and entered the room. His sons followed and began looking around. There was a curtained-off four poster bed with velvet drapes. Lan pulled them back and placed Ake down on the bed. He checked her wound and noticed no lasting damage had been done. He turned as he watched Amities run through another doorway. The boy came back and smiled.

'Father, we have a bed like this one.'

'Great, I get to share with you,' grumbled Mandami.

Lan's eyes settled on the two comfortable chairs in the centre of the room and dragged one over near the bed and sat down.

'Boys, go find something to do please.' Lan sighed. 'Hand Caoimhe to me, Amities.'

Amities gave his father the baby. 'Our belongings have been placed on the bed in our room. We will go sort it.'

'Okay.' Lan smiled.

The boys entered the adjoining room and closed the door.

He looked down at his daughter and smiled. 'What a hectic

first week you have had.'

The baby smiled.

Lan smiled back and forgot his worries for a little while.

———

Lan jolted awake. His arms were empty, and he looked around. *Where is the baby?* His gaze settled on Ake as she sat nursing the baby in a chair by the bed and he breathed a sigh of relief. He smiled, throwing back the covers and sliding out of the bed.

He walked over to her. 'Are you okay?'

Ake ignored him and stopped nursing. She leant the baby forward and patted her back, encouraging her to bring up any wind. The infant sneezed and pulled an amusing face. Lan laughed. Ake continued to ignore him.

Lan pulled a chair across from her and sat. He watched her until she could no longer avoid his gaze.

'I admit I acted recklessly.'

Ake stared at him.

Lan sighed. 'I seem to always get it wrong. I protect you and our baby when a stranger grabs our newborn and has a guard detain you. Somehow that is wrong and ends with you ignoring me. Don't you think you are being unreasonable?'

Ake placed the baby in her padded crib that was situated on the floor and ignored Lan as she bent down to lift it off the floor. Before she could do so, Lan had picked up the baby and crib.

'You shouldn't bend down.'

'You don't do as I ask. Why should I do as you suggest?'

'Finally, a reaction.'

'I asked you not to hurt the king.' Ake glared at Lan.

'I didn't hurt him. I also stopped when you asked me.'

Lan placed the crib down on the chair.

'So, I shouldn't protect you and our baby when a king man-handles her?'

Ake eyes filled with anger, and she walked away from him and sat on the bed.

'Were you worried I could have started a war?'

Ake looked at him like he was crazy. 'One elf against—' Her eyes filled with fear. 'I hadn't thought of that.'

Lan's eyes darted away, and he blushed. 'You were worried about me. Forget about my previous comment.'

'You took on Cephas's army. You could easily incite a war.'

'We are getting a little carried away here. I understand you were angry for putting myself in danger when simple words could have rectified the situation.' Lan turned his head to the clock on the wall. Amities had spent the later part of the prior evening showing him how to read the time. The clock read half past six. 'We have to meet the king for breakfast.'

Ake's gaze settled on his bruised eye. 'Why are you sporting a black eye? The damage appears small but I can notice it.'

'The king had me punched in the face as punishment for my actions.' Lan grinned. 'Then he ordered the same treatment for having detained you and grabbing our baby. Then he invited us to breakfast.'

Ake began to laugh. 'That is amusing.'

There was a knock on the door. Lan opened it to see Orilan in the doorway. Mandami and Amities were with him.

'These children of yours came into my room. The younger one bounced on my bed and the older one stood in the doorway glaring at me.' Orilan smiled. 'We are off to breakfast.'

A servant cleared their throat and Orilan stepped out the way.

'Please follow me.' The servant turned and walked away.

Lan picked up Caoimhe and took Ake's hand. 'I trust I am forgiven.'

'I am pleased you want to protect me and our children, I am not pleased you could have gotten yourself killed and our friend and his people.'

Lan released her hand and gave her a stern look. 'I am in control of the darkness, Ake. I wouldn't be around you if I wasn't. It is awful of you to suggest I would harm our friend. You either trust my judgement enough to protect you and our children when necessary or you don't. The rules seem to change when you see fit.'

Lan walked through the doors and pushed past Orilan.

Ake mumbled to herself as she followed. 'How dare he walk away in the middle of a conversation. He is somewhat right, I guess.'

Lan grinned to himself. *That I am, my stubborn bride.*

They reached a large set of guarded double doors. One of the guards swung open the doors and the servant announced them.

'We welcome the elven princess, Telewanake, and her consort, the brooding god, Lord Bás.'

Ake noticed Lan glare at the guard. She stepped forward and bowed and walked through the doors. Lan followed suit and the king laughed at Lan's serious expression.

'I thought that would get a reaction. Take the stick out your arse and enjoy yourself.' The king gestured to the spread in front of them. He was seated at the head of the table. A huge selection of roasted meats, pates, breads and sweet meat were on offer. Wooden mugs were filled with ale.

Orilan, Ake and the boys took a seat and waited patiently for Lan to be seated. Lan sat down gently and cradled the baby against his chest.

'Eat and enjoy yourselves.' The king turned to Borrush and they slammed their mugs together and began to drink.

Mandami began to pile his plate high. Orilan took some of the finer cuts and Amities looked sad.

Lan reached out and put his hand on his shoulder. 'I understand.'

'So many animals just for a few people,' whispered Amities.

'You can't control other people, Amities. Take what you need and be happy that your actions align with your values.'

Amities nodded and began to nibble at a few slices of the sweetmeats. Lan did the same as not to offend anyone. Lan began to sip his cup of the ale before putting it down.

'I promised your mother I would not overindulge in alcohol too often.' Lan smiled at Amities. 'Stick to your word, my son.'

Ake's eyelids felt heavy and she stood up. 'I apologise, your highness. I must take my leave.' Ake yawned and blushed with embarrassment.

'You are welcome to your rest.' The king waved her away.

Lan stood. 'I request my leave too, your highness.' Lan bowed.

'I will bring the boys back later,' said Orilan.

Ake turned and left, and Lan hurried after her.

'She really has him on a leash.' The king laughed.

Ake looked back at Lan and saw him grin. He walked over to her and handed her the baby. Lan tuned and walked back through the doors. Ake stood in the doorway and watched Lan approach the king, grab a mug and raise a toast.

'To all husbands who are at the beck and call of their wives as they tug on the cords that bind them. Be honoured that she still gives you the time of day. If she doesn't, it is likely she pulled away as you ignored her stretching the cords that bind you beyond repair.'

'That is true. If you experience silence from your wife, it is likely you dug a shaft void of coal, and it will take a miracle to mine for more to keep the embers of marriage burning.' The king smiled. 'I was about to mention to Borrush here that my wife's demands are greater than your wife's.'

'I assure you all the demands are mine. She asks very little.' Lan smiled. 'I am sure with your large personality and appetite—' Lan spread his arms wide and grinned. '—your demands on your wife are higher than her needs from you.'

Ake gasped and everyone fell silent.

The king began to laugh. 'He is funnier than you, Borrush, he doesn't cater to my station. I see why he amuses you.' The king stood up. 'Make your sons leave and I will continue this conversation. It would be best if your wife left too.'

Lan teleported his younger sons out of the room. 'Ake, you should go rest.'

Ake shook her head. The king shrugged and turned back to Lan.

'At least I have an appetite. My wife's needs are truly met.' The king took a sip of his ale and puffed out his chest.

Lan pointed to Mandami and Amities in the hallway and then at Caoimhe. He turned and grinned at the king.

'Well, that's at least thrice. More than most elves.' The king turned and smiled at Ake. 'It seems even elven men are as proud of their virility as dwarves are.'

Ake rolled her eyes. 'No, apparently just this one. I never heard Dane or Serenade brag about the number of their children. Or mention how they satisfied a lover.'

Borrush laughed. 'That is not quite true.'

Ake stared at Borrush in shock.

'In negotiations, Serenade often brought his children along. Virility for kings shows stability for the crown. A kingdom without a surplus of heirs often falls.' Borrush smiled at her kindly. 'Don't take it to heart, lassie, a gentleman never talks like that in front of a lassie. Especially his own lady.'

Lan blushed and turned to stare at Ake. 'I took it too far. I saw a chance to counter his quip and took it. I am sorry for the insinuation about our love life.'

'I thought it was very tasteful. I never heard you say look how many children I have. This proves my wife is satisfied,' said Orilan who stood and grinned at Ake. 'This is how dwarves banter and build bonds after the women and children have left. It is good your husband is trying to counter the animosity between them. It is no place for a lady. It would be best if you left.'

The king laughed and held out his hand to Lan. 'You are welcome to stay in Rock Fell as long as you like. It is an honourable thing among dwarves when a man and wife have a strong love life.'

Lan shook his hand and bowed. Caoimhe began to cry and Ake rocked her.

'I'll bring the boys back later if you like,' said Orilan.

Ake nodded and began to walk away slowly, her strength giving out. Lan hurried after her and grabbed her hand as she swayed on her feet. He picked her up and cradled her and the baby against his chest. As they walked back to the room. She looked up into his eyes.

'I am sorry I was offended by your innuendo.'

'It doesn't matter. You are bound to be a little upset lately. You just had a baby.' Lan smiled. 'I am sorry I overreacted before with the king. I know a fair bit about the forwardness of dwarves and reacted poorly. You were in pain, and he took our baby and I just reacted.'

They reached the room, and he placed her gently on her feet and opened the door.

'All is forgiven.' Ake smiled.

They entered the room and Ake went and lay down while Lan took care of Caoimhe. Ake closed her eyes and fell asleep.

CHAPTER FIFTY-ONE

Ake had spent three weeks resting, being waited on by Lan while Orilan had taken the boys to visit the wonders of the dwarven city. They saw everything from lifts to deep mines full of gems and gold. Dwarven technology was advanced. Rock Fell had everything, from steam-powered engines to pot belly stoves, to metal rods that vibrated when they neared metal and more. Amities was in his element.

The baby was asleep. Lan sat in a comfortable chair reading through the detailed information about Drianna's hives. Ake was on his lap enjoying a romantic moment. She was almost healed. He looked at her, trying to gauge her thoughts.

Ake sighed.

'What is it?' asked Lan.

'What great wonder are we going to see next?'

'There it is.' Lan mumbled and looked back at his documents.

Ake grumbled and went to get up. Lan exhaled and put his papers down.

'You know me well enough to realise what I am going to say. Then there will be a battle of wills and one of us will make a ridiculous decision.' Lan pulled her back down.

'Not necessarily. You made a promise that we would travel.' Ake grinned.

'That was before you put yourself at risk, sweetheart. I am a better healer than most and where they failed to turn Caoimhe

I most likely would have succeeded. If I had failed, at least I wouldn't have butchered you. Can I trust you to not put yourself in danger if we travel?' Lan gave her a worried look.

'I will try harder, Lan,' charmed Ake.

'Hardly reassuring, honey. What's next? Healing an evil dragon while surrounded by poison gas?' asked Lan.

Ake laughed at him. 'An evil dragon, now that would be a sight.'

'Are you trying to ease my worry or strengthen it?' he asked.

There was a knock at the door. Orilan opened it and brought the boys in. Amities was chattering excitedly and Mandami was blocking him out. Orilan listened kindly. Amities rushed over to his parents. He launched into a vivid description of his adventure. His parents listened patiently for as long as they could.

'Breathe, Amities. You are your mother's son. She is the same when explaining something she is passionate about.' Lan laughed.

'That's ridiculous,' said Ake.

'Hmm. The long explanation about elves to an elf,' said Lan.

Ake scowled. 'To an elf who pretended he was a human.'

Lan shrugged. 'True, but you were very cute, like your son. You both get caught up in your explanations.'

Orilan watched her as she sat on Lan's lap. Ake got up, feeling awkward. Caoimhe fussed and she went over to settle her.

'What are your plans?' asked Orilan.

'I'm thinking we finish our travelling, then take on these hives. I want to make some memories before dealing with that evil lot. What do you think, Ake?' He turned and gave her a radiant smile.

Ake squealed, then composed herself. She was about to launch into a happy tirade and stopped herself.

'That is acceptable,' she said with all the eloquence she could muster.

'That's even more adorable,' said Lan.

Ake glared at him, and her face blazed a vivid red. 'Cut it out.'

Orilan cleared his throat. Mandami and Amities stared at their parents, puzzled.

'I believe they have forgotten their children are here,' said Mandami.

'It's sweet,' said Amities.

'Awww. Look at father being sweet and adorable to his wife. It's so wholesome and cute,' teased Orilan.

Lan stood up and tried to hide his smirk. 'Look at my adorable sons. They are so tiny and the bigger one is playing sweetly with his brothers.'

Ake looked at them as if they were all insane. She spoke to Caoimhe. 'So glad you are here. These males are odd. Aren't they, my little girl?'

'I guess we could leave in a few days, Ake.' Lan wandered over.

Ake ignored him and turned to Orilan.

'Yes, we will go in a few days,' she said.

Orilan nodded. 'I will return to Caelestis in the morning then.'

Amities complained and rushed over to hug his brother. 'Come with us Ori.'

'I don't think that's appropriate, little brother,' said Orilan.

'Why, Ori? Unless you are in love with my mother, how is it weird?' Mandami asked.

Ake and Lan had a whispered discussion.

'Did he ever try anything on you?' Lan kept his eyes on Orilan.

'There were a couple of hugs, but I set him straight.' Ake blushed. 'During the ceremony where he was cured—'

Lan and Ake watched Orilan and Mandami walk over to them.

'I took a bite out of her and have kissed her several times. While my feelings haven't changed, I have.' Orilan refused to meet Lan's angry glares and his gaze dropped to the floor.

Ake's cheeks burned.

Lan frowned. 'And after that?'

'Nothing,' said Ake.

'Do you trust him?' asked Lan.

Ake nodded.

'Ori, that is weird. Even for you.' Mandami made a noise of disgust.

'I don't behave like that anymore. I am happy to leave as I don't want it to be awkward.' Orilan blushed.

'Are you in love with her?' asked Mandami.

'Butt out, brother. I no longer have such designs on a friend. Why are you making a good situation uncomfortable?' asked Orilan.

'Mandami, stop pushing your brother's buttons,' reprimanded Ake.

'I trust Ake's judgement. You can come if you wish,' said Lan.

'I would love to spend time with my family.' Orilan grinned.

Amities and Orilan began to discuss possible destinations.

Lan turned to Ake. 'He bit you before Caoimhe was conceived? I am grateful he did, or we might not have conceived our beautiful baby. It undid the blood he gave you.'

Ake stared at him aghast. 'Deas said the gods in us were enough to create Caoimhe. How can you be pleased he bit me and kissed me?'

'I never said I was pleased he kissed you.' Lan's eyes bored in to Orilan's and Orilan's eyes darted away, unable to face the disappointment in his father's eyes. 'Maybe inviting him is a bad idea.'

Ake turned his head towards her. 'Are you okay?'

He nodded.

'Ori is no threat to us, Lan. It is important he spends time with his siblings. He needs to see us together with our children as a family so he realises how family works and what is considered acceptable behaviour.'

Lan grinned. 'I know. The thought of another kissing you makes me jealous even now. I am sorry.'

Ake smiled. 'It would be unnatural if you weren't jealous of that.' Ake caressed his face.

'Ouch,' cried Orilan.

Ake and Lan turned and saw Mandami throwing heavy items at Orilan. 'That's for kissing my mother, you dirty devil.'

Amities stood up and placed himself in front of Orilan. 'Stop it, Mandami. If Father isn't offended by Ori's presence, why are you? I am sure Orilan is remorseful.'

Mandami dropped the object in his hand. 'I won't hurt you, little brother.'

Orilan sighed and strode towards the door. 'It's best I leave.'

'Orilan, get back here!' Lan's eyes blazed with authority as Orilan turned to stare at him, his mouth open in shock.

Lan walked over to him and dragged him by the ear towards Ake. Orilan's cheeks were red with humiliation. 'Apologise to Ake for kissing her.'

'Let me go, Lan.' Orilan pulled away and Lan released him.

'It's Father to you.' Lan gave him a gentle smile.

Orilan sighed. 'I am sorry for kissing you. I should not have done that without your husband's consent.'

Lan stared at him. 'I think you need to reword that.'

Orilan's eyes widened in bewilderment, and he rubbed his jaw. 'Ah, right, I should never have kissed you without your consent and because of the fact you belong to my father.'

Ake pursed her lips in annoyance. 'I accept your apology, but I don't belong to anyone.'

Lan grinned at Ake. 'He is trying at least.' He turned and smiled at his son. 'Orilan, you will be coming with us so you can learn how families work.'

Orilan nodded. 'Here I thought it was going to be a joyous holiday.'

'Go sit with your brothers while we make our plans,' said Lan.

Orilan walked over and sat down on one of the armchairs and Mandami approached him.

'Wow, that was humiliating. I actually pity you. Father is treating you like a child.' Mandami patted Orilan on the shoulder.

'He is young, Mandami, and still learning. An elfling by Sidhe standards. Unfortunately, he had a terrible childhood among immoral fiends,' said Amities.

'Like I said, he has paid for his misdemeanour by telling our father the truth and suffering his wrath. I have never seen father so stern.' Mandami held out his hand to Orilan. 'Welcome to righteousness and our family, brother.'

Orilan shook his hand.

Ake smiled at her husband. 'That was very clever, Lan. Showing Mandami Ori has been punished clears the bad air between them.'

Lan smiled and began packing their things into a bag. Ake began to help him.

CHAPTER FIFTY-TWO

Ake mumbled in her sleep and began clutching at her abdomen. 'He isn't dead, he killed our freedom …' She reached out her hand and slapped at the air. 'I couldn't be with him, you know.' Lan reached out for her hand, and she screamed. 'I hope I'm not soiled.' Ake's eyes fluttered open and she looked dazed for a moment before she closed them and snuggled into him. Lan lifted his gaze to the night sky. Grey clouds threatened rain and a few merry stars twinkled, reminding him of his insignificance in the infinite tapestry of life.

They had camped under the large sheltering boughs of a cypress tree. Orilan had taken the boys and camped another tree over and Mandami had refused to let Caoimhe out of his sight so she lay curled up in the crook of his arm. The baby fluttered her wings, and they shimmered in the moonlight.

Lan sat up and grabbed a nearby stick and poked the embers of their banked fire. A cold draft made the embers flare, and he threw on a few pieces of wood. The wood began to smoulder and catch alight. A sharp breeze whistled through the trees shaking the boughs and a light rain began to fall gently, creating a comforting patter. His hand tickled as Ake reached out and made intricate circles on his palm, the elvish sign for lovemaking.

He laughed and dove under the blankets. He gasped as her hands caressed him and pushed her hands away as she tried to loosen his trousers.

'Not yet. I don't know if you are healed yet.' He kissed her. 'We can make out though.'

'Caoimhe is five months old. I am sure I have healed enough,' she whispered.

'At least give it another month.'

She sighed. 'Okay.'

He entwined their legs and pulled her against him as he kissed her with reckless abandon.

She took a deep breath when he relented. The fire hissed as raindrops rolled off the leaves and dripped on to the fire. Lan felt the hairs on his arms prickle.

'Death herself comes riding in on a pale horse,' whispered something in his mind. Dark shadows seeped from his hands and Ake gasped, capturing his gaze.

'Your eyes are crimson.'

'Yours are golden. I think some foul thing of Drianna's is hunting us.' Lan threw back the blankets and scrambled to his feet. He kicked out the fire as Ake rose and dressed. There was a gentle rustling nearby and Lan turned his head to see Mandami staring at him. The boy's dark eyes glowed briefly before the boy tucked Caoimhe into his bed-roll and stood.

'Did you see that? His eyes resembled a wolf's just now,' asked Ake.

'Probably a trick of the light.' Lan turned his head as the gentle clip-clop of hooves threatened their peace. 'It is here,' Lan whispered.

Mandami lifted Amities into the bed-roll with Caoimhe. The boy grumbled and rolled over to hug the infant. Mandami booted Ori awake and the young druid grumbled before throwing off his blankets. Orilan stretched and slowly stood.

'Why are we up so early?' Orilan grumbled.

The wind began to reach a crescendo, howling through the

trees like a pack of rabid wolves. Branches groaned in response and water splattered onto them. A startled bird cried out and several more followed until the noise pressed in on them and suddenly went out. The silence was crushing. A thud, followed by another, broke the silence as a cluster of tiny birds fell to the ground, their eyes wide open in shock, their tiny wings frozen in flight as if they had tried to make a hasty escape. Ake began to sob.

'Poor things.' Ake began to pick them up and screamed when thud, thud, thud hundreds of death's defenceless victims rained down upon them including bats, birds and small rodents.

'Bow to me,' something hissed as a pale horse trotted into view, its golden horn shimmered in the darkness.

'A unicorn.' Ake began to wander over to it before Lan grabbed her and thrust her behind him.

The unicorn's muzzle opened and it bared yellow teeth in various states of decay, saliva dripped down, and it hissed. 'Please bow to Drianna before she kills you all.'

The unicorn reared up and Lan noticed huge stitches running along its belly. A wave of despair washed over him, and he shuddered. *Trust Drianna to corrupt something so innocent.* There was a ripping noise and Lan felt the bile rise in his throat as the stitches were ripped open. Hundreds of dead fairies fell from the cavity. Ake screamed and a cry of anguish involuntarily passed his lips.

The stitches began to sew themselves up as if an invisible needle and thread was guided by death itself.

The unicorn collapsed on the grown and nickered, its eyes rolled about wildly. 'The last of them. She killed the last of the fairies in tribute to your new baby. I tried to rescue them, and she stuffed them inside. I am now free of their burden. Stay safe.'

The poor beast nickered in pain before its shuddering breaths stopped, its eyes wide and fixed as if staring death in the face.

Lan approached the unicorn and petted it before closing its eyes. 'Be at peace, gentle one. Go home to Dee.' Its body burst into flames as he set it alight. He knelt down and picked up a handful of the fairies. His eyes darted over their tiny forms. Their heads were missing, and a small wooden mask had been sewn onto the neck. They all wore masks with the same dreadful expression painted on; a jagged, twisted mouth full of fangs, a bulbous nose and wolf-like eyes and jutting demon horns. There was a clicking noise and Lan blinked in surprise as the neck of the fairy moved and it hoisted its mask. The painted mouth opened as the sound of creaking wood reached his ears. Its fangs latched down onto his hand. The trees above him swung their branches in anger as a ferocious wind ripped through them. Lan glanced down at the pile of fairies, their wings fluttering in response to the wind. The bodies began to squirm, and he took a step back.

'Get ready to defend yourselves,' he yelled as the bodies rose in the air and hurled themselves at him. He was pressed down in a mass of whirring wings and undead that smelt of decaying flowers and honey. He yelped as hundreds of pincer-type teeth bit at him. He unleashed a wave of flames and the bodies hissed and threw themselves off him.

Ake screamed and Lan scrambled to his feet. He turned and witnessed some of the fairies tearing chunks of her hair out. One flew up her dress and Lan saw blood well on her thigh as it bit her leg. He threw his knives and took down the two harassing her hair. Ake pulled the fairy from under her clothes and winced as its bite was broken and blood ran down her leg.

'Hungry ... Blood ... More,' yelled the fairy.

Mandami was thrusting his dagger at the fairies within his grasp. Amities woke up, screamed and clutched Caoimhe to him. The infant chittered and the fairies fluttering above the trees drove towards them, screeching.

'Abomination.'

'A memory.'

'Angry we can't be the same anymore.'

Orilan yawned and teleported Amities and Caoimhe out the way. The fairies slammed into the ground, their masks cracked as they lay writhing in pain.

'Free us.'

'How is it they can talk and Caoimhe can only whistle, laugh or cry?' asked Ake.

Orilan grinned. 'When there is more than three of a creature, a druid can cast speech and translate the language for all those around.'

'Useful.' Lan ducked as twenty more of the fairies swooped him. He gagged as the fairies began tearing the heads off the dead animals and lapping at the blood.

'Not sweet.'

'Not flowers.'

'Not cream … miss cream.'

Several of the fairies alighted on a bough and began jumping up and down. Lan gasped as a cold wave of water washed over him. Caoimhe giggled and the fairies hissed and fluttered towards her.

Ake grabbed two of the creatures and shoved them into a bag. They scratched at the inside of the bag. When they became silent, Ake opened the bag and a creature growled and leapt at her, tearing at her hair as well as biting and scratching her.

Mandami and Amities grabbed their packs and began stuffing the fairies into the bags, when they were full, they grabbed more packs and threw the full ones onto the ground. The bags rolled about as the scampering fairies tried to escape.

This seems like more of a distraction than a direct attack. The howling wind suddenly stopped, and Lan turned as a dreadful scream rent the air. All light, both natural and created, went out and they were left in absolute darkness. Caoimhe's eyes glowed softly in the dark. Mandami's eyes flashed briefly. One patch of darkness seemed to writhe and rushed towards them, growing bigger. Lan was thrown from his feet as the wave of darkness washed over him. He felt the air drawn from his lungs and clutched at his throat. His face began to burn, and he raised his hand to the puckered skin and screamed as a hideous memory tormented him.

—⁓—

Ake lifted her arms out in front and took a tentative step. She shuddered as her bare feet crushed delicate bones and she felt warm blood spurt on her toes. She heard Lan scream and walked in the direction. A large hand was placed on her shoulder, and she was thrown to the ground as a mass pressed into her.

'Do not think to deny me or I will beat you.' Ake felt the tears run down her cheeks and she averted her gaze.

Ake screamed and kicked out and the darkness pressed in on all sides.

—⁓—

Amities felt the emotions rush in, and his breathing came in ragged waves. *Why must I feel their pain?* He tried to block it out and the sound of tearing pages crowded in on him. He covered his ears as the cacophony tormented him.

Caoimhe giggled and the sound disappeared. Amities smiled and held up the infant. Her wings blazed a brilliant rainbow hue and the crushing darkness seemed to lighten. Amities saw Mandami curled up in a ball.

'Don't take Mother from me again,' cried Mandami.

Amities noticed his brother weeping. Caoimhe fluttered her wings and floated briefly in the air before Amities snatched her up and placed her between his brothers. Orilan was tearing at the bag, his fangs glistened white and he went to bite a screeching fairy.

'No, I mustn't give in. If the vampyr wins, Ake will withdraw her kindness and Father will despise me yet again. I am a good man,' whimpered Orilan.

Caoimhe whistled excitedly and hugged each brother. Orilan shook himself and grinned. Scrambling to his feet, Orilan ran in the direction of Ake. Mandami stood and brushed himself off and cursed. Amities blushed and Mandami ran towards the sound of Lan's anguished cries. Caoimhe fluttered her wings and bobbed up and down before landing on the ground.

The infant chittered and held up her hands to Amities. 'Up.'

Amities picked her up and sprinted after Mandami. They came across Lan clutching at his face.

'I cannot protect her. How can a broken man do so?' cried their father.

Mandami shook him. When Lan grabbed his throat and squeezed, the tiny fairy fluttered out of Amities' arms and pressed her little face against Lan's cheek, chittering sweetly.

'Daddy, stop.'

Lan released his grip and his eyes fluttered open.

Mandami coughed and punched his father. 'You strangled me, Athair.'

Lan sat up and pulled Mandami into a hug. Tears welled in his eyes as he wept. 'I am so sorry.'

Mandami pushed him away. 'It's fine.'

'Daddy, Caoimhe help. Death darkness go away. Where's Mama?' Caoimhe smiled.

Lan blinked in surprise and scrambled to his feet. 'Fairies must have a whole language of their own.'

'Fairies smart. Hive mind gone now. Caoimhe last.' Caoimhe began to cry.

The bags caught fire and began to explode. Sweet smoke billowed in the air.

'I can't talk to you—' Caoimhe frowned as her words turned in to whistles enunciated with clicks.

'I am sorry, Caoimhe, I don't understand.' Lan hugged the chittering infant.

'She's feeling love for Mother,' Amities whispered before sprinting in the direction of Ake's sobs.

They jogged after him and came across Orilan kneeling next to her, shaking her. Ake tried to lift her arms and they appeared pinned down and her legs were splayed. Her wrists were marked with fingerprints and her eyes were scrunched up. Caoimhe hefted herself from Lan's arms and fluttered under her mother's hair and whistled to her, nuzzling into her neck. Ake opened her eyes.

Lan retrieved the infant. 'Thank you, Caoimhe.' Lan hugged his daughter and handed her to Orilan.

Tears welled in Ake's eyes and Lan winced and turned his head away.

'Go,' roared Lan.

Orilan stood and grabbed Caoimhe and ushered the boys after him.

'Why can't we stay with mother?' asked Amities.

'Probably lovey-dovey stuff. Gross,' said Mandami

Orilan sighed as he stacked a pile of wood and lit it with *Druid*

Fire. The flames licked the wood greedily, as if starved of comforting light after Drianna's attack. He turned and the boys met his gaze.

'Sometimes humans do terrible things to each other. That memory can resurface and cause pain.' Orilan smiled sadly. 'What happened to your mother happened to Father and that is how I was born. We could never understand their pain, so it is better to let them comfort each other.'

The sky began to lighten and Orilan smiled. 'Drianna's reach should weaken as Mercury greets us, his delightful rays warming the aftermath of a wicked night.'

'Very poetic,' mumbled Mandami.

Orilan smiled as Ake and Lan joined them at the fire. Lan's eyes were fixed on Ake's as she sat and warmed her hands.

'We have no supplies, Father,' said Orilan.

Lan sighed and frowned. 'Right, the packs. Okay, we shall find a town as soon as the sun is up.'

Ake reached for his hand as the sun made his slow journey into the sky.

Chapter Fifty-Three

As Lan and his family had continued their journey, they had encountered strange lands with creatures they had long heard tales of but never witnessed. Nine months had passed since Caoimhe's birth, and they were nearing the end of their holiday.

Ake stared up at the enormous, grey-skinned animal. Two white tusks jutted out from either side of its head. Its long nose reached out towards her and was about to caress her face.

'Ake, this is one of your more dangerous ideas,' said Lan.

'He's majestic, isn't he?' Ake grinned.

'We don't even know what that is,' mumbled Lan.

'It's an elephant. I read about them. Even saw a crude picture in the ancient part of Caelestis's library,' announced Amities.

The beast trumpeted.

Lan yelled over the din. 'It will probably eat her.'

Ake went running and took her Anwyn form. She glided onto its back without a second thought. The beast turned and thundered away. Ake laughed and bounced about as she held on to the creature's ears. Lan swore.

'Language, Lan,' yelled Ake.

Lan shouted back. 'Really, wife. You are worried about that?'

Lan sprinted towards the beast. With great agility he used the side of a nearby tree as leverage and somersaulted onto the beast. Ake smiled at him.

'That was amazing,' she said.

The beast began to slow and came to a stop. The elephant used his trunk to lift Ake off his back. Lan stiffened as the beast did the same to him. It caressed them both with its trunk. Then it turned and thundered off into the foliage.

Ake turned towards Lan, jumping up and down on the spot. 'That was incredible.'

'You are crazy, my darling wife.' He smiled.

Lan was about to kiss her when Mandami came over and handed him his daughter. The baby looked human as she was wearing Deas's necklace. She was swaddled tightly to prevent her from flying away.

Caoimhe had learnt to fly a few months ago and had become a handful. The baby struggled and whistled in agitated song. She wanted to fly off and explore. Lan was concerned she wasn't growing as she was still tiny. He sighed and pulled out a small harness, altered to fit over her wings. Lan unwrapped her and captured her in the harness. She kicked and flapped trying to get away. Lan didn't like the harness, but he couldn't let an infant fly off into the wilderness. The baby flapped around above his head, and he attached the strap to his wrist. *I look ridiculous.*

'I'll take her, Father. You will probably have to run after Mother again at some point,' offered Mandami.

Mandami was often a serious and astute child. When he was with Caoimhe, he let his guard down. His father handed over the fluttering infant. Ake ran off towards a large cat with a shaggy mane. Lan followed and grabbed her hand.

'Lion,' said Amities.

Amities explained the nature of the beast to Lan. Mandami rolled his eyes. Orilan was documenting unknown species of plants and drying samples to take home.

'Ake. Come back here,' yelled Lan.

Ake had let go of his hand and walked towards the lions. Lan sprinted after her. Mandami wandered over to Orilan and sighed.

'What's wrong?' asked Orilan.

'What is it with her?' Mandami asked.

Orilan looked up at him. 'She is a goddess of life and mercy. That means a spirited woman with an unnatural zest for life.'

'But Father is so reserved,' said Mandami.

'Thank goodness. We can't have three like that.' Orilan laughed.

'Three like that?' asked Mandami.

'Dear little brother. You killed a hellhound without batting an eyelid. What about that jaguar? The one you stared down a few weeks ago when you were on watch. He bolted.' Orilan grinned. 'You are both impulsive.'

'Sod off, Ori,' cried Mandami.

Orilan laughed.

Caoimhe became tired and floated down to sit on Mandami's shoulder. She chirped softly in his ear. He recognised the gentle coos that meant she was hungry and handed her a wreath of flowers. She began chewing on the petals and cooed happily.

'You are very cute, Caoimhe.' Orilan tickled her under the chin.

Caoimhe noticed a new flower in his hand. She swiped it and crammed it into her mouth. Orilan grabbed her and fished it out. She bit down on his finger with tiny, pointed teeth. Amities roared with laughter and Mandami smirked too. Caoimhe began chittering apologetically and grabbed his thumb with her tiny hand.

'It's okay, Caoimhe. I know you didn't mean it. No eating random plants, baby. That could have made your tummy very sore,' he said.

'Ye gods,' yelled Lan.

The others turned and saw a lioness nuzzling Ake as she scratched the belly of a cub. Lan approached carefully and Ake grinned at him. She crooned softly to the lioness and grabbed his hand. Without warning, she placed it on the lioness's head who butted it affectionately. Lan smiled and relaxed a little.

'Are we done in this part of the world now, Ake?' asked Lan.

'Yes. Weren't those pyramids amazing? I can't believe we are due home today. Forget Drianna and travel with me,' she said softly.

Lan grabbed her hand and slowly backed her away from the family of lions and back over to the others.

Lan sighed. 'I would do that in a heartbeat if it meant we were safe. Drianna is on the rise. There have been skirmishes in Mencrey. Our small force of mystics has managed to keep it in check. But for how long?'

He felt Ake's tears fall on his hand and pulled her into a loving embrace. She sobbed against his chest. Soon they were all standing outside Caelestis.

'Could have warned us, Father.' Orilan signed the symbol for father.

He sometimes still signed single words with his one good hand. It was second nature to him.

Caoimhe signed *father* and pointed at Lan. She whistled with excitement.

'Ake, look,' whispered Lan.

Ake looked up, eyes red with tears and smiled at the baby.

Ake dried her tears on her sleeve. 'This is wonderful. We will be able to understand her. It is so sad I didn't get to hear her speak.'

'I am so glad you had her. I missed so much.' Lan kissed her.

Ake's shoulders slumped with dejection.

'Ake, I will buy us as much time as I can. That is why we need to reduce the number of casualties by destroying these hives. I need you to be strong like you always have. You must help me with this. Please,' he begged.

Ake nodded and composed herself. Caoimhe flew over and sat on Lan's shoulder and signed father.

Lan smiled up at his dear daughter. Well done, he signed back.

They all went through the gates of Caelestis. Ake turned and looked at the clouds gathering on the horizon. She knew one day Lan would be taken from her because of their choices.

CHAPTER FIFTY-FOUR

Lan placed the gifts he had made on the decorated table. The marble table had a green tablecloth and Ake had decorated it with branches of holly. Red candles burned brightly in golden holders in the centre.

It was mid-winter, and they were to celebrate the elven festival of family. *I have a beautiful family,* he thought proudly. Some of the students and teachers had gone home to their families for a few days. Caoimhe sat near the hearth. The fire crackled warmly and lent the room friendly cheer. The toddler was stacking the brightly coloured wooden blocks he had made for her birthday a few months ago. Every time they crashed to the ground, they made various sounds from bangs to pops and the toddler laughed.

I can hardly believe it's been over five months since we've come home. We have settled into family life with no fuss. The time has gone by so fast.

A log split and shattered loudly. Caoimhe cried and got to her feet, toddling towards her father. He held out his arms and called to Ake with his mind. She entered the room as Lan swept up their daughter who had just taken her first steps, wanting to be consoled by her beloved father.

'Well done, my baby,' said Lan.

Scared, signed Caoimhe.

Lan had been teaching Ake, Caoimhe and the boys the elven

sign language Qwena. Lan handed the baby to her mother and Ake rocked the tiny toddler, soothing her.

Down, Mama, signed Caoimhe.

Ake placed the toddler on the floor, and she toddled back to her blocks and began to play. Lan walked over to Ake and took a piece of holly from his pocket and held it above Ake's head.

Lan leant in and whispered in her ear. 'Fair maiden, your elven lover has held this token above your brow, will you reward him with a kiss now?'

Ake giggled. 'Did you just invent that?'

Lan grinned. 'Maybe, or is it an elven tradition?'

Ake smiled. 'I grant you that reward.'

Lan tilted her chin and brushed her lips lightly with his own. Lan drew back.

'I'll add to that later,' he said.

'I will hold you to that.' Ake smiled.

There was a knock at the door and Lan went to answer it. Orilan entered with Borrush and a young dwarven girl. The men were arguing as usual.

'Like your gifts are going to be any good, elf. Probably some berries and twigs,' said Borrush.

Orilan laughed. 'Knowing dwarves, you will hand out mining picks and lumps of coal.'

Borrush looked at the bag in his hand and grinned. 'At least that is practical.'

They turned to greet their hosts.

Caoimhe signed *brother* and held out her hands for Orilan. He put his bag down and picked her up with his one good hand. Borrush kissed Ake warmly on both cheeks then enveloped Lan in a crushing bear hug and released him.

'This is my daughter, Beryl,' said Borrush.

'Hello,' said Beryl.

'Where's her mother?' asked Lan.

Borrush gave him a sad smile and sent his twelve-year-old daughter to play with Caoimhe as Orilan placed the toddler on the floor.

'Dead three years ago, killed in a dark alley by gugglies,' said Borrush.

'I am sorry for your loss, Borrush.' Lan patted Borrush's shoulder. 'Why didn't you mention this before?'

Borrush clapped him on the back. 'Kind of ye to say so lad. Dwarves don't mention the dead in case it wakes them from their rest; dooming them to wander aimlessly for eternity.'

Ake shivered.

'Sorry to change the subject. But what are gugglies?' asked Lan.

'They have the bodies of large spiders with a serpent head. They are carnivorous and venomous and hunt in packs. Rissa took a wrong turn. We miss her every day.' Borrush frowned as his gaze settled on his daughter.

Ake wandered over and hugged him. 'I am sorry, Borrush. Would you be offended if we toast her tonight?'

Borrush smiled sadly. 'Not at all, lass. Thank ye kindly.'

The door slammed open and Amities and Mandami came in. They were playfighting. Mandami poked Amities in the ribs and Amities swatted at him.

Borrush laughed. 'You have fine sons, elf.'

Ake left the room, and everyone talked among themselves. When she returned, she brought in glasses and a variety of jugs. Lan swore and raced from the room.

—◈—

Lan hurried to the kitchen to check on their dinner. He had dwarves install a pot belly stove a week ago and was still learning how to use it. Without thinking, he pulled open the handle and burnt his hand. He blew on it before grabbing a tea towel and pulling the door open. He gave a sigh of relief and removed the trays and placed them on a bench. *Thank Dee, nothing is burnt.* The elven festival of Glendanoch encouraged hearty vegetarian dishes made with root vegetables and herbs, standard winter foods. He had prepared Camash, an elvish dish made of creamy mashed potatoes, cabbage and aromatic herbs. Potato candy— small sweets made with cream cheese and sugar shaped like potatoes and covered with cinnamon—was for dessert. He had roasted carrots, parsnips and pumpkin and prepared a simple gravy. *Borrush probably won't like the lack of meat.* He grabbed the last tray, a seasoned cabbage soup and placed it with the others.

Mandami and Amities entered the kitchen, arguing.

'It's your fault, Mandami,' said Amities.

Mandami glared at him. 'No, you jumped on me and I knocked the table, spilling the mead Mother made.'

'That was because you kicked me,' said Amities.

'Boys. Stop it,' said Lan.

'Mother sent us to help you,' said Mandami.

Lan nodded. 'Good, start taking in these dishes. I will grab some plates.'

Amities picked up a tray. Mandami used a spell to levitate his trays out of the room, poking his tongue out at Amities as he left. Lan rolled his eyes.

'Aren't you going to use magic too, Father, and humiliate me?' asked Amities sadly.

'No. Sometimes it's more satisfying to complete tasks without it, Amities.' Lan smiled at the child.

They grabbed the rest of the dishes and returned to the others.

Everyone sat in comfortable chairs with bowls of nourishing food on their laps. Ake filled everyone's glasses with homemade mead for the adults and sarsaparilla for the children.

'Please raise a toast to family past and present as we celebrate their lives. We miss you Dane, Regona, Melowy, Het, Flo, Hau, Falcon, Serenade and Rissa.'

Everyone bowed their heads in their honour then lifted their glasses in a toast.

Lan heard the whispers of the dead and felt a warm breath on the back of his neck and shuddered. He looked around and saw a shadow disappear through the wall. He stood up suddenly, his empty bowl clattered to the floor. A log cracked and the two simultaneous noises made everyone jump.

'I think we should move on to happier things,' said Lan hastily.

Orilan and Ake looked at him with concern.

'Are you okay?' asked Ake.

Lan ignored her and began to hand out his gifts. The gifts had to be practical in nature. The idea was to receive a useful tool from loved ones to help you through a harsh winter.

Everyone opened their gift from Lan. To Borrush he had gifted an axe and the druid smiled. He had given Amities vials of ink and Mandami a whetstone, they were pleased. Orilan received some potion vials and shook his hand. He gave Beryl and Caoimhe a tiny cup engraved with fairies; the girls were delighted.

Orilan handed everyone bottles of willow bark tea and cold and flu remedies. Borrush gifted everyone small pickaxes and bags of coal and he grinned at Orilan.

Orilan laughed. 'I knew it.'

'I was correct as well, elf.' He held up the willow bark tea. 'See berries and twigs all crushed up for remedies.' Borrush grinned.

Ake had been working on perfecting bottles of mead and handed them out. She gave cakes and sweets to the children.

Borrush put the bottle to his lips and drained the whole thing. 'It is a good brew, lass.'

Lan looked impressed and put Ake's present aside. He walked over to her. 'It's a special occasion. Would you be upset if I drank a fair bit?'

Ake smiled. 'It is a special occasion. If you think it won't lead to you drinking all the time, I guess it's fine.'

Lan walked over to Borrush. 'I challenge you to a drinking contest.'

Borrush laughed. 'Sure, lad.'

'It is late, let me settle the children first.' Ake picked up Caoimhe. 'Follow me, children.'

'We aren't tired.' Amities yawned.

'I am nearly a man, let me stay,' said Mandami.

Ake shook her head with a smile and left the room and the children followed.

Orilan left briefly and returned with two large bottles and four shot glasses on a tray. Ake returned and the four adults pulled their chairs into a semi-circle around a small table.

'I asked Teyra to watch over them. She opted to stay over the holidays.' Ake sighed. 'She is one of Amities' favourite teachers and he told me all her family were killed when Caley fell. I offered for her to join us a little while, but she declined.'

Lan frowned. 'Cephas's actions affected so many families.' Ake winced and Lan grabbed her hand as she brushed passed him to the seat nearby. 'I'm sorry for mentioning him.'

Ake took a shuddering breath. 'I'm fine.'

'I am going to beat you, elf.' Borrush grabbed a shot glass of whiskey Orilan had poured and downed it.

Lan gave him a sad smile. 'I doubt it.'

'This halfling drinking game is called riddles. Each round, everyone asks one riddle and whoever gets it wrong has to down a shot. Borrush, you go first as you have already drunk a bit.' Orilan poured four more shots.

'I power the dwarven world and keep you warm,' said Borrush.

Orilan rolled his eyes, and everyone answered coal.

'I weep with empathy and my skin heals your pain,' said Orilan.

Borrush took a shot. 'Bloody, elf.' He laughed.

'Weeping willow,' said Lan.

'Willow bark,' said Ake.

'The bark is the skin. I meant the tree. Ake take a shot,' said Orilan.

Ake drained her drink and coughed. Lan patted her on the back.

'I am the grain of the earth, the sweetness of the plants. A bird's gift is part of me. Apply the heat and taste my goodness,' said Ake.

'Flowers,' said Borrush.

'Bad food.' Orilan laughed.

'Take a shot both of you,' said Ake.

'Cheers,' said Orilan, just wanting to drink.

'Cake,' said Lan.

'Correct,' said Ake.

Lan took two shots, not to be outdone by the other men.

'But you got it right,' said Ake.

Lan grinned at her and shrugged. 'It doesn't matter, my little sweet tooth.'

Ake took a small cake out of her pocket and began to eat it. Lan pulled her on to his lap. She swatted his hands away but didn't get up.

'My typical Ake,' he nuzzled her neck.

Lan poured her a shot and handed it to her.

'That's against the rules,' she said.

'You won't get the next one.' He grinned.

Orilan and Borrush had just started competing against each

other and ignored the couple. Lan and Ake watched them for a bit, amused. After many shots the men started belittling each other for fun and soon fell asleep. Borrush snored loudly.

Ake downed the shot. 'Ask away.'

'My white flowers sometimes blush pink as I burrow the roots of my sacred body into the earth,' said Lan.

Ake took a shot, Lan did too.

'What am I thinking?' asked Ake.

'That is a ridiculous question.' He drained his glass and laughed.

Lan whispered in her ear. 'What are you wearing under that dress?'

Ake refused to answer and took a shot. Lan could see she was drunk as she could barely maintain her upright posture and he steadied her with his hand.

'Have you ever been drunk?' asked Lan.

'Nope.' Ake giggled.

'That's enough for you then.' Lan took her glass.

Orilan woke up and booted Borrush. Borrush groaned and opened his eyes. The men got up and stumbled from the room. Ake leant over, picked up a bottle and drank from it. She spluttered and Lan took it from her.

'Spoilsport,' she mumbled.

'Slow down.'

Ake grabbed another shot and offered it to Lan. He shook his head and finished the bottle he had taken from her. Ake finished her drink.

'Oh no, it's all gone.' Ake stumbled over her words. 'Hawthorn … Hawthorn tree was the answer,' she mumbled.

Lan laughed. 'So, you knew the answer. You just wanted to drink with me.'

Ake nodded. 'I don't feel well. How can you like this feeling?'

Lan hid the bottle behind him. 'See it's all gone.'

Ake struggled to focus on him. 'No, it's not, Lan, it's behind your back. Stop controlling what I do.'

Lan sighed and pulled the bottle out. 'You will feel awful tomorrow if you continue.'

Ake laughed. 'So what. That's my choice. What did you get me anyway?'

She reached for the gift on the table and almost fell. Lan hauled her up. He reached over and handed it to her. She unwrapped it. Lan had made her a simple crown of hawthorn flowers and twigs. It represented love and protection.

'Put it on me, please.'

Lan placed it gently on her head as she swiped the bottle from him and took a drink.

She smiled at him. 'See, I'm a queen with a crown now and I declare I have won the contest.'

'My blessed Queen Ake. Your humble warrior is at your service,' said Lan.

Ake smiled and played along; her inhibitions gone. 'I demand either a kiss or for you to take a drink.'

'Alas, it would be a most foul deed if I were to kiss a drunk woman as she knows not what she asks. I have no choice but to venture forth and risk the poison that will wreak havoc on my body.' Lan grabbed the bottle from her and swallowed the contents and hiccupped. *I am drunk too.*

Ake leant against him, her breathing slowed and he dropped his gaze to her face. Her eyes were closed, and he smiled. He leant back in the chair, content and drifted off.

CHAPTER FIFTY-FIVE

Four-year-old Caoimhe peered out over the bushes and saw her parents checking the rows of plants in the kitchen garden. She was angry at them for telling her off. She had taken a liking to the flowers in the memorial garden and had eaten them all over the last few days. *They were just so tasty. I couldn't help it and now Mother and Father hate me. They will be sad when they can't find me.*

She ducked back down as Ake walked by. She could blend in with any plants and knew they wouldn't be able to find her.

'Come out, Caoimhe. We aren't angry anymore,' said Lan.

'We must find her, Lan, she could be anywhere. I am worried about her. I hate to do this. It feels like I am summoning a pet,' said Ake.

'Ake, she's a tiny child. We need to know she is safe. We will never find a fairy among plants and trees. Do it,' said Lan.

Caoimhe giggled and moved away towards the gate, hoping to make an escape. A wonderful scent reached her nostrils and she turned to look at her mother. Ake had taken out a bowl and poured milk and honey into it. Caoimhe tried to fight the urge to not run over and take the bowl. Her feet betrayed her, and she ran over to her mother and picked up the bowl and drank its contents.

Lan grabbed her. 'Don't ever make us worry like that, Caoimhe. You are too young to be on your own, it's not safe.'

Caoimhe gave him an annoyed whistle and he carried her inside. Ake followed.

—⁓—

Everyone clapped and cheered as Caoimhe blew out the birthday candles. It was her fifth birthday. Caoimhe felt lonely despite being surrounded by people. Orilan and her parents had left her in search of the hives of someone called Drianna. She was left in the care of her teachers and her seventeen-year-old twin brothers. Amities was caught up in his work and had forgotten about her. Mandami had arranged a party at the last minute. She sat in a classroom surrounded by teachers, a couple of students and Mandami.

Mandami cut the cake and handed her a slice. She took a bite. It was crunchy and tasted burnt. Mandami smiled at her and ate some. He swallowed his mouthful and put the plate down.

'Ah, yes, I'm not really one for sweets,' he said.

You baked it, signed Caoimhe.

The sound of footsteps could be heard down the hallway and the door opened. Ake, Lan and Orilan entered the classroom. Caoimhe whistled in happiness. *They remembered me.*

Mandami's eyes darted to his parents. His father was leaning on Ake, and he had done his best to cover his injuries but looked pale and unwell, like he was fighting illness. Ake hoisted Lan up as he began to falter. Orilan reached out a hand, steadied her, and yawned, looking as exhausted as Ake.

Lan steadied himself and declined their help. He walked over to his daughter and hugged her. 'Happy birthday, Caoimhe.'

Ake kissed her and gave her the best gift in the world, a bag of mixed sweets. Caoimhe hurried into a corner and began to eat them.

Ake laughed and called out to her. 'Happy birthday, daughter.'

Caoimhe gave her a big smile and continued to eat her treats.

Ake turned to Mandami. 'I know you will graduate soon. We have found the hives. They are full of vicious, disease-carrying monsters. We need your help next time.'

Mandami nodded. 'Okay, Mother.'

Lan collapsed. Caoimhe ran over to him, weeping.

What's wrong? Father, get up, she signed.

The large Mandami picked up his ailing father and strode through the open door.

'He will be okay, Caoimhe.' Ake hugged her daughter. 'Orilan, can you stay with her for a little while?'

Orilan nodded and sat down on a chair. Ake rushed after her husband and son.

—⁓—

Lan moaned and thrashed about on the bed as the poison coursed through his body. Borrush was surrounded in a green light as he lay his hands on the deep scratches across Lan's body.

'Did he take most of the damage?' asked Borrush.

'Yes. Orilan uses spells to fight. While I can fight, I am not a warrior.' Ake continued to apply cold compresses to various parts of Lan's body that felt hot. The skin was angry and red.

Lan opened his eyes briefly and cried out. 'Please don't do this.' His eyes were full of fear.

Orilan pounded the mortar into the herbs in the pestle as he mixed them for a poultice. It was three hours since their return and Lan was getting worse as time progressed.

'I didn't mean to. How can anyone ever forgive me for what I have done?' Lan whimpered.

'The poison affects the soul. The poor lad is reliving some

horrible trauma.' Borrush took a break momentarily and turned to Ake. 'Your turn to try, lassie.'

Ake nodded and placed her hands on Lan's wounds. 'Dee and Sorendee, please bless me with the ability to heal one of your loyal warriors.'

Green light flooded from her hands and engulfed Lan. Lan thrashed about again.

'Father, mystics never marry. We dedicate our lives to research and fine-tuning our bodies for self-defence only. Why are you pushing me to marry her? How can she want a sinner like me? I am soiled.' Lan's eyes fluttered open, rife with fever. He rung his hands in frustration as he battled some inner thought. 'Shame on you for daring to dream she would lay beneath you, welcoming your passion and your love.'

Orilan shoved the herbs into a small pouch and poured liquid from two vials onto the outside of the pouch. He cleared his throat. 'Here is the poultice. I am going to give you two some privacy.'

Borrush grinned. 'It's a bonnie thing to hear a husband speak so of his wife.'

'Some things are better kept between couples.' Orilan grinned.

'Snobby elf.' Borrush stood and clapped him on the back. 'Your father is not as reserved as the rest of you elves it seems.' Borrush winked at Ake and she blushed.

Orilan smiled. 'True.' Orilan waved and opened the trap door and left.

'I am exhausted, lassie. I am going to get ale. Want some?' Borrush squeezed her shoulder.

Ake nodded. 'Sure. And thank you.'

Borrush left and Ake took a break from healing and began applying the poultices. Lan winced and then cried out. Lan tried to grab at the wounds where she had applied the poultices and Ake held him down.

'I will have you. I wish I didn't have to hold back but you are so sweet and innocent.' Lan grinned in his sleep.

Ake smiled and ran her hands through his hair. His fever seemed to be receding.

Lan opened his eyes, and they were full of a desperate need. 'You are mine?'

Ake nodded. 'Of course.'

Lan smiled and closed his eyes and drifted off into a more relaxed sleep. She climbed in next to him, exhausted and fell asleep. She heard someone place something down next to her and mutter, 'There you go, lassie.'

A blanket was thrown on both of them and Ake drifted further into sleep as she heard footsteps receding.

Ake released Lan's hand as he let her through a small gap in the overgrown shrubbery. It was early morning and a gentle breeze whipped the loose tendrils of hair that had escaped her braid and crowned her face. They were in a small, secluded grove she had no idea existed. Situated near the ancient oak forest this part of the grounds had fallen to neglect and wasn't worth the expense to maintain it. She glanced around at four stone benches set in a circle with a large fountain in the middle. The water was murky and the contents were a mixture of algae and rotting vegetation. An elven youth, clad in a skirt of leaves, sat astride a large fish whose mouth was wide open, revealing piping where water would flow. The area was surrounded by large overgrown bushes and eight wooden dummies had been placed around the area.

'Do you want to know the tale behind the youth?' Lan caressed her shoulder in passing and walked over to the fountain. 'A pity it's overgrown.' Lan began pulling out the decaying plant matter.

'Urrgh,' he muttered. He walked past Ake quickly, who noticed a small dead bird in his hand.

'Oh, poor thing,' Ake said sadly.

'I tried to not let you see it.' Lan slipped into the bushes and returned. 'It is dealt with.'

Ake walked over to the fountain and stroked the fish, running her hands over the very detailed scales. She let out a sharp breath and sucked her finger as she cut it on the jagged stone.

Lan took her hand and inspected the finger and winked. 'You will be fine.'

Ake laughed. 'You don't need to look over every wound.'

Lan expression turned serious. 'Infection can attack the smallest wounds. Sometimes people die from small cuts from dirty surfaces rather than wounds gained in battle.'

Ake imitated his serious expression. 'And you must let me heal you just in case.'

'You cheeky lass.' Lan laughed and turned back to the statue. 'I chose this spot for the tale that involves the statue. The youth was called Ge or, simply put, on the move. He was always restless. The story says a traumatic event in his childhood always caused him to run whenever things got too tough. There came a day when Ge fell in love with a maiden called Eon. Eon was highly affectionate and, as her name indicates, loved to embrace others. When the relationship became too serious Ge ran, as usual. Eon followed close behind and when Ge took the rite of adulthood at one hundred years old he failed and fled, fear written on his face. He ran until he hit the ocean, but, as if death was still chasing him, he clambered into the sea's cold embrace.'

'Unfortunately, Ge couldn't swim and began to drown. On knees, her head bowed, brave Eon begged the gods to turn her into a fish to save her beloved. They granted the wish and she swam to Ge who rode the giant fish to safety. Ge turned to thank the fish. In a familiar voice, the fish answered, "Farewell my beloved, live a good life free of terror. I will always be here for you." Ge assaulted the sand with his tears as Eon swam away. He had let the one good thing in his life go because he had allowed fear to overcome him. I recently remembered this story. My mother told me it before I left for Caelestis. She tried to teach me not to let fear prevent me from living my life.' Lan smiled. 'My poor mother, it didn't work. I made the same mistake as Ge. When you found me again, I had given up on us as I thought I frightened you and it seemed pointless as every time I returned home, I couldn't stay. I had given in to fear and despair.' Lan turned to Ake, took her hand and led her over to a stone bench.

Ake backed away from the two familiar spears, their points glistened in the sun. She felt the fear squeeze her heart. *How could he have kept those dreaded spears from the fall of Caelestis?* Lan picked up the Empon Seato and held it out to her.

'I won't touch it. You can't force me to,' Ake stammered.

Lan placed the spear down and picked up Mbel Daoine. It was only a few days after Lan's bout of fever and he was still very weak. He walked towards a target and had to steady himself from fatigue.

The tip flared into life. He pointed it towards the target and fire erupted from the spear, destroying the target. The fire continued and burnt nearby decaying bushes.

Ake sent jets of water to put them out. Lan dropped the spear and the fire stopped.

'You aren't strong enough to control it yet,' said Ake gently.

'Drianna cares very little for my recovery.' Lan picked up Empon Seato and held it out to Ake. She backed away and he followed her.

'Ake, we need every tool to defeat her. I won't push you, but you should at least try.'

'Do you not remember the horror it caused?' Ake shivered.

'Of course, I do. But fear won't help us against Drianna.' He grabbed her hand and placed it on the spear. She gulped in a large amount of air too quickly and choked on her saliva. He let go of her hand and patted her on the back. She closed her eyes and when she opened them he had clasped her hand in his and hefted the shaft of the spear.

Ake glared at him. 'How dare you.'

Lan gave her a winning smile. 'I can be cheeky too.'

'This isn't a game. This spear is dangerous.'

'Any tool when in the hands of an untrained youth is danger- ous.' Lan removed his hand and Ake realised she was still holding the spear. She hurled it away from her. There was a thud as it embedded itself in a dummy.

Lan blinked in surprise. 'When did you learn to hurl a spear like that?'

Ake shrugged and gave him a secret smile.

'Do I have to get it out of you?' Lan sauntered up to her and reached for her. She backed away and he grabbed her and began tickling her. 'Do you yield up the answer.'

Ake was near breathless. 'Okay, Het taught me to hunt. Bows were his thing; I favoured the spear.'

Lan laughed. 'What weapon couldn't he use?'

Ake pondered for a moment. 'Not sure, he could use a trident, short sword, long sword, bow, staff and axe. As far as I know there may have been more.'

'Damn.' Lan gave her a look of envy.

'He was a big man, Lan. You aren't built for heavy weapons.'

'So, not only was he impressive in combat, he was taller and stronger than me too.' Lan gave her a sulking look and Ake rolled her eyes before Lan burst into laughter.

'I thought you were actually upset.'

'Nope.' Lan grinned at her. 'I have an idea. Let's try hunting with that spear. If it is used as a simple weapon, it may not seem so menacing.'

'I guess. Be prepared, I was never good at hunting. The animals were—'

'Too cute.'

Ake blushed. 'Yes.'

'That's okay, we can try something else.'

'No, I want to hunt now.'

'You don't have to prove you can do it, honey. I am sure you did some hunting.'

'Well, actually I haven't.' She hoisted the spear and dashed into the forest.

'Hey, wait you don't know what is in this ancient forest.' Lan swore, grabbed the other spear and chased after her.

—⟶⟶—

Ake snuck along an overgrown path. She had slipped off her shoes like Het had taught her. *I need to become one with the earth so that I remain undetected.* She wriggled her toes, the ground was hard, any sound would vibrate across its surface, easily alerting creatures to their presence. She picked up her shoes and trod lightly over sticks and rocks. She gasped as someone grabbed her from behind.

'Hello, sweetheart,' Lan whispered in her ear.

'You don't even have to try to remain undetected in the forest,' she grumbled.

'Advantages of being an elf, I guess.' Lan stepped in front of her, his eyes scanning the forest. He tilted his head, staring at a coppice of trees. There was a rustling, and a kingfisher flew past. She smiled and turned to Lan.

'It's beautiful.'

'My bird is better looking.'

Ake blushed. 'Cut it out, we are supposed to be hunting.'

'I love the red spots on my bird.' He reached out and caressed her cheek.

Ake stomped past him. 'Bloody elf, always making me almost swoon with his endearments.'

'Hey, wait.' Lan followed close behind. They walked further into the trees, content in each other's company, listening to the sounds of birds and the wind rustling the leaves. Lan grabbed her, pulling her behind him as the area fell silent. They covered their noses as the smell of sewerage assaulted them. A large whooping noise filled the air as something crashed through the undergrowth chasing a herd of deer. A heavily pregnant doe faltered and the beast dragged the defenceless animal towards it.

The gambion was a large ape-like creature whose skin was as rough as stone. Its jagged flesh was a great defence against stronger monsters and the smell deterred most creatures. The creature whooped again as it tore off a leg of the deer. The crunching of teeth on bone reached their ears and Ake turned her head and retched.

'Can't have that thing so close to the school,' muttered Lan.

'That poor deer.' Ake's eyes filled with tears.

'That too. It didn't stand a chance.' Lan gave the deer a sad glance and pointed the spear at the gambion. Fire burst from the tip and pummelled the monster. It howled and rushed towards them. Its flesh began to singe, and it threw itself to the ground in an attempt to extinguish the flames. Lan's shoulders drooped and the flames stopped.

'I'm not fully recovered yet.'

Ake watched him sway on his feet. The beast rose and lunged at him. Lan barely dodged the blow.

'You really aren't well.' Ake grabbed up her spear and the monster whooped and charged her. She stepped back and hurled the weapon. The beast turned and stared at Lan; the spear embedded deeply in its forehead before it dribbled blood and collapsed on the ground. Ake retrieved the spear. Her annoyance caused the spear to glisten as it was pulled from the body covered in the water of life. Ake walked over to Lan and offered him a hand up, still holding the spear. As their hands made contact, Lan's body tensed and she watched his arm change form into a serpent. She concentrated on the spear's essence and willed it to change Lan back. Lan narrowly avoided the serpent's poisonous fangs as it tried to strike his face.

'Honey, concentrate on your own will, like you do when you manipulate water. Sense it—' Lan grabbed the serpent's head with his other hand and squeezed. 'Ouch. It appears to be its own being, yet I feel it as if it's still my own arm. How bizarre.'

Ake closed her eyes and sensed the pull of magic. To her it felt like a raging river pulling her towards it. 'How does magic feel to you?'

'Like silk, seductive.'

Ake giggled and opened her eyes. Lan blushed.

'Lusty elf, aren't you. I've heard like a building storm, cold as ice or like the flames of the underworld. But never seductive.'

'Ake, this is serious. Sense it, like a raging river pulling you towards it then manipulate it to your will.'

'How did you know my magic manifested like that for me?'

Lan grinned. 'When you were in my body I did a little exploring of your senses.'

'While being overwhelmed by basilisk poison? You could barely fight it.'

Lan winked. 'You helped me defeat it. In the few seconds our souls connected, I needed to understand why it felt like we had met each other lifetimes ago. Now, Ake, bloody concentrate or you will have to put up with a husband who has a serpent for an arm.' Lan grinned.

Ake felt for the magic and began to manipulate it like she did all water magic. Slowly, Lan's arm returned to normal. Lan sighed and sat on a nearby rock.

'I did it.' Ake jumped for joy, her squeals echoing in the forest. An angry crow swooped her.

'Sorry, Mr crow.' Ake laughed. The crow swooped her again and flew back to its nest. Ake walked over to Lan and knelt by him. 'Are you okay?'

He nodded. 'Just give me a few moments, then we will head back. I believe you are no longer frightened of the spear.'

Ake gave him a slight smile. 'Less so.'

'Please practice with it.' Lan glanced at his arm. 'Maybe when you're alone.'

'I will try.' Ake held out her hand and he took it, then stood and they left the forest.

——〜〜——

Ake walked along the beach with Empon Seato in her hand. She turned and stared at the waves. *If I have to wield it like water then I may as well be near its influence.* She had tried to use the weapon's magic several times since the incident with the gambion and had failed. She closed her eyes and breathed in deeply. She felt for the pull of the raging ocean and held up the weapon, pointing it out to sea. She felt the ebb and flow of the spear in tune with her own sense of self and began to manipulate the magic emanating from the spear.

'Are you okay, miss?' Ake opened her eyes and saw a fisherman carrying a simple rod made of a stick and rope. His face suddenly froze in shock and his mouth began to droop as the flesh peeled away. Ake threw the spear into the ocean and grabbed the man as he collapsed.

'Help,' she screamed. She lay the man down and ran from one end of the beach to the other, looking for help. She saw no one so lifted the heavy man up and ran towards Caelestis, sobbing. She felt the man's breath become shallower and she stopped and lay him on the ground. The last of his breaths faltered in his chest at he succumbed to the horrific injury. Ake began to weep. Someone knelt down beside her.

Ake turned her head to Amities. 'It's not your fault, Mother.'

'You followed me.' Ake's lip trembled. 'I murdered an innocent man.'

'It was an accident. You are not ready to wield that spear, Mother. I have taken care of it.'

They turned their heads at the pounding footsteps behind them and Orilan rushed towards them. His eyes darted around, taking in the scene.

'Go get Father, Amities. I will deal with the body.' Orilan picked up the body as Ake stood.

Ake watched Orilan's eyes fill with worry.

'This isn't your fault. Father insisted you try to use it.'

'This is hardly Lan's fault.'

Orilan shrugged. 'What's done is done. What matters is if you're okay.'

Ake turned on him in anger. 'Aren't you worried about the poor dead man and his family?'

Orilan grinned. 'He doesn't feel anymore and as for his family, they aren't my family.'

Ake growled at him. 'You are acting evil, Orilan. Have you no feelings or empathy for the innocent?'

Orilan grimaced. 'How can I feel for those I don't know?'

'That is part of being a decent person. Helping the sick, injured and vulnerable.'

Orilan became lost in thought before he smiled at Ake. 'So, I should learn advanced healing and help others so I become more humane.' Orilan turned and strode away.

Lan teleported in front of Ake and she ran into his arms, sobbing out her grief.

'It's not your fault.' Lan gave her a gentle smile. 'I will find out who he was and try to help his family somehow.' Lan's mouth was set in a hard frown, his brows furrowed with concern. 'The mayor of the village may seek justice.' He pulled her close. 'I'll sort it.'

'No, I must endure any punishment thrown at me.'

Lan sighed. 'I won't allow that. I am responsible for encouraging you to train with that spear.' Lan teleported them to Mencrey. He gripped Ake's arm as she tried to run towards the mayor's house. She struggled, pulling her hand away.

'Let me go.'

'I will not.' Lan hauled her along towards the large wooden shack. He knocked on the door. There was some scuffling within, and the door opened.

A portly, well-dressed gentlemen greeted them. 'Why, if it isn't Trebrelan. I assume this is your bride I married you to all those years ago.'

Ake pulled her hand away and glared at Lan before turning to face the mayor.

'Hello—'

'Yes, this is my bride and by that law I invoke clemency for a crime committed by her. As you know, a woman cannot be held accountable for her actions as a husband is responsible for her.'

Ake stomped on his foot. He winced and ignored her.

'That isn't how this works. If I committed a crime I am responsible for it.' Ake gave the mayor a beatific smile. 'As you can see, your honourable mayor, I am quite capable of being responsible for my actions.'

The mayor laughed. 'You are a pretty thing and young by the looks of it. What crime could a mere slip of a girl commit that would cause a husband to beseech clemency for her?'

'I killed someone. I used a magic spear crafted by a goddess and melted the poor soul's face. I had closed my eyes and invoked the magic but he walked in front of the spear.'

The mayor's mouth dropped open in surprise. 'What does your husband say about this admission?'

Lan frowned 'She didn't want to use the spear and I insisted she learn.'

'I see.' The mayor glanced away, his fist on his chin, lost in thought. 'Are you not the headmaster of that magic school?'

Lan nodded. 'Mystic school, but yes.'

'So, you would be well aware of the danger of such items but insisted she use it?'

Ake scowled at the men. 'I did this. He had nothing to do with it.'

'Is there evidence? I need to see this body and this spear before I pass judgement. I will wait here with the woman while you go and find me the evidence, Lan.'

Lan nodded and teleported away.

The mayor turned to Ake. 'Wish I could do that.'

Ake smiled again at the mayor. 'Now my loyal husband is gone, I beg you to punish me and not him.'

The mayor scratched his head and looked away awkwardly. 'I am sorry, miss, even if your husband hadn't asked for clemency, the law still holds him accountable. It is wise he brought it to us straight away or we would believe he is trying to circumnavigate the so-called crime.'

It was nearly nightfall, and a cold wind blew. Ake shivered.

'Come inside, Madam Scryer.'

'My name is Telewanake.'

The mayor scoffed. 'I can't call you by your name. It is customary to address you with your husband's last name. In our tongue he is Star Scryer, therefore you are Mrs Scryer. I see why your husband is concerned for your well-being when you don't even know our customs.'

'I am aware of the custom,' growled Ake.

'Very temperamental girl too. You must give your husband trouble.'

Ake poked her finger into his shoulder. 'How dare you treat me as inferior.'

The mayor slapped her hand away and whistled. A guard approached; his gaze fixed on the mayor. Ake lowered her hand and gave the mayor a sheepish grin.

'Take this woman over to the inn. Her blood is heated by the guilt of her husband's crime and it has meddled with her senses. See to it she drinks a dram of ale to refresh her wits.'

Ake's wrist was grabbed, and she was pulled along. 'This isn't over. I am responsible.'

'As far as I'm concerned you are too prone to anger and loss of wits. Your testimony can't be trusted. I will settle this with your husband.'

'Orilan saw the body too,' Ake yelled out. 'He is a witness to my crime.'

The mayor turned and entered his home.

—⁓—

Doors slammed and hurried footsteps echoed along the corridor. As he lay on his bed, the door to his bedroom swung open and Orilan grinned at his father.

'Where is the body, Orilan?'

'What body?'

Lan strode over to him, his face darkening with anger.

'If looks could kill, I would be dead.' Orilan got off the bed and smiled at his father. Lan took a step back as he took a step forward.

'This is serious. I could hang for this.'

'Only if there is evidence.'

Lan growled and grabbed the collar of Orilan's shirt. 'What did you do with the spears and the body?'

An evil grin spread across Orilan's face. 'I am sorry, you won't find them. If you ask Amities his thoughts will be hazy. You see, we shared a very humane brew. Your dear sweet Ake said I needed to consider others' feelings and my brother was distraught. I gave him a memory brew. His memories of where he hid the spears shall return in a few years. I had some of the brew too so I honestly don't know what I did with the body.'

Lan unclasped his collar and began to shake with rage. 'I am sick of all this horror. My poor Ake must be so distraught.'

Orilan gave Lan a gentle smile. 'It's okay, Father.'

Lan tensed as Orilan gripped him in a hug.

'Let me go, Ori. This is very awkward.'

Orilan released him and Lan sighed before teleporting away.

As if I would drink the brew. I own my actions whether evil or good. No one will hurt you or Ake if I can prevent it. Now I have time to bury the body. Orilan drew back the covers on the bed.

'You made yourself quite at home.' Orilan hoisted the body and opened his wardrobe. Inside was a shovel he had hastily thrown in there. He grabbed it and teleported a distance away from Caelestis. He placed the body down.

'Corruptus mortus,' cried Orilan. The ground cracked open, and a skeleton clawed its way out.

Orilan handed it the shovel. 'Bury him.' *Pity it can only be summoned once a day.*

The skeleton buried the body and as the spell waned the skeleton collapsed. Orilan pushed it back into its grave with the toe of his boot. *What would Ake do now?*

'Rest in peace,' Orilan said over the freshly turned dirt and smiled to himself. *Now to track Father.*

Lan had handed over the gold when a woman carrying a fishing rod approached the mayor. Her eyes darted about looking for someone and her eyes appeared puffy from weeping.

'Sorry to interrupt, mayor.' The woman bowed and held the rod up. Lan's eyes were riveted to the shaft; it was engraved with initials.

'My husband is missing. I found his rod on the beach.'

The mayor turned and glared at Lan. 'I see.'

The woman's gaze kept darting from one to the other. 'What is going on?'

The mayor gave the woman a disarming smile. 'Here, take some gold. When we have news of your husband we will let you know. Can I borrow that for now?'

The woman nodded and handed over the fishing rod. 'Leave now, please.'

The woman wandered away.

'I will have to confirm your wife saw this rod. Unfortunately, I will have to discipline you. According to your wife, it was an accident so you will not hang.'

Lan shuffled his feet and looked towards the tavern. 'I insist she goes home. She has been through enough. Tell her I am doing community service.'

'I can do that.' A guard wandered over and the mayor had a quiet conversation with him. The guard approached Lan. 'Hold out your wrists.'

Lan held out his wrists and they were tied together. The man prodded him in the chest. 'Get moving, you are in for a rough night.'

Lan grumbled and began to walk.

———

Ake tapped her foot impatiently and tried to rise again. The guard pushed her shoulder down.

'Sit still, my lady. Your lord husband will return soon, do not fret. I am sure he will sort it out.'

Ake let out a sound of annoyance. 'I am not my husband's charge. I can take care of myself.'

The guard sighed. 'This display of impertinence is ill-befitting of an elven noble woman.'

'I see common women share their feelings often.'

The guard grinned. 'We all know they act common because they are common.'

'That's prejudiced.' Ake tried to rise again. 'I am no elf.'

The guard ran his fingers over her slightly pointed ears.

'No human woman has ears shaped like this and the tilt of your eyebrows and eye shape indicate you are probably half-elven or a parent was.'

Ake pushed his hands away. 'Don't touch me, you brute.'

'Not very timid for an elven woman. They usually shy away or politely decline touch. You haven't been raised well.'

'And how many actual elven women do you know?'

'A few before they were massacred. Timid in public, great lovers.'

The barkeep whistled. 'Elf's drink's up.'

The guard fetched Ake's drink and held it out to her. 'Courtesy of the mayor.'

Ake took it. 'Thanks.' She stared at the guard. 'I am not elven. Why are people now referring to me as such when they have never done so before?'

The guard smiled and appeared to relax as Ake stopped trying to flee. 'Elves are rare. Anyone associated with their heritage is almost akin to fae. Their race is now cursed, and anyone associated with them is said to meet a fate worse than death.'

'That is ridiculous.'

The guard laughed. 'I know, but townsfolk are very superstitious and rumours spread like religious doctrines and become almost the recognised truth.'

The mayor entered the tavern and approached Ake.

'Do you recognise this rod?'

Ake swallowed and nodded. 'Yes. It's the fisherman's.'

'You are free to go, lass. There is no body and no weapon so there is really no evidence of any crime. Your husband has paid reparations and will be volunteering for community service to make up for it.' The mayor pointed towards the door.

'Please, no. I need to be absolved of my crime. What community service is my husband doing?'

'Mucking out stables in the local farms. He insisted that you wouldn't let this rest unless reparations were made.'

'When does he start?' Ake rose to her feet.

'He insisted he begin immediately. He also asked us to tell you to return home.'

Ake sighed and left the mayor and guard staring after her.

'No manners,' she heard the mayor say.

I will find you, Lan. You won't disappear on me again. Ake smiled as she saw Orilan run past and followed.

Lan rubbed his sore wrists and looked around. They had entered a cemetery. An elderly man was digging many graves. Lan looked at the bodies piled up nearby in various states of decay from disease and other ailments. He made a quick count. *About one hundred*. The guard handed him a shovel.

'Bury them.'

Lan nodded and approached the bodies. The smell hit him and he gagged. He took out a cloth and put it over his mouth and nose and tied it behind his ears. He began to dig. After several hours the guard offered him a flask, the aroma of strong wine wafted from the vessel.

Lan pointed to the elderly gentlemen. 'That man is older. He should be the first to drink.'

The guard laughed. 'He has buried one body you are on fifteen. You have earned a sip or two.'

'If he can't drink I shall not either.'

The guard shrugged and went and perched himself on a rock and began to scull the wine.

Lan sighed and went back to his work. He was startled as Orilan appeared next to him with a shovel.

'What do you want? I am busy.'

Orilan grinned. 'Ake made me feel bad about the body's disappearance. I didn't want you hung. I am here to help.'

'Oi.' The guard approached them. 'Get out of here, you.' The guard pointed to Orilan. 'Before I belt you one.'

'Sorry, Father.' Orilan wandered over and sat down on a dirt mound and watched his father continue his work.

Orilan turned and there was a yelp as he hauled Ake up from behind the mound. 'Why did you follow me? I don't like to be followed.' He smirked at Ake.

'Get out of here, Ake,' yelled Lan not even turning to look at her. 'This is no place for you.'

'He is right you know.' Orilan grinned at Ake. 'This is hideous work, even for stalwart men.'

Lan turned and rolled his eyes at Orilan. 'She's seen enough death. It is not a matter of her being a woman.'

Ake stood with a smug look on her face, hands on her hips, staring at Orilan. 'See.'

'Aren't you childish.' Orilan laughed and ran away as Ake swatted at him.

'Enough!' Lan crossed his arms and frowned. 'I have enough to do without being distracted by you two.'

Orilan watched the guard fall asleep, drunk from his wine. Ake stopped to stare at the guard. Orilan's eyes widened in surprise when he realised Ake was holding his shovel. 'How did you do that?'

Ake ignored him and walked over to the old man. She took him by the hand and led him over to the mound, passing the guard. 'Sit, please.' Ake helped the old man lower himself and handed him the guard's flask. 'Drink.'

'Thank you, lass.' The man touched her hand and began to drink.

'What the hell?' Orilan grinned. 'Now you have the flask too.'

Ake strode past him and began to dig. Lan wandered over to her as he saw her gag. He withdrew his spare handkerchief and tied it around her face and returned his work. Orilan shrugged and began lifting bodies and throwing them into holes the others dug.

'Show some respect, Ori,' said Lan.

'They are dead.'

'Imagine if that was Dane's body you were tossing in there.' Ake stared at Orilan, disgust on her face.

Orilan looked down at the aged male body in his grave. 'Yeah, you didn't even think to ask me to say goodbye and you wonder why I don't understand certain things. Everyone leaves me out. I'm an inbred demon not worthy of care.'

'I am sorry we left you out, Ori. But you kissed my wife and tried to kill me once. At that time I don't think we were worried if you were hurting.'

'True.' Orilan shrugged. 'It doesn't matter.'

'It obviously does. I am sorry.' Lan glanced up at Orilan. 'You are worthy of care.'

Orilan looked away, a variety of emotions flittering across his face. 'I'll be gentler with the bodies.'

They quickened their pace and finished the job as the sun rose. Orilan and Ake left before the guard woke and Lan eased the old man to his feet.

The guard groaned and opened his bleary eyes. 'Well done. You can go now.'

Lan nodded and began the hour's walk home, needing exercise to relax his exhausted muscles and clear his mind. As he approached Caelestis Ake was waiting out the front, dozing in the sun. She had changed. He picked her up and she opened her eyes.

'You came back.'

I said I would.' He kissed her. 'How are you coping after that fisherman's death?'

Tears filled her eyes. 'Not so good.' She wrinkled her nose.

'Yep, I smell awful.' He rubbed his face against hers.

'I just bathed.'

'Now you will have to join me.'

Ake laughed and he carried her inside.

Lan entered the classroom and looked around the brightly painted room. His eyes alighted on the new painting Ake had done of a proud griffin soaring over a herd of horses. Lan had described Cory to her, and this had been his secret birthday surprise a week earlier. He smiled at the memory.

He had been eating his breakfast, trying to avoid his wife who was insistent on him having a cake in front of the staff. He heard Ake laughing in the hallway outside the cafeteria and rose. He sculled the cup of tea and grabbed a piece of toast and his textbooks and began to walk towards the doorway. He saw her talking to Orilan.

'I'll get him for you. Fancy avoiding his gentle wife.' Orilan turned and grinned at Lan.

'I am not avoiding Ake. I am avoiding the embarrassment of the human need to sing to family members and indulge in sweets on the anniversary of their birth.' Lan smiled.

Ake withdrew a cloth from her pockets. 'So, it's okay for you to spoil me and our children on our birthdays but it is not acceptable for you.'

'Damn, you have me there.' Lan grinned. 'I will accept any gift you give me but no singing.' Lan's eyes trailed down Ake's body and he winked at her. Ake blushed.

Orilan looked away. 'That was awful, Father. In front of your own son.'

Lan shrugged. 'It was harmless enough.'

Ake walked over to Lan. 'Close your eyes.'

Lan closed his eyes and grinned in amusement.

'I'll leave you to it.' Orilan strode away.

Lan felt soft silk lowered over his eyes and felt it tighten as Ake tied the blindfold. 'I like this.' He turned sensing her movement and pulled her into his arms.

'Lan—'

Ake giggled as he kissed her nose and cheek and then found her mouth. Lan broke the kiss as he heard the sound of footsteps approaching. Ake took his hand and led him down the corridor. He felt each turn and his familiarity with the layout of the fortress suggested she was taking him to his history classroom. He heard a door open and close and she led him towards a wall. She began to untie his blindfold but before she could, he pushed her against the wall.

'Are we alone?'

'Yes.'

His mouth found hers and she responded. He pulled away and she removed the blindfold and stepped away from him laughing.

'Wanton elf.'

Lan gave her a flirtatious smile until the picture caught his eye and he stared at it in shock. He turned and smiled at Ake with tears in his eyes.

'Thank you,' he whispered.

'You're welcome. Happy birthday. I have to go teach gardening now. But keep that blindfold for later.' Ake winked and strode from the room.

—◦◦◦—

Lan ran his hand over the detailed artwork and sighed. 'I miss you, dear friend.' He went to his desk that sat to the left side of the front wall and grabbed some chalk. In the centre of the front wall was a large blackboard. He began to write.

Today's lesson: The history of Din and Dage and the Alliance.

Lan placed down the chalk and brushed his hands together. He picked up three textbooks from his desk and placed them on the three desks with two seats a piece. He heard the sound of his students arriving, the door swung open, and they came through the door talking among themselves. They sat down and Lan went and stood near the blackboard.

'Please turn to page fifteen and continue yesterday's dictation.'

A student read aloud before Mandami stood up and took his turn.

'Din and Dage argued over the best possible place to build Caelestis. The two brothers parted ways, and each sought an isle of their own. Din came upon the Anwyl elves and their king, Swan Rider. Swan Rider invited both Din and Dage to attend a feast and dancing. The king's wise words allowed the brothers to reconcile their differences and they settled on the island of Man'hannon. The unmarried brother, Din would dedicate his life to research, learning and teaching others to hone their bodies for defence so that when the child of prophecy was born, the chosen mystic among them would take her as a bride, breaking all taboos to protect her. Dage was the last great elven smith. His line eventually declined resulting in one half-elven descendant, Regona ...' Mandami stared around as the classroom was filled with an awkward silence.

Some of the students whispered among themselves.

Lan picked up the book from his desk and blushed as he read the passage. He gestured to Mandami. Eighteen-year-old Mandami rose and walked over to him.

'I have never read this information before. Where did your mother find these books?' asked Lan quietly.

'Orilan retrieved them from the restricted area after the fall of the druid academy.' Mandami shrugged.

'Okay, return to your seat, please.'

Mandami sat down. Lan walked over to the desks and began retrieving the books the students had been sharing.

'Headmaster, that's unfair,' said one student.

'Mystics never hide knowledge,' muttered another.

'He just doesn't want us to know that his wife is the child of prophecy,' whispered a girl.

'He should be proud,' said a boy.

'He doesn't like to be the centre of attention,' said Amities.

Lan raised his hand for silence. 'I will have to read the book to see if it is appropriate for students. Please take out your old copy of *The History of Eriu* please.'

Lan went back to his desk and flipped through the pages. 'Chapter six, page one, *The Alliance*. Amities, please read.'

Amities mumbled quietly. 'It was at the beginning of the seventh age of man that the Daione Sidhe, the dwarves and the halflings felt pity for humankind. Drianna's corruption had caused the species to almost destroy itself. The Alliance was formed to aid humankind. Din and Dage founded the mystic order, vowing to treat humans and elves equally and educate them to better themselves. The dwarves vowed to pit their strength against monsters but refused to divulge their secrets to the weak species of humankind. The elves of Caley worked with the wiser of human folk and created the first druid academy. They vowed to share their healing and knowledge with all—'

The bell rang and the students closed their books and stood. Lan bowed to them, and they bowed back. As the students left the room Lan grabbed one of the four textbooks and went to meet Ake to discuss the reading material.

Orilan listened intently, hoping to discern his prey's whereabouts. He heard tiny feet running across the grass and opened his eyes. Caoimhe stopped and glared at him before signing rapidly at him.

You cheated, Ori, no peeping.

Orilan grinned. 'I don't remember that rule.'

Caoimhe squealed with delight as Orilan began to chase her.

'Raargh, I am the big, scary monster come to eat a tiny girl.' Orilan laughed.

Caoimhe ran towards the field where Ake was teaching horse care to five of the students. She had read countless books on the topic over the last six months and had daily care lessons with local farmers.

'Caoimhe, stop,' yelled Orilan.

Ake ran towards Caoimhe.

The little girl stopped in front of a horse who reared up and began to lash out.

Caoimhe screamed. Just before the hooves crashed down onto the child, a book was thrown at the beast, and it backed off disgruntled. Ake looked around as Caoimhe was nowhere to be found. Ake began to shake, and her heart skipped a beat. She turned as she heard Caoimhe giggle.

Caoimhe sat astride a gentle mare. Lan held her upon the horse.

'Not all horses are temperamental, Caoimhe. You must take care from now on, horses are prey animals and will run or act out in fear. You must approach them gently and quietly. Promise me.' Lan smiled at his daughter.

Caoimhe nodded. Okay, Father.

Ake rushed over and grabbed Caoimhe in her arms, sobbing as she cradled the child. Her face drained of all colour.

Orilan approached Lan. 'I am so sorry. It happened so quickly.'

Lan shrugged. 'Accidents happen. Caoimhe is fine.'

'I don't think she is.' Orilan gestured to Ake.

'You are correct.' Lan dismissed the students and began leading the two mares into the barn.

Orilan followed as Lan handed the reigns to the stable hands.

'What about Ake?' Orilan asked.

Lan turned to Orilan. 'Take Caoimhe back to the fortress. I will see to her.'

Orilan strode from the barn and approached Ake. 'I'll take her back to the fortress. Are you okay?'

Caoimhe struggled in her mother's arms, signing rapidly. Put me down, Mother, I am fine. I am almost grown.

Ake put Caoimhe down. 'No, you are not. Go with your brother now. I am glad you are okay.'

Caoimhe stomped her feet. I can go on my own.

Why are you so stubborn? Ake signed back.

Caoimhe began to sprint towards Caelestis and Orilan ran after her.

Ake watched as Lan exited the barn. 'I'll be right back. I'll will check on Caoimhe.'

'Wait—' Ake watched teary-eyed as Lan disappeared on the spot. She turned to leave when her eyes alighted on Lan's stallion, Brady, was unattended. Ake hugged her arms to herself awaiting his return.

—⁓—

Caoimhe raced past the doorway and felt a hand reach out and grab her. She whistled angrily and stared up into her father's face.

'My stubborn daughter, I knew you would try to avoid having to stay in the fortress.' Lan smiled at her angry expression.

I am not a baby, Father. Put me down.

'Not until you agree to stay inside. Your mother and I were terrified.'

Caoimhe nodded. Fine.

'Are you injured at all?'

No.

Lan gave her a brief hug. 'I am relieved. I must attend your mother now.'

See, Mother, needs you more than I. She is sensitive, so tend to your wife.

Lan laughed. 'Your mother is just being a mother. She is fiercely independent when necessary, just like her indignant daughter.'

Caoimhe poked her tongue at him.

He grinned. 'Just like her.'

Orilan rushed up and took Caoimhe by the hand. Lan smiled at him and disappeared.

Lan teleported next to Brady. He laughed and led his temperamental stallion over to Ake. 'Caoimhe is like you.'

'I am not so stubborn.'

Lan rolled his eyes. 'Sure.'

'I don't want to startle the poor thing.' Ake backed off from the horse. 'Is Caoimhe okay?'

'Yes, she is fine.'

'I should go check on her.'

'Trust me, she is fine. You already checked her for injuries, and I have just seen to her now.' Lan smiled.

'I guess so.' Ake looked back towards Caelestis, concern on her face.

Brady pawed the ground. Ake turned back to Lan.

'Shouldn't you put Brady away? He is very nervous.'

'I don't want you to use Brady for your classes until I have had a chance to train him further.'

'I thought he was okay.'

'He is with me. But he is still young.' Ake cried out as Lan lifted her onto the horse who nickered nervously. He leapt up behind her. With pressure from his knees the beautiful stallion leapt forward, its long luxurious mane and tail whipping in the breeze. Its huge powerful muscles drove it forward with great agility. Lan ran his hand down the shiny coat and the horse began to slow, lifting its hooves in a delicate trot, the feathers on its feet fluttered in response.

Ake laughed with delight as he encouraged the horse to gallop towards the oak forest. The horse slowed and wound its way through the trees. The sky was beginning to streak with orange and red as dusk crept in.

'Are you okay?' Lan whispered in Ake's ear.

'I am now.'

Lan whistled and the horse stopped. He slid down and pulled her off the horse and into his arms.

'Caoimhe gave me the fright of my life too.'

'She is so lucky you where there.'

Lan nodded. 'Lucky I came to discuss those books on history.'

Lan let go of the reins and Brady began to nose the ground, eating emerging shoots of tender grasses.

'What about them?'

Lan sighed. 'They mention our lives in great detail.'

Ake shrugged. 'It's one person's interpretation of history. Our future isn't set in stone. Apart from one more passage mentioning how our son and I must destroy Drianna, there is very little else.'

Lan sighed with relief.

Ake laughed. 'We wouldn't want a mystic in the limelight, would we?'

'I prefer—'

'A quiet uneventful life. I am sorry, Lan, but that isn't our fate.'

'Okay, I will return the books to the classroom tomorrow then.' Lan smiled.

'I do have a question though.'

'What is it?' asked Lan.

Caelestis is over forty thousand years old, an ancient place for humans. Flo once said it really wasn't very old, only six elven life-times. How can that be if elves can only live up to two thousand years?'

Lan grinned. 'You won't get elves to change their version of the facts. It is said elves used to live over six thousand years. Some elves even believe a few of our kind can still do so.'

Ake laughed. 'I guess Flo had her pride too.'

Lan looked up at the sky as the first few stars began to twin-kle and the moon began to rise. 'I am glad we have these sweet moments.'

'I agree.'

'Let's go home.' Lan lifted Ake up onto Brady and joined her in the saddle.

Brady reared up at Lan's abruptness and Ake cried out as the horse galloped. She turned and smiled at Lan, her eyes alight with the thrill of their race. *She drives me wild.*

Lan's hands slid around her waist, and he turned her in the sad-dle to straddle him. His mouth took hers and she was lost in the passionate embrace. He released her hair from its ties, and it flared out behind her. Brady began to slow, and Lan released her. Her cheeks were hot with passion and her lips swollen from his kisses.

'Damn, you're beautiful and you're all mine.' He grinned charmingly at her.

Ake blushed.

Lan whistled and the horse halted as they approached the sta-bles. Lan jumped down and Ake slid into his arms. He took the reins in one hand and her hand in the other and lead Brady into the barn and removed the saddle. Ake curried the stallion with a comb before he was led into a stall. Lan picked her up and tele-ported them into the loft.

'This stallion will have his mare.' He pushed her down into the hay and nickered in her ear.

Ake laughed at the ridiculousness of it. 'You are so cute some-times.'

'A cute elf, that's new.' Lan grinned and began to unbutton her gown.

He drew off his clothes and flung them away. Brady kicked his stall in anger as the garments landed on him.

They both laughed.

Lan withdrew the blindfold from his pocket and tied it over his eyes.

Ake giggled. 'I had forgotten about that.'

'Now, let's see how well I know you.' Lan's mouth found hers and she was swept up in his passion.

Eighteen-year-old Amities gasped and put his bleeding finger into his mouth and sucked as the warm metallic taste coated his tongue. After the bleeding had stopped, he tried to jam a small blade into a hollow metal chamber. It clicked into place. 'Woohoo,' he cried.

'ZZZZZZZZZZ,' whispered something in his ear.

Amities jumped and scrambled to his feet, knocking over his chair and stumbling in the process. His eyes darted about the room looking for any intruder. He shuddered, noticing the door ajar. *I closed that.* A slow clapping began and sweat beaded down Amities' forehead as he slowly turned his head towards the sound, his lips trembling with fear.

'You finally got it in place.' Orilan grinned at him. Seated in a chair, he was rocking back and forth, the legs hovered precari-ously before landing on all fours. Scowling, Amities sprinted over to him and shoved Orilan in the chest.

'S—.' The chair crashed to the floor.

Orilan laughed and pushed Amities off him and stood.

Amities leapt to his feet. 'That was horrible.'

'Shows how vulnerable you are. While Mandami is training to defend himself, you have secreted yourself away with tomes and cogs.'

Amities scoffed. 'I am working on items to help others in battles.'

'Okay, great inventor, I need your help. I sensed something enter Caelestis. Father, Mandami and Ake are still exhausted from defeating the last hive and I would let them sleep.'

Amities smiled. 'No one ever asks for my help.'

'They can never find you.' Orilan laughed. 'Also, how would you defend yourself?'

Amities held up the strange new invention. 'You see this blade attached to this chamber? The chamber is hollow and contains more blades. The cog on the side of the weapon can be turned and this window will change to various elvish symbols including fire, earth, water, air, ice and lightening. The user then enchants the chamber with various spells for each symbol and the device stores them. There is a button on the top that fires the blade by using a simple internal sling shot and the dagger is imbued with the magic as it hits its target.'

'Sounds impressive. But does it work?' Orilan snatched the weapon and turned the dial to earth. 'Dee ro.' The device vibrated and a puff of brown smoke wafted from the inner chamber.

'Earth arrow. A good choice,' said Amities.'

Orilan grinned. 'How—'

Amities stayed him with a hand. 'I sat in on every magic class. Just because I can't cast magic, doesn't mean I am not aware of how it's done. The basic element spells are *Earth Arrow, Mystic Fire, Water Jet, Ice Puddle* and *Static*.'

'We will start with one in case it blows up on you.' Orilan

handed Amities back the weapon. 'What's with the two gold-en-knotted interlocking hearts engraved on the side?'

Amities shrugged. 'Appears every time they talk …' *Better not to say anything. Even Ori will think I'm odd.* Amities cleared his throat. 'Appears whenever I try to combine science and magic.'

'We better go. We have lingered enough.' Orilan jogged to the door and stuck his head out into the hallway. 'It's headed to the guest room.'

'What is?'

Orilan stepped out into the hallway and Amities followed. They strode quickly down dark hallways, taking turns until Orilan pushed himself against the wall, Amities did the same. Orilan turned his head, his eyes riveted on Amities; fear lurked in their depths. 'Drianna's apostates,' he mouthed. Orilan hugged himself as several shadows passed them. A coldness crept up through Amities' toes, stopping his breath in his lungs. His blood felt like it froze within his veins and his heart thudded dully in his chest like it was forgetting its purpose. *Accept the darkness. Give in to power and death. Drianna awaits,* something screamed in his mind.

Amities clawed at the being who shook him. 'Snap out of it, little brother.' Amities pushed Orilan away. 'What the hell was that?'

'Drianna's apostates trying to convert the disparaged, the cruel and the lost dreamers to her cause.' Orilan's gaze dropped to the floor, and he sighed. 'My earliest memory.'

'That's horrible.'

Orilan blinked in surprise as Amities enveloped him in a hug. They stayed that way for a few minutes before they walked down the corridor; their soft footfalls a welcome sound in the deadly silence.

—⁓—

Borrush gripped his buxom bride in the throes of passion, he groaned and opened his eyes trying to capture her eyes with his own. 'F—!'

He tried to throw off the being that clung to him; a corpse almost stripped of its flesh. Its wet straggling hair was gripped around his wrists. It moaned and its jaw became unhinged, and a vile green liquid spewed from its mouth. The smell was wretched, and he gagged.

'Come on, lover boy. Drianna awaits.'

The tendrils of hair writhed and tried to drag him closer. A foul, yellow tongue licked his mouth and he coughed. He yelped in pain as the hair found his tender regions and wrapped itself around him. Black druid fire erupted from his hands and the entity screeched and released him, Its head spun in circles, and it scurried up the wall, hung from the roof and began to spew the foul contents from its decaying stomach. Borrush grabbed a broom nearby and smacked it off the roof. Its body snapped in half. Screeching, it dragged itself towards the open door.

'Borrush, we are coming in,' cried Orilan, rushing in through the door as the creature crawled over his bare toes.

Amities squealed and Orilan ignored it.

'Are ye not disturbed by Drianna's spawn?' Borrush shoved Orilan out the way and closed the door.

'In my younger years that would have appeared as a magical fairy or a beautiful servant. When the blindfold was pulled from my eyes, I saw them for what they were, and my mind tried to protect me and normalised it.' Orilan shrugged.

'No wonder you were a messed-up git.' Borrush shook his head. 'How many of these things are there and how did they get in?'

'I originally had protective wards up. When my father came home, accepting that he was the former Lord of Death, I had to weaken the shield. I never renewed them, or Father would have been kept from us again. They have weakened and become almost non-existent,' said Orilan.

'What do they want?' asked Amities.

'Ake and Mandami,' said Orilan.

'Hell.' Amities ran to the door and opened it. 'Father and Mandami have been taking turns patrolling the forest in the hours before dawn and just before dusk. Father said he had felt Drianna's influence creeping ever closer.'

Borrush yawned. 'What of it?'

Orilan's eyes widened in shock, and he ran from the room.

Amities blushed as Borrush grabbed a pair of scissors and cut the hair loose. 'It's not good when a man is tense.' Borrush laughed. 'Stop being so bashful, lad. We are both men.'

Amities shook his head. 'No shame. We need to hurry; my mother is exhausted and alone.'

'Hell lad, why didn't you say so?' Borrush threw on a robe.

'I did.'

They sprinted down the hallway. 'Yeah boy, I'm a dwarf, don't sugar-coat it boy.' Borrush grinned. 'You look perplexed boy.'

'I am,' said Amities.

Ake's screams rent the air as they turned the corner. Orilan was flinging paralysis spells as a horde of undead shuffled towards him, while six green imps had wrapped themselves around him, biting and slashing at him with their claws.

'This really is the epitome of a slow death,' cried Orilan as he tried to pull the creatures from his body.

Ake was held against the wall by the foul creature that had failed to enter the wards years ago. Fate's beautiful face whispered against Ake's ear as her reptilian appendages held her against the wall.

'As Drianna grows more powerful, she creeps closer. I know you sense her and have been putting up wards to protect the island, my little divine one.' The beast shuddered and sniffed her hair. 'It has left you exhausted. The little divine essence still left leaves its delicious mark on you.' Fate's head licked Ake's cheek and she shuddered.

Borrush sent wave after wave of druid fire into the masses of undead. They exploded and were replaced by shadows. The shadows weaved in and out of human and demon-like silhouettes. Horns and claws were replaced with humanoid limbs before reverting back. Borrush grunted as the shadows charged. He tumbled to the floor and was thrust against another wall as the shadows cascaded over him like a giant wave. The never-ending onslaught mimicking the deadly depths of a bottomless ocean. He gasped for breath. Amities was splattered with water and the smell hit his nostrils, raw sewerage.

'Help,' cried his mother. She conjured fire, tossing it at the monster's face.

The monster bellowed before it raked a claw across her bosom. Ake screamed and thrashed about as it tried to chew on her ear, mumbling, 'Give in.'

Ake kicked it before biting its face. Blood dripped down her chin and onto her white nightgown.

Ori grinned at her. 'I taught you well.'

Ake rolled her eyes before she tried to release a jet of water at the monster, her shoulders slumped with exhaustion.

Borrush scrambled to his feet as Orilan threw off the imps and stomped them into oblivion before his and Borrush's druid fire began to obliterate the shadows and undead that were reforming.

'I can—' Amities shuddered and dropped his weapon. It clattered to the floor and he turned to run. Mandami cleared his throat and withdrew his sword as he strode down the hallway towards them. 'It is okay, little brother, I will protect you.'

'No.' Amities squared his shoulders and aimed his weapon.

The weapon roared with life. The Fate monstrosity howled in pain as a bolt hit her between the eyes. Ake dropped to the floor and her head smacked against the wall.

'I got you, lass,' said Borrush, steadying her.

The creature swept towards Amities and Mandami. Mandami bowed and stepped aside.

Amities reloaded the weapon. 'Throw you? Why?' he whispered to the weapon.

Amities shrugged and tossed the weapon as the creature reached for him. There was a ticking noise and Amities jumped out of the way as the monster and the weapon blew up, the roaring heat engulfed him and he felt his skin blister a little.

Mandami patted him on the back. 'That was helpful.'

'I need an ale,' said Borrush.'

'So do I.' Ake sighed. 'Lead the way, Borrush.'

A cleaner armed with a mop and bucket turned the corner and swore.

'Have fun,' said Orilan, tossing him a coin.

CHAPTER FIFTY-SIX

Nineteen-year-old Mandami stood on the stage and accepted the scroll and medallion from his proud father. Lan hugged him as he left the stage. He walked over to his mother and sister who made a fuss of him. Orilan shook his hand and congratulated him.

Amities looked up from his sketch book and clapped as his brother received his graduation scroll. He had never graduated as he hadn't mastered magic and had dropped out a few months ago. His mother had insisted he should be there for his brother. He had reluctantly agreed to attend. *Mother doesn't understand I am working on a project of the greatest importance. I understand family and friends are important. That is why I need to finish my work before they take on those monsters again.* Amities sighed and stood up as his twin wandered over.

Amities hugged his brother 'Congratulations, Mandami.'

'I am glad you could make it. You are always holed up at Rock Fell hoping to get into their engineering school,' said Mandami.

'You don't understand, brother,' said Amities.

Mandami patted the small elf on the head. 'We miss you, Amities. Life is going on without you.'

'Quit treating me like a feeble child, Mandami.' He punched his brother playfully.

Mandami pushed him away with one of his big hands and laughed. 'Little brother, I am just looking out for you. At least eat with us.'

Amities nodded and joined his family for a meal. The huge graduation ceremony had been done away with and replaced with simple meals shared with the students and their families. Amities and Mandami sat down at a table with their family which included Borrush and Beryl. Everyone began to eat and talk joyfully among themselves.

Lan squeezed Ake's hand. 'We did it, we got them to this point, my darling. Our Mandami is grown.'

Ake squeezed his hand back and leant in and kissed him.

Amities hurried his meal and said goodbye to his family and left. Mandami sighed and sprinted after him.

'Amities, stay a little longer,' said Mandami.

Amities smiled sadly. 'I can't. Meet me outside the forge in Mencrey in three nights. Please come.'

Amities hurried away and Mandami's shoulders drooped. Someone tapped him on the shoulder, and he turned to see Beryl looking up him. Mandami went to kiss her, and she pushed him away.

'We can't, Mandami. My father won't allow it. I must marry a dwarven noble.' Her eyes shone with tears.

Mandami pulled her to him and held her tightly. 'Don't do this. You know how I feel. I—'

'Don't say it, Mandami, it will make it worse. Father says you will likely die in the battle against Drianna. I can't be caught up in that, especially now—' she faltered.

'What are you doing with her, Mandami?' asked Borrush.

The dwarf strode over and pulled his daughter away.

'I want to marry your daughter, Borrush.' Mandami bowed.

'I can't allow it. She is leaving with me today. She is not your destiny, Mandami.' Borrush turned and pulled his daughter after him.

'Wait, Father.' She let go of her father's hand and smiled sadly at

Mandami. 'Mandami, it's over … I never loved you.' Beryl turned and ran away sobbing.

'I love you, Beryl,' he shouted after her. Mandami sniffled and wiped his face on his sleeve.

'Dwarven duty overrides any summer flings, Mandami. Contacting her will mean the end of my alliance with your parents.' Borrush glared at him.

'I thought you were beyond blackmail, Borrush. Fine, love is for the weak anyway.' Mandami turned and walked away, his head held high while his heart ripped in two.

—w—

Amities pumped the bellows until the flames burned blue. He poured the molten steel into the mould and proceeded to hammer the blade while reciting elvish incantations.

'*Elnamo Anam Imeall.*'

There was a puff of green smoke. Amities grabbed the large tongs and pulled out the heavy weapon. He dipped it into a barrel of water, then took it over to an anvil and began to hammer it again. When the blade was finished, he attached the unusual hilt.

Amities carried the blade over and placed in on a table next to a green bow, a hammer and an unusual weapon. Amities picked up the strange weapon and carried it over to a wooden box lined with velvet. The box contained a mysterious powder and round projectiles. He cocked the hammer and tested the trigger. It appeared to be in working order. He put the weapon in the box and placed the lid on top. *For you, Father. One day.*

'Hello,' called a familiar voice.

'Come in, Mandami,' said Amities.

Mandami entered the smithy and hugged his brother. Amities returned the hug, relieved his current projects were completed.

Mandami saw the sword and hefted it into his hands.

'You made this?'

Amities nodded. The sword flared in Mandami's hand, and he grinned.

'A magic sword, brother. So, your magic is in your creations, far more powerful than mere spells. Who would have guessed.'

'You think so?'

'I know so. When was the last great elven engineer?' asked Mandami.

'Dage, in the time of the Alliance,' said Amities.

Mandami took a swing and cried out in pain as the sword attuned to his soul. He dropped the weapon and it hummed at him in annoyance.

Mandami stared at Amities in shock 'Is it sentient too?'

'Yes. I learnt of sentient weapons when reading the tomes in the great library of Rock Fell. I can do so much more if I study there. I can spend time with you and Beryl when you marry her and move there. Have you told our parents yet?' asked Amities.

Mandami winced. 'I decided love isn't worth it. Mother will be devastated when she loses Father. If I die, I couldn't imagine that fate for Beryl or any other woman.'

'Oh, I will miss you, Mandami. Are you okay?' Amities patted him awkwardly on the back.

Mandami grinned. 'A drink for the road, brother?'

Amities smiled and they left the forge.

CHAPTER FIFTY-SEVEN

The sun rose high above them as they trotted the horses along the dirt track towards the village of Axeton. Amities had left for Rock Fell a few weeks ago and it was now time for Lan to travel the island of Man'hannon offering help to its citizens. As the Lord of Caelestis he was responsible for the upkeep of the houses their tenants lived in and the general wellbeing of the island's inhabitants. In accordance with tradition, the check was required twice a year. Lan had decided to bring his wife and daughter along to break up the monotony of hours on horseback.

Ten-year-old Caoimhe was seated on the mare in front of Ake and Lan rode Brady. They came to a small farmhouse with a roof in need of repair. Lan slowed his mount and Ake did the same. They both dismounted.

A farmer looked up from where he was tilling the soil and waved. 'The lord is here. Brigid bring the list.'

A woman milking a cow stood up from her stool and picked up her pail. She entered the house and came out and walked towards Lan and Ake and bowed.

'Here is the list my lord.'

Lan smiled at Brigid as she lifted her head. 'Please don't bow, Brigid. I never allowed your father to bow to me all those years ago.'

Brigid curtseyed to Ake. Brigid gasped when Ake responded in kind.

'This is my Ake.' Lan laughed. He grabbed Ake's hand. 'The locals aren't used to a lady curtseying back, they believe it is beneath you.' He gestured to his daughter. 'This is our little Caoimhe.'

Ake shrugged. 'If one is polite to me, I will be polite to them.'

Lan let go of Ake's hand and she took Caoimhe down from the horse and placed her on the ground.

'You married?' asked the farmer wandering over. 'I had heard rumours of that. Isn't that taboo among mystics? And a child as well.'

Lan shrugged. 'Change happens and I am glad it did as I have a wonderful wife and four children. But enough about my life, how can I help you prosper?'

'Well, as you can see the roof needs fixing. We need seeds and new tools for the harvest. That's about it.' The farmer scratched his head. 'If you follow me, I can show you the state of things.'

'I am going to go with Eric here and see how much money he needs to get things in order,' said Lan.

Lan followed Eric over to a small shed and they began looking at some rusty tools.

Ake noticed the woman's dress was worn. She heard an infant cry and Brigid wandered over to a basket hung from a tree that was gently swaying in the breeze. The woman withdrew a very small infant wrapped in a frayed blanket.

'How old is your baby?' asked Ake.

The woman scowled at Ake suspiciously. 'She's fine I can take care of her.'

She is wary of me. 'She's beautiful. It's been a long time since I held a baby.'

Brigid gave her a proud smile. 'She is a pretty wee thing. Her name is Louise.'

'I know it's common for the lord to aid the master of the farm. I have been Lady of Caelestis for a few years now and its now part of the law to ask after the needs of the lady of the farm as well and offer our support.' She gave Brigid a charming smile. *I better mention this new law to Lan.*

'Do you want to hold her? She is just over half a year. I am mighty proud of her, she has outlived my other babes.' Brigid's eyes filled with sadness.

'I would be honoured to.' Ake held out her hands.

'Lan, we should be helping the women and children as well. Did you ever consider that?' Ake spoke to him using telepathy.

Lan turned to stare at Ake as Brigid placed the malnourished baby in her arms.

Lan blushed. *'I had assumed by helping the head of the household all would be accounted for. We must do better.'*

'Eric, I have changed the laws of Caelestis lately.' He winked at Ake. 'As you can see, I am a family man, and a man takes care of his own. We offer a stipend for housekeeping now, bolts of cloth for clothing and monthly staples.'

Eric glared at him. 'Did your wife just make that up now? I can take care of my own family.'

Lan gasped, acting shocked. 'Did you hear my wife make that up just now? I assumed you had just heard me mention it to you just a few moments ago.'

'We aren't charity. We may be struggling but village folk look out for each other. How can a lord and Lady possibly understand the situation?' Brigid took her baby back.

Lan and Eric watched in horror as Ake turned on Brigid.

'You would allow your pride to hurt your baby?' Ake glared at the woman.

'How dare you? What would a lady know of such things? Sitting in a castle with servants and food all around her.' Brigid slapped Ake. 'I would give my life for my baby. What would you know of loss?'

Eric stammered. 'Fo-give her my lo-rd. Brigid is impa-ssion-ed as your lady dared question her commitment to Louise.'

Lan grinned. 'It's fine, Ake will handle it.'

Lan walked over to Caoimhe and grabbed her hand and took her to see the cow.

Ake waited until the men were out of earshot and spoke quietly. 'I was starved and beaten in my formative years watching my mother suffer at the hands of the men of her tribe. I have lost four children. Their deaths hit me harder than I would have imagined considering they were conceived against my will. And before you assume it was my husband, it was not. It is callous of you to assume one has not suffered because of their current station in life. I have accepted help from others when I could not provide for my own son.'

Brigid began to weep. 'I am sorry I slapped you.'

Ake gave her a gentle smile. 'It is fine. You do not have to accept, but if it is okay for your husband to do so why not his wife and child? When you are all healthy the farm thrives and that benefits Caelestis and all of the isle.'

Brigid stifled her tears. 'It's not much of an apology but do you want some tea?'

Ake nodded. 'I would be grateful. Riding is thirsty work in this heat.'

Brigid smiled and rushed into the house. Lan wandered over to her. Ake's cheek was beginning to discolour. 'Quite a back hand. You will bruise.'

'I'll wear it as a badge of honour. I believe I may have reached her. Sometimes harsh words encourage others to lash out and convey their feelings. Then a real discussion begins.' Ake smiled.

'I have married a wise woman.' Lan caressed the cheek and Ake winced.

Brigid wandered over with a pretty cup. The fine porcelain was slightly cracked but it had once been a beautiful piece covered in butterflies in a tall wheat field. She handed the cup to Ake. 'Was my mother's. I would be honoured if you kept it.'

'I can—'

Lan shook his head.

'Of course.' Ake took the cup and began to sip the tea. 'Refreshing.'

Brigid smiled and turned to her husband. 'Did you hear about the wife's stipend?'

'Yes, I did. You can make wee dresses for Louise.'

Lan began to count out fifty coins and handed them over to the couple. They gasped at the generous amount.

'Consider it a bonus for all your hard work over the years. We will be back in a few days with the bolts of cloth, tools and staples. Farewell.'

Lan proceeded to help Ake onto the mare and lifted Caoimhe onto her lap. He mounted Brady. 'We best be off then.'

Lan turned his horse and set a quick pace. Ake smiled and waved at Eric and Brigid before following.

Lan smiled to himself as he heard their conversation, his elvish hearing picking up the distant words.

'What a strange couple,' said Brigid.

'Even after all their generosity?' asked Eric.

'Never said I didn't like and appreciate them,' said Brigid.

Eric laughed.

―⁓―

Twelve-year-old Caoimhe sighed as she stared out the window. She breathed on the window and traced her fingers through the condensation on the frosty pane. She turned her attention back to her mother who was filling in for her father. Lan and Orilan were in Rock Fell trying to arrange a meeting with Borrush. Things had soured between the dwarven druid and her father after Mandami's graduation and Caoimhe was curious. Lan had sent many letters and even tried to visit the palace. The new king refused to see an elf and Lan had left. Year after year he had returned and been treated the same way.

'That's it for today, class. Try and stay warm, this winter is really harsh,' said Ake.

Caoimhe stood and waited for the other students to leave.

Mother, why does Borrush dislike Father? They used to be fond of each other, she signed.

Ake sighed. 'I honestly don't know. Things haven't been the same since Mandami graduated.'

When does Father return?

They both turned as they heard someone cursing in the hallway. They opened the door and stuck their heads out of the classroom. Lan was pacing.

'Father, you should calm down.'

'What have we done wrong? I thought Borrush enjoyed my company.' Lan went to curse again.

Orilan gestured to the eavesdroppers. 'Your womenfolk are present.'

Lan stopped himself and smiled at his wife and daughter. 'Sorry.'

Caoimhe ran over and hugged her father. What is wrong?

'The king told us Borrush has left Rock Fell. The king met with us and will not give us the details of Borrush's whereabouts. He doesn't believe that Borrush and I were friends.' Lan sighed. 'He has declared the alliance between dwarves, elves and humans over. Without the elves upholding their end due to their near extinction, and the natural weakness of humans, the king said it was in the best interests of the dwarves to break their pact. I am no longer welcome there but at least Amities is.'

Ake walked over to her husband and embraced him.

He held her to him. 'We seem to lose all our good friends, don't we?'

Mandami came down the hall whistling to himself. The skin on his arms glistened with sweat from his workout and his shirt was drenched, he held his sword in his hand.

He stared at his family. 'Why are you all in the hallway looking subdued?'

Lan released Ake and looked up at his tall son. 'Borrush doesn't want anything to do with us anymore.'

Mandami shrugged. 'Dwarves can be flippant.'

'Dwarves are stalwart and loyal. Borrush's behaviour is unusual for a dwarf,' said Ake.

'I have my own opinions on that.' Mandami smiled. 'Father, I know what will cheer you. I will test my mettle against yours. I may even let you win.'

Lan grinned. 'I can still best you.'

Ake rolled her eyes and laughed. 'Caoimhe, do you want to go and have supper?'

Caoimhe whistled in excitement. There better be loads of honey and cream.

'Of course.' Ake winked at her. 'Ori, want to join us?'

'Very tempting, but I want to see my father fall on his rear. You could always bring the supper to us.' Orilan smiled.

'Done.' Ake strode towards the cafeteria with Caoimhe.

'Ori, go help them. Ake and Caoimhe are not your servants,' said Lan.

Orilan grinned at Lan. 'I was going to do so.'

Lan watched Orilan's retreating back and turned back to Mandami. 'Where shall this skirmish take place?'

'Outside in the frigid weather. It will give you the upper hand with your ice magic.'

Lan laughed. 'I don't need any help, my son.'

Lan turned as he heard Orilan shouting down the hall.

'There's going to be a fight between Mandami and the head-master. If that isn't tempting enough, we have snacks.'

Mandami rolled his eyes. 'Ori and his showboating.'

'I guess he could be attempting to raise morale. It has been a harsh winter. Lives have been lost on the island due to illness and the cold,' said Lan.

A crowd began to gather, and Lan opened the front doors. Sleet was falling and the cold temperature hit him, and he shivered. Mandami didn't seem to notice the cold and strode through the doors. His heavy boots left small holes as he trudged through the thick snow. Lan walked over the surface with ease and left no tracks. They chose a frozen lake for their fight and after a few moments, others joined them, dressed in warm cloaks, gloves and scarves in defence against the bitter cold.

'Magic and combat,' said Mandami.

Lan grinned. 'The loser is the first to lose his footing three times.'

'I know your weaknesses, Father. You helped train me.' Mandami took several steps back holding the large sword in his hands.

Lan turned to watch Ake, Caoimhe and Ori bring out huge pots of tea and cups and saucers. The trio began handing out hot drinks.

'Mother, that kind of takes away the seriousness of our battle,' grumbled Mandami.

Ake turned and smiled at them. 'What else would you have me do?'

'Well, I need a beautiful damsel to give me her favour before I teach this rogue a lesson.' Lan winked at Ake.

'Well, there goes my appetite for battle.' Mandami frowned.

Ake drew back the hood of her cloak and took the ribbon out of her hair and handed it to Lan who bowed and kissed her hand. The women in the crowd made sounds of adoration. The men booed.

'That's right, I don't need no damsel's boon.' Mandami grinned. 'I fight for the thrill of besting a worthy opponent.'

The men in the crowd cheered.

Caoimhe ran up to Mandami. Then I guess you are unwilling to accept my token.

'A brother is always a champion for his little sister. I will accept your token.'

The crowd laughed as Caoimhe handed him a toffee. Mandami held his head up proudly and pocketed the sticky sweet.

Thank you, Mandami.

'Any time, Caoimhe.'

Lan turned back to Mandami as Ake joined Caoimhe among the crowd.

Orilan stepped forward. 'Keep it civil you two. Begin.'

Lan charged Mandami, moving gracefully across the snow. Mandami didn't expect Lan to make the first attack and countered the blow from one of Lan's knives as it blurred across his field of vision. The knife clanged against his sword and Mandami's weapon burst into flames. Amities had insisted the sword could do more than produce flames, but Mandami had laughed as he had yet to see it happen.

Mandami kicked his father in the chest and swung his sword down towards him. Lan rolled out the way. Lan stood and Mandami watched in fascination as clumps of snow began to form into snowballs and levitate around his father.

'You can use ice, Father, I am not frail.'

Lan grinned. 'I would rather not seriously injure my child.'

Mandami grunted and changed his stance as he was besieged by a tirade of snowballs. Lan continued the onslaught and Mandami fell to one knee. Half the crowd cheered, and the other half made sounds of annoyance.

'Round one to the headmaster,' announced Orilan.

Mandami stood and charged Lan. Lan went to counter the blow and Mandami changed direction mid-strike. Mandami cast *Mystic Fire* at Lan and his robes caught alight. Lan threw his knife at Mandami, the throw went wide as Mandami noticed his father's deliberate attempt to miss. Lan patted out the flames.

'You disrespect my skill, Father.' Mandami tried to sweep Lan's feet out from under him. As he did so, Lan leapt up and delivered a kick to Mandami's opposing knee, avoiding Mandami's strike.

Mandami winced at the blow. Hefting the sword, he went to deliver a strike to Lan's side. He suddenly dropped the sword and his fist crashed into his father's nose. Lan stumbled backwards, his hand to his nose. Blood dripped down onto the white snow. Lan grinned and shook his hand free of the blood and charged Mandami.

Mandami hurled steam at the ground and Lan lost his footing briefly. The sword hummed as Lan regained his stride. Lan gasped and stumbled down onto his knee for mere seconds as the sword fired jets of steam into the ground and he slipped.

'Second round to Mandami,' shouted Orilan.

'Well done, son. The first time you have bested me.' Lan smiled proudly at his son.

'Must you announce that here, Father?' Mandami charged Lan.

Their weapons rang out against each other, interrupted with *Mystic Fire* as they each avoided the other's flames. Lan sported several lacerations, his robes torn across his arms where Mandami's heavy blows had struck. Mandami's shirt was in tatters on the ground, shredded by Lan's knives and a handful of light scratches adorned his skin where the blades had made contact with him.

Mandami growled. 'You could have given me many nasty injuries. You insult me by holding back. You do not see me as an equal.'

'That is not the reason I hold back.' Lan countered another blow.

Mandami smirked. 'How will I stop Drianna if I cannot defeat you?'

He charged Lan and his father continued to evade him. Mandami made a sound of frustration and thew the sword down in anger. 'This thing is useless.'

The crowd began to point to the sky talking among themselves. 'What is that?'

'Look at the sun.'

The sun peaked out from behind the clouds and glowed a brilliant orange. Lan delivered a kick to Mandami's side. Mandami grabbed him in a bear hug, lifting his father off the ground.

'Third round goes to Mandami. The headmaster's feet are technically off the ground,' said Orilan.

'Bull, that doesn't count.' Mandami dropped Lan.

Lan stood and brushed himself off. 'Take it, Mandami, it was well played.'

'I refuse. You gave your word you wouldn't go easy on me and have done the opposite.' Mandami turned and began to walk away.

Lan turned his head as he heard Ake whisper, 'The gods are watching, look at the sun.'

Lan's gaze settled on his son as the light appeared to follow him; the beams darting across the sky as Mandami moved.

Mandami turned as the air suddenly turned static with electricity. Streaks of lightning crashed into the ground inches from Mandami and almost struck him as he dodged out of the way. He grabbed the sword, and it flashed briefly as it sparkled in the sun's light.

Lan summoned hail and hurled them towards his son. Mandami grinned and the crowd cheered. The sword gave off a flash of light, blinding Lan. He closed his eyes and Mandami used the sword to hit the hail back at his father. Lan struggled to catch his breath as the hail hit his chest. He stumbled and his foot caught in a drift. Mandami rushed him as Lan pulled his foot out. Mandami grinned and pushed him over into a snow drift.

'Mandami wins,' cried Orilan.

Mandami lifted his father onto his feet. And turned to the crowd. 'That is false. He even held back with the lightning. He has won.'

'It doesn't matter,' shouted someone in the crowd.

'It was entertaining,' said another.

The crowd began to disperse and Mandami turned to his father. 'I know why you held back.'

Lan smiled. 'Well, that is good then.'

Mandami watched as Lan turned and walked over to Ake and grabbed a drink.

'I love you too, Father,' whispered Mandami.

Lan turned and bowed to his son before continuing his conversation with Ake.

Mandami blushed. *That's right, he can hear me from over there.*

Mandami walked towards Caelestis. Caoimhe stood in front of the doors.

You cannot go through until you return my favour. Caoimhe held out her hand.

Mandami laughed and handed her the toffee. Then they both entered the fortress.

CHAPTER FIFTY-EIGHT

Caoimhe snuck through the decaying foliage. The sky was overcast and nearly dark despite it being early morning. The area surrounding Drianna's hives was racked with decay and disease. She was careful not to touch the plant life. Orilan had warned her not to give into her instinct to save the plants. A prick from a diseased roaming thorn could kill her.

The fifteen-year-old fairy was no bigger than a three-year-old human child. She was dainty with long blonde hair, blue eyes and fair to almost translucent skin. She could hide almost unseen in any foliage and was the perfect scout for her parents.

Caoimhe peeked out among the bushes and watched closely. The hive looked like any other of Drianna's. It was jet black and constructed to look like a wasp hive. It would soon spew out horrors reeking of death and evil. The fairy shuddered and gave the barely audible whistle that meant the coast was clear.

Lan's elven hearing picked up the signal and his eyes glowed red. He turned to Ake and nodded.

'Mandami, I've tuned the weapon again. If you keep pushing it to the extreme it is going to come out of sync,' said Amities.

Amities had studied with the dwarves of Rock Fell for the last three years and was finally home. He had produced some truly remarkable pieces of engineering. His most famous item was Mandami's long sword Anam Imeall. It was a focal point for Mandami to channel his innate magic. Mandami favoured solar magic like his mother.

Mandami was six foot and heavily muscled. His black elven eyes acknowledged Amities. Both twenty-seven-year-old men had the dark hair and eyes of their father. Mandami was tanned and Amities was pale. Amities kept his hair medium length and was a light build at five foot two. Mandami was clean shaven with short hair in the Regian style. Scars from talons and weapons appeared randomly across Mandami's chest and back. He was dressed only in grey trousers and red boots. Amities wore the standard black mystic robes.

Lan brought the shadows up to conceal them. Ake's eyes glowed golden as she took her Anwyn form. Lan felt the pull of death drawing him in. It was like this every time. He felt the overwhelming urge to let the power seduce him and to give into dark whims. He shook himself and growled.

'Let's do this thing,' he roared.

Hordes of horned guards poured out of the hive. Ake looked at the abominations in disgust. Their horns were part of their human bone helmets, two upright humeri. The guards wore nothing apart from helmets and a loincloth made of human skin. They carried wooden spears hardened in fire which ended in a glass blade. The blade would shatter into fragments when they wounded someone.

The creatures were blind. They had supernatural hearing and an unearthly sense of smell. Maggots and tics crawled in the sockets of their eyes and nasal cavity. Their mouths were empty except for two extremely sharp canines. Their skin was grey and drawn tightly against their bones. The fingernails were yellow and dried with blood, one slash of their diseased claws was the cause of painful, lingering death. Their breath rasped in their diseased lungs and smelt of blood.

Ake shivered and looked at her scarred son and husband.

The heavy scars on Lan's wrists and legs were a grim reminder of their fingernails and the sicknesses the monsters had inflicted on him. Mandami had the reach of a long sword and the strength to wield it, giving him better protection. Lan's need to get in close to deliver deadly blows with knives and unarmed combat put him at risk for deeper cuts and infection upon infection.

They had little choice but to defeat these hives if they wanted to stay together. Lan had told her every time a hive was destroyed, the darkness was kept away for a little longer. This was the seventeenth hive they had come across in ten years and apparently the last.

Orilan could no longer fight with them. Something ailed him and he would no longer let anyone treat him. He was growing weaker and kept to himself a lot these days. Ake and Lan hoped to cure him with the destruction of this last hive.

Mandami channelled his magic into his sword, and it caught fire. The heat radiated down the blade and was absorbed in the heat proof hilt. He rushed into battle. Horned guards bounced off the blade. They burst into flame then rose in the air as ash.

Ake opened up cracks in the earth and the monsters fell into them, melting in hot molten lava. She concentrated on closing the vents when Mandami and Lan got too close. Lan took down countless numbers with hail stones, lightning bolts and *Mystic Fire*. He called on the powers of Lord Bás and sent a vortex of shadows to hurl creatures into Ake's vents. He held out until he felt the power overwhelming him and pulled back. Then he rushed into combat, knives ready.

It was hours before they defeated the hordes of weaker creatures, and they retreated for a short rest. They would need their energy to fight the Shadow Masters within.

Hundreds of human slaves came running out of the structure. All looked injured and malnourished. Mandami kept watch. This ploy was used often. Sending out humans to disarm them and distract them, while some were Shadow Masters in disguise.

'Ake, ready *Starlight*,' yelled Lan.

Shadow Masters could only be killed with a specialised druid magic known as *Starlight*. It took great effort and willpower to use and maintain it. When cast, a huge bright light with many colours swirling in its depth surrounded the druid. The druid was tempted to step into the portal as it tempted them with visions of all their wishes becoming fulfilled.

Only druids of the highest rank could control it. There had been many a time when a minor druid had tried to control *Starlight* but had been lost to the spell. The light destroyed all evil in an explosion of magnificent colours. Orilan had been the last druid capable of casting *Starlight*. Now just Ake was left. The spell was a gift from her divine heritage.

The number of Shadow Masters had become vast over the years. Ake knew there would be many and would not be able to take them all out in a single hit. She relied heavily on her son and husband to fight the numbers off until she could.

Sixty of the humans threw off their disguises and took the form of the dreaded Shadow Masters. Dark blood poured continuously from their eyeless sockets. They were devoid of the normal facial features. They had a pig's snout instead of a nose and screeched through their beak-like mouths. Their ears were daggers, tipped with poison. The creatures had a serpent-like body with mere stumps for arms. The main weapon was the trident-like tail. The monsters were blind but could see through the eyes of a person at will.

Their most destructive weapon was a mind attack. Wails of the banshee echoed off the sconces of one's skull, as the pressure mounted, the brain internally combusted. The mind weapon was very rarely used as the creatures were charged with the blood of dragons and gifted with their strength. They preferred to use brute force to overcome their victims.

Mandami clashed his sword against one of the monsters' tails. He held his stance but still felt his feet budge a little. He summoned sunlight into his sword and the creature backed off, screeching momentarily. Another one whipped his feet out from under him and he rolled out of the way. It drove its poisoned prongs into the ground where he had been.

'It is screaming in my mind!' Mandami dropped his sword.

Ake heard him cry out and sent *Starlight* hammering into the two monsters. They were destroyed.

Several looked through the eyes of Ake and she withdrew *Starlight* and closed her eyes. Ake opened vents in the earth and trapped them. She sent *Starlight* sweeping over them and they were obliterated.

Lan stomped on the head of a monster. He had tied two of the monsters' tails together by weaving and ducking between them. He darted out of the way as the creatures tried to fight each other.

Mandami picked up his sword and leapt over Lan's head in an extraordinary display of strength and acrobatics. A third monster had aimed at Lan and its tail crashed down upon Mandami's sword. It screeched in pain as the flaming sword surged with rays of sunlight. The blade began to lose its magic and Mandami forced more power into it.

'Mandami, you're pushing it to the extreme again,' yelled Amities.

Amities continued to fire his emerald bow. He pulled back the glowing, green string. Waves of endless arrows struck the creatures, causing them to writhe in pain. The earth magic Amities had used to create the bow countered the monsters' evil taint.

Eventually they were able to defeat the creatures and the hive imploded on itself. The family ran and dove for cover as waves of decay filled with unknown diseases came sweeping towards them. Caoimhe sprinted from the bushes and was swept up in Lan's arms. Ake saw some slaves about to succumb to the waves. She glided and picked up the people and crashed just out of the way. The disguised monsters turned on her and drove their daggers into her. The pain wracked her body. She screamed as hot waves of evil latched on to her divine light and began to drain her. Her veins began to pulse black as the poison wove through her bloodstream.

Waves of dark energy slammed into the monsters, pushing them back as Lan welcomed the darkness. Mandami rushed in and hoisted his mother up.

'Mother, cast *Starlight*,' he cried.

'I am too weak,' she said.

'I order you to. For Father's sake,' he commanded.

Ake nodded and cast the spell. Mandami's sword hummed, and he channelled her magic into it. The fibres of the sword screeched against overuse. Mandami grinned and charged it harder. He threw the sword at one creature. A spectacular array of colours burst through both monsters, eliminating them.

Lan walked over and took his wife's hand to steady her. Mandami went and retrieved his blade. He shook off the blood and sheathed it in the holder across his back. Amities rushed over and gave Ake one of the antidotes Orilan had concocted. She drank it and the poison was nullified.

They all huddled together, trying to draw strength from each other. Then Lan teleported them home.

CHAPTER FIFTY-NINE

Orilan drew off the glove and looked at his skeletal hand. He sighed. They had defeated another hive. That meant the deaths would draw out the darkness in Lan and eventually call him to the underworld. Orilan had sacrificed his own body to give Lan and Ake more time. Only his face, back and chest were untouched.

Another sacrifice was due. Orilan grimaced in pain as his back took on the skeletal form. He didn't know how long it would give them. They had given him a home and loved him like a valued person. After Drianna, that was the ultimate gift. He was happy to give them his life.

Orilan limped over to a chair and eased himself down. He replaced his glove. He ran his hand through his curly red locks. As the vampirism had left his body, so did Drianna's magic and his body was slowly returning to its original design. Ake and Lan would come to check on him and he threw a blanket over himself. There was a knock and Caoimhe pushed open the door.

Caoimhe smiled. Hello, Ori.

Hello, kiddo, he signed back.

He held open his arms and she ran into them chirping happily. Caoimhe handed him some pretty wildflowers she had found. Orilan held back tears. Lan and Ake knocked and entered.

'How are you, Ori?' asked Ake.

'All is as it should be,' said Orilan vaguely.

Lan went to shake his hand and Orilan drew back.

'Borrush just sent me this.' Orilan handed Lan a slip of paper. Lan's eyes glittered with tears as he read the note.

Ori, we have found Drianna. Here are the coordinates. I am sorry. Good luck to all of you. Thank you, Ori, Lan and Ake for your friendship. Sincerely, Borrush.

Underneath a set of familiar coordinates were scrawled.

Ake read the note when Lan handed it to her. Ake's eyes widened in surprise. 'Borrush has contacted you after all this time?'

Orilan nodded. 'We will have to reach out to him.'

Lan eyes filled with despair. 'We all know those coordinates. Drianna's on the island.'

'I tried my best to give you more time.' Orilan sighed.

Orilan stood and nearly stumbled. He removed his glove and shirt. Ake screamed.

'Ori, what have you done?' Lan frowned.

'I kept her away. She made me a demon. With that link I have been able to feed that thing inside you, Father, and satisfy it, keeping it at bay. We had fifteen extra years. Forgive me. I have loved you both and appreciated the family you built for me.' Orilan's eyes, now blue, filled with tears.

Lan embraced his child and Orilan sobbed on his father's shoulder. Orilan had found his redemption. Lan ended the hug and smiled at his son.

'I am proud of you, Ori. You are a good man and I love you. Thank you for the extra time. I will need you to guide them when I leave. My wonderful children will eventually come home to me. But my beautiful Ake ...' Lan frowned.

'Will eventually walk alone,' said Orilan.

Caoimhe whistled at them in anger and began to sign rapidly.

Mother will never be alone. I am here. A fairy doesn't die unless killed directly. I will look after Mother for my father and brothers. I will share the good memories with her.

I thank you, Caoimhe, I couldn't ask for a more caring daughter. Look out for each other, Lan signed back.

'I have to prepare her,' Lan muttered.

'I understand.' Orilan opened the door to see Amities and Mandami waiting patiently outside. 'Come in you two.'

The twins entered the room. Lan and Ake hugged each of the children.

'We love you all. We are proud of who you are,' said Ake.

'Mandami, you are a gallant warrior, always defending those in need,' said Lan.

'My gentle Amities, you are unmatched when it comes to magical engineering. Orilan, you have become a wise and caring man. And Caoimhe, you are a bright innocent light in a harsh world,' said Ake.

Lan looked at his beloved children and began to weep. 'Please look after her for me, children.'

'Of course, we will,' said the boys proudly.

Ake smiled at Orilan. 'I am proud of you, my good friend.'

Orilan smiled. It was a bittersweet moment, one worth living for. Orilan sat and talked to his siblings. Lan led Ake from the room.

Chapter Sixty

Ake and Lan stood alone in a field of flowers facing each other, despair etched into every fibre of their being as they clung to each other. Ake's lip trembled, tears threatening to overflow as Lan drew away. Lan was dressed in a blue shirt with a V neckline and long sleeves, a belt and black pants. Ake wore a white dress split at the sides, showing her legs. The dress was beautifully designed and accentuated her slim form.

'I know the new custom is to exchange gold rings that represent eternity. I, Trebrelan, take Telewanake as my wife forever. You were the best thing that ever happened to me. The natural zest you have for life was contagious and it taught me life was meant to be fun. You are my lover, confidant and best friend. Your pure kindness and mercy kept me going when I was at my lowest. I love you, Ake.' Lan put the ring on her finger.

Ake let the tears slip from her eyes and stared up at him, almost lost for words.

'I, Ake … Oh, Lan, you will always be my husband. You are gentle and kind and yet you have a strength that defies gods. My life was worth living because you were in it. You are at the heart of my compassion and mercy. When I falter, I remember your love and protection and it inspires me to forgive. You drove me to do my best and it made me a better person. It is the memory of you that will keep me going. I love you.' Ake slipped the ring onto his finger.

Lan kissed her. 'I wish it ended now and we could stay like this forever.'

'Why me, Lan? Why must I endure without you?'

'Despite everything you have endured you never give up. You are the strongest person I know. Only you have the ability to watch all the horror and forgive. You are the epitome of love. When the end comes it is you who will bring those beautiful memories to the gods, Ake. It has been an honour to love you.' Lan caressed her cheek.

Lan pulled out the needlework he had made for their wedding certificates and handed it to her. Her eyes widened with surprise, and she smiled.

'I will keep it close. It is truly beautiful. Thank you.'

The sound of pounding feet interrupted them.

'No! I'm not ready to let you go,' cried Lan.

He grabbed her hand and led her away to a grove of trees. *We will have this moment.* Lan took her mouth with his own, defiantly. Ake trembled against him. Lan lifted her up against the trunk of a tree and unbuttoned his trousers.

Lan whispered in her ear. 'Are you ready for me?'

'Yes.' Ake kissed him.

Ake gasped as he took her passionately. He was driven to a frenzy at the thought of losing her. Ake saw stars and cried out. Lan captured her mouth with his and he pushed her further until he was spent. When their breathing had slowed, they smiled at each other. They fixed their clothes and walked hand in hand towards Caelestis.

Chapter Sixty-One

As Ake and Lan neared the main doors Amities came running up.

'Father, Mother, I have been looking for you. We believe she is here,' said Amities.

There was a deafening roar, and the sky began to darken.

'Lan,' cried Ake.

'This is it, my darling. I am so sorry.' Lan whispered against her ear.

Ake felt his tears slide down her cheek. He grabbed her hand and led his goddess to the battlefield.

The mystics of Caelestis were evacuating the island with the inhabitants of Mencrey and Axeton. Louise and her mother bowed to them.

'I will return on my honour, my lady,' said Bridgid, before running away with the other villagers. Eric had passed in the great winter years earlier. Others also vowed they would come serve Ake and her children after the battle was won. Ake curtseyed to them, and they bowed back.

The sky began to rage, a harsh wind began to blow, and rain hammered down. Lightning streaked in the sky and tried to kill the fleeing inhabitants. The earth began to shake and crack. Several people screamed as they lost their footing.

Mandami stood strong, sword ready to defy this thing while Amities stood back, his bow drawn. Orilan and Caoimhe began helping injured villagers nearby.

'Let's take this fight to a field, away from the main buildings. We will give everyone a chance to escape,' yelled Lan over the din.

The others nodded and they raced towards an open field. The air began to fill with the stench of decay.

Ake felt the Anwyn flow through her in response to Drianna. She was sick of her world being driven to despair by the jealousy and evil in others. Her wings glowed with celestial fire in the rank darkness.

'Drianna, I command you to show yourself. I am ready to seal your fate,' she cried.

Ake was no longer demure when faced with such utter evil. There was a roar, and the beast clawed its way out from the depths of hell.

'Great-niece, spawn of all I hate, I hear you. But it is I who will devour you all. And man will turn on fellow man so that he dooms himself.' Drianna cackled.

She towered over them all, some twenty feet tall. There was a collective gasp as everyone stared at the beast in horror. Her body was a bulging mass made up of tortured souls writhing in pain. She had thousands of legs made from an assortment of human spines. Drianna's head was a collection of human skulls twisted into shapes resembling eyes, and a maw filled with fangs.

'All those that did evil, writhe within me. They torture the good souls I have stolen. I am filled with their glorious and undeserved pain,' Drianna bellowed.

She opened her cavernous maw. There was a faint buzzing noise that began to grow louder.

'Move,' yelled Ake.

Mandami ran forward, his blade burning with sunlight. He dodged the maw as a radioactive beam shot forth at them all. Ake glided out the way.

Lan's eyes glowed red and a vortex of shadows shielded Orilan and Caoimhe. Drianna turned to Lan and hit him with her beam. He fought against it and the darkness tried to consume him. With incredible skill, he maintained concentration on the shield and teleported behind Drianna. The monster screamed as he summoned lightning and it hammered into her, destroying several rows of legs. She turned and tried to coil her insect-like body around him and hollered as hail slammed into her, forcing her to back up.

'Here, Father.' Lan glanced briefly at Amities who blew on a whistle from a cord around his neck. A spear shimmered into view next to both Ake and Lan. 'It's a summoning spell I attached to your spears.'

Lan grabbed the spear quickly and aimed it at Drianna. 'Well done, son.' Fire burst from Mbel daoine into Drianna. Drianna burrowed underground and he leapt onto the retreating figure and fired *Mystic Fire* into her behind with little effect. He dove out of the way and landed hard, the ground suddenly becoming uneven as Drianna dug her way back out.

'This spear is useless against her.' Lan threw the spear at Drianna. It burst into flames and drove itself into her body. Drianna clawed at the spear.

'It hurts,' she screamed, tearing at the weapon. Thirteen of her legs disintegrated before the spear exploded, leaving damage to her body.

'Get out of the way, Lan,' yelled Ake.

Lan ran as Ake spoke words so dark it would make the very demons in the underworld shiver.

'*Magma manas crono.*'

The earth began to shatter, and steam seeped up from the cracks. Drianna howled and began to claw her way out as Dee's blood, magma hot and strong, poured out through the wounds in the earth. Drianna opened her cavernous maw. She groaned and rows of fangs shot out of her mouth towards her combatants. Ake winced as the projectiles pierced her skin. She screamed as the fiery poison began to burn through her body. Ake bent over, heaving with the effort to breathe. Relief flooded through her as Orilan cast a healing spell.

Mandami drove his sword into the monster, and it howled and turned its sight on Lan. The air was rent with the sounds of hundreds of bone jaws clacking together in skeletal laughter. Hundreds of skeletons emerged from Drianna's body. Lan rushed towards the monsters. His son leapt into the fray, joining his father in destroying the skeletons.

Several skeletons surrounded Lan and he delivered a punch to their necks, skulls went flying. The skeletons rushed forward, blindly clawing as him. He slipped under them, turned and delivered a roundhouse kick and his two opponents collapsed in a pile of bones.

Three more jumped on his back and scratched and tore at him, their nails filled with venom, his robes shredded. Lan grabbed the limb of one and flung it to the ground before him. One raked his face, and he grabbed its arm, pulling it out of the socket. The creature fell to the ground and rose. With his arms free, he reached behind him and pulled off the skull of the other one clinging to his shoulder. It slid of him, and he kicked it towards the other skeleton. They became entangled and fell to the ground. He turned to face the horde.

Mandami used the flat of his blade to deliver strikes to the skeletons. Bones shattered and went flying past him. He turned the sword and raked it through the unrelenting horde, trying to clear the way to his father. Lan dodged the claws of the sixteen that were trying to overwhelm him backflipping over the skeletons and landing in front of Mandami, breathing heavily.

The skeletons crowded in on the pair. Lan placed his knives back in their guards and picked up a large stick. Skeletons rushed him and the stick was used as a barrier between himself and the onslaught. He drove the stick into the dirt and used it as leverage to hoist himself into the air, delivering a variety of kicks in one long arc until he landed gracefully at his starting place.

Mandami saw Amities firing at some of the skeletons. A skeleton collapsed in a pile of bones. Mandami channelled the earth magic into his sword. He closed his eyes and spoke to the sword. 'Destroy the skeletons in a wave of earth magic but avoid my father.'

'Mandami, they have surrounded us,' cried Lan.

Mandami opened his eyes, reached forwards, and hauled his father behind him. The sword hummed to life. The ground began to shake as stones rose in the air and shot towards the skeletons. Limbs and skulls went flying as the attack continued. Eventually the horde was defeated.

'Well done, Mandami,' said Lan.

'You are an impressive fighter, Father.'

Lan smiled at his son.

They turned to survey the battle.

—◠◠◠—

'*Magna crono*,' said Ake.

Fire erupted from the ground in a large column and moved towards Drianna, forcing her back. Ake walked forward controlling the spell. Drianna burrowed under the ground and came up behind her. Ake turned and faced her. Drianna opened her mouth and copious amounts of blood flowed down onto Ake from all the death Drianna had caused. Ake wiped the blood out of her eyes as huge, blood red serpents swam in the pooling blood and wrapped themselves around her. She drew her short sword and slashed at them. They hissed and delivered bite after bite. Ake dove out of the way as more chased her. She kicked and sliced at them. Three of the serpents weaved their way up her legs and coiled themselves around her, and as their grip tightened, her eyes glowed golden. The serpents exploded as she summoned divine light to counter their attack as more latched onto her arms and tried to coil around her.

'*Waterius.*' Her bubble shield burst forth, enveloping her as she struck the serpents with her short sword, slaughtering them with swift, deadly strokes.

Drianna turned and light pulsated from her open maw, hitting Lan directly from behind. Lan's eyes glowed red and a vortex of shadows surrounded him and Mandami. The light continued to pulsate against the shadows. He fought against it and the darkness consumed him. He turned and shouted to Ake, 'I love you.'

Lan's words were lost in the noise. His defences disintegrated and he succumbed. Lan slumped to the ground. He closed his eyes, and his last thoughts were of Ake.

Ake screamed and rushed over to Lan. She sat next to him and cradled his head in her lap. Drianna laughed, the sound a hideous parody to genuine joy.

Mandami rushed up the monster's legs. His sword was a blur as he hacked at the beast. Drianna bellowed and turned her attention to this annoying flea who cut at her body. She lashed out with her many legs and struck herself. Mandami grinned.

Ake placed Lan's head down gently and kissed him. She stood and marched over to face the monster. Tears slid down her face and she thought of all those she had lost.

'I cut you here. I cut you there. Every cut a mark for the lives you take.' Mandami laughed as he easily dodged Drianna's attacks.

Drianna bellowed. The tortured souls in her hide moaned.

Acid oozed from their mouths and spurted at Mandami. It covered Mandami's boots and began to burn his feet.

Ake looked up. Drianna turned her strange eyes towards her. Ake began to glow, and the rain and lightning halted. Stars began to twinkle in the sky. They suddenly became brighter.

Drianna felt strange as whisps of souls began to leave her body and float about Ake. They began to take on solid form and behind Ake stood her friends and family.

Drianna roared and spat more acid at Mandami. It burned his back and he screamed. He ran up the monster's neck and tried to strike at its head.

'Run, Mandami,' Ake yelled.

The sky filled with a thunderous roar as meteorites began to fall and strike at Drianna. Ake kept aiming but the monster destroyed them with its beam.

Drianna thrashed about in pain as more souls left. She aimed at Orilan and light streaked towards him. He shielded his sister with the last of his druid magic. Orilan was consumed in a blast of light.

Amities raced towards his sister and picked her up.

'Run, Amities, and don't look back,' Ake shouted.

Mandami had a few moments to think as poison began to seep from Drianna's pores. His eyes began to burn. Mandami drove his blade into the monster. He opened a pocket under her skin and hid. She bellowed and turned her attention back to Ake.

Poison dripped down onto Ake as the monster towered over her. Drianna opened her maw to swallow Ake. Mandami darted from his hiding spot and Drianna screamed as Mandami sliced open her skull. Ake fired a meteorite into the monster's brain. Mandami ran and leapt off Drianna's back as she crashed to the ground. Ake strode over to her. Her eyes were full of bitterness.

'Let all this hate go, Drianna. Let go of the jealous woman who craved Sorendee's love above all else. You warped it beyond recognition, and it turned you into this monster. When your body dies, your underworld goes with it. You will fade away into nothing. A forgotten story,' said Ake.

———

Drianna felt the strength leave her. Her power over death was waning and she felt mortally afraid. *This is what mortals must feel before they die, faced with the unknown as their souls leave their fragile vessels. I will not die. I will prey on her weakness, mercy.*

———

Shadows began to coil themselves around Drianna. Mandami channelled this darkness into his blade.

'Free me,' cried Drianna.

'You want me to give you mercy? Everyone I ever loved was never given that option. You tormented those pure souls in death and in life,' growled Ake.

Ake began to cast *Starlight*. She shook with rage and glared at Drianna. She felt a hand on her shoulder.

'The healer in you would never do that, Ake,' said a familiar voice.

She turned. Het picked her up and spun her around. He put her down.

'Sorry, Het, you are dead because of her,' said Ake.

Het smiled sadly and disappeared.

'Ake, remember the prophecy. Your son will be her downfall, but you will be her saviour,' said a kindly voice.

Ake turned and looked for the wise voice. Dane stepped forward and clasped her hands.

'Sorry, Dane. You were always wise. But she doesn't deserve freedom as she spoiled ours.' She gave him a sad smile as he dissolved into nothingness.

Ake began to draw in the starlight. *I will destroy this foul creature's very soul. She killed all those I ever loved.* Ake turned as a spear appeared next to her in a hazy light. She plucked the spear out of thin air and pointed it at Drianna. 'You will feel what they felt.'

'Please, don't torture me,' begged Drianna.

The spear glistened red and Ake's face contorted in a mixture of pain and rage. 'You dare beg me not to torture you? You forced my husband into sin with his sister, corrupted his son, enslaved and murdered millions and killed my friends and family. You deserve every bit of this.'

Ake drew on her rage. She felt heat spread throughout her body, the anger making her blood almost feverish. She began to sweat and wiped it away as Drianna was encased in a white flame. Her bones broke away and took on primordial forms as she watched ancient creatures of the earth form. From sponges to a trilobites to amphibious animals that had once crawled from the primordial ocean. These were a testament to Drianna's ancient beginnings. As voice boxes began to form in these creatures their screams and howls rent the air as bone, shell, and flipper were shredded from the constantly evolving form as if a serpent had shed newly dead scales. Soon Drianna took on a more human form, her bright red hair was torn from her head with Drianna's own hands, her blue eyes wracked with pain.

'Please, just end it.'

Something broke in Ake and she began to weep. Fond memories flooded in. Tendrils of light danced around her born from her feelings of pure love. Ake gazed at Drianna and her face softened with pity. She snapped the spear in half over her knees and flung the two halves away from her.

'I will not allow anyone to use this evil spear again.'

A sly grin spread over Drianna's face. 'You are too kind to defeat me. You are clever though. I forged that spear. Over time its influence would have corrupted you.'

Drianna's evil laughter washed over Ake, and she shivered as Drianna's form began to change and grow in size, taking her other form, still battered and bruised from the ongoing battle.

—⁓—

Mandami rushed over to the body of his father on a whim. He pushed the sword to draw in all the magic it could find. The magic, good and bad flowed into the blade. Mandami drove his sword into Lan's heart.

Ake screamed and rushed over to him. Mandami pulled out the blade. Green light erupted from the sword and was absorbed by Lan's body. Drianna cackled and drew in the left-over remnants. She fired a beam straight towards Ake. Mandami leapt in front, blade blazing when a vortex of shadows engulfed Drianna.

This gave Mandami a chance and he dove down the creature's throat. Drianna exploded from the inside out as he drove his flaming sword into her heart. Mandami was thrown from the explosion and caught by a hooded spectre. The creature drew back his hood, grinning from a skeletal face that was strangely familiar.

The vortex receded and Lan stood there holding a small dark sphere in his hand. A strange eerie bell began to toll.

'Ake, I need you to decide what to do with this soul,' said Lan.

'You're alive?' Ake wept.

'In a sense, darling. I am now the Lord of Death. I will create an underworld that would make you proud. I will need flowers, paint brushes and cakes and maybe even an elephant.' Lan gave her a sad smile.

She smiled and reached out to touch him, but he shook his head.

'I am death, honey. You are life,' he said.

Ake frowned. 'This isn't fair, Lan. We did everything the prophecy said.'

'Ake, you must decide. Remember your mercy, my darling,' he said.

Ake reached out and touched the soul.

'I want it to be reborn again and again. Maybe through pain and suffering it may feel something. When it does, maybe it will find love and happiness,' she said.

A tear ran down Lan's cheek. 'That's my Ake.'

The soul flared up and disappeared. Ake and Lan heard an infant cry.

Mandami touched the skeletal face.

'Boo,' it said loudly.

Mandami jumped. The spectre removed the spell and Orilan grinned at Mandami.

'Grim Reaper, my brother, link between death and life. Got a stylish costume and an important job. I'll be bringing the souls for Father to sort,' said Orilan.

'As weird as you, brother.' Mandami crushed Orilan in a bear hug.

The bell began to toll louder.

Ake reached out for Lan. 'You once promised you would never leave me alone. Please don't break that promise again. I love you. Let me come with you.'

Lan shook his head sadly. 'I made a pact to save your life and now the debt must be paid.' He reached out to caress her cheek then pulled it back. 'It's not forever, my sweetheart. Your choice has lessened our time apart. When the last elf dies, I will come home to you. Be joyous, Ake. Live and explore that beautiful world of ours. I will always love you.'

He blew her a kiss and turned away from her. All the souls followed. There was a chorus of tolling bells and they disappeared. The sky lightened into the brightest blue and the sun shone brightly, bringing comfort to all that saw it. But not for Ake.

CHAPTER SIXTY-TWO

The old man telling Ake and Lan's story stretched his ancient bones.

'That's it, Grandfather?' asked his grandchild.

'No, my boy. Mandami stayed with his family a while but as he aged, he decided to take up the rule of the Regian empire. He lived longer than most and was wise and kind. He protected women and children, changing the rules around how they were treated. Mandami was a great, religious king. Where others debased the word of their god to hurt others, Mandami upheld those words to raise up his people. He never married as he vowed never to break a woman's heart like his beloved mother's had been.'

'Caoimhe eventually managed to warm her mother's heart and they travelled, enjoying their world. Ake guided new souls to earth, but she was never the same. Amities went on to be a great explorer. Sometimes he travelled with his mother and sister. They had glorious adventures and discovered many hidden secrets. But that is another story.

'Eventually Amities found and married Carolina. They had a daughter. A golden-haired, golden-eyed baby girl they named Anwyn after her grandmother. The child was long lived and brought her grandmother and parents great joy. Sadly, Carolina died before her child was grown.' The old man gave his grandson a sad smile.

'Were Ake and Lan ever reunited?' asked the lad.

'Now you see, my dear Alwin, your father, Arlys, married my dear Anwyn. She had you late in life and you are my joy. She was long lived like me,' said the old man.

'That is ridiculous.' Alwin laughed.

The old man stood and removed Caoimhe's necklace. His elven ears stood out.

'I can only tell you this story because I was there. I am the last elf, and I didn't want their legacy to be forgotten. While plague and disaster did run its course, my parents' sacrifice kept the earth from being overrun with evil. The gods, bolstered by my parents' devotion, occasionally intervened.'

'My mother chased death, hoping to catch Orilan. Sometimes she succeeded and was able to relay messages to my father,' said Amities.

'Why tell me?' asked Alwin.

'You are their legacy. Darkness is growing. Man is turning on his fellow man to enslave his brother. Many are forced into poverty for another's greed. I am asking you to find Ake and Caoimhe and fight the darkness as my parents once did. I know you are only nineteen, but I believe in you. I love you Alwin,' said Amities.

An eerie bell began to toll. There was a knocking at the door and Alwin opened it. A fairy chittered and flew past him. Alwin blinked in surprise.

Hello, Caoimhe, Amities signed.

Amities hugged her. There was a gentle rustling near the doorway and Ake stood there in her Anwyn form. She still looked young, having never aged past thirty. She smiled sadly at her elderly son.

'Hello, Amities. You asked us to come. Why did you request me to show this form?' Ake walked over and embraced him.

Alwin's eyes widened in shock as they alighted on her golden wings.

'That is Anwyn's lad. Evil is gathering and it won't be long before we all feel its reach. Train him, Mother, and you three may stand a chance at defeating it. Alwin needs to see that the story I told him is true,' said Amities.

Ake nodded. 'When will this darkness ever leave?'

Ake heard a bell toll and looked around.

Amities clutched a hand to his chest. 'I love you all.'

Ake's eyes brimmed with tears, and she embraced her son. She began to cast healing magic on him.

'You must stop, Mother.' Amities pushed her away.

'Lan, I'm begging you. I've lost everyone else. Please don't take our son,' cried Ake.

Amities fell to the ground. Ake knelt down and checked for any sign of life, there was none. Alwin screamed and his father came running. Ake reverted to her human form and fled the little house, trying to run from her grief. Caoimhe was sad but stayed to watch over Alwin.

CHAPTER SIXTY-THREE

Ake ran until exhaustion overwhelmed her. She fell to her knees and sobbed; her tears wet the parched earth. She felt weak with grief and lay down. Ake closed her eyes and succumbed to fitful sleep.

Someone lifted her into his arms and whispered against her mouth. 'When the last elf dies, I will come home to you.'

Ake's eyes fluttered open and stared into Lan's. Tears rolled down her face and he kissed them away.

'Don't grieve for our Amities, sweetheart. He had a long and glorious life. He has taken up my job now, reunited with his brothers. Boys, show yourselves,' said Lan.

'Hello, dear Mother.' Mandami wrapped her in a hug.

Amities waved. 'Can't touch you now I'm death, you are life. But I am fine, Mother. Anwyn and Carolina are here. It's a beautiful place, built on Father's memories of you.'

'I believe in our last game of let's chase death, I was it. I just tagged my father. He can chase you now,' said Orilan.

Ake laughed and Orilan grinned.

'Time to go,' said Amities.

'I love you all,' said Ake.

'We love you too,' they called out.

Several bells tolled and the boys disappeared.

Lan grabbed Ake's chin in his hands and kissed her with intense longing. She closed her eyes but didn't respond. She believed it to be another dream that would disappear as soon as she woke. Tears streaked down her face.

'Ake, look at me,' he demanded.

She opened her eyes; he was still there. Ake noticed something different about him.

'What happened to your ears?' she asked.

'Darling, I must look human for this modern world. I can't spend the next few centuries trying to hold back the darkness looking like an elf. Remember, I'm a man not an elf.' Lan smiled.

Ake laughed, his words bringing back an early memory.

'Let's go find one of those hotels. We have some catching up to do,' he flirted.

Ake kissed him and he responded with such intensity she had to catch her breath when he relented.

'You are real,' she whispered.

Lan winked at her. 'I kept my promise.'

'You can put me down.' She laughed.

'Nope, you belong in my arms,' said Lan.

Ake snuggled closer.

The clerk barely looked up as Lan threw coins on the desk. Lan refused to let Ake out of his reach and carried her to a room. It was there they became reacquainted.

The Stars Fallen Family Tree

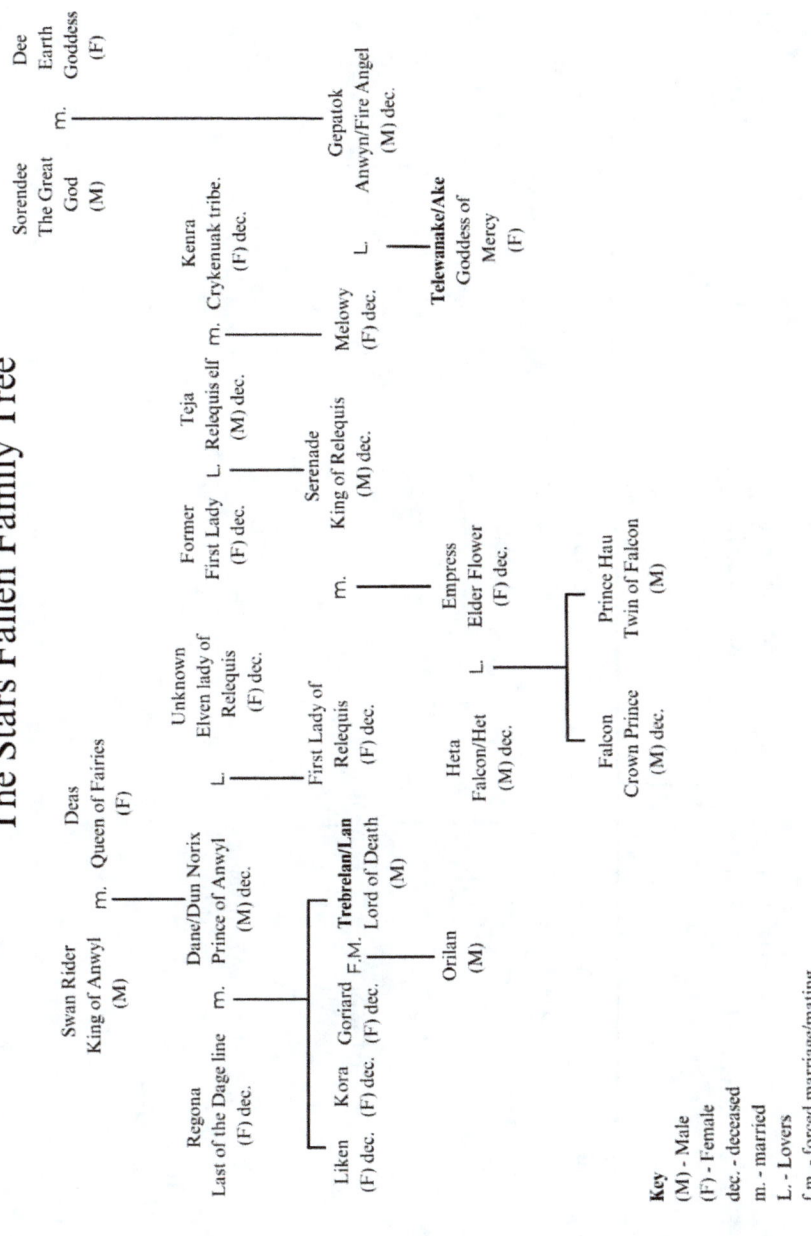

Key:
(M) - Male
(F) - Female
dec. - deceased
m. - married
L. - Lovers
f.m. - forced marriage/mating

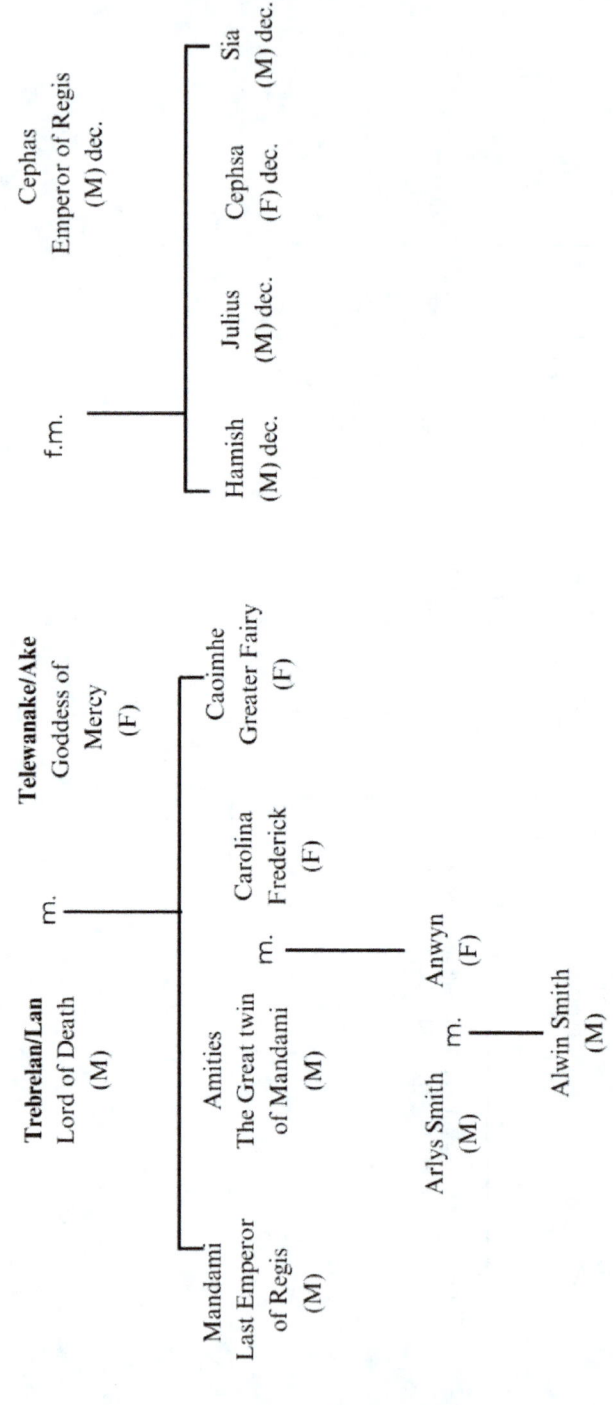

Key
(M) - Male
(F) - Female

Glossary

Ake is pronounced Ar-key.

Anam Imeall translates to Soul's Edge.

Caelestis means celestial.

Caley means Forest's Heart and was home to forest elves who were healers and hunters.

Caoimhe is pronounced Kee-va.

Cathal is pronounced Ka-hal.

Hau is pronounced Hey-ooh. It means spiritual essence.

Telewanake (pronounced Tel-a-wa-nar-key) means Stars Fallen and is shortened to Ake.

Trebrelan (pronounced Treb-re-lan) means Star Scryer and is shortened to Lan.

Relequis means the remaining.

Star Stone very precious gem. It has a gold base and tiny slivers of silver crystal weaving its way to the heart of the stone.

NADINE ABRAHAMS

The Primal Heartbeat: Book One in The Stars Fallen Series

Born into a world where humanity has been corrupted by evil, can one tribal girl fulfil a prophecy and defeat a dark goddess?

Ake's peace is fragile. Trying to carve out an existence in a land torn by strife and famine, her destiny has made her the target of terrible creatures. And as her divine nemesis's power grows ever stronger, the young mage knows she must awaken her own otherworldly heritage if she wants to survive.

Enduring endless hardships with aid from her soulmate, Ake bravely battles the forces attempting to tear them apart. But being fated to save the world and actually doing it are two very different things...

Ad' Astra

Ad' Astra is a collection of short stories centred around the magic store Ad' Astra. The strange goods within can either help or hinder the purchaser. In this collection of kooky short stories will you learn a lesson?

RPG Muintir Game

The inclusive RPG Muintir is set after a great catastrophe. The people must come together and battle mutagen in this shout out to home brew. The simplified six-sided dice system allows for quick and easy play. Those with diverse needs are celebrated, often having unique gifts that allow them to thrive in the world of Muintir.

Acknowledgements

Special mention to my editor Jenn Zabinskas of RedInk Creative. Jenn is a talented and dedicated editor who pays special attention to consistency and flow. Her comments are clear, and her suggestions are inspiring. I look forward to collaborating with her again.

Deborah Daken is a talented proof-reader and editor. Her keen eyes pick up on subtle errors that are easily overlooked, and she makes excellent suggestions to any changes she has recommended. She is incredibly fast and thorough. I found her to be amicable, flexible and approachable.

To all my friends and family members, thank you for your support and to my little sister for your important insights. Special thanks to my dearest friend and fellow storyteller Amy and my ARC readers including Roseline Briyai and Noemi Grey.

Meet the Author

Nadine has been an avid reader and writer since her early childhood, from publishing poems to creating her first novel at thirteen, *The Primal Heartbeat*, and publishing it in her early adulthood. *The Primal Heartbeat* has since been edited and updated.

Nadine is an avid gamer and role-player, as well as creator of fiction and fantasy novels. She also loves archery and nature.

After dealing with adversity and overcoming it, Nadine writes books that show even powerful characters are inherently flawed. That these weaknesses can often become our strengths as long as we remain true to ourselves. Nadine's writing reflects on the dark side of humanity as well as the good side and how, even though we think we are worthless, we can change our destiny, just as her memorable characters do.

Nadine's other books were written on a whim, designed for and dedicated to a special needs child who didn't relate to any of the books on the market. Seeing a representation of themself in the children's book encouraged them to improve their reading skills and develop a love of reading.

The next book of the Stars Fallen Series will be coming later this year.